Cane and Abe

Cane and Abe

James Grippando

An Imprint of HarperCollins*Publishers*

This book is a work of fiction. The characters, incidents, and dialogue are drawn from the author's imagination and are not to be construed as real. Any resemblance to actual events or persons, living or dead, is entirely coincidental.

HarperCollins books may be purchased for educational, business, or sales promotional use. For information, please e-mail the Special Markets Department at SPsales@harpercollins.com.

FIRST HARPERLUXE EDITION

Library of Congress Cataloging-in-Publication Data is available upon request.

ISBN: 978-0-06-234414-4

15 ID/RRD 10 9 8 7 6 5 4 3 2 1

For Tiffany

Chapter One

*U*nbelievable was the word for her. Samantha Vine was unbelievably beautiful. It was unbelievable that she'd married me. Even more unbelievable that she was gone.

It was also pretty unbelievable that I'd fallen in love again and remarried. But resilience is more the rule than the exception, isn't it? People fall in love. People die. People somehow pick up the pieces and move on, accepting or not the soothing spiritual song that death is nothing more than a major change of address. But the most unbelievable thing about Samantha had nothing to do with us. Strictly speaking, it wasn't even about *her*. It was about her father. Luther Vine was once an African-American slave.

Bullshit, you say, and not because you think I'm just a crazy white guy trying to insinuate himself into black history through marriage. Or maybe that is part of your thinking. But mostly, it's the generational disconnect.

I totally get the skepticism. Slavery was outlawed in 1865 with the adoption of the Thirteenth Amendment to the US Constitution. Samantha wasn't even conceived until then president Jimmy Carter pulled on a cardigan sweater in a chilly White House and asked all Americans to be like him, conserve energy, and turn down the thermostat to fifty-five degrees at night. All winter long, Luther and Carlotta Vine had crawled into bed and heated things up the old-fashioned way. The point is that racism persists, but Samantha was so far removed from the end of slavery as an institution that she had never known a US Supreme Court without a black justice. She had no memory of the NFL without a starting black quarterback. She couldn't even name a hit song by Prince until he was officially the artist formerly known as Prince, and she wasn't old enough to party like it's 1999 until it actually was 1999.

So, back to that troublesome timeline. Even if Samantha's old man was literally an old man at her birth, it doesn't add up. In fact, it flies in the face of history. The last American slave died in 1971. Not one of Sylvester Magee's children was alive to see the headstone finally laid in his honor in Mississippi more than four decades after his death—coincidentally, the same year I lost my wife.

Samantha Vine, the daughter of a slave?

"No way," people tell me. "Not unless I'm missing something."

"You're missing something."

"What?"

"You don't know sugar."

"Fuck you, Abe. It's you who doesn't know shit."

"No," I say. "You don't know *sugar*."

I mean Big Sugar.

In the fall of 1941 a group of men traveled across the Deep South and visited the black part of towns like Memphis and Biloxi, offering "steady employment" to "colored farm workers" eighteen years or older. It didn't matter that Luther Vine was only sixteen. Nothing about the offer was legit. "Enjoy Florida Sunshine during the Winter Months," the ads promised, "while harvesting Sugar Cane on the plantations of the National Sugar Corporation." Luther wasn't stupid. Swinging a machete all day, cutting down twelve-foot stalks of sugarcane as thick as a man's wrist, and loading tons of cane onto a truck wasn't for college boys. "Any way you slice it," Luther often said, pun intended, "you're talkin' stoop labor." But the company promised good wages, as much as thirty dollars a week. Good living conditions, free rent, free meals, free transportation to Florida, free medical attention, and recreation were all part of the package. He signed up and got on the truck with the other recruits.

Their destination had been Clewiston, the "world's sweetest town," where thousands of acres of sugarcane butted up against the south shore of Lake Okeechobee in the Florida Everglades. The ride took two days. The men were fed twice, bologna and a slice of bread. Upon arrival, each recruit was handed a bill for eleven dollars—the cost of the "free" ride from Memphis. More charges quickly piled up. Seventy-five cents for a blanket. Fifty for a machete. Another thirty for a file to sharpen the blade. A dollar for a badge that identified a worker as a company employee. Fifty cents for water that wasn't too dirty to drink. Recruits were up to their eyeballs in debt before the first workday, which started with breakfast at 3:30 a.m. They were in the field by 4:30, broke for a short lunch, and cut more cane until dark. Wages for the first day were a dollar eighty, four bucks short of the amount promised. Superintendents patrolled the fields, armed with blackjacks and pistols, threatening anyone who wasn't working hard enough or who grumbled about wanting to go home. The best chance to escape was at night. After three weeks—twenty-one straight workdays, rain or shine, sunup to sundown—nine workers ran off from the barracks at the company camp. Luther was one of them. The plan was to hitchhike back to Memphis. They were arrested eighteen miles from Clewiston, fined forty dollars for "vagrancy," and returned to the field. The only way to pay off the fine was to cut more cane. Naively, Luther asked for permission to convert the fine to prison time, preferring jail. The superintendent cracked him with a blackjack and told him sure thing, as soon as he paid off what he owed the company, a debt that was getting bigger every day because he drank too much water in the field and needed medical attention for a snakebite.

There were enough runaways for word to trickle back home, and from there to the Department of Justice in Washington, DC. Herbert Hoover himself approved the FBI's sixty-page investigative report. A federal grand jury in Florida indicted National Sugar and several employees for "conspiracy to violate the right and privilege of citizens to be free from slavery under the Thirteenth Amendment."

So, in my book, calling Luther Vine a former slave was no stretch, even if the indictment had technically been dismissed. "The grand jury was tainted," the sugar lawyers argued, "because there weren't any farmers on it." Right. And Timothy McVeigh should have complained about the lack of terrorists on the grand jury that indicted him for the Oklahoma City bombing.

Anyway, Samantha's father was coming up on his ninetieth birthday. The old man and I were still close, or as close as we could be. Luther was showing signs of dementia, and even though he had good days, he still told folks at the skilled nursing facility that his son-in-law was Abraham Lincoln. A stretch, to be sure, even if I was a tall white lawyer with four score and seven murder trials under my belt. I just went along with whatever Luther said. It only confused him to hear that I was senior trial counsel at the Office of the State Attorney for Miami-Dade County, the go-to guy in capital cases.

"I'm looking for FBI agent Victoria Santos," I said to the state trooper.

Her black-and-tan vehicle, beacons flashing, was one of six Florida Highway Patrol cars blocking the entrance to a mile-long bridge across the heart of the Everglades. The Tamiami Trail was the main route connecting east and west Florida below Lake Okeechobee, the second largest lake in the continental United States.

"And you are?" she asked.

"Abe Beckham, state attorney's office," I said as I flashed my badge.

It wasn't my job to visit every crime scene in Miami-Dade County, even when there was a possible homicide. But when the FBI was tracking a serial killer, it was critical for someone more senior from the state attorney's office to stay on top of the investigation. The chief assistant to the state attorney had personally asked me to follow up on the report of a body in the Everglades that had all the markings of a fifth victim in south Florida.

"That way," the trooper said, pointing toward a gathering of law enforcement agents beside the bridge. They were standing on the old two-lane stretch of highway that ran parallel to the new bridge, and which was no longer in use.

I thanked her, ducked under the yellow crime scene tape.

"Abe, hey, what's going on?"

I stopped at the sound of the familiar voice. It was the crime-beat reporter from Action News. We were two miles from the western frontier of urban sprawl, too far from downtown Miami to discern even the tallest skyscrapers, but I could see the microwave towers of media vans in the long line of traffic that stretched toward the morning sun. Helicopters were sure to follow. It wouldn't have surprised me to see a camera crew or two arrive by airboat—anything to be first.

"Nothing to say, Susan."

"Oh, come on, Abe."

Susan Brown had covered at least a dozen of my murder trials, and I usually gave her what I could. But I truly had nothing. I turned and continued down the embankment.

The old road had undergone many improvements since Model Ts first rolled across it in 1928, and to many folks a new elevated bridge seemed a waste of money. But it was part of a multibillion-dollar Everglades restoration project, much of which was geared toward undoing the negative impact of the well-intended but catastrophic work of the Army Corps of Engineers in the twentieth century. Levees and canals built by the corps opened the saw-grass plains to sugarcane growers and other farmers, and roads like the 275-mile-long Tamiami Trail made the watery sloughs passable by motorists. The casualty in all the construction was the water flow essential for a healthy Everglades. The new bridge was raised on pilings, adjacent to the old road, to alleviate the damming effect.

I hopped from the embankment onto the old road but came up short. I was halfway up to my knees in muck.

"Ah, *shit*." It wasn't just the wet shoes and pant legs. It takes a thousand years of decomposition to create a foot of peat, and I'd just unleashed the rotten stink of nine hundred and ninety-nine.

"Let me help you out there, pardner," said one of the troopers. He tugged me by the arm, and the muck puckered like a suction cup as my foot emerged from the Everglades version of quicksand. I considered rinsing off the black mess in the standing water near a culvert, but the nine-foot alligator sunning itself on the bank changed my mind.

"Welcome to Shark Valley," said the trooper.

I assumed that it was just a name, that there weren't actually any sharks around, but I was nonetheless glad to be on dry land. Not that there was much of anything dry around me. From the southern lip of Lake Okeechobee, tea-colored water flowed for a hundred miles, south to the tip of mainland Florida and west to the Gulf of Mexico, much as spilled milk spreads across the kitchen table. Covering these millions of watery acres, flat as a Kansas wheat field, were endless waves of saw grass, a rare species of swamp sedge that has flourished for over four thousand years. This legendary "river of grass" divided the east coast of Florida from the west, an environmental marvel where visitors found exotic reptiles, manatees, and rainbow-colored tree snails, roseate spoonbills and ghost orchids, towering royal palms and gumbo limbos. Here, biblical clouds of mosquitoes could blacken a white canoe within seconds, and oceans of stars filled a night sky untouched by city lights. There was no other place on earth like it. I rarely went there, except when passing through at sixty miles per hour on the drive to Naples.

Or, on a day like today, recovering a body.

"Freakin' cold out here," I muttered, but my trooper friend had already moved on to pull some other moron out of the muck.

Fifty-one degrees in February is downright frigid by Miami standards, and the FBI agents were readily identifiable in their dark blue windbreakers with yellow lettering. The feds were part of a much larger, multijurisdictional task force. Miami-Dade police were at the scene, including two homicide detectives I knew well and a team from the South Florida Homicide Clearing House, which played a key role in any investigation involving interagency cooperation. The medical examiner's van was parked alongside the road. I saw only one woman who was marked FBI, and even though she probably had no memory of our previous meeting, I recognized Victoria Santos. I went toward her. She was talking to a member of the road-striping crew who had been repainting the markings on the new bridge. His sharp eyes had spotted the body in the saw grass alongside the old road.

"Didn't really look human at first," the worker told her.

I was standing off to one side, close enough to hear. Santos was a good-looking woman with short, dark hair that reflected hints of crimson in the Florida sun. As the coordinator in residence for the National Center for the Analysis of Violent Crimes, she was on the front line as primary liaison between the FBI and local law enforcement. She was new to Miami, however, and I'd met her only once before, as an FBI instructor in an invitation-only course for prosecutors presented at the national academy in Quantico. Santos was a twenty-year veteran and a bit of a legend at the FBI, not just because she was good, but also because she wasn't afraid to buck the system, which didn't always win friends at FBI headquarters. I had to wonder if that was the reason she'd been reassigned from the prestigious Behavioral Analysis Unit, a nationwide responsibility, to the field office in Miami, where her first case landed her neck deep, so to speak, in Everglades muck.

"What I noticed first was the ring," the witness told Santos. "The diamond caught the sun and gave off this sparkle that you really couldn't miss. I was riding in the bed of the pickup truck, passing traffic cones down to the road crew. But when this sparkle down in the saw grass catches my eye, I squint to take a closer look, and I think to myself, What the hell? I'm pretty sure the ring was still attached to a hand, so I bang on the roof and says 'Charlie, stop the truck!' And then both Charlie and me walk over to the guardrail along the bridge, and we're still a good twenty yards away, looking down into the swamp. And Charlie agrees with me. It's definitely a ring on someone's hand. And so I throws a rock in the general direction, and this monster bull gator scurries off thataway." He pointed to a mound about twenty feet away. "That's when we saw the rest of the body come floating to the surface."

Santos was a professional and showed little reaction, but the crime scene photographer was already doing his job, and I knew that someday—soon, if we all did our jobs—I would have to show a jury some pretty gruesome exhibits. I eavesdropped for another ten minutes and let Santos finish with the witness before introducing myself. She replied by telling me that she was leading the task force investigation of a serial killer known as Cutter. It was pretty much SOP for the FBI to remind local law enforcement that the bureau was in charge, but in this instance Santos wasn't just posturing. Cutter's four previous victims had been residents of Palm Beach County, seventy miles to the north, their bodies found in the sugarcane fields just outside Clewiston. Like everyone else from Miami-Dade County, I was an outsider to the larger investigation and not yet an official member of the task force.

"Can we talk a minute?" I asked.

Santos nodded, and we found a place away from the crowd. Behind us, beyond a copper-brown stretch of saw grass, a flock of egrets found a place to rest above the tangled roots of mangroves. The reflection of the white birds on the flat, black water was straight out of a Clyde Butcher exhibition.

"You think this is victim number five?" I asked.

"Hard to know just yet," said Santos. "So far we have some common indicators. Young woman. Unclothed body. I count at least one grievous blade wound already, probably a machete. But it would be Cutter's first strike outside Palm Beach County."

"Or it could be a Palm Beach County victim and the first disposal of a body in Miami-Dade," I said. "Which would make some sense, wouldn't it? After four victims dumped in Palm Beach County cane fields, it must be pretty risky to dispose of another body there. He has to believe that law enforcement is on heightened alert in that area."

"Totally with you on that," she said. "But at this point, we're very preliminary on whether it's the same killer. Definite similarities, but we'll have to wait for confirmation on sexual assault and some other indicators."

"What are the other indicators?"

She paused, knowing what I was asking for: the signature. Much had been reported in the media about Cutter, the killer who mutilated his victims with a cane cutter's machete and dumped their bodies in the cane fields. But law enforcement always held back something in serial killer investigations, a key characteristic of the crimes that was so unique that it served as the killer's signature.

"Facial markings," she said. "But we are going to have to do some serious searching to confirm that."

"Searching for what?"

Santos glanced in the direction of the medical examiner's van, where the remains of the victim lay beneath a white sheet on a gurney. Then her gaze swept the acres of saw grass along the roadside, as if to measure the daunting task before them.

"We're still looking for the victim's head."

I breathed in and out. Those trial exhibits for my jury just got more gruesome.

The assistant medical examiner called Santos over. I followed her to the van. The FBI might have been in charge of coordinating the Cutter investigation from an administrative standpoint, but homicides were generally local matters, and the Miami-Dade County medical examiner's office was my territory.

"I wanted to point out one major deviation from the Cutter profile," the assistant ME said.

"Tell me," said Santos.

"We're a long way from a positive ID, and the accelerated decomposition we get in the Everglades can make it more difficult than you might think to determine a victim's race. But I can say this much with confidence: If this was Cutter, it would be his first victim who isn't Caucasian."

I glanced at the gurney, then up at the cloudless blue sky, my eyes drawn by the whirring sound of a helicopter. The first media helicopter was over the crime scene, and I could feel the pointed questions about to rain down on us.

"A victim's race is usually a key component of the killer's psychological profile," I said, knowing that I wasn't telling Santos anything she didn't already know. "Does that change your thinking about whether this was Cutter?"

She thought for a moment before answering. "Do you have time to take a ride up to Palm Beach County with me?"

I had just plea-bargained a death penalty case down to life without parole, so my trial calendar was unusually clear. "Sure. What for?"

"I'm a big believer in a fresh set of eyes on the evidence," she said. "Would love to hear you answer your own question."

"You got it," I said.

"But do me just one favor before we go."

"What?"

She glanced at my muck-covered shoes. "Lose the Gator Man from Okefenokee look."

"Yeah. I can do that."

Chapter Two

We drove toward the smoke, thick clouds that rose from the fields and blackened the crisp blue sky. I closed the AC vent on the passenger side of Agent Santos' car.

"I can smell the smoke," I said.

"A little like roasted corn, isn't it?"

"Too roasted."

"Be glad you don't live around here," said Santos.

Smoke from controlled fires was a familiar part of the winter landscape in the vast and privately managed sugarcane fields of the Florida Everglades. Only after the leaves and thick undergrowth had been burned away could the blades of men or machine get at the base of the twelve-foot sugarcane stalks.

Nobody was quite sure how it was discovered that burning a cane field would facilitate the harvest without reducing the yield. But I knew from my father-in-law that National Sugar Corporation had been doing it since at least 1941, when Luther and the other "recruits" had shipped down from Memphis. After beating the Justice Department's criminal indictment for slavery, National and the other growers gave up on Americans and hired only foreigners for seasonal labor under the H-2 visa program. Jamaicans, Haitians, and Dominicans perfected the burns—and the cutting. Each season for the next fifty years, ten thousand men would leave their families in the islands, live on top of each other in cheerless barracks, ride buses to fields before dawn, pull on protective caps and boots, and fasten aluminum safety guards on their shins, knees, and hands. Armed with machetes, they'd march onto the soot-covered fields like black gladiators. One in every three would cut himself or be cut by another worker, puncture an eye or an eardrum on the sharp spear of a cane top, or lose a day's pay to heat stroke, snakebite, or an attack of angry fire ants. They raced to cut a ton of cane per hour, and with a proper burn, they were expected to cut it *low*. "No stubble, mon," the better-paid Jamaicans, the ones who had curried favor with the company, would tell the newbies. "You leave a inch o' stubble, National lose a ton o' cane. Bend yo' bok, mon."

By the mid-1990s, machines had taken over. But the fires endured.

"It's a pretty amazing sight," said Santos, her gaze fixed on the road. "Forty acres will go up in fifteen minutes."

I was staring out the passenger-side window, transfixed by the fire's intensity. The orange wall of flames reached thirty feet or more above the cane tops. Bursts of heat pushed the ashes even higher into the sky. Thousands of birds took flight, escaping with their lives. It was like a scene out of *Bambi*, and I wondered about the rabbits, raccoons, and other critters that had made the thick cover of cane their home.

"Victim number one was burned pretty badly," said Victoria.

"You don't mean burned alive, do you?"

"No," said Santos. "I'll show you. It's just ahead."

We were suddenly beyond the burn zone. Long tongues of fire and blinding orange heat gave way to leafy waves of sugarcane. The reeds were taller than the saw grass fifty miles to the south, but they were similarly beautiful, which made sense: sugarcane is a grass.

Santos steered onto the shoulder of the road and parked. The thick brown field outside my door looked impenetrable. The other side of the road, however, was a postharvest wasteland. Machines had taken all that the land could offer. Tons of cane had been cut and hauled away. All that remained was the blackened stubble of a burned and harvested field.

"This way," said Santos.

I followed her across the deserted two-lane road and into the field. I could still see the fire in the distance, but a cool breeze carried the smoke in the other direction. The ground was soft, but it wasn't the thick soup that had nearly swallowed me whole in Shark Valley. Mostly it was covered with shredded brown debris left by machines, but occasionally a puff of ash and gray dust rose up from my footfalls, the remnants of the preharvest burn. It was easy to see where long, orderly rows of cane had once stood, and beyond it was another field, yet to be cut. I thought of Samantha's father, sixteen years old, standing out in this field with a machete in his hand and wanting to go home to Memphis, waves of sugarcane as far as the eye could see. It was a little like handing a kid a teaspoon and telling him to empty the ocean.

Santos stopped and pointed to a clearing several rows over. "Victim one was there."

"Who found her?"

"One of the burners. They spray the perimeter with water to prevent jump fires and then go into the field with firepots to light it up. There is a standard walk-through before the burn, but they don't find every-thing. They do another walk-through after the burn to clear away things that might clog the machines, which could be anything from a cooked alligator to an old washing machine dumped by one of the neighbors. That's when they found the body."

Santos squatted, sifted through the debris on the ground, and gathered a small amount of ash. She worked it into her fingertips as she rose, blackening the skin.

"This is Cutter's signature," she said.

"Ash?"

"White female victims, their faces blackened with ash."

I glanced again toward the clearing, where victim number one had been found. "How were you able to ascertain that with a charred body?"

"We have an ID on the victim. Charlotte Hansen. We know she's white."

"I understand that much. But if the body was burned, how were you able to tell she had ash smeared on her face?"

"We weren't. Cutter put her too deep into the cane field. I believe that's why victims two, three, and four were so much easier to find. Cutter left them on the perimeter, where the cane is watered to contain the burn. He learned from the first drop and corrected his mistake. He wanted us to see his signature."

I reached down and gathered some ash. I was already into the mind of the killer, already had my own theory, but I wanted to hear it from Santos. "What does it mean, his signature?"

"All four women dated black men."

The Cutter profile was writing itself in my head. White female victims. Black boyfriends. Angry sexual assault. Brutally violent death. *You want to be black? Okay, bitch, I'll make you black.*

"So we have a definite aberration in Miami-Dade," I said. "A black victim."

"Yes, we do."

"My guess is you didn't see that coming."

"Nope."

"And if it turns out that the black victim had ash smeared on her face, what does that tell you?"

"The ash on the face was something the task force never shared with the media. So if it's there, we'll need to rethink our profile of the angry white racist killing white women who date black guys."

"And if there's no ash on the black victim's face?"

Santos brushed the ash from her fingers. "Then we may have two killers."

"A copycat?"

She didn't answer my question, but she didn't have to. She dug her car keys from her jacket. "Let's wait to hear what the medical examiner has to say."

Chapter Three

At 3:00 p.m. I was on my third pair of pants for the day. Pinstripes. It was the oldest suit in my closet that still fit, and I wore it to court whenever I needed luck. Lots of luck.

"State of Florida versus Jayden Tayshawn Vine," said the bailiff, calling the case.

Criminal Courtroom 9 of the Richard E. Gerstein Justice Building was familiar territory to me. It was where I'd cut my teeth as a "pit assistant," a C-level prosecutor in my first year of adult felonies, working sixty-hour weeks under my supervising attorneys, earning the astronomical sum of forty thousand dollars a year. But this was the first time I'd stood on the defendant's side of the courtroom.

Jayden Tayshawn Vine was Samantha's older brother.

"What do we do now?" J.T. asked, whispering.

"Have a seat," I said in a soft voice. "It's going to be fine."

Every family has baggage. In Samantha's family that baggage was J.T. Another widower might have walked away after Samantha's death, but I was J.T.'s rock. He had no one else. And I didn't want to see him end up homeless. Again.

"Mr. Beckham, it's good to see you," the judge said. "A familiar face in an unfamiliar place."

"Yes, Your Honor," I said, rising.

"What did she mean by that?" J.T. asked me, some urgency in his whisper.

"The judge is just being polite," I whispered back. "It's going to be okay."

The prosecutor on J.T.'s case was Leslie Highsmith, a young pit assistant who was getting the opportunity to serve as first chair on what was a fairly routine sentencing. Simple assault normally would have landed J.T. in misdemeanor court with a slap on the wrist. Unfortunately, the victim was a transit worker, a bus driver, which was right up there with taking a swing at a police officer. A prior conviction from J.T.'s days of living on the street didn't help.

Highsmith rose from her chair—my chair, once upon a time—and addressed the court. "Your Honor, the state is willing to accept a plea of no contest with thirty days' house arrest."

The judge checked the case file before her. "Refresh me, Counsel. This is all over a passenger wanting to get off a bus?"

"That's correct," I said.

The question had been directed at the prosecutor, but I intercepted it. Not that I didn't trust Highsmith; in an office of three hundred plus attorneys, I hardly knew her. But J.T. had his own version of everything he'd ever done in his life, and he didn't react well to strangers who mischaracterized one step of reality as he knew it.

"Abe, you're not the prosecution this time," the judge said, smiling at me. "Let's hear from Ms. Highsmith first."

The prosecutor thanked the judge and continued. "Mr. Vine was reportedly walking up and down the aisle of the bus and bumping into other passengers. When the driver asked him to take a seat, he refused and continued pacing. The walking intensified, and eventually he started skipping."

"Skipping?" asked the judge.

J.T. grabbed my sleeve. "Not true!" he said, angry, but managing to keep his voice low.

"Yes," said Highsmith. "Mr. Vine then demanded to get off the bus. The driver told him that he would have to wait until the bus came to a stop. Mr. Vine then raised his voice, saying that he needed to get off immediately, and he ignored the driver's repeated requests to take a seat. When the bus stopped at a red light, Mr. Vine ran to the door. The driver explained that it was not a bus stop. Mr. Vine started to pound on the door. The driver got up to stop him from breaking the glass and injuring himself. Mr. Vine then pushed him, and several passengers came forward to restrain him."

"Abe, she's a liar!" said J.T., his voice just above a whisper. But it was too loud for a courtroom.

"Alcohol or drugs involved here?" asked the judge.

"We don't believe so," said Highsmith.

"They were not involved," I said.

The judge glanced in my direction. "Something you'd like to add, Mr. Beckham?"

"Mr. Vine does not drink alcohol or take drugs. He went off his prescribed medication, and what the prosecution just described is what happens when he doesn't follow his course of treatment."

"That's why we are accepting the plea of no contest on the condition of house arrest for thirty days," said the prosecutor. "That will allow time for the medication to restore Mr. Vine to a less agitated state. Mr. Beckham has agreed to monitor the defendant and take him to his regular doctor visits during that time period."

"Fine," said the judge. "But I do see several prior arrests for public intoxication."

She was referring to J.T.'s homeless period. "That was years ago," I said.

"That may be," said the judge. "But I want Mr. Vine's monitoring to be done through a SCRAM bracelet."

SCRAM—Secure Continuous Remote Alcohol Monitor—was an ankle bracelet that detected the wearer's alcohol intake through perspiration. The judge was talking about the two-in-one device that included traditional house-arrest radio-frequency monitoring.

"The state has no objection," said Highsmith.

J.T.'s eyes were like saucers. SCRAM wasn't the end of the world, but it was a deviation from what I had laid out for J.T. before the hearing. "It's okay," I told him. "Really, it will be okay."

"No objection," I told the court.

"Very well," the judge said. "Thirty days, house arrest. The court is extending you a very generous second chance, Mr. Vine. Don't blow it."

The transcript wouldn't reflect it, but the judge had been looking straight at me as she spoke.

The state attorney's office was right across the street from the criminal courthouse, but it took me two hours to get there.

The fitting for the ankle bracelet had gone as expected. *Too tight, too loose, do you have another color?* I drove J.T. home, laid out his medications in the daily pill dispenser, and made him promise me on Samantha's grave that he would take them. I was seated behind my desk, reviewing a transcript from a suppression hearing in a murder case set for trial in two weeks, when my phone rang. It was Victoria Santos.

"You sound stressed," she said, thirty seconds into our conversation.

My desk phone rang. Caller ID told me it was J.T. I let it go to voice mail, though it was probably full from the six previous messages he'd left, each one longer than the last.

"Me? Stressed? Nah."

"I just wanted to touch base," said Santos.

"Thanks. How close are we to an ID on Jane Doe?"

"Search is ongoing to recover the victim's head. Decomposition is complicating the fingerprint analysis. Forensic team is working around the clock, so hopefully soon."

I grabbed a pencil to take notes. "What do you have so far?"

"Not much more than you already know. African-American female. Early thirties. Five feet, six inches tall. Factoring in the average weight for a human head, total body weight is estimated at one hundred twenty pounds. Red nail polish on fingers and toes."

My pencil point snapped. It was a total overreaction on my part, but I missed Santos' next question.

"Abe, you still there?"

"Sorry. I had . . . a little distraction."

"Is everything okay?"

"Yeah, fine."

"Can you meet me at the medical examiner's office tomorrow at seven? Doc Hernandez is going to do wound comparisons on the victims for me, and I'd like you to be there."

"Sure. I know Doc well."

"He's the best, and it gives me a good feeling that he's on it. We are going to catch this guy."

"I know."

"One other thing," she said. "I'm pushing the Miami-Dade investigation hard and fast. No offense to Palm Beach County, but I like the team we're putting together here. If this latest victim is another Cutter killing, my preference is to prosecute in Miami first. And I want you to take the case to trial."

"That'll be the state attorney's call."

"I understand. I'm asking for your permission to request you by name."

I didn't need to think long. "Permission granted."

"Thanks, Abe. I'll see you tomorrow at seven."

"You bet."

I hung up, breathing in the silence of my office. The broken pencil lead lay on my yellow notepad, tiny gray shavings sprayed across the last word I had written: *red.*

Santos had provided only basic and generic information, and it could have fit thousands of women. But every now and then, sometimes out of the blue, and even after the passage of nineteen months, I still got little reminders of how raw and recent my own loss could feel, which made it disconcerting to hear a homicide victim described in such a familiar way, down to the race, age, height, weight, and choice of nail polish.

It could have been Samantha.

Chapter Four

I headed home around nine thirty, the end of a fifteen-hour Monday. I called my wife from the car to let her know I was on my way. Angelina sounded as tired as I felt.

"Okay, see you soon," she said.

We were newlyweds, technically speaking, married just seven months. But Angelina and I had met pre-Samantha, having dated a year before we moved in together and shared an apartment for eighteen months. No breakup was easy, but sometimes it was best to move on. I fell in love with Samantha and got married; Angelina dated a couple of different guys, nothing serious. When Samantha died, Angelina reached out on Facebook. The friendship rebuilt itself, and with time, it became a relationship renewed. All told, pre- and post-Samantha, I'd been romantically involved with Angelina longer than with any other woman in my life. Still, it's weird when you're white and everyone, black and white, finds it a little strange that you married a white woman. Some folks were more discreet about it than others. J.T.'s toast at the wedding reception, an awkward attempt at humor, hadn't exactly endeared him to my new wife: "Damn, Abe. From black to blond. Now you's just like a brotha."

Angelina was on the couch watching *The Bachelor* when I got home.

"I made dinner for you," she said, staring at the TV.

"Thank you." I leaned over from behind the couch to kiss her, but got only her cheek.

"Two hours ago," she said. "It's cold now."

I laid my suit jacket on the chair and went to the kitchen. Angelina was a great cook, and her spaghetti Bolognese was awesome, even if microwaved. I brought my plate out and sat beside her on the couch.

"This is delicious," I said.

"Glad you like it. How did it go with J.T. today?"

I drank some water, then breathed a sigh. "Poor guy. He's kind of a mess. But he's back on his meds, so hopefully—"

"This is what I mean," she said, stopping me.

"What?"

She hit the mute button on the TV, then sat up straight, squaring her shoulders toward me. "You give so much to him, and then you come home all worked up."

"I'm not worked up."

"Yes, you are. Listen to yourself. You're home less than five minutes, and all I hear about is J.T."

"You *asked* me about J.T. So I answered."

"Of course *I asked.* I have to ask. I need to know if I'm going to have all of my husband, half of my husband, a quarter of him—what part of Abe are you going to give to your wife this week?"

This was becoming her M.O. Angelina prepared her words in advance, and no matter how our conversation developed, no matter how forced the route to the trigger point, Angelina would unload the speech on me.

"I'm really tired, Angelina. Can we talk about something else?"

She got up and went into the kitchen.

"Shit," I muttered, but there was no one to hear me. I grabbed the remote and found the Heat game. They were up by thirty-five in the fourth period, so at ten o'clock I switched to the local news.

"Serial Killer in Miami?" was the lead story, the question mark reflecting the lack of confirmation that the most recent victim was connected to the Palm Beach murders.

Angelina came out of the kitchen and stood behind the couch, watching from over my shoulder.

"Are you working this case?" she asked.

"Yup. Sure am."

"A machete," she said, wincing. "Horrible."

"Yeah. It is."

"Why are they being so cagey about whether the murders are connected? Five women all hacked with a machete, all found in the Everglades."

"It's the first one found in Miami-Dade. And it's the first black victim."

"Yeah, and I suppose it could also be the first body recovered on a Monday with the wind blowing out of the northwest at thirteen miles per hour. I swear, sometimes I think you guys overanalyze these things. Do you really believe this is a coincidence?"

"It's more complicated than you might think."

"If you say so."

Our landline rang. Angelina answered it. The serial killer coverage was wrapping up on television when she handed me the phone.

"It's J.T.," she said, her tone colder than the dinner she'd left me in the kitchen.

"Tell him I'll call him first thing in the morning."

"No, take it."

"I don't want to take it."

"Yes, you do."

"I really don't."

"Don't put him off just because you think I'm mad. He sounds a little wired. Last thing I need is you blaming me if J.T. goes off and hangs himself."

"That's not funny, Angelina."

I took the phone. "Wired" was an understatement.

"Abe, I gotta get this thing off me!"

He was so loud that I had to hold the phone away from my ear. "Calm down," I said. "What thing?"

"The thing! The fucking bracelet!"

"Listen to me, J.T. This is very important. You cannot take off the bracelet. If you do, the judge will put you in jail."

"They're listening to me."

"What?"

"That's what this thing is for. They can hear everything I say."

I wondered who might be on the other end of a conversation with a guy who lived alone, but that was another issue. "It's just a bracelet," I said. "No one is listening."

"Yes. Yes, they are. They can hear me, and they can see me, too. I gotta get it off, Abe!"

"J.T., no one can—"

"I gotta get it off right now!"

"J.T., please. I want you to breathe for me. Nice and deep. In and out, in and out, all right?"

I listened, but I didn't like what I was hearing. J.T. was practically panting.

"Slower, J.T. Much slower." I gave him a moment. "That's better. I'm going to hang up and—"

"No, don't!"

"Listen to what I'm saying, J.T. I'm going to call you right back on my cell phone, and then I'll drive over. Promise me you won't touch the bracelet till I get there. Will you promise me that?"

I could hear him breathing. It sounded like such a chore.

"J.T.? Will you promise me that?"

More breathing on the line. "Still too fast, J.T. Slower. Breathe slowly, and I'll be there in just a few minutes."

"Okay," he said. "But hurry."

I hung up, grabbed my cell phone and car keys, and went to Angelina. "Sorry, honey. I'll be back as soon as I can."

She just shook her head, more resignation than anger. "I'll see you tomorrow."

"No, I'm not staying over this time."

She just looked at me, both of us knowing the truth.

"Go, Abe," she said in a flat, detached voice. "Go take care of your family."

I went out the door and closed it, but before I was even halfway down the front steps I heard Angelina lock it with the chain. I was about to turn around, try to find the right thing to say to her, when my cell rang. It was J.T.

"Abe, where are you, man? I gotta get this thing—"

"Okay, okay, I'm on my way."

He kept talking, and I kept listening and telling him that it was going to be okay as I got in my car and drove to his apartment. Again.

Chapter Five

My meeting with Agent Santos was set for 7:00 a.m. at the medical center. Fifteen minutes before the hour I was still crawling along in traffic on the 836 expressway. Miami's rush hour seemed to peak earlier every time I got in the car.

"Gonna be a little late," was the message I left on Santos' voice mail.

My sleepover with J.T. had involved very little sleep. No fault of my brother-in-law—he got plenty of rest. I was the problem. The way Angelina had locked the door with the chain, telling me to stay with my "family," hit me like a message not to come home. That alone was enough to keep me awake all night. The complicating factor was that any visit to J.T.'s apartment was a trip to my past. Samantha and I had once lived there. The furniture had been ours. The draperies, rugs, wallpaper, and every other touch had been Samantha's. It had been Samantha's wish that J.T. have a place to live, and I was doing my best to make it happen. A nice thing, if good intentions counted for anything; but I still felt guilty about it, the kind of guilt that kept a man up all night. It had set in long after J.T. had gone to sleep, when I'd headed upstairs to the guest room. I'd ended up sleeping on the couch. No way I could sleep in the bed that had been *our* bed, where I had lain next to Samantha, whispered in the dark, listened to her breathe, felt her heartbeat, discovered and rediscovered those legs of silk. She had killer legs. So firm, so strong, the way they squeezed my head in a vise grip as she reached climax. One night stood out for me.

"I love doing that to you," I'd told her.

"I'm glad you love it."

"I mean, I *really* love it."

"I'm just happy to have a man who wants to do something other than hit it from behind."

It was a joke, but she would have done better to save it for her girlfriends. "TMI, Samantha. Way too much information."

"Sorry."

"You kind of killed the mood."

She kissed me, and I saw that look in her eye that every man wants to see, a look that made the past irrelevant, because going forward, no man but me would get it from this beautiful woman who had promised to be forever my wife.

She threw her leg over my waist, mounting me, the fullness of her breasts staring me in the face, the smell of her hair drawing me in.

"I'll fix that," she said as she slid beneath the sheets. "I'll fix it *real* good."

The Miami-Dade County medical examiner's office is in the Joseph H. Davis Center for Forensic Pathology, a three-building complex on the perimeter of the University of Miami Medical Center campus and Jackson Memorial Hospital. Mornings were always busy around Jackson. Medical breakthroughs in everything from spinal injuries to cancer were woven into the institutional fabric here, and every day patients flooded in from across the country and beyond to see some of the most respected doctors in the world. In a way, that had made it even tougher to accept Samantha's prognosis.

I parked as close as I could to the examiner's office and ended up being just five minutes late for the meeting.

"Dr. Hernandez is ready for us," said Santos.

I knew Doc Hernandez, and I knew well enough to leave my jacket on when entering his examination room. Frigid air gushed from the air-conditioning vents like the north wind from Canada. Bright lights glistened off the white sterile walls and buffed tile floors. Doc Hernandez waited for us behind the stainless steel table, a white sheet covering the mound before him. Doc adjusted the spotlight overhead before lifting the sheet.

"Now, be forewarned," he told us. "Nothing that comes straight from the Everglades to the medical examiner's office is ever a pretty sight."

"I understand," said Santos.

I wondered if she really did. Even though Santos was an experienced agent with forensics training from Quantico, nothing had really prepared me for that first autopsy of a victim recovered in the Everglades.

Doc pulled back the lower corner of the sheet. I braced myself, but the body was in much better condition than I had expected. Bloated, to be sure. The victim had been properly bagged while still in the water, and we were seeing firsthand how the organism-rich Everglades enhanced the usual release of acids and gases during putrefaction. I had to look away as my gaze drifted to where the head should have been.

"If this was July," Doc said, "and if we were talking about days instead of hours in the Everglades, we'd see highly accelerated decomposition, not to mention evidence of predators. But with the lower winter water temperatures and relatively quick recovery, we have much more to work with."

"When you say 'relatively quick recovery,' what timeline are you estimating?" I asked.

"Twenty-four hours," said Doc. "Perhaps a little longer. I'd say we're looking at a late Saturday night homicide."

"Any evidence of sexual assault?" I asked.

"Not vaginally or anally," Doc said.

Santos chimed in with the unspoken variable. "There was evidence of forcible oral sodomy in all of Cutter's previous victims."

Doc shone the spotlight on the very place my eyes did not want to go. "Obviously that's something we can't determine, given the incomplete condition of the cadaver."

"It also prevents us from confirming Cutter's signature," said Santos. "Unless your examination has found traces of sugarcane ash elsewhere on the body."

"Negative," said Doc. "But let's talk about the wounds."

The doctor brought his laptop computer to the table. He scrolled through dozens of forensic photographs, searching for the right one. "Here we go," he said, freezing the image.

It was an autopsy of a young woman, her naked body on the steel table, positioned much the same way as victim number five before me. "This is Elizabeth Gowan," said Doc, "victim number three. Her body presented much the same as all of the Palm Beach victims. We see multiple strikes against the victim with a machete or similar blade," he said, using the cursor to point out each one.

"Lots of anger," said Santos.

I glanced at the body on the table. "We don't see that on this victim."

"Exactly. And there's something else."

He clicked forward to the next image on the screen. It was a close-up shot of the side of the victim's neck, a horrendous gaping wound. Some law enforcement officers could remain clinical about these things, as if the autopsy were a medical textbook. Even after dozens of murder trials, thousands of gruesome exhibits, it still pained me to look.

"Here's what I find interesting," said Doc. "In the Gowan case, like all the Palm Beach cases, the fatal blow was probably a strike to the side of the neck, which severed the carotid artery. This is a gaping wound with exsanguination, massive blood loss."

"But there was no beheading in any of the Palm Beach cases," said Santos.

"That's correct. Truth is, unless you are a skilled executioner, it requires several strong blows to take off someone's head with a machete or a sword."

"But we have a beheading here," I said.

"In fact, we don't," said Doc.

Both Santos and I glanced at the body, the obvious contradiction.

Doc shook his head. "Predator. Alligators have razor-sharp teeth. They don't do well with large prey, so it's no surprise that one might happen by the body, bite off what it could, and then move on. Look here," he said, shining his light on the wound. "These are alligator teeth marks. And here," he said, pointing, "the flesh is torn. This is not a cutting or chopping motion with a machete. This is the typical alligator ripping and tearing, which from the standpoint of the average five-foot-long alligator is way too much work for a meal. That's why even though Florida Fish and Game gets twelve thousand complaints about alligators every year, we see only four or five actual attacks on humans. And in the last seventy-five years, only a couple dozen fatalities. They like birds and turtles that they can swallow whole."

"So this is not a dismemberment case," said Santos.

"Correct."

"Which brings it in line with the Palm Beach cases, where there was no dismemberment."

"That's true," Doc said. "But again, we don't have the multiple blows to the torso that we had in Palm Beach. We see no defensive wounds on the hands or arms, which we would expect if the victim were fighting off her attacker. And there are no ligature marks on the wrists or ankles, which would indicate that she was bound and restrained."

"Those are all significant differences," said Santos.

"And I may be able to explain them," said Doc.

"Please do," said Santos.

"As I mentioned, while we see multiple blows in the Palm Beach cases, the fatal blow was probably the neck wound. My initial fear was that the alligator attack would make it impossible to determine whether this victim had a neck wound like the Palm Beach victims."

"Are you saying you *can* make that comparison?" asked Santos.

"Not definitively. But I have a preliminary leaning," said Doc.

He shone the spotlight on the cadaver, focusing on the neck wound. "It's hard to see from this angle, with the cadaver on its back. Let me show you the photos I took earlier." He went to his laptop again, brought up the image, and then zoomed in. "Do you see this laceration at the base of the neck?"

"I see it."

"Again, we have the confounding effect of the predator. But focus in particular on that smooth edge right there."

I leaned closer. It was surrounded by the ripping and tearing of the alligator's teeth, but an inch-long section of the wound did have a smooth quality. "It does look different," I said.

"I'm reasonably certain that this was a knife wound," Doc said.

"So this case is like the Palm Beach cases?" I asked.

"Ah, that's where this gets interesting," said Doc. "The wound suffered by each of the victims in Palm Beach was to the sternocleidomastoid muscle. That's the same muscle that football players bulk up to get that no-neck look. If you're a Trekkie, like me, it's the muscle that good aliens always have and bad aliens never have, because this particular muscle is a uniquely mammalian feature that makes creatures appealing to the human eye."

Doc had a tendency to digress. I brought him back, as I had done several times before on the witness stand.

"The blow was to the side of the neck, is that what you're saying?"

"Yes. Sorry. My point is that here we have an anterior blow to the cervical spine, between the C1 and C2 vertebrae. And if I'm correct, the cause of death here may have been a single strike to the back of the neck, which severed the spinal cord."

"Like a stalk of sugarcane," said Santos.

"Your term, not mine," said Doc. "The important point is that it's a single blow."

"So death would be instantaneous?" I asked.

"Not even a guillotine is instantaneous death," said Doc. "The French Revolution is replete with historical accounts of blinking eyes, gnashing teeth, and blushing cheeks after execution. But certainly there would be instantaneous loss of consciousness and awareness, and death within seconds. Which explains why we see no defensive wounds with this victim, no evidence that she fought back. That's very different from what we see in the Palm Beach cases."

Santos and I exchanged glances, and she said exactly what I was thinking.

"So, the technique in this instance seems— . . . well, this may not be the right word—but it seems almost merciful, compared to the previous victims."

Doc paused, considering his words. "We can hypothesize with some degree of confidence that this victim did not see the blow coming and that she instantly lost all conscious awareness. The same cannot be said with any reasonable degree of medical certainty for Palm Beach. Whether it's 'merciful' is a question for a forensic psychologist."

He switched off the spotlight and closed his laptop.

"But the pathology of the wounds is very different," said Santos. "Which makes me ask: Are they so different that you think we have two killers?"

He hesitated.

"Or one killer," I said, "who has different feelings toward victims of a different race."

Doc glanced at me, then at Santos, as if it were a toss-up. "We need more."

I thought of the ongoing search for Cutter's signature in Shark Valley, the missing body part that may have been lost forever to a hungry alligator.

"Do we keep looking for the ashes?" I asked.

"We have to," said Santos, her gaze drifting back to the cadaver. "But I wouldn't hold out much hope."

Chapter Six

I met Angelina for lunch at noon. After a night at J.T.'s, I had some serious making up to do.

Lunch was something we rarely did together. Angelina was a loan officer for a bank downtown, working nine to five on the fourth floor of one of those waterfront skyscrapers that, some predicted, would have three floors submerged in warm water before the end of this century. The state attorney's office was much farther west, on the other side of the Miami River. Not that far as the crow flies, but when the drawbridges were up, we might as well have been on opposite sides of the Grand Canyon. I got lucky with the traffic flow and reached the restaurant on time. Angelina was already seated at an outdoor table, looking like a movie star beneath the shady umbrella, her designer sunglasses up on her head. I took a shot with a kiss hello, and this time I didn't get a turn of her cheek.

"I ordered conch fritters," she said.

That was a good sign, thoughtful on her part. "My favorite. You remembered."

The Big Fish restaurant, right on the river, was in my book the perfect lunch spot. It was nothing fancy, just a relaxing place to eat fresh dolphin, tuna, or shrimp ceviche while soaking up a historic stretch of river, a piece of old Miami where mariners from houseboats at the west end of the river sidled up alongside bankers and lawyers from the office towers to the east.

"I'm sorry I was such a bitch last night," she said.

An apology was unexpected, but it made me smile. "I needed and deserved a good slap upside the head. No worries."

"J.T. just scares me sometimes."

"I know. But his psychiatrist assures me that he's perfectly fine living alone, and that he's not violent."

"He hit a bus driver."

"No, that's not what happened. But let's not go down this road, okay?"

The waitress brought our fritters. "Something to drink?"

Angelina smiled at me. "I have an idea. Why don't we order a pitcher of sangria and call in sick for the afternoon?"

It was the kind of thing we used to do, before we got married—way back when, in the pre-Samantha phase of our relationship.

"That's very tempting," I said.

"Really? You want to?"

I hated to say no, but the Cutter investigation was just a small part of my overall caseload, and the way things were going, I would be lucky to make it home for dinner. "I do. I really want to. But I'm sorry, I just can't. Not today."

"It's okay. Neither can I. But a girl can dream, can't she? Iced tea," she told the waitress.

"Same," I said. The waitress left the menus for us and headed inside.

"It was lonely last night without you," said Angelina.

"I'm sorry."

"I was up late, going over so many things in my head. And I was wondering. What do you think about trying to have a baby?"

I did not see that coming, but that probably wouldn't have been the right thing to say. "Wow. A baby."

"What does that mean?"

What it meant was that I had no idea what to say. "A baby," I said, still searching. "Wow."

"Wow. A baby. A baby. Wow. Either we're on TIVO and I accidentally hit rewind, or you're not very excited about the idea."

"No, it's not that. It's not that at all. It's just . . . a baby."

"Please don't say 'wow.' "

The waitress brought us two sweaty glasses of iced tea. I quickly opened the menu and ordered Peruvian ceviche. "You want anything?" I asked Angelina.

"You mean like a baby?"

The waitress took my menu. "That's your department, boss. I'll get the fish."

Angelina waited for her to leave. Then she reached across the table to take my hand. "I want to start a family, Abe. *Our* family."

She squeezed my hand for emphasis, and the baby discussion no longer seemed so out of the blue. This was about *our* family. As opposed to Samantha's.

"Do you think I'm ready to be a father?"

"I think you'd be a great dad."

She reached out, pressing my hand between the soft palms of both of hers. I was looking across the table into eyes as big and blue as the ocean.

"Okay. Let's make a baby."

I heard a shriek of excitement as she hurried to my side of the table and kissed me. Then I heard my cell phone. I let it go to voice mail.

"I'm so happy," said Angelina as she returned to her chair.

"Me too."

My cell rang again. It was Agent Santos. I apologized to Angelina and promised to make it quick.

"Are you near a TV?" asked Santos.

There was one at the bar inside the restaurant. "I can be."

"Turn on Action News now. We have an ID on the victim."

"Who is it?"

"A thirty-four-year-old lawyer from Miami. Her name was Tyla Tomkins."

I gripped the phone. "I'm sorry. Say that again."

"Tyla Tomkins. Do you know the name?"

"No, no," I said. "Just a bad connection. Lost you for a second there."

"Turn on the television. It's important to stay on top of the media reports. Then we should talk. Are you available for a conference call at two?"

"No, I'm in court from one thirty on."

"Call me when you get out," she said, and we hung up. Angelina looked at me from across the table.

"What was that about?" she asked.

I told her quickly, promised to come right back after the news clip, and hurried inside to find the TV set.

Tyla Tomkins.

People all over Miami were staring at their TV sets in disbelief and saying it couldn't be her, it couldn't possibly be her. But my head wouldn't go there. I skipped right past that first stage of shock and denial.

It's her.

Chapter Seven

Agent Victoria Santos was alone in her FBI sedan on the MacArthur Causeway, the Port of Miami a blur in her passenger-side window. The mega ships that made Miami the cruise capital of the world were out to sea, but container vessels aplenty were in port, and tugboats towed several others down the Government Cut shipping lane. Victoria weaved through three lanes of eastbound traffic, doing seventy in a fifty-mile-per-hour zone, eager to reach South Beach.

Victoria was new to the FBI's field office in Miami, but not unfamiliar with Miami. Her first year in Quantico, she'd battled minds with a geographically transient serial killer with a half dozen known victims. The only lead was an anonymous newspaper informant who had an uncanny ability to predict each murder, time, place, and victim. Or was he the killer? On the receiving end of the tips was Mike Posten, a crime reporter for the *Miami Tribune*. The nationwide manhunt had been an unusual coordination between law enforcement and journalism, and there had been many a late-night meeting and deep conversation between Victoria and Mike. She was single, but Mike was married, which had nixed "coordination" on any other level.

Water under the Tamiami Bridge.

Victoria passed a slow-moving truck and continued toward South Beach. But Mike was still at the back of her mind. Back then, the *Tribune* headquarters had buttressed the water's edge at Biscayne Bay, and the newsroom enjoyed drop-dead views of Miami Beach to the east. She remembered one night, late, when the silence and distance between her and Mike had become ambiguous, until Mike suddenly broke eye contact, nervously walked to the picture window, and started to play tour guide, just to change the subject. "Did you know that Miami Beach is actually a man-made island?" he'd asked. "The Army Corps of Engineers dredged it up, just so there'd be some hurricane protection for the mainland." She wasn't sure if Mike had used the words "billion-dollar sand bar," or if she was recalling those from some other account of how this narrow strip of dredged-up land had drawn millions to work, play, and live.

Tyla Tomkins had been among them, and her South Beach apartment was officially the newest homicide crime scene in the county.

Victoria shook off her memories and glanced in the rearview mirror, catching a glimpse of downtown Miami and the fifty-five-story office tower where Tyla had practiced corporate law for one of the city's high-powered firms. Deeper into the mainland, west of the jagged skyline, was where Victoria's day had begun—at the medical examiner's office, Tyla's temporary place of rest.

Victoria cut through an older residential area several blocks south of the glitz and glamour of legendary Ocean Drive and its party-hearty kid sister, Washington Avenue. Tyla's condominium had been built in the South Beach revival style of the 1980s, not the classic Art Deco of original Miami Beach, but there was something to be said for breathtaking waterfront views coupled with plumbing and air conditioning that actually worked. Every parking space on both sides of the street was taken, which was normal. The row of double-parked squad cars was a definite aberration, particularly for the middle of the afternoon. Victoria pulled up behind one of the white-and-green cars from the Miami-Dade Police Department, left her beacon on the dashboard, and headed into the building. She flashed her credentials to the uniformed Miami Beach police officer who was posted outside the double-door entrance to the ground-floor lobby.

"Here to see Lieutenant Riddel," she said. Riddel was with the homicide squad.

"Seventh floor," he said. "You'll have to use the stairway, which has been cleared. CSI is still processing the elevators."

"No problem," said Victoria.

The officer turned his attention to a group of complaining residents who weren't allowed to enter their own building. Victoria ducked beneath the police tape and climbed the stairs.

It was easy to imagine Tyla Tomkins walking these stairs, opting for the exercise route over the elevator after a long, sedentary day at the office. By all accounts she was a fitness buff, blessed with both a brain and striking good looks. A missed spinning class had been the first red flag. "Tyla never missed the six a.m. class," her instructor told police, "no matter what she was doing the night before."

Victoria found another officer stationed in the stairwell at the seventh-floor landing. He escorted her down the hallway to Tyla's apartment. The door was open. Inside, a team of crime scene investigators was at work, searching with penlights, combing over every detail, bagging, labeling, and photographing anything that might be important. Victoria was drawn straight to the balcony and the view of the Atlantic, but the CSI team was already immune to it, focusing on the task. She found Detective Riddel in the living room.

"Pretty clean," he said. "Not a drop of blood anywhere."

Victoria had worked with Riddel before, their paths first having crossed three years earlier, when MDPD had called on Behavioral Analysis Unit 2 for assistance with a kidnapping that, tragically, became a homicide case. She knew him to be thorough and dedicated—so dedicated, rumor had it, that he shaved his head just to avoid possible contamination of a crime scene with one of his stray hairs. It probably didn't hurt that it made him look like Taye Diggs.

"That's consistent with our prior victims," said Victoria. "Not one of them was attacked where she lived. We have yet to pinpoint an actual murder site."

"Having seen the autopsy photos, I would have to say that he did his machete work someplace else. But it's still possible that the killer was here. Also can't rule out that the victim died here and was taken somewhere."

"Any sign of a struggle?"

"Nothing yet."

Victoria's gaze swept the room. The furniture was modern, the pricey kind that wasn't especially comfortable. The chairs were essentially hard leather straps on chrome frames, softened somewhat by small throw pillows. The sofa was not nearly long enough or soft enough to flop on after work, and there was no television to watch anyway. Fear of despoiling the Tibetan silk rug would have been likely to paralyze any guest entrusted with a glass of red wine. The look and feel was straight out of a home-design magazine, the tony apartment of a young professional who lived alone, spent far more time in the office than relaxing at home, and earned more than enough money to hire an established decorator and empty out a Roche Bobois showroom.

"Let me show you the bedroom," said Riddel.

It was a two-bedroom apartment, but the smaller room was a home office. Victoria followed him into the master suite, which wasn't unusually small for a South Beach condo, but definitely not big enough for the king-size bed that dominated it. There was barely enough space to walk between the foot of the bed and the bureau. The mirror over the bureau, facing the bed, was also oversize for the room.

"Apparently she liked to watch herself sleep," said Riddel.

Victoria understood that cop humor was part of homicide squad survival, but she shot him a look that conveyed zero tolerance for jokes about victims. He caught her drift.

"Sorry," said Riddel.

Victoria walked around the bed. The linens had been stripped, leaving only the bare mattress. "Any sign of blood or body fluid on the sheets?" she asked.

"Not that we detected. The lab may tell us otherwise, but I doubt it. The bed was neatly made up when we got here. It didn't appear to have been slept in or otherwise utilized."

"So if she was killed Saturday night, which is what the medical examiner thinks, Tyla probably went out and didn't come home."

"That's my bet," he said. "I spoke to Mrs. Elias, the seventy-year-old resident busybody who lives down the hall. According to her, Tyla hardly ever slept here on weekends."

"Did she have a boyfriend?"

"We're checking into that. No one special we've identified so far. But here's something interesting."

Riddel led her to the jewelry box on the dresser. The box was open, revealing a top tray lined with maroon velvet. The assortment of earrings and gold chains was pretty, but it was the diamond rings that caught Victoria's eye. There were two of them, each with a gold band.

"Bridal sets?" she asked, confused.

"That's what they look like to me."

Victoria took a closer look but didn't touch. The diamonds were the classic round cut in a Tiffany-style setting. "The one on the left looks to be about a half karat. The other one is probably close to two."

"That's quite a ring," said Riddel. "If it's real."

"Tyla was wearing a one-karat diamond ring when her body was found. It was real."

"My understanding is that she has never been married. Is that the same info you got?"

"Right," said Victoria. "Never married."

"So a gorgeous unmarried woman goes out on a Saturday night wearing a wedding band and an engagement ring? And she has two other bridal sets in her jewelry box at home."

"Looks that way."

"What's up with that?" asked Riddel. "She strings men along, gets them to buy her a diamond engagement ring, and then dumps them?"

"Could be," said Victoria. "Or she buys them for herself."

"Either way, this is kind of interesting, don't you think?"

Victoria glanced at the ginormous bed, at the oversize mirror, and then back at the rings. "Yeah," she said. "Kind of interesting."

Chapter Eight

It was almost 10:00 p.m. when my workday ended.

My court appearance had run into the evening, followed by two hours of witness prep in my office. I would return early in the morning. The official name for the main facility of the Office of the State Attorney for Miami–Dade County was the Graham Building, but I called it the Boomerang. The building had two wings, and the footprint was angled like a boomerang, but the appellation had more to do with the fact that it seemed I could never leave without coming right back.

I dialed Agent Santos from my car and left a short message: "Any news?"

Since our phone conversation at lunchtime, I'd heard from neither Santos nor the MDPD homicide unit. It would have been standard investigative protocol to visit Tyla's apartment and interview anyone who knew her, which should have triggered some kind of update. I double-checked my smartphone for messages while stopped at a red light. None from Santos. Several from J.T.

The light turned green, but I kept my foot on the brake for a moment, debating my next move. Angelina probably would have preferred that I leave J.T. alone, but she was at a baby shower for a friend—which surely had something to do with our conversation at lunch—and I saw no urgent need to go straight home to an empty house. Thirty days of house arrest without at least one visit a day from someone seemed like cruel and unusual punishment. I hung a right and headed to J.T.'s apartment. He was so glad to see me that I could barely say hello through his bear hug.

"Thank you, Abe. Thank you for coming."

I followed him inside. He was dressed in jogging shorts and a T-shirt, ready for bed. His mouth was foaming with toothpaste, and the brush was in his hand.

"I took my medication a little while ago, so I'll be asleep soon."

"That's fine."

"I'll be right back. Make yourself at home," he said, brushing his teeth as he climbed the stairs to the bathroom.

Make yourself at home. I wasn't sure if he was trying to be funny or if he'd simply forgotten that I'd once lived there with his sister. I went into the TV room and turned on the local news. The lead story was the brutal murder of Miami attorney Tyla Tomkins, which immediately sucked me in. Neighbors described her as "the nicest person you would ever want to meet," but the report also mentioned that Tyla was "just the second African-American woman to become a partner at Miami's oldest and largest law firm, Belter, Benning & Lang." The gray-haired managing partner, Brian Belter, spoke of "a brilliant Harvard-educated lawyer who was determined to give back to her community."

Tyla's photograph flashed on the screen again, and I found myself transfixed.

"Abe, did you hear what I just said?" asked J.T.

"Huh?"

J.T. stepped farther into the room. His mouth no longer foamed with toothpaste, but he was still brushing between sentences.

"Jeez, Abe. Can't you at least pretend to listen? I'm wasting my breath here."

"Sorry. I was focused on the TV."

He plopped down on the couch beside me. He was brushing furiously, but there was still no foam.

"Are you using toothpaste?" I asked.

"Just water. I'm brushing off the toothpaste."

"Why?"

"Everybody brushes off the toothpaste."

"No, they don't, J.T. And stop brushing so hard. You're going to make your gums raw."

He continued to brush, his gaze locking onto the television screen. "Is that the murder case you're working on?"

"Yes."

"Did you know her?"

"Know who?"

"The victim."

"Why would you ask that?"

"Why would you work all day and then sit your ass down in front of the TV to hear more about her? I get ESPN, you know."

I grabbed the remote and switched the channel.

J.T. brushed his molars, then stopped. "You still didn't answer the first question I asked."

"You mean the one I didn't hear?"

"Okay, I'll ask again. When we was in court yesterday, why did you have to tell the judge I'm bipolar?"

"I didn't."

"You should have told her the truth, that I have post-traumatic stress disorder."

"J.T., you don't have PTSD."

"So you had to let the whole world know that I'm bipolar, is that it?"

"I didn't tell anyone you're bipolar."

"People aren't stupid, Abe. All those medications I take are for bipolar disorder."

"I didn't mention any of the medications by name."

"Yes, you did."

"No, I really didn't."

"I heard you," he said firmly, slamming the wet toothbrush down on the sofa cushion. "You *told* them."

I was certain that I hadn't, but I more than understood how counterproductive it was to argue with J.T. when he "knew" he was right. He'd dig in his heels, get assertive, then get agitated. Then he'd feel the compulsion to walk, and walk, and walk. Sit, stand, walk some more. In the chair, out of the chair, bouncing up and down. Maybe even skip his way across the room, still brushing his teeth and arguing the point. He'd be up all night, maybe two. Maybe jump on a bus for a three-hour ride, J.T. prancing up and down the aisle.

It wouldn't end well.

"I'm sorry, J.T. I should have been more careful."

"Sorry doesn't cut it, Abe. We've talked about this before."

Yes, we had. Countless times, the same conversation over and over again. "Rumination," was what his doctor called it.

"I'll be more sensitive next time," I said.

He started brushing again, his bizarre mission to remove every speck of toothpaste, then stopped. "I'm tired," he announced. "I'm going to bed. Are you staying here tonight?"

"No. I'm going home to Angelina."

"What about tomorrow night?"

"I don't think so."

"What about the night after that?"

"J.T., you need to—"

I started to say what I wished I could say, in the tone I wished I could use, but stopped. This wasn't J.T.'s fault. But, dear God, it was exhausting.

"J.T., let's touch base tomorrow, okay?"

"Okay. Oh, one more thing."

"What?"

He came to me, putting his head on my shoulder in an awkward embrace. "Thank you, Abe."

"You're welcome, J.T."

"I know it ain't easy for someone of average intelligence to have a brother-in-law who's a genius."

Again, it wasn't easy to tell when J.T. was kidding around, but finally he laughed.

"Had you goin' for a second there, didn't I, homeboy?"

"Good night, J.T."

I waited until he was upstairs, then switched the channel back to the local news. The nightly if-it-bleeds-it-leads coverage had switched to a convenience store robbery in Hialeah. I settled back into the couch and texted Angelina to see what time she planned to get home.

Soon, she texted back. *11-ish.*

I texted back but didn't tell her where I was. I honestly wasn't sure what would have bugged her more, the fact that I was with J.T. or that I was in the apartment Samantha and I had once shared. We didn't talk much about Samantha. The name seemed to come up only when Angelina and I were arguing about J.T. Not that a new wife should make the old wife a nightly topic of conversation, but at some point I would have expected at least one meaningful conversation. *When was the cancer diagnosed? How long did you know she was going to die? Did you talk about what you would do after she was gone? Do you think everything happens for a reason?* I couldn't really recall any questions of substance that Angelina had ever asked about Samantha, save one. It was late, we were in bed, and I had drifted off to a semiconscious state after making love. I felt Angelina's arm slide across my chest, smelled the wine on her breath.

"Was Samantha your only black lover?"

My eyes blinked open in the darkness. "What?"

"You heard me."

"Why does that matter?"

"I want to know. So it matters."

I wasn't sure why Angelina had wanted to know. Perhaps she didn't even know why. But her question had been a cold reminder of what a complicated place my head was. Answers were never simple. In high school I used to read the sports pages of the *Miami Tribune* before leaving the house each morning. During the O. J. Simpson trial, my favorite columnist wrote a piece on racism. The subtleties of racism, he called it. For most white people, he wrote, it was easier to imagine black people having sex than to imagine them getting sweaty palms at the high-school dance. Later, as an adult, I came to understand what he was saying. As a teenage boy, not at all. All I knew was that whenever I looked at Shawna Jones sitting next to me in tenth-grade homeroom, I pretty much wanted to have sex. The sweaty palms and dancing didn't come till much later. So all those nights I'd lain in bed alone thinking about Shawna, I bore the double guilt and shame of having sprayed my bedsheets, which only proved that

I was, in the eyes of my favorite sports columnist, a racist.

My cell rang. It was my boss. Actually, my boss's boss. The call was from Carmen Jimenez, the four-term state attorney who had hired me out of law school and approved every promotion since. It wasn't often that Carmen called me after ten o'clock at night. In fact, the last time I could remember a call at this hour had been during a street riot.

"What's up, Carmen?"

"Are you alone?"

"Yeah, why?"

"Abe, normally I'd say this is none of my business, but I think you know why I have to ask: Were you having an affair?"

The question threw me, but that was Carmen's style. Most lawyers would start a deposition by asking a witness where he lived, his employment history. Carmen, in her day, had gone for the jugular with the first question.

"Was I having an *affair*?"

"Yes, that's what I'm asking," she said. "Were you?"

As a prosecutor, I understood better than most that the only way to answer a direct question is with a direct answer. I couldn't count the number of times I'd stood before a jury and painted a witness as a liar for dodging a question by responding with a question of his own. But there I went.

"Why would you even ask that?"

"Say no more," said Carmen.

"Hold on a second. I didn't say I was. I'm not."

"Did you know Tyla Tomkins?"

"Yes. That was a long time ago."

"Okay, stop right there, because now I know you've lied to me at least once. And when you lie to me, this becomes a personnel matter."

"I'm not lying!"

"Abe, chill, okay? This is not hostile fire. But you are going to have to answer some tough questions, and you need to do better than you just did with me. Victoria Santos has demanded a meeting with us first thing tomorrow morning."

"What? Why is the FBI getting involved in this?"

"It's her prerogative. And anytime the bureau sticks its nose into my office, I have to go strictly by the book."

"I don't see the big deal. I was going to tell you about Tyla tomorrow anyway."

"Good. Let's leave it at that. I want you to sleep on this, sort it out in your head, and tomorrow morning all will go smoothly. Don't say things that dig a deeper hole than the one you're already in."

"What hole?"

"Abe, I can't coach you. That's as far as I'm going to take it on the telephone. Santos is one smart cookie. Don't lie to her. We'll talk in the morning. My office. Eight a.m."

"Okay. See you tomorrow."

As we hung up, my own words echoed in my mind. *Why would you even ask that?*

Why that had been my answer, I'll never know. Carmen was on my side, and if I'd given her a flat no, she might have gone to bat for me and told Santos to take her list of questions and pound sand. I'd given her no choice but to let the meeting proceed, to "do this by the book." She hadn't specified what "this" was, but I wasn't clueless. It had been a bizarre day, from the bloated and headless cadaver at the medical examiner's office to my wife asking for a baby within minutes of the official identification of what appeared to be Cutter's fifth victim. I was operating under awkward circumstances that blurred the lines between personal and professional. But I also knew that Carmen Jimenez wasn't just being nosy. Of course I would have to answer questions about any relationship with a murder victim, and the state attorney had a right to know if it was old news or a potential flashpoint that could be tomorrow's headline. I wasn't quite sure how I would word it, but in substance, I would be answering the question that

Angelina had put to me in the privacy and darkness of our bedroom.

No, Samantha Vine had not been my only black lover.

I pulled up my calendar on my smartphone and scheduled the meeting for 8:00 a.m. In the state attorney's office. Top floor of the Graham Building.

The Boomerang.

Chapter Nine

I made a point of being a few minutes early for the 8:00 a.m. meeting in Carmen's office. She hated to be kept waiting, which was ironic. In my experience, and without exception, a meeting with Carmen would be interrupted in the first two minutes for a phone call that she absolutely had to take, which kept everyone else waiting.

"Hold my calls," Carmen told her secretary.

We were apparently playing by different rules this morning.

Carmen naturally had the most spacious corner office in the building. Top-floor views of the Miami River and the criminal courthouse stretched behind her tall leather desk chair. I was the fifth person in the room, counting Carmen and the director of human resources, which was what "by the book" meant. I hadn't expected Lieutenant Riddel—"Rid," I called him. We'd worked several homicide cases together, and I liked him, too. At one point Samantha and I had double-dated with Rid and his wife, and I still considered him friend enough never to call him by his first name, DeWitt, which he thought sounded like *dimwit*, and that some really hilarious guys over at the station reconfigured into "dumb shit."

Agent Santos was in a chair beside Carmen's desk, facing me. The American flag was a fixture in Carmen's office, and Santos had managed to sit directly in front of it, making hers the position of power in the room.

"Well, we're a big group," I said as I greeted each of them with an awkward smile.

"Have a seat, Abe," said Carmen. "Before I turn this over to Agent Santos, is there anything you'd like to tell us about Tyla Tomkins?"

It was a friendly lob, and I took it. "Yes. Ever since I saw Tyla's name on yesterday's newscast, I knew I would have to disclose our relationship."

"So you admit that you knew her?" asked Santos.

"A long time ago."

Carmen laid a notepad on her desktop, pen in hand. "Why don't you start at the beginning, Abe."

"I met her at a job fair convention here in Miami. You sent me to it," I said, glancing at Carmen. "I had just started working here. Tyla was a first-year law student at the time. She wasn't interested in a job with the state attorney's office, but somehow we started talking. We ended up going to dinner together. Kind of hit it off."

"And?"

"And what?"

"That was it. She went back to school in Cambridge. Tyla was Harvard Law. Very smart woman. Very attractive."

"When you say you 'hit it off' . . ."

I shifted in my chair. "This is getting really personal, don't you think?"

"My lead prosecutor in a serial killer investigation had a relationship with one of the victims. If I'm even going to consider keeping you on the case, I need the whole picture."

I knew Carmen well, and I read between the lines. Either she was going to ask these awkward questions, or I would have to face them from Santos. Better from Carmen.

"Okay, here's the poop. I was twenty-seven years old and single, working my ass off and not meeting a lot of women. I'm not proud of it, but I'm not apologizing for it either. A one-night stand was out of character for me, and it was my impression that it was out of character for her as well. But that's all it was. I never saw her again after she went back to school. That was the beginning, and that was the end."

"That's it?" asked Carmen.

"That's it."

"Nothing more recent?"

"Nope."

Carmen sighed, as if wishing that I'd answered differently. "Agent Santos, please show Abe the telephone records."

I glanced at Santos, then back at Carmen. "Phone records?"

Santos rose and handed me a printout. "Detective Riddel found a prepaid cell phone in Tyla Tomkins' apartment."

I caught Rid's eye. We had just worked a case involving prepaid cell phones. Criminals, especially drug dealers, loved the anonymous dial tone. No name required. No ID check. No billing information. No questions asked. Thirty bucks bought a working phone line that was virtually impossible to trace.

"Why would Tyla have a prepaid cell phone?" I asked.

"Maybe you can tell us," said Santos. "These are the records from the calls made from that phone over the past two months. There are five calls of interest. The highlighted ones."

I checked the printout, then froze. "That's my cell number."

"Which is precisely the problem," said Santos.

I looked up from the printed page, meeting the accusatory eyes of the FBI. "This isn't possible," I said. "I've never spoken to Tyla on the phone."

I looked at Carmen, who looked away, as if pained to see me in this position. "It *is* your number, Abe," she said.

I took another look at the printout. "I don't understand this. Honestly, I don't."

Carmen glanced in Santos' direction, as if deferring to the FBI, no longer able to help me.

"Our tech agents have already looked into this," said Santos. "There were five calls in all to your number. The first four were voice-mail messages."

"Well, I never got them."

"The tech report shows otherwise," said Santos. "Voice-mail messages are not like texts or e-mails. They don't float around in cyberspace forever. Once a voice mail is deleted, the message is gone. But our techies can confirm when the message was left, when it was deleted, and when it was permanently deleted. Each of these four voice-mail messages was deleted the same day it was left."

"Then I must have deleted them before listening to them. I never got a voice-mail message from Tyla Tomkins."

Santos looked skeptical. "Is it your practice to delete voice-mail messages before listening to them?"

"No, of course not."

"Do you have an assistant who checks your messages for you?"

"No. It's my cell. I check it myself."

"Is your cell password-protected?"

"That's office policy," said Carmen. "Our attorneys can't use any mobile device unless it's approved by our tech department and protected by a password. Each attorney creates his own. It can't be something simple, like one-two-three-four, and it's absolutely forbidden to share the password with anyone, even other attorneys in the office."

"It was a secure password," I said.

"So you accidentally deleted four new voice-mail messages on four different days? And all of those messages happened to be from Tyla Tomkins?"

I hesitated, fully aware that Santos had framed a question that didn't lend itself to a believable response.

"All I can tell you is that I never got any of these voice-mail messages. Maybe it has something to do with this prepaid phone she used."

"People use prepaid phones all the time. They work fine."

"And then there's the last call," said Santos. "It's two minutes long, and our tech agents found no evidence of a voice-mail message. That's an actual conversation."

"Two minutes could be a hang-up."

"The entire Gettysburg address was delivered in two minutes, Abe."

"I never spoke to her on the phone."

"Then how do you explain the phone record?"

"It must be a mistake."

"So four inadvertently deleted voice-mail messages, and a two-minute billing error? Is that your story?"

"I understand it looks fishy."

Santos nodded, her first sign of agreement with me since the start of the meeting. "Given the fact that you admit to a past intimate relationship, I would say more than fishy."

"What do you mean by that?"

Carmen intervened, putting it as delicately as possible. "It's the question I asked on the phone last night, Abe."

Were you having an affair?

"I was not sleeping with Tyla Tomkins, if that's where this is going."

Santos said, "That's exactly where this is going."

"Which, again, would be none of our business," said Carmen. "Except that it was with the victim of a serial killer you may be called upon to prosecute, and you didn't disclose it."

"Carmen, it didn't happen."

Santos retook control, speaking as much to Carmen as to me. "It actually goes deeper than a question of whether Abe should continue on the case or not."

"Deeper in what way?" I asked.

"I realize that this is a serial killer investigation," said Santos. "Nonetheless, in any homicide investigation, a married man who was sleeping with the victim is always a person of interest. Especially when the married man is lying about the affair."

"I'm not lying, and I wasn't having an affair."

"Hold on," said Carmen. "Before this thing spirals out of control, let's make some simple adjustments. Abe, I love you, but I have a lot of talented prosecutors. You're off the Cutter investigation."

"I was going to suggest that," I said.

"Which is the stand-up thing to do," said Carmen. "Now, as for this person-of-interest discussion. Agent

Santos, I understand the cheating-husband angle. But Abe didn't kill Tyla Tomkins. So if you feel compelled to put him on some list that the task force is maintaining, I urge you to be extremely discreet about it. This is a fine man's professional reputation at stake, not to mention his marriage."

"Discretion is a good thing," said Santos.

"Thank you," said Carmen. "So, I think we're all good here?"

No one disagreed. Carmen rose, thanked us, and showed us to the door.

Rid had work to do with another prosecutor and headed one way. Santos went the other way, toward the elevator.

It bothered me that things had turned icy between Santos and me. I was off the Cutter investigation, so it was no longer essential that we get along, but I hated to lose the respect of any law enforcement officer. I followed her down the hall.

"Agent Santos?"

She stopped, and I caught up with her at the bank of elevators. "I feel like there's been some damage to our relationship here."

"You think?"

"I want you to know that I did not have an affair with Tyla Tomkins."

I got nothing from her—nothing but an eye of disapproval for a man whose wife was the last to know. The elevator bell chimed, and the doors opened.

"I'll be in touch, Mr. Beckham."

Suddenly I was Mr. Beckham.

She stepped onto the elevator, and Santos was gone.

Chapter Ten

I drove to Coconut Grove after work. I needed to talk to Rid.

George Washington Carver Middle School is a top-ranked magnet school in an area that was once known as the Grove Ghetto. The Grand Avenue neighborhood isn't the war zone it had been when Janet Reno was state attorney in the 1980s. Back then, butting right up against Miami's most expensive real estate was a ghetto that could accommodate just about anyone's bad habit, from gangs with their random hits to doctors and lawyers who ventured out into the night to service their addictions. That had been Samantha's neighborhood. Carver Middle was the first punch in her ticket out. J.T. wasn't as lucky, having wandered the streets too late at night for too many years.

The neighborhood wasn't quite so bad anymore, but it was fair enough to call it hardscrabble, especially after dark. One thing surely had not changed: basketball ruled. I knew I would find Rid coaching his eighth-grade boys' team in the Carver gym.

"Be with you in a minute, Abe," he shouted from across the court.

His players were running "suicides" up and down the court, the sprint-until-you-puke ritual that the toughest coaches imposed on the best teams. I took a seat in the bleachers, ready to dial 911 or administer artificial resuscitation, as necessary.

"This ain't a walk!" he shouted to his team. "Everyone under thirty seconds!"

My friendship with Rid went beyond the cases we'd worked, deeper than the double dates with Samantha and his wife for dinner or whatever. He'd even convinced me to be his assistant coach for one season. I loved it so much that I'd decided to coach my own team. It wasn't easy to land a head coaching job at a school, so I formed a "travel team," which operated in a private league completely outside the school system. I lasted one season. My team was getting slaughtered, fifty-point blowouts or more. We had no height. I wondered how the other coaches were able to find fourteen-year-old boys who stood six-foot-four and could dunk with either hand, dribble behind their back, and shoot free throws with their eyes closed; how they persuaded parents to move the entire family from as far away as Orlando or Jacksonville just so their extremely talented son could play for Coach Nobody in a south Florida travel basketball league. Then I snagged my own ringer from Pompano Beach, and my eyes were opened. It started after our first big win. Ringer's momma came up to me before the ink was dry on my stat sheet. "Coach, uh, the phone company canceled my phone. Can you loan me two hundred bucks?" Next win: "Coach, uh, my car—I'm two payments behind." And on it went. "Coach, you know, the rent's a problem for me this month." "Hey, Coach, my new boyfriend says I'd be bitchin' with a weave."

"Coming back to be my assistant?" asked Rid.

I rose and smiled. "I wish."

His team was in the locker room, and it was just the two of us courtside. "Give me a hand with the equipment?" he asked.

"You got it." I draped a dozen jump ropes around my neck, gathered up as many basketballs as I could carry, and followed him into the storage room.

"You were pretty quiet in this morning's meeting," I said.

He shoved a stack of orange training cones onto the top shelf. "Maybe you should have been, too."

"Did I talk too much?"

"You denied too much."

"You mean the voice-mail messages?"

"You've got shit for brains if you expect anyone to believe that Tyla Tomkins dialed your number for no reason, that you never listened to her messages, and then you deleted them by accident. And even if that's true, it doesn't even begin to explain the two-minute phone conversation where there was no voice-mail message."

We stepped out of storage, and Rid locked up. "Answer me this," I said. "Do you honestly think I had something to do with Tyla's disappearance?"

"Shit no, Abe. I think you slept with her, and this song and dance is the typical married man's bullshit denial."

I followed him back into the gym, across the court to the exit. "That's not what this is."

"That's how it's coming across."

"Then I need to fix that."

We stopped at the metal exit doors behind the bleachers. "Abe, let me give it to you straight. You violated rule number one of being interrogated: Always assume the guys asking the questions know more than you think they know."

"Okay. You gonna tell me what Santos knows, or you gonna make me beg?"

"Let me give you a hypothetical."

"Is her name Tyla?"

"Yeah. Tyla Hypo. She's young, gorgeous, great body, smart, and married to her career. No time for a relationship, never been married. But she owns three different diamond engagement rings with wedding bands. Different size diamonds, from half karat to two karat. What's your take?"

"I don't know. She collects rings?"

"She was wearing a set when her body was found. She doesn't just collect them."

"So she wants people to think she's married."

"Not *people*, Abe. Men. She wants married men to think she's married."

"Why?"

Rid shook his head and pushed open the door. "Damn, Abe. Don't play dumb on me."

I followed him out of the gym. The sun had set, and the yellowish glow from the fire department's five-story training facility next to the school was the only light in the parking lot.

"I'm not playing dumb," I said, walking. "Really, why would she do that?"

"You missed the key fact. She has no time for a relationship. The only men she wants are men who don't want to move into her apartment and complicate her life. Men who are too afraid of creating a message trail to text her all day long and interfere with her work. Men who have no expectation that she'll hang on their arm at some fancy-pants gala that she has no time for, because she needs to be out doing her own business development. Men who have no interest in taking her home to meet Mom and Dad. You get it?"

"That all makes sense. But her friends, people at her law firm—everyone she knows—would think she's crazy. They know she's not married."

"She doesn't wear the rings around people she knows. Tyla worked for a high-powered law firm. She was in London one week, San Francisco the next, Hong Kong the week after that. Instead of eating in a hotel room alone, she hooked up with lonely married men who spend two hundred business days a year away from their wives."

"But she doesn't have to pretend to be married to have an affair with a married man."

We stopped at Rid's car. "Are you really this dumb?"

"Apparently."

"Abe, go get yourself a copy of *Cheating for Dummies*. Chapter one: Never cheat with someone who has more to lose than you do. If I'm married, and I'm banging a single woman, she's got the power. I live in fear that she's going to want more from 'us,' call my wife, and bust me. But if I'm banging a woman who's also married—who has something to lose—we're equal."

"So if Tyla wears the rings . . ."

"The world is wide open," he said. "Single guys, married guys, even married guys with something to lose. Married men who are too smart to risk everything for some gold digger will sleep with a married woman. They're all in play, and they all want the same thing she does. A good time, no strings attached."

"That's pretty calculating on her part, if you're right."

Rid unlocked his car door. It creaked as he opened it. "No one said Tyla Tomkins was stupid."

"No one ever will," I said.

Rid climbed into the driver's seat and started the engine. "By the way, Abe. About that list of phone calls you saw this morning from Tyla's prepaid?"

"Yeah?"

"There were six different numbers she called on that cell. So far, we've tracked down five of them. Every one of them was a married man. Including you."

It was like a punch to the chest. That explained the late-night telephone call from Carmen, why she'd dropped the gloves and popped me right between the eyes: *Were you having an affair?*

"I got your back, Abe. But do yourself a favor. Have a talk with Angelina." He closed the car door and backed out of the parking space.

I watched the red taillights disappear into the darkness, standing alone in the parking lot, right outside Samantha's old middle school.

Chapter Eleven

Victoria Santos rode the express elevator in silence, fifty-five stories up. The paneled doors opened, and she stepped onto inlaid floors of polished Brazilian hardwood. Silk wall coverings and museum-quality rugs softened the conservative decor, and the Baccarat chandeliers were an added touch. Just beyond the grand staircase was the main lobby, an atrium in the sky, three stories in height and enough floor space for a basketball court. The entire east wall was an arched window that, this close, was much larger than it had appeared to Victoria from street level. Seated behind the mahogany and glass reception desk was a young woman who could have been a *Cosmopolitan* model. Behind her, mounted on the wall, was a larger-than-life oil painting of three old white men, who Victoria could only assume were the late Belter, Benning, and Lang.

Victoria wondered if any of them had ever bumped heads with J. Edgar Hoover.

"Can I help you?" the receptionist asked.

Victoria stepped toward the desk. Her appointment was with Brian Belter, BB&L's managing partner and the grandson of the firm's founder. Belter's assistant had specifically asked that Victoria not announce that she was an FBI agent, so she obliged, giving only her name and the time of her appointment with Belter.

"It should be just a few minutes, Ms. Santos. If you'd like to have a seat, I'll call you when Mr. Belter is ready. Mr. Riddel is already here."

"Mr. Riddel?"

The receptionist double-checked her appointment screen. "Yes, he's part of your meeting. I'll call you."

Victoria went to the seating area. Riddel rose from the leather couch to greet her.

"Wasn't expecting to see you here," said Victoria.

"That's because you didn't invite me. I called Belter yesterday to set up my own appointment and found out that he already had a meeting scheduled with the FBI. I suggested we consolidate. Hope you don't mind."

"Actually, I do mind."

"Why?"

"Abe Beckham is your friend."

"So?"

"My goal is for the FBI to sift through every e-mail, every voice mail, every text message, to or from Tyla Tomkins over the past six months. I don't want any communications between her and your friend Abe to, shall we say, fall through the cracks."

"Nothing is going to fall through the cracks."

"Call me paranoid, but maybe once or twice in the history of the universe a man has probably covered for another man who cheated on his wife."

"Abe denies he had a relationship with Tyla Tomkins."

"Great. Two more times, and the cock will crow."

Riddel smiled a little, as if he liked her style. "Okay. Look, I have my doubts, too. But even if Abe had a little indiscretion, it has nothing to do with Tyla's death."

"Nothing would make me happier than to look at all the e-mails, all the evidence, and come to that conclusion. And I do mean *all*."

The receptionist came for them. "Mr. Belter will see you now."

Riddel stepped aside for Victoria and said, "After you," making it clear that he wasn't leaving and would be right behind her.

The receptionist led them down the center hallway to a double-door entrance to a conference room. The door weighed much more than she did, and she nearly fell off her four-inch heels trying to open it.

"Let me know if there's anything else you need," she said as Victoria and Riddel entered. The door closed, and Belter crossed the room to greet them.

Belter was a handsome man in his late forties, much better looking than his grandfather in the oil portrait. Two other lawyers were with him. One was a young associate who would surely say nothing, but who would probably be up all night drafting a forty-page memorandum for Belter that summarized the meeting, identified all potential legal issues, and analyzed every legal precedent since Blackstone that favored their position. The other lawyer was Maggie Green, a former federal prosecutor who had recently joined BB&L as a new partner, earning at least ten times her annual government salary to develop a white-collar criminal defense practice.

"Very nice to meet you," said Victoria, conveying not an inkling of her true feelings for prosecutors who cashed in.

The players took their seats, law enforcement on one side of the long walnut table, the lawyers of BB&L on the other. Victoria began with an update on the status of the investigation. Maggie Green interrupted several times with questions, not all of which Victoria could answer.

"Question," said Green. "You mentioned that in the Palm Beach cases, the killer left a signature on the victims. Exactly what kind of signature are you talking about?"

The sugarcane ash on the victims' faces was still not public information. "Sorry, I can't discuss that with you."

Belter spoke up. "Agent Santos, I appreciate that law enforcement has to be discreet in these circumstances. But as you know, this law firm has represented Cortinas Sugar for over half a century. Two of the four Palm Beach County victims were found in sugarcane fields owned by our client. On our advice, the company has been nothing but cooperative. One of our young partners is now dead, and she may be victim number five of this monster. Surely it's time to bring us into the loop."

Victoria shook her head. "I'm sorry, I don't have that authorization."

"Happy to let you call on our dime and get it," said Belter. "The phone is right over there."

"All I can tell you is that we have not yet confirmed the existence of the killer's signature in the murder of Tyla Tomkins."

Maggie Green nodded slowly, eyes narrowing, and Victoria could practically see the mind of a former prosecutor at work. "Not to be gruesome about this," said Green, "but is that because you have not recovered the victim's head?"

Victoria didn't want to get into all the other differences between the cases. "That's correct," she said. "And that's more than I should be telling you. But I share this with you in that same spirit of cooperation you alluded to earlier, Mr. Belter. There are things I need to ask of you and your law firm."

"Ask away," said Belter.

"It's very important that the FBI have full access to Tyla's computer and e-mail accounts."

Belter glanced at his partner. "I anticipated such a request," he said. "That's Maggie's area of expertise."

Victoria smiled a little, trying to lighten the mood. "So what's the expert's answer?"

"No," she said flatly.

"We can get a subpoena," said Victoria.

"We can fight it," said Green.

"That would be really unfortunate."

"Probably not very good PR, either," said Riddel. "Old *My-ama* white-shoe law firm blocks investigation into murder of its young African-American partner."

"I don't see what race has to do with this," said Belter.

"I'm just sayin'," said Riddel.

Green leaned forward, palms flat on the table. "Here's what this is about, folks. We're a law firm. We have clients. Tyla represented many of those clients. We can't just turn over her computer and e-mails. We have to protect the attorney-client privilege."

"Who were her clients?" asked Victoria.

"Tyla was in high demand by all our clients," said Belter. "She was extremely talented."

"What clients did she do the most work for?"

"Hard to say."

"Did she do work for Cortinas Sugar?"

Belter exchanged a quick glance with his partner. "Yes."

"Was she doing any work for Cortinas when she died?"

"Probably. Which is nothing unusual. Cortinas is this law firm's biggest Florida client."

"What was she working on for Cortinas?"

"Whoa, whoa," said Green, intervening. "Now, see how quickly we can get into sensitive areas? We need to sort out the attorney-client privilege issues in an orderly fashion."

"What are you proposing?" asked Victoria.

"First, I would suggest you submit your questions to me in writing."

"That's ridiculous."

Green continued, unfazed. "While you're preparing those written questions, we will review Tyla's hard drive and e-mails. We will then provide you with a privilege log that lists all documents we are unable to produce based on the attorney-client privilege."

"We're trying to catch a serial killer, Ms. Green. This isn't corporate litigation. We don't have the luxury of time."

"We'll move as expeditiously as we can," said Green. "I'm sorry, but this is an obligation we have to our clients. No law firm in America would simply lie down to law enforcement and turn over the computer files and e-mails of one of its partners."

Belter folded his hands, obviously ready to wrap things up. "Anything else?"

Victoria answered quickly. "Just let me know which one of you wants to accept the subpoena. That seems like my next move."

"Do what you have to do," said Belter. "Maggie is our point person."

Victoria was about to push away from the table, but Riddel stopped her. "I have one little thing," he said.

"Certainly, what is it?" asked Belter.

Riddel reached inside his coat pocket and laid a copy of Tyla's phone record on the table. "Ms. Tomkins had a prepaid cell. She used it only to call a handful of numbers. I was wondering if you could help me identify this one," he said, pointing.

Belter leaned forward, looking carefully at the number on the printout. "That would be my cell."

Victoria showed no reaction, silently enjoying the detective's pay dirt. She would have loved to take over, but Riddel had earned the right to make his point.

"Any idea why she would have called you from a prepaid cell?" he asked.

"We talked a lot," said Belter. "I didn't keep track of every phone she ever used. Maybe it had to do with international travel."

Riddel retrieved the printout, folded it slowly, and tucked it away in his breast pocket.

"Are you married, Mr. Belter?"

Belter seemed surprised by the detective's question, but he answered. "Yes, happily. Almost twenty-two years. Two children. A son at Amherst, and our daughter is a freshman at Duke."

"Do your children use prepaid cell phones?"

"Not to my knowledge."

"Parents like them because it's a way to keep their kids from overusing their cell. Once the minutes are used up, no more phone. But law enforcement hates them because they're virtually impossible to trace. In fact, we never would have linked this prepaid cell to Tyla if we hadn't found the actual phone in her condo. They're very popular with drug dealers, terrorists. Adulterers. Mistresses."

"Excuse me?"

The detective glanced at Victoria. "You want to tell him what we know about Tyla's call list? Or should I?"

Victoria appreciated the lob, but she was happy to leave things just as they were. "I think Mr. Belter gets the point."

Belter seemed poised to launch an indignant denial, but a subtle glance from his partner sent a clear message: *Say no more.* Belter cleared his throat, rising. "I apologize, but I have a ten a.m. conference call and unfortunately must wrap this up. Is there anything else, Agent Santos?"

"No. I got what I need. You, Detective?"

"I'm good," said Riddel.

The parting handshake was a formality, and Belter asked the junior associate to escort the law enforcement officers straight to the elevator, as if they might sneak into Tyla's vacant office and walk off with her computer if left to their own devices. The elevator doors parted, and they were the only passengers. They rode side by side in silence, eyes forward.

"Well?" asked Riddel.

Victoria's ears popped with their rapid descent. "Well, what?"

"Any doubt in your mind that Belter was doing her?"

It wasn't precisely the way Victoria would have phrased the question, but she was beginning to think Riddel was a guy she could work with nonetheless. She let the blinking number line of fifty-five floors tick all the way down to the lobby before answering.

"None whatsoever," she said as the doors opened.

Chapter Twelve

At four o'clock I left the courthouse for the day. By four fifteen I was back in the Graham Building, summoned by the state attorney herself.

Boomerang.

I could go weeks without setting foot in Carmen's office, so two visits in as many days under such uncomfortable circumstances exceeded my quota. Her follow-up didn't come as a total surprise. The morning *Tribune* had run a story about Cutter and the multi-county investigation, and the quote by an "anonymous source" regarding my "reassignment due to a potential conflict of interest" raised more questions than it had answered. I had no idea who the source was, but the state attorney's office was no different from a police station: both could be information sieves.

"We have a problem, Abe," said Carmen.

It was just the two of us this time, Carmen behind her desk and me in the armchair facing her. She'd left out Human Resources, which I took as a good sign.

"I know, I read the *Tribune* article," I said.

"That's not the problem."

She slid her iPad across her desk. The screen was alight with six boxes, each a separate photograph. Each was a black-and-white image, a little grainy, with a date and time stamp on the bottom. They appeared to be frames from a security camera video. My hand shook as I tapped the screen, enlarging each image and moving on to the next one. I had never seen them before, but there was no mistaking the images: it was me and Tyla Tomkins.

I swallowed hard, looking across the desk at Carmen. "We had dinner."

"I can see that from the photographs," she said as she took her iPad from me. She brought up one image in particular and laid the device on the desk, the image facing me. "I see a bottle of wine on the table between you."

"It was after work hours."

"You two appear to be having a good time."

"Nothing happened," I said. "I ran into her at a bar convention in Orlando. She invited me to dinner to meet a friend who was thinking about coming over to the state attorney's office. When I got to the restaurant, it was just her. We had dinner, some wine, and that was the end of it."

"Fine, Abe. Whatever you say. The problem is that you told me in my office that you hadn't seen Tyla in over a decade. These are date-stamped photos from a security camera. Are you saying the dates are off by a decade?"

"No. The dinner was last September."

"So you lied to me?"

I swallowed hard, busted. "That was wrong."

"Why did you lie?"

Why. Of course it had started the way all lies started, with a little one. "Nope," I'd said in response to Agent Santos' question about any recent contact with Tyla. One word, one syllable, had painted me into a corner. From that point forward, I was wedded to the lie.

"Because I could see that Agent Santos had already made up her mind that I had a thing going on with Tyla. I knew I was going to be pulled off Tyla's case based on what happened ten years ago. But I didn't want it going around the office that I got yanked because I hooked up with Tyla again and cheated on Angelina. That never happened, Carmen. But rumors become reality. So I kept the dinner to myself. I didn't expect pictures."

"Or phone records showing calls to your cell from Tyla's prepaid phone?"

"Carmen, I swear. I never got any voice-mail messages from Tyla, and I never talked to her on the telephone. Last night I wasted almost two hours on the phone with my carrier trying to sort this out. I can't get an explanation from anyone, but I still think it has something to do with the prepaid cell Tyla was using."

She sat back in her chair, then glanced out the window. "You shouldn't have lied, Abe."

"I know. I'm sorry."

"This is a mess."

I couldn't disagree. "Can I ask a question?"

"Go ahead."

"How did you get these photographs?"

"They were attached to an e-mail. Anonymous sender from an Internet café. But I have a theory."

"Can I hear it?"

"Detective Riddel and Agent Santos had a meeting with Brian Belter and Maggie Green at BB&L yesterday. Belter's cell number was on Tyla's call list from the prepaid phone. Riddel raised it simply to test the waters and see if Belter and Tyla may have had more than a professional relationship."

"Really?" I said. "What did they come away with?"

"Fire in the hole," she said, "if you'll pardon the pun. As Detective Riddel aptly put it, if you ask a man if he's married, and his reply is not a simple 'Yes' but 'Yes, *happily*,' the red flags go up."

"Do you think Belter e-mailed these photos to you?"

"The timing raises an eyebrow, don't you think? We fired a salvo across their bow; they fire one right back? They have access to Tyla's e-mails and appointment calendar. There could have been a reference to dinner with Abe Beckham. BB&L certainly has the resources to send out an investigator to check the tape from the restaurant's security cameras."

"So their objective here is to forge the uneasy alliance of assured mutual destruction: the state attorney messes with BB&L; BB&L messes with the state attorney."

"That's my assumption," said Carmen.

I sat in silence, thinking of the jam I was in. "I can't tell you how sorry I am about this."

"You know I should suspend you, right? You lied to me."

I nodded. "How long?"

"Two days, without pay."

That was actually a relief. "Thank you."

"Lucky for you, Abe, I'm feeling merciful. I do things by the book around here, even brought in HR yesterday. But this time we're outside the book. I'm leaving HR out of this. I'm not going to suspend you."

That surprised me, but I was grateful. "Thank you."

"What I'm trying to say is that I'm worried about you."

"You don't have to worry about me," I said.

She sat back, her gaze drifting toward the framed photograph on her desk. It was her late husband. Pancreatic cancer had taken him in a matter of months.

"After Sebastian died, people gave me a little time to get myself together. But it wasn't long before they started to ask, 'So, Carmen, when are you going to start dating?'"

"I got the same question with Samantha," I said.

"Of course you did. There's no right answer, except for this: Don't start until you're ready."

"That's good advice."

She leaned forward, her eyes clouded with concern. "I wish I had given it to you a year ago. But I'm your boss, and I didn't want to interfere. I kept my mouth shut. Pardon me for speaking up now, but I've always feared that you started too soon. I understand that you and Angelina dated before you met Samantha, that there's a history between you. But healing takes time. I'm speaking to you as a friend now, not as your boss. I see Tyla as a symptom of a grieving man adrift."

"I did not cheat on Angelina."

"Abe, I'm not blind. Tyla is a beautiful woman. And she looks one heck of a lot like Samantha."

It was true. I'd thought it to myself, but this was the first time I'd ever heard someone else say it. "Nothing happened, Carmen."

"Just listen to what I'm saying. You're a good person. You went through hell with Samantha's death, and now you've got your hands full with a new wife, not to mention your brother-in-law under house arrest. If you made a mistake, own it. Not to me. This is not my business. It's between you and Angelina."

I didn't answer, but I understood what she was saying.

"Okay, Momma's through talking," she said with a weak smile. "Take a walk, Abe."

"Thank you," I said rising.

"No need to thank me. Just don't ever lie to me again."

"Never again," I said. And I meant it.

Chapter Thirteen

I smelled osso buco when I opened my front door.

Angelina was a terrific cook, and her traditional osso buco with truffle oil risotto was absolutely my favorite dish in the world. I closed the door and followed my nose through the living room and toward the dining area. The lights were dimmed. Candles were burning on the table. A bottle of wine stood between two place settings. I picked it up. Empty. One of the wineglasses was missing.

"Angelina?"

I heard something in the living room. She was seated on the couch. The lights were so low that I'd walked right past her. I went toward her.

"What's the occasion?" I asked.

She looked up at me, a glowering that turned away my kiss. Her face was red and puffy. She'd been crying. "I thought we were going to make a baby," she said.

Thought?

I sat beside her. She scooted a few inches away, shaking off my attempt to put my arm around her.

"What happened?" I asked.

She reached for the large envelope on the cocktail table in front of us. Without a word, refusing to even look at me, she handed it to me. I didn't need to open it to know what was inside.

"This is not what it looks like," I said.

Her eyes refused to meet mine. "There are dates on the photographs, Abe. It was after we were married. *I* was your wife."

The emphasis on *I* was telling; somehow, Samantha was to blame. "Angelina, I promise you that nothing happened."

She swallowed the rest of her wine, and her unsteady effort to put the empty glass on the cocktail table ended with a shatter. "Shit!" she said, rising, but she fell right back onto the couch. An entire bottle of wine was way beyond her limit.

"I'll get it," I said.

"Don't do me any favors."

She pushed herself up from the couch. I tried to help her stand, or at least keep her from falling onto the table, but she shooed my hand away.

"Angelina, please—"

"I don't want to hear it, Abe."

She crossed the room, ambling in the general direction of the hallway, even staggering a bit. I followed tentatively, then stopped when she wheeled and stared me down.

"I'm going to bed," she said. "Your dinner is ready."

"Who sent you these photographs?"

"I don't know who sent them, Abe. They were in our mailbox. No postage, no address. Just the blank envelope. Obviously, it was someone who thought I should know."

My first thought was the law firm, Carmen's theory about retaliation from BB&L, but the immediate problem had nothing to do with who had sent the envelope. Angelina was quick to remind me.

"What difference does it make, Abe? Is that you with Tyla, or isn't it?"

"Yes. We had dinner. We're not in bed."

"You might as well be. Look at the pictures! Look at how you're looking at each other! That woman is five seconds away from crawling under the table and—"

"Angelina, stop!"

We were both getting loud, and I was losing. Angelina turned and stormed down the hallway. Part of me wanted to call out to her and fix this right now, but I let her go. The door slammed at the end of the hallway. The living room went silent. I gathered up the shards of glass from the carpet and laid them beside the rest of the broken wineglass on the table. The envelope was inches away, calling to me.

If BB&L was playing games, I wanted fingerprints to prove it. I used a napkin to pick up the envelope by its corner, letting the photographs slide onto the cocktail table without touching them. The first one was identical to the one I had seen in Carmen's office, a frame from a security video at the Orlando restaurant. Still using the napkin, I went through the stack, confirming that all six were a match for the others. At photo number six, however, I did a double take. There was a noticeable smudge. I looked closer. It was a black smudge. And it was right over Tyla's face. I lifted the corner of the photograph, and tiny black speckles ran to the bottom of the photograph like sand spilling downhill. I froze.

It was ash. Black ash smeared on Tyla's face.

It was suddenly hard to breathe. With great care, so as not to disturb any more of the ash, I lowered the corner of the photograph until it lay flat on the table.

Slowly, I backed away and got my cell phone. I dialed Carmen at home.

"Hey, it's Abe. About those photographs of Tyla and me."

"It's taken care of, Abe. You don't need to be worrying about this at home."

"No, this is important," I said, catching my breath. "They're not from BB&L."

Chapter Fourteen

Before the osso buco was cold, our house was a crime scene.

I was convinced that the photos were from Tyla's killer, which meant that a serial killer had stood on our front porch and reached into our mailbox. The photographs and envelope were bagged and sent to the lab. The mailbox was dusted for fingerprints. Our driveway was checked for tire tracks; the yard and walkway, for footprints. A uniformed police officer was parked on our street, keeping an eye on our house, and he would remain there overnight. It was every prosecutor's worst nightmare that his work would put his family in danger, and I wasn't taking any chances.

Angelina kept to our bedroom. She didn't answer my knocks, but Rid was able to get through to her, and he was talking with her privately, taking her statement. The front door was wide open, members of the forensic team coming and going, when Agent Santos arrived. Her attention was immediately drawn to the broken wineglass on the cocktail table. I had prosecuted enough domestic violence cases to know how that must have looked.

"A little accident," I said.

"I see."

"Just some spilled wine."

She didn't answer. I was beginning to think that the stars had aligned against any hope of regaining her trust.

Rid entered from the hallway and joined us in the living room. The statement he'd take from Angelina was on his clipboard.

"Not much to add," he told us. "The envelope was in the box with the rest of the mail. She's sure that she checked the mail yesterday and it wasn't there, so we can focus on the last twenty-four hours when talking to neighbors about anyone they might have seen."

Santos took the clipboard and gave it a quick once-over. "I saw ash only on the last photo," she said. "Did you ask if she brushed off any of the others?"

"She didn't," said Rid. "In fact, she had no idea what I was talking about when I mentioned ash. She never got to the last photo. After the third one, she ran to the bathroom and vomited."

That hurt. As if I needed to feel worse than I already did.

A crime scene photographer entered the living room, begging our pardon. I moved our group toward the kitchen, allowing Santos to enter first, managing to get a couple words in privately with Rid on the way.

"How's Angelina?" I asked.

"Drunk as a skunk."

"You think she'll talk to me tonight?"

"I'd wait till the morning if I were you."

I trusted his read, and I wondered if we all might be working till morning. Technically, I was off the Cutter investigation task force, but the photos had drawn me back in, at least to this limited extent. We took seats at the kitchen table, and I was about to pick up the conversation, but Rid went in another direction.

"Man, it smells awesome in here. Is that oxtail?"

"Veal shank," I said. "Angelina's an amazing cook."

"You're a lucky guy, Abe," said Santos.

"I know I am. I may not deserve her, but I'm a good husband."

"I hope you work it out," she said, nothing snarky about it. "I mean that."

"Thank you." Maybe those stars were realigning after all. Or she was playing good cop/bad cop all by herself.

"So what's really up with this ash?" asked Rid.

"I have no doubt the lab will confirm that it's sugarcane," said Santos.

"Let's assume it does," I said. "In terms of profiling, do you consider the ash on the photo to be the equivalent of the signature in the Palm Beach County murders?"

Santos thought carefully before responding. "First off, I can say that we are never going to know whether there was ash on Tyla's actual face."

"Have you given up hope of recovering the rest of her body?" I asked.

"Not entirely, but we're coming up on six full days. With predators, parasites, and the general acceleration of decomposition in the Everglades, it's unlikely we'll find skin, let alone traces of sugarcane ash."

"Let me ask my question a different way, then," I said. "Is the photograph enough for you to officially say that Tyla is victim number five for Cutter?"

"I would be leaning more in that direction if Tyla were white and had a black boyfriend, like the other victims."

Rid rose to check out the platter of osso buco on the counter. "Interracial thread is still there. Tyla's a black woman who has hooked up with white guys."

I did not let on that Carmen had told me about Tyla and Brian Belter. "I assume you mean me ten years ago," I said.

"Right, sorry," said Rid.

"Whoever, whenever," said Santos. "The fact remains that we have our first black victim, with no way to know if ash was smeared on her face like the previous white victims."

Rid grabbed a fork. "Can I try some of this?"

"Go for it." I kept my focus on Santos, who in my opinion was being too cautious. "If I were still on the case, I'd have no problem arguing to a jury that this is the work of the same killer."

"His lawyer would point out that the photo came five days or more after Tyla was murdered," said Santos. "Almost like an afterthought."

"What do you mean, an afterthought?"

"I can't rule out a copycat killer," said Santos. "You heard the medical examiner describe how different Tyla's wounds were from those of the victims in Palm Beach County. So let's say we have a copycat who watches the news and decides that attacking victims with a machete is Cutter's signature. He whacks his victim on the neck and disposes of the body in the Everglades. Afterward, he somehow learns that Cutter's signature isn't the use of a machete, that it's ash on the victim's face. What can our copycat do? Well, one option is to send photographs to the lead prosecutor's house with ash smeared on Tyla's face."

"How would he find out that ash was the signature? That's been kept under wraps."

"Our task force is growing, the number of people in the know is increasing, media attention is expanding, leaks happen."

"I see your point," I said. "But that raises another question. Whether we're talking about Cutter or a copycat, how did he get those photographs of Tyla and me off a restaurant security camera in the first place?"

"I'm working with FDLE and the Orange County Sheriff's Department on that. But there's only one way the killer would have known that Tyla was having dinner with a white man on that night at that restaurant. He must have been stalking her."

"All the way back to September?" asked Rid.

"It's not unusual," said Santos. "I've looked inside the computers of serial killers and found photos of victims going back years."

"I've prosecuted a few of them," I said. And hearing myself say that raised my concerns for Angelina once more. "Not to change the subject, but I know we have a squad car on our street overnight. What are we doing long-term? God forbid if the message being sent here is that my wife is next on the list."

Santos shook her head. "Angelina doesn't fit the victim profile. She's not a white woman dating a black man or a black woman who dates white men."

"I don't take huge comfort in that," I said.

Rid was still at the counter, his mouth full. "We can get increased patrol in this neighborhood, Abe. That's no problem."

"Thanks."

"Good sticky rice," he said.

"It's mushroom risotto."

The landline rang. It was on the counter right next to Rid. "You want me to get this?" he asked.

"Who is it?"

Rid checked the caller ID. "It's you," he said.

"Let it go," I said.

"Yeah, I don't answer your calls either."

The ringing stopped. "It's J.T.," I explained. "He lives in the apartment Samantha and I used to live in. He has no credit. All the utilities are still in my name."

The ringing resumed.

"It's you again," said Rid.

"Leave it."

"Okay, but if you call one more time, I'm going to have to take you downtown for stalking yourself."

"Very funny," I said, but the joke suddenly took on a different twist. The elephant in the room was that those photographs of Tyla and me, our dinner last September, couldn't be viewed in isolation. She had followed up with phone calls to my cell. The records showed five from her prepaid phone. Maybe not enough to constitute "stalking," as Rid had joked. But I was suddenly wondering if there had been others. Tyla had a persistent personality. She wasn't the type to dial a man's cell, get no response, and leave it at that. I wondered if she had tried more than just my cell. My old number, for instance, which was the *only* number she would have retrieved through directory assistance if she had asked for the listing for Abraham Beckham. The home number for Angelina and me was listed under her name.

A third round of ringing started on the landline.

"Okay, that's it," said Rid. "You're under arrest."

I pushed away from the table and answered. The voice on the line was calm by J.T. standards.

"Hi, Abe. The judge said I could visit the old man once a week during house arrest. Can we go tomorrow?"

The "old man" was my father-in-law, Luther Vine. "Sure," I said. "We can do that. I'll be right over."

"No, not tonight. Tomorrow," said J.T.

It was a long shot, but I was eager to get over there and check J.T.'s answering machine—*my* old answering machine. "I understand," I said. "I'll be there in a few."

I hung up and apologized to the Cutter team in my kitchen. "Stay as long as you need. I have to go."

Santos watched me, and Rid made himself a plate, as I headed out the door.

Chapter Fifteen

J.T.'s apartment was a short car ride from my house. Our conversation on the landline had clearly confused him, so I called him on the way and explained what was going on.

"What answering machine?" he asked.

J.T. had no clue, which came as no surprise. He'd been living in our old apartment for over a year and had only recently mastered the coffee machine. Forget the computer. And an answering machine?

"I actually don't trust them," said J.T.

I didn't even ask.

The machine was connected to the landline on the kitchen counter. It was a bit of a dinosaur in the world of voice mail, but I'd changed very little about the apartment Samantha and I had shared, so the answering machine remained. The digital memory was completely full. *You have eighty-seven new messages,* the mechanical voice informed me.

J.T. had truly never checked the thing. The newest message was about a month old. The oldest "new message" went back more than a year, to his first day in the apartment. I should have started at the most recent and worked backward. Instead, I ventured into the most dangerous territory of all: old messages that had been played long ago but not erased, messages from Samantha to me. Some were random gems, just the sound of her voice. "Abe, why aren't you answering your cell? Call me." Others made me smile all the way to my toes. "It's eleven o'clock, do you know where your wife is? *Work.* So sorry, baby. Don't wait up." One tugged at my heartstrings. "Hi sweetie, are you there? It's me. Pick up if you can hear me . . ."

And then there was the dagger to the heart. "Abe, I hate to do this, but can you move our dinner reservation to tomorrow night? Dr. Berch wants me to drive all the way over to Jackson for a couple of tests, and seven o'clock tonight is the only time the lab can squeeze me in this week on short notice. I'm sure this is nothing, but Dr. Berch is such a nervous Nellie that she's even got me worked up. I'll make it up to you. Promise. I love you. Happy anniversary."

So there it was: the pain-in-the-neck doctor order- ing the abundance-of-caution test that would mark the beginning of the long and painful road to the point of no return. Funny thing was, the first time I'd listened to that message, I'd taken Samantha's word at face value and agreed that it was probably "nothing." A few weeks later I would be glued to cancer websites, learning that mammograms missed plenty in women with denser tissue, and praying that Samantha wouldn't be another number in the grim statistical fact that black women were twice as likely to develop triple-negative breast cancer and twice as likely to die from it before the age of forty. Knowing all that, and knowing how the story would end, I could hear the concern in Samantha's voice on this replay of the old message on our answer- ing machine. Samantha had known something was wrong with her. So wrong that she'd canceled dinner on our wedding anniversary.

"Me again, Abe."

I froze. Tyla Tomkins' voice was coming from my old answering machine.

"You obviously have chosen to ignore my messages, but this is not a ruse that I'm playing to hook up with you. This is real. I said more than I should have said in my last message. This is damaging to my firm and my client. I'm trusting you to be discreet, so please delete

this message and the other ones I left on your cell. If you don't want to talk to me, that's fine. But at least have the sense to follow up with that old cane cutter I mentioned in the last message. He knows everything."

There was silence, but the message wasn't over. Finally, her voice returned with one last thought: "*Angelina, you don't know me and I don't know you, but if you pick up this message, I'm not an old girl-friend trying to hit on your husband. Please make sure Abe gets this. It's important.*"

End of message, the machine told me. I rewound to get the date and time: December 12; 8:31 p.m.

I hit stop and grabbed a pen and paper from the junk drawer to create a timeline. I didn't have the exact dates in my head, but I knew from the prepaid phone record that the last of the four deleted messages on my cell phone had been the first week of December. This message asked me to delete the earlier ones. They in fact had been deleted, and I knew I was going to have a tough time convincing anyone that *I* had not deleted them.

I replayed Tyla's message and wrote it out verbatim in longhand, jotting down a few notes and questions as well. I had more questions in my head, and I hoped to find a more recent message from Tyla that might provide some answers. It took nearly half an hour to play through to the last message. The memory card had reached maximum capacity on December 29. It was all solicitation calls after December twelfth; nothing more from Tyla.

J.T. entered the kitchen and went to the refrigerator. "I'm out of everything," he said, holding the door open. "Can you go to the store for me tomorrow?"

"Yeah, sure, J.T.—I'm going to have some people come over here tonight and pick up this machine."

"I'm going to bed."

"You go ahead."

"Did you find what you were looking for?"

The notepad was still on the counter, and I glanced at the message from Tyla that I'd written out in longhand. "I honestly don't know what I found."

The answer seemed to satisfy him. J.T. went to bed. I dialed Rid on my cell, so eager to talk to him that I was counting the rings. But something made me hang up before he answered. It bothered me that there was still so much ice to thaw between me and the FBI, and if it was melting away at all, progress was glacierlike. My first call about this breakthrough had to be to the right person.

I dialed Agent Santos.

I was recording Tyla's message on my smartphone when Santos knocked on J.T.'s door.

I had replayed it several times while waiting on Santos. Suddenly, a terrifying image popped into my head, an old *Mission Impossible* moment of the answering machine sizzling and self-destructing before my eyes, taking Tyla's message with it. The smartphone backup kept *me* from self-destructing.

"Come on in," I said.

I was glad to see that Rid had come with her. He tagged and bagged the answering machine as evidence in the Cutter investigation while Santos and I listened to a recording of the message on my smartphone, over and over again.

"Play it one more time," said Santos.

Rid joined us at the table for the fifth replay. In the span of two hours, we'd basically swapped Angelina's kitchen for Samantha's, transplanting ourselves from the present to my past, which seemed almost metaphorical, given the way the night had unfolded. Santos created another page of notes on her yellow pad as Tyla's voice-mail message played yet again. When it finished, I was more than ready to hear Santos' impression.

"What do you think?" I asked.

"Let's start with the obvious," she said. "It appears that Tyla was trying to tell you something about one of BB&L's clients, presumably something that is damaging to the firm and the client. The reference to the 'old cane cutter' who 'knows everything' would suggest that the client is Cortinas Sugar."

"I'm with you so far," I said.

"Which is interesting," said Rid, "because Brian Belter told us that Tyla was working for Cortinas Sugar before she died."

"But she couldn't have been calling Abe about anything she was working on recently," said Santos.

"Why not?" I asked.

Santos checked her notes. "Tyla's exact words were that an old cane cutter 'knows everything.' It's been two decades since the sugar companies replaced manual labor with machines. So Tyla had to be talking about something that happened at least twenty years ago. Maybe longer."

"That raises an important point," I said. "As a lawyer, Tyla would understand that after a certain period of time, the statute of limitations would bar criminal prosecution. So, if she was calling to tip me off about a crime, very few crimes have a limitations period that reaches back two decades or more."

"Murder does," said Rid.

"That's definitely one of them," I said. "Basically we're talking about a felony that results in death or one that carries a punishment of life imprisonment or the death penalty."

"A felony that results in death could be any kind of criminal negligence," said Santos. "Let's not be too quick to say she was talking about cold-blooded murder."

"But let's not be too quick to jump back in time, either," said Rid. "Maybe Tyla wasn't talking about an old murder. Maybe she was talking about an old *murderer.*"

"I know what you're saying," said Santos. "But I think it's a stretch."

"I'm asking, more than saying," said Rid. "Is it possible that when Tyla mentioned an old cane cutter who 'knows everything,' she meant Cutter? As in *our* Cutter?"

"An old serial killer does not fit our profile," said Santos. "In fact, it doesn't fit any profile I've ever seen."

"I'm not talking geriatric," said Rid. "Some of the H-2 visa cutters were eighteen or nineteen years old. An 'old' cane cutter could still be in his late thirties, early forties."

"What was the date of the first Palm Beach murder?" I asked.

"November twenty-ninth," said Santos. "Almost two weeks before Tyla left this message."

"So I may be on to something," said Rid. "The old cane cutter who knows everything could be Cutter?"

I shook my head. "It still doesn't make sense. Why would Tyla have any reluctance to pass along information about a former sugarcane cutter who might be our serial killer? She asked me to be discreet because it could be damaging to her firm and to her client. Passing along information about a murderer is not that kind of sensitive information."

"There's another possibility," said Santos, her gaze shifting squarely toward me. "Maybe she just wanted you to call her back."

"Well, clearly she wanted to talk to me," I said. "That's how a whistle-blower operates."

"What I meant to say is, that's *all* she wanted," said Santos. "There was no other purpose for her call."

"Let me be sure I understand," I said. "You're saying that she pretended to be passing along information about a crime just so I would call her back?"

"Sounds crazy," said Rid. "But when I was a patrol cop, I ticketed a woman who ran her car into some guy driving a Porsche just so she could meet him."

"A woman who does something like that is not a successful partner in Miami's largest law firm."

"Don't be so sure," said Santos. "Tyla seemed to be going out of her way to try to convince you that this was not a ruse. She even reached out to your wife by name in case she listened to the message, trying to put Angelina at ease that she wasn't hitting on you."

"Santos may have a point," said Rid. "When a woman with Tyla's track record tries that hard to convince a man that she's not gunning for him, I say hold on to your underwear."

"This can't be," I said. "Tyla would have to have been some kind of sociopath."

Santos gave me the proverbial if-the-shoe-fits expression. "We're talking about a woman who owned three different diamond engagement rings with matching wedding bands, who called married men on a prepaid cell phone to avoid detection, and who apparently was sleeping with the managing partner of her law firm. You knew Tyla better than I, Abe. But what I've learned about her so far doesn't rule out at least some sociopathic tendencies."

"Well, I didn't know her very well either," I said. "We had our thing ten years ago. We had dinner last September. That was it."

"Truth?" asked Santos.

"Yes. That's the truth."

"Did she want more than dinner?"

"What difference does that make?" There I went again, answering a question with a question.

"A big difference," said Santos, "to someone of her psychological makeup. If you blew her off, that makes you the one who got away. You're a challenge, a mountain to climb, the deal that never closed."

"I get it," I said, shutting down the raging river of metaphors.

Santos narrowed her eyes, pressing the point, as if switching to interrogation mode. "That goes double if you led Tyla to believe that you wanted her, but in the end you were just playing her. You spit the hook, so to speak. You went back to your hotel room, and she went back to hers. Or maybe things got even murkier than that. Maybe the two of you were on your way up to her room, still feeling that bottle of wine, standing too close or even some touching in the elevator. But when she opened the door and invited you in, maybe in words, maybe just with her eyes, something stopped you. Something made you say good night and walk away."

"Where are you going with this?" I asked.

"Just looking inside her head," said Santos, "trying to see if Tyla had something other than crime tips on her mind when she called you. But there's no way for me to know, is there, Abe? Only the two of you were there, and one of you is dead. You're the only one who can tell us if Tyla wanted more than just dinner."

I considered what Santos was saying, considered all of her insinuation. I can't say that I was comfortable

studying Tyla's motives in Orlando. But it was interesting to me from a tactical standpoint how Santos had
managed to frame her question strictly in terms of
Tyla's intentions, and not mine. Without having been
there, without ever having met Tyla, Santos seemed to
have a better handle on how it had gone down than I
did.

Or she simply understood how the male ego would
like to remember it.

"There's no question," I said. "Tyla wanted more."

Chapter Sixteen

It was almost midnight when I got home. The police officer was parked on our street, as promised. How much he was actually "keeping watch" was debatable. He was texting on his phone as I drove past him.

The front door was locked. I tried not to make too much noise, inserting the key gently, turning the latch slowly, and praying that the alarm didn't sound as I pushed open the door. My catlike entry was partly out of courtesy, a genuine effort not to rouse Angelina from a deep sleep. The more powerful force at work, however, was that waking her would mean a midnight conversation about Tyla. I'd had enough of Tyla Tomkins for one night, but there seemed to be no avoiding the issue. Angelina was on the couch, wide awake and watching Lifetime.

"I didn't expect you to be up," I said as I closed the front door behind me.

She was wearing her nighttime comfort outfit, a big terry-cloth robe with fuzzy slippers. She didn't look at me. Her gaze remained fixed on the flat-screen. "Neither did I," she said.

"Were you . . . waiting up for me?"

Her head turned slowly in my direction, and her expression said it all.

"Sorry, my bad," I said. I hung my car keys on the hook by the door and took a seat in the armchair.

"What's up with the squad car outside our house?" she asked.

"It's a precaution," I said. "There's a possibility that Tyla's killer sent those photographs to you."

That made her head turn. "Are you kidding me? A serial killer stood on our doorstep and dropped off those photographs of you and Tyla?"

"Possibly."

"Wonderful. Some wives have Dr. Phil on their side. I got Ted Bundy watching my back."

"No one's watching."

"Said the man who thought so until the photographs proved him wrong." She looked away, embarrassed. "Sorry."

She was clearly still feeling the bottle of wine she'd finished by herself, her drunk and sober halves clashing. "Don't apologize," I said. "I deserved that."

"We'll get to what you deserve," she said coolly. "But seriously. If no one's watching, why is there a squad car out there?"

"We're just being careful," I said. "Agent Santos does not believe there's any danger."

"No danger? Really?"

"No."

She looked at me again, this time even more intently. "And what do you think, Abe? Do you think there's any danger?"

I was pretty sure she wasn't talking about the serial killer, but I had no idea what the right answer was.

"To put a finer point on it," she said, "what about us? Do you think we're in any danger?"

Definitely not talking about a serial killer, but I was still looking for that right answer. "I hope not."

She exhaled loudly, something between a scoff and a mirthless chuckle. "Oh, Abe. You are such a piece of work."

I moved forward in the armchair, still seated but leaning toward her, beseeching her. "Do you want me to tell you what happened that night?"

Angelina switched off the television with the remote, then looked me in the eye. "I know what happened."

"No, I don't think you do."

"Photographs don't lie, Abe. You were having a very good time."

"It was a nice dinner."

Angelina should have unloaded on me for such a stupid comment. But she didn't. "I've been to nice dinners," she said in a calm, even voice. "That's not what this was. I saw the smile on your face. I saw the look in your eye."

"Angelina, I'm telling you the truth: I did not sleep with Tyla."

"I wish that's all it had been."

"What? No. Seriously? You think I was *in love* with Tyla?"

She shook her head, as if to emphasize that I just didn't get it. "No, Abe. I don't think for one second that you were in love with Tyla. You're in love with Samantha. And for two hours at that dinner, Tyla was your dead wife."

Angelina pushed herself up from the couch. She stood there as if debating whether to say more, then gathered up her long blond hair and put it up in a clip.

"I know you didn't sleep with Tyla, Abe. But you and I both know that it had nothing to do with how much you love me."

I didn't move. I couldn't move. I stayed in the armchair as Angelina walked alone to our bedroom.

Chapter Seventeen

I juggled Friday's workload and whittled it down to one early hearing at the courthouse. I was out by lunchtime. My afternoon was full, starting with a drive to Palm Beach County for a visit with a legal aid hero. At least he thought of himself as a hero.

Ed Brumbel was an ideologue, a relic of the 1960s and a magna cum laude graduate of Harvard Law who had shunned the Wall Street law firms and devoted his entire career to epic legal battles that pitted farmworkers against huge agricultural conglomerates. One of his first cases as a young lawyer had gone all the way up to the US Supreme Court, where he was lucky to find just enough holdovers from the liberal Warren Court era to produce a landmark ruling that children of Mexican aliens must be allowed to register in schools. He spent another ten years in Texas legal aid, fighting for migrant workers who swam across the Rio Grande to pick cotton in Hereford, Texas. He took on the poultry industry in Arkansas, where processing plants ruled over local farmers like feudal lords. He battled apple growers in Maryland and lettuce farmers in California. Success was fleeting after that early Supreme Court victory. He drifted from one legal aid clinic to another. When he was in his prime, women were drawn to his aura of romantic self-regard, taken by this passionate Ivy Leaguer who played Mozart on the piano in his spare time and went mountain climbing in Tibet every summer. His personal relationships were short-lived, however, usually ending when a new girlfriend discovered that he had no apartment and slept on the couch at the legal aid office.

Then Ed took on Big Sugar. And his life really fell apart.

"Mr. Lincoln, how are you, my friend?" he said, greeting me with a warm embrace.

Ed was one of the few lawyers who knew that my father-in-law called me Abe Lincoln. He knew Luther Vine's cane-cutting story in detail.

"I've been better," I said.

Ed invited me back to his office, which had all the charm of a warehouse. The Florida Farm Aid legal clinic was in Belle Glade, a mostly dirt-poor community that had once been a late-night destination for lonely cutters in search of a good time. Twenty years after the demise of the H-2 program, Belle Glade still had one of the highest HIV infection rates in America. The legal aid clinic was a few miles east of the noisy grinding mill for the Sugarcane Growers Cooperative, of which Cortinas Sugar was part owner. It was also just a few blocks west of a rat-infested trailer that housed an undocumented dozen of the estimated forty-five thousand migrant workers who still traveled to Palm Beach County each winter to harvest something other than sugarcane. Ed's office doubled as the clinic's file storage room. Stacks of banker's boxes covered all four walls from floor to ceiling. I assumed there was a window somewhere, but no one would ever find it.

"Have a seat," said Ed.

There was only one guest chair, and I had to clear away three boxes to get into it. Ed went to the wobbly chair behind his desk, resting his elbows on armrests where the leatherette had worn away and duct tape saved the day. I noticed a patch of rust at the corner of the desk, and the stain in the ceiling confirmed that it was from the leaky roof.

I'd first met Ed when I was engaged to Samantha. He'd wanted to see Big Sugar criminally indicted—again. He knew my future father-in-law's history with the National Sugar Corporation in the 1940s, and he thought I might warm to the idea of an indictment that would actually stick. The criminal prosecution never got off the ground. It was Ed's last shot at breathing some measure of success into his disastrous class actions. Big Sugar had cheated a generation of Jamaicans, his lawsuit alleged, because paying the workers not by the hour but by the number of rows they cut worked out to less than 60 percent of the legal minimum wage. After more than a decade of litigation, a jury rejected the claim. Big Sugar switched to machine harvest anyway, tired of being cast by everyone from *Vanity Fair* to *60 Minutes* as an antebellum plantation that exploited humanity. Ed's clients didn't get a dime in back wages. *And* they were permanently out of a job. Everybody hated Ed. Except Ed. "It was the principle of the thing," he'd told the media on the courthouse steps, his eyes tearing with bitter disappointment.

"So you want to know everything about the sugarcane lawsuit?" he asked, smiling.

I glanced at the wall of cardboard boxes around the room. "Well, not *everything*. In fact, it's not so much the case I'm interested in. It's more about your clients."

"Good men, all of them," said Ed, his smile fading. "Wish I could have done more for them."

"There's one in particular I'm hoping to talk to."

"Who?"

"I don't know his name."

"What years was he in the H-2 program?"

"I'm not sure."

"Which country was he from?"

"Jamaica, I think. But I don't know for sure."

"Which sugar company did he work for?"

"Cortinas."

"Okay, that's a start. We've narrowed it down to about forty thousand possibilities."

"That many?"

Ed gestured toward the dusty stack of boxes behind him. "The class action was filed on behalf of every cane cutter who was part of the H-2 program from 1980 going forward. Ten thousand cutters came here every year, mostly Jamaicans. Some returned year after year, so we're still talking more than a hundred thousand in total. Cortinas Sugar had about forty percent of them."

"I'm looking for one who might have been a witness to a crime."

"They witnessed it every day," said Ed. "The whole program was a crime."

It was a well-trodden road in Ed's life, and I didn't want to go down it. "That's not what I'm talking about. This would be the kind of crime that could be prosecuted twenty years or more after it was committed."

"Not many crimes with a twenty-year statute of limitations. You mean like a homicide?"

"Possibly. Or at the very least criminal negligence that caused someone's death."

He scratched his head, thinking. "Criminal negligence could be a lot of things in agriculture. But the only outright murder I remember involving cane cutters was in the mid-nineties."

"Tell me about that."

"These cutters lived in barracks for months at a time. About one level above Dachau, if you ask me. Tempers flare when you throw hundreds of grown men on top of each other, work them all day long, and give them no privacy at night. Throw a sharp machete into the mix, and someone is bound to snap."

"What happened?"

"One cutter lost his cool and swung his machete at another cutter. Cut his head off. Horrible. The victim had a wife and kids back in Jamaica."

"What happened to the killer?"

"Went to prison. I presume he's still there, but I don't know."

My interest was piqued, but I had to believe that Agent Santos would have already investigated a cane cutter convicted of beheading a coworker, as part of the Cutter investigation.

"My focus wouldn't be on an open-and-shut crime that's been resolved. I'm looking for a cane cutter who would know everything there is to know about a very serious crime, possibly as serious as homicide. And the crime has never been publicly known, much less solved by law enforcement."

"Wow," said Ed. "That's not a needle in a haystack. That's a needle in a needle stack."

"That's what I was afraid you'd say."

"But hold on," said Ed. "Let's think this through. Do you have reason to believe that this cane cutter is still alive today?"

I replayed Tyla's words in my mind. "Yes," I said. "I was told pretty recently that I need to talk to an old cutter, and that he knows everything about it."

"Okay. If a cane cutter had information about a serious crime, why would he not come forward? Assuming he's not dead."

"He's afraid," I said.

"That's one good explanation. There's a better one. Remember, we're dealing with Big Sugar."

I caught his drift. "He was bought off."

"Bingo."

I sat back in my chair, as did Ed, each of us trying to figure out how our deduction might narrow our list of possibilities from forty thousand. It took a minute, and then Ed's face lit up.

"Opt-outs," he said.

"What?"

He leaned forward, elbows on his rusty desk. "My class action was like any class action. The court required us to mail notices to all cane cutters who were part of the H-2 program and tell them that they were named in the class. It was a total pain in the ass. I had to get a hundred thousand addresses from the Department of Labor. But here's my point: the notice gave each member of the class a chance to opt out and say that they wanted no part of our lawsuit."

"How many of those did you get?"

"About seventy-five."

"I like that number better than forty thousand."

"Don't get too excited," he said. "A lot of the addresses we used were old, the mail didn't get delivered, whatever. But I always wondered about these seventy-five characters who actually took the time to fill out the form, check off the box to opt out of the lawsuit, and mail it back to us."

"That does seem strange."

"It's beyond strange," said Ed. "In my mind, the only explanation is that these guys were in Big Sugar's back pocket. If I'd had the money in my legal aid war chest, I would have deposed every single one. I was convinced that they opted out of my lawsuit because they knew something about the way Big Sugar cheated the workers on their wages and got paid off to keep quiet. But who knows? Maybe they saw dumping of toxic waste in the Everglades and got bought off. Maybe they witnessed OSHA violations and got bought off. Maybe . . . well, use your imagination. It could be anything."

"Anything," I said, nodding.

I still didn't know if I was onto something, if Tyla had truly called about criminal activity that could be seriously damaging to her law firm and her client. But I surely didn't buy into the idea that Tyla had made this up to reconnect with me, that she had the psychological makeup of some neurotic who might run her car into a Porsche just to meet the driver.

"Where do I find this list of opt-outs?" I asked.

Ed walked around his desk to the stack of boxes behind me. It was leaning to the left, the legal aid version of the Tower of Pisa. "Maybe in one of these," he said, and then he walked toward another tower. "Or here."

It was pretty clear that he had no idea.

"You don't have it on computer?"

Ed laughed. "That's a good one, Abe."

"Yeah," I said, only half smiling. "Hilarious."

Chapter Eighteen

I bought groceries on the way home from Belle Glade and dropped them at J.T.'s apartment. The world nearly ended when he saw that I had purchased his root beer in twelve-ounce cans instead of twelve-ounce bottles, but I had the perfect diversion: we were off to see Luther.

It was three in the afternoon, the geriatric version of happy hour, when we reached the Sunny Gardens nursing home in Miami Shores, which meant a bunch of old folks in wheelchairs parked in a semicircle in the courtyard and watching the Friday-afternoon entertainer. My father-in-law had a prime spot, dead center, near the fountain. The magician had his undivided attention.

"Keep your eye on the queen of diamonds," the magician told his geriatric audience.

"She's in your left pocket!" shouted Luther. He'd seen the act before. About a hundred times. But I was happy to see him engaged and with it. That wasn't always the case. Nighttime was generally tougher than daylight. Sunset was worst of all—sundowner syndrome, they called it. Thankfully, we'd caught him before dinner.

"Abe!" he said.

"Your son's here, too," said J.T.

"Devon?"

"No, Devon's dead, Pop. It's J.T."

An old woman shushed us. The even older man next to her scowled and shouted, "Shut up, yourself, lady! What happens in Vegas, stays in Vegas!"

I had no idea what the poor old guy was talking about. I wheeled Luther to the other end of the courtyard where we could talk.

"You look good, old man," I said.

"Don't you know it," said Luther.

Truthfully, I barely recognized him anymore. He'd shed twenty pounds in the last year, and it showed in his face. The barber had given him a buzz cut to keep him from yanking his hair out in the occasional fits of confusion, but it made him look even more skeletal.

"How's your girlfriend?" I asked.

"Oh, she's old news. Got my eye on a sweet thing from Carol City. She just moved in Thursday."

"Good luck with that."

"How you doing?" asked Luther. "You dating yet? Samantha would want you to find someone, you know."

I'd told him many times that I'd remarried. Either he kept forgetting, or it just never registered.

"Life's good," I said, rolling with it.

"Good. That's good. Life *is* good."

"Abe's been working in the sugarcane fields," said J.T.

I shot him a look, making it clear that I would have rather not brought that up.

Luther's eyes clouded with concern. "Oh, no, Abe. You don't want to do that. They gonna charge you for the blanket, they gonna charge you for the knife, they gonna charge you for the water you drink and the pot you piss in. You ain't never gonna make no money cuttin'—"

"Luther, it's not that. Don't worry. I'm not cutting sugarcane."

"He's trying to catch a serial killer," said J.T.

Luther's eyes widened. "A killer?"

"Somebody murdered his girlfriend."

"J.T., that's enough."

"Girlfriend?" said Luther. "You got a girlfriend?"

"Not anymore," said J.T. "Somebody whacked her with a machete."

"Oh, my," said Luther.

"J.T., stop," I said.

"They think Abe did it."

I grabbed J.T. by the wrist and asked Luther to excuse us for a moment. Luther's hearing was poor, especially in his right ear, so I didn't have to pull J.T. very far to light into him.

"J.T., what the hell are you doing?"

"You think I couldn't hear you talking to the FBI agent and the detective last night? I was wide awake in my bedroom. It's like a tin can in that apartment. I can hear everything."

"Agent Santos never said Tyla was my girlfriend, and she sure as hell never said that I'm suspected of killing her."

"Not in so many words. I could hear it in her voice."

"You don't know what you're talking about, J.T. Just stop it. You weren't even in the room, and you heard no such thing in Agent Santos' voice."

"Sure I did, Abe. I'm good at hearing voices. Remember? You told the judge I'm bipolar."

Now I understood. He was still ticked off at me about the court hearing. "J.T., just because you're bipolar doesn't mean you're delusional and hear voices. That's a stereotype."

"Just because you think I'm bipolar doesn't mean I am bipolar."

"It's your doctor's diagnosis."

"The doctor's wrong, which is one more reason why you shouldn't have told the judge I'm bipolar."

"J.T., for the last time: I never told the judge you're bipolar."

"How do *you* like being hit with bullshit accusations? Not cool, is it?"

"I have never accused you of anything, J.T."

"You should've told the judge the truth. Should've told him that I have post-traumatic stress disorder."

"J.T., you don't have PTSD."

"All those years cutting cane gave me PTSD."

"This is not funny, J.T. And it's not cool to be making jokes about being a cane cutter when my office is investigating these serial killings."

"How do you know I'm joking? Maybe I'm being delusional."

"I never said you were delusional."

"There you go, then. I do have cane cutter PTSD."

"You didn't cut cane. Your father cut cane."

He paused, and I hoped he was tiring of this game, which is usually what he did, so long as I didn't lose my cool. But then his eyes narrowed, and he turned his glare in Luther's direction. "That crazy son of a bitch is not my father."

"Don't ever say that. Your father loves you."

"If he's my father, then why didn't my bone marrow match Samantha's?"

It was the five hundredth time we'd had this conversation. High doses of chemotherapy and radiation were supposed to kill Samantha's cancer cells, but they'd also destroyed bone marrow, where blood cells are made. J.T. had been our last hope.

"It's like the doctors told us: siblings are usually the best shot, but it's not a guaranteed match."

"If I had given bone marrow, Samantha wouldn't have died."

"You weren't a match, J.T. That's not your fault."

"Maybe another test would've showed I was a match."

"We did all the tests," I said, "and then some."

"Maybe they made a mistake. Another test might've caught the mistake. Did you ever think of that?"

"They didn't make a mistake."

"Don't tell me doctors never make mistakes," he said sharply.

"Keep your voice down, please. I didn't say doctors never make mistakes."

"Then how do you know my doctor didn't make a mistake when he said I'm bipolar?"

I was on the verge of losing it. "J.T., this whole conversation is getting stupid."

"Take that back, Abe. Just because I was a cane cutter don't mean I'm stupid."

"J.T., you never cut cane."

"You sayin' I'm stupid?"

"No, I'm saying—" I stopped for air. I could hardly believe that I was playing along as if this were a rational conversation, but patiently walking J.T. through these episodes of verbal combativeness was the only way to make sure it didn't end badly, with J.T. pacing all night or skipping across the room till dawn. "J.T., the last time any American cut sugarcane in Florida was 1941. You're African-American, not Jamaican, and you never cut cane."

Luther leaned forward in his wheelchair and shouted, "Stop talkin' shit, motha' fucka'!"

The old man's hearing was apparently better than he let on. Or maybe we were louder than I'd thought. J.T. and I exchanged one final glance, my last effort to bring him under control.

"Take a deep breath, J.T."

"I'm still pissed at you, Abe."

"I know. Just breathe for me, okay?"

My cell rang. I told J.T. to hold tight, stepped a little farther away from him and Luther, and took the call. It was Ed, still at the Farm Aid office.

"Don't you ever go home?" I asked.

"This is my home."

I'd forgotten. "What's up?"

"I was going through these boxes—"

"Ed, please. You don't have to do that." We'd left it that I would come up over the weekend and do it myself.

"It's no trouble," he said. "If there's a chance that we could uncover a crime committed by Big Sugar, I'm all over it. Anyway, I have the name of a cutter for you."

"Okay, but if you tell me his name is J.T. and you hear a loud pop on the line, it's just me blowing my brains out."

"What?"

"Nothing, go ahead."

"Vernon Gallagher. Kingston, Jamaica. He cut cane for Cortinas Sugar from 1981 to 1986."

"What makes him stand out?"

"I checked the pay records. Cortinas kept daily task tickets for each cutter because they paid these guys by the row. Some guys took two days to cut a single row. Gallagher could cut two rows in a single day. For six years he cut more tonnage than almost anybody else on the field. The guy was a stud, the freakin' Michael Phelps of cane cutting. He stood to gain more than just about anybody from this class action."

"But he opted out of the class," I said, intrigued.

"He opted out. Remember, if a cutter did nothing and just ignored the class notice, he was in the lawsuit and shared in whatever money we might collect. But Gallagher took the time to read over this eight-page legal document in small print, sign the opt-out form, put a stamp on the envelope, and drop it off at the post office. He wanted no part of suing Cortinas Sugar."

"Interesting," I said.

"Either he was in the company's back pocket," said Ed, "or he was scared to death of them."

"That's a pretty big leap at this point."

"For you, maybe. But not for me."

"Why not for you?" I asked, and somehow I knew that he was smiling on the other end of the line.

"You don't know the history," he said. "But I do. There was some big shit going on at Cortinas in 1986. Really big."

Chapter Nineteen

Pumpkin hour for J.T. was 6:00 p.m., so I drove him straight back from the nursing home. The court's order on house arrest gave us a three-hour window to visit Luther each week, which meant that I was off the hook until next Friday. I'd been leaving messages all day for Angelina and tried her one more time from my car in the parking lot outside J.T.'s apartment. This time she picked up.

"Hey," I said, a little startled not to get her voice mail. "How are you?"

"Fine."

Fine. Delivered the right way, at exactly the right moment, it was the most vulgar of all four-letter words.

"I was thinking maybe we could meet for happy hour and get some sushi."

"I'm having dinner with my mother."

Not fine. "Your mother's in town?"

"I'm picking her up at the airport in thirty minutes. Don't worry, she's not staying with us. She insisted on a hotel."

"I could join you at the restaurant if—"

"It's dinner with my mother, Abe. Just us."

"Okay. Well, say hello to her for me. Maybe you and I can get a drink later?"

"Mom will probably want to see a movie after."

That sounded bogus, after a flight from New York and dinner. "Sounds like fun. What are you going to see?"

"Truthfully, Abe, I couldn't care less. I'll see you later at home, okay?"

"Okay," I said, not wanting it to end on that note, but there was only silence coming back from her. "Angelina?"

"What?"

"I'm sorry."

No response. Just a moment of hesitation, and then she hung up. I laid my phone on the dashboard, started the car engine, and blasted the air conditioning to help me breathe again. After a full day of straight-to-voice-mail, I supposed it was a good sign that Angelina had finally answered my call, and that she was planning on coming home later tonight. But I was still betting on *Ice Age*—not for the movie they were supposedly going to see, but for our indefinite future. Which left me with a huge dilemma.

Friday night was the memorial service for Tyla Tomkins.

My intention had been to steer clear of all services for Tyla. Over the years, I'd paid my respects to dozens of homicide victims, and I'd never missed a service where I was the prosecutor assigned to the investigation. But I was officially off Tyla's case. With all the media coverage of the Cutter serial killer investigation, Carmen had planned to attend Tyla's service herself. The Miami-Dade state attorney is, after all, an elected official. So it had come as something of a surprise when Carmen pulled me into her office earlier in the day and asked me to accompany her to the service. She'd made a fairly compelling case.

"Rumors are flying, Abe. No matter how firmly I say that I pulled you because of a personal relationship with the victim that was over and done with ten years ago, people talk. If you come with me to the service tonight, it reinforces our public position that nothing recent and nothing untoward was going on between you and Tyla."

"I appreciate the offer," I'd told her, "but I'm not going."

It was a position that I had staked out with personal and professional conviction, but I'd been rethinking it all day. Not for the reason Carmen had given. One much more compelling was weighing on my mind. I knew Carmen well enough to finally come to the realization that this other reason, the one she'd only implied, was the real reason behind her invitation.

I glanced in the rearview mirror, as if to check my own resolve. Then I dialed Carmen on my cell and told her that I would meet her at the funeral home.

"That's a good decision," she said. "We don't have to stay long."

"That's fine," I said. "This won't take long."

We hung up, and I was certain that Carmen understood what I had meant by "this."

I wanted to meet Brian Belter man-to-man, face-to-face. I didn't want to miss the opportunity to see him at a time, and at a place, where I could look him right in the eye and see all the way to his soul.

And I needed to do this—for me.

Chapter Twenty

A memorial service was scheduled for seven at Seaver's Funeral Home, just off Miami Avenue. It was closer to six thirty, half an hour past sunset, when I found a parking space and killed the engine. There was no rush, but if I intended to go through with this, I needed to do more than sit frozen behind the wheel, unable to open the car door. The internal conflict was on many levels. Angelina and Tyla were obviously at the center of it, but there was more. Seaver's was where we'd held the memorial service for Samantha.

Just do this, I told myself.

Tyla had been part of a large professional family, a mega law firm that numbered more than three hundred attorneys in the Miami office alone, not to mention administrators, staff, and the spouses of all of the above. Friday evening's service was for the broader group, with a more intimate service for her family and closest friends scheduled for Saturday morning at the Mission Hill Baptist Church of Coconut Grove. A necktie was in order, and fortunately, mine was still in the backseat, along with my jacket, from the morning court appearance. A shave wouldn't have hurt, but the best I could do was run a comb through my hair. I drew a breath, clutched my keys, and stepped out of the car into the early-evening darkness.

You have to do this.

The parking lot was filling up quickly. Visitors came from various directions, some having parked a block or more down the street, others in the overflow lot across from the funeral home. One woman was sobbing and dabbing away tears. Others appeared numb, or at the very least at a loss for words. I looked away, only to catch sight of the black hearse parked beneath the porte cochere alongside the building. The thought of Tyla heading to a cemetery was almost incomprehensible, but she wouldn't be laid to rest any time soon. The family didn't want to put off the service any longer, but the burial plan was on hold until law enforcement advised that there was absolutely no hope of ever recovering the rest of the body. The search in the Everglades was ongoing, and it seemed that all but

Tyla's immediate family had come to accept that her head would never be found.

"Wait up, Abe."

It was Carmen. I stopped long enough for her to catch me, and together we walked to the entrance.

"You okay?" she asked. Carmen knew the history with Samantha at Seaver's.

"Better than I thought I would be."

There was a small gathering of guests at the sign-in register in the lobby. I let Carmen sign first, and it somehow made me feel better about showing up at Tyla's memorial to see my name directly below hers, as if that made it more legitimate, or at least okay.

Several other clusters of quiet conversation dotted the room. Bouquets of white roses and chrysanthemums adorned antique tables. It was all very subdued and traditional, except for the poster-size photographs of Tyla that greeted us in the parlor. Her childhood was to the right. On the immediate left was Tyla the track star, not an ounce of fat on her body as she flew across the finish line in the 800-meter run. Next was Tyla in her crimson robe, graduation day from Harvard Law. And on it went, all along the wall, one shot from each stage of her life.

"You sure you're okay with this?" Carmen asked quietly.

"I'm sure."

Barely had the response crossed my lips before I took a turn for the worse. It was surely the photographs, but whatever the reason, the words Carmen had spoken to me in her office, that Tyla was "a symptom of a grieving man adrift," were rushing through my mind: *Abe, I'm not blind. Tyla is a beautiful woman. And she looks one heck of a lot like Samantha.*

It all left a knot in my stomach.

"Thank you for coming," a young man said.

I turned, but he was addressing Carmen. He introduced himself as Tyla's brother. "It means a lot to our family for the state attorney to make the time to be here," he said.

Carmen expressed her sympathies and introduced me. I shook his hand, making no mention of how long I'd known Tyla.

"This is so painful," he said. "We didn't want to have to do two services, but the outpouring from Tyla's law firm was overwhelming. BB&L was so good to her."

"It's obvious she was very highly regarded at the firm," I said.

"Very," he said, his gaze drifting toward Tyla's law-school graduation photo. "Last Thanksgiving Tyla and I had a nice talk. She told me how she was promoted from doing the work for Cortinas Sugar, which everybody at BB&L does, to doing the legal work for the Cortinas family, which is like an invitation to the inner sanctum. She was so proud. I work in DC, and the only person I've seen happier about a promotion was a friend of mine who got a White House press pass."

Her brother smiled wistfully at the memory, and I smiled with him, but it was the first I'd heard of Tyla being part of the Cortinas family "inner sanctum." It put yet another shade of light on her voice-mail message.

"Y'all go ahead and find seats," he said. "We're going to start soon."

He stepped away. I followed Carmen down the side aisle. There were more photographs, each one separated from the next by an impressive stand of flowers. We passed a magnificent arrangement of roses on our way to an open row of seating. It was by far the largest single assortment in the room, and I checked the card.

"With deepest sympathy, the Cortinas family."

It certainly backed up what Tyla's brother had just told me.

We found open seats on the aisle, and I checked the printed program on the seat. Another image of Tyla was on the front, but I went right to the list of speakers. Brian Belter was the first eulogist. I was about to point

out his name to Carmen, but Maggie Green had strate-
gically grabbed the seat beside Carmen and snagged her
attention. I didn't know Green well, but Agent Santos
had told me that the former federal prosecutor was part
of the meeting she and Rid had attended at BB&L.

Green was working Carmen hard.

"This isn't the appropriate time," said Green, "but I
need to follow up with you on the search of Tyla's computer files and e-mails at the firm. I received a subpoena today from the feds, and I'd like to coordinate
with both your office and the US attorney."

"Maggie, you are so right," said Carmen. "This isn't
the appropriate time. But I'm available."

A young lawyer approached, beyond obsequious,
clearly a first- or second-year associate with little more
standing in the firm than a messenger. "Sorry to interrupt, Ms. Green."

Green looked annoyed. "What is it?"

"It looks like you're going to have to speak."

"What?"

"Mr. Belter can't make it this evening."

Carmen glanced in my direction. His sudden no-
show was intriguing, but Carmen played it cool. "Oh,
no. Has Brian taken ill?"

"Called out of town," the young lawyer said.
"Unexpectedly."

"I see. These things happen," said Carmen.

Green shook the state attorney's hand and thanked her. "I'll be in touch."

"I'll wait for your call," said Carmen. Green and the BB&L associate left, and Carmen and I returned to our seats.

"Out of town, my ass," Carmen whispered through her teeth. "Coward."

"The worst kind," I said.

"But I'm still glad we came," Carmen said.

I was thinking of those words from Tyla's brother, curious to know what Tyla might have learned in that "inner sanctum," and wondering what the "Michael Phelps of cane cutting" might tell me when I followed up on Ed Brumbel's lead.

"Me too," I said.

Chapter Twenty-One

Agent Santos attended Tyla's memorial service, but no one would ever know it. That was the way she wanted it.

The disguise was not elaborate, and it was certainly nothing like what an agent might do for an undercover operation. But the blond wig, funeral-appropriate hat, and general low profile were enough to keep anyone from recognizing her. Even Abe Beckham had walked right past her. Wandering the room, with no one aware that she was an FBI agent, was an excellent way to pick up a stray comment that might not otherwise be shared with law enforcement—some unvarnished truth about Tyla or someone she knew that might help catch a serial killer. It could be a friend expressing her suspicions of one of Tyla's old boyfriends. Or maybe a relative wondering out loud about a cousin who was just a little too fond of Tyla.

By Victoria's estimate, Tyla's service had drawn close to seven hundred guests. It was to be expected, given the tragic death of such a young and successful woman, a partner at a prominent law firm, killed so senselessly. At one point or another Victoria had her eye on each of them. Most were from BB&L or other prominent law firms, many of them sad or even grief-stricken. A few had come purely out of professional obligation, signing the registry, expressing brief condolences to the family, and leaving before the eulogies. Still others had nothing to do with Tyla's life at BB&L. Older guests consoled Tyla's parents, occasionally taking a seat on the couch to rest their swollen feet. Some were there for Tyla's two older brothers. Some barely knew anyone in the room, speaking to no one, perhaps old friends from high school or the neighborhood where Tyla had grown up, having lost touch with Tyla years earlier but feeling the loss nonetheless.

Victoria's interest was in none of them, but not because she didn't care. She was looking for the lone wolf in the crowd. She knew from years of experience, both at Quantico and in the field, that when it came to serial killers, the stereotypes were often true. It heightened the thrill to return to the scene of the crime, help in the manhunt, even watch the funeral and visit the victim's grave. The memorial services for Cutter's previous victims had been very private affairs, too risky for a stranger to drop in unnoticed. Tyla's was very different. If it was in his psychological makeup at all, Cutter would make his appearance here.

Victoria stepped away from the crowd and found a spot behind a stand of white mums and daisies, where she checked in with local police who were monitoring the parking lot. She wasn't miked up, but text messaging was a less conspicuous way to communicate with a uniformed officer in this setting.

Anything? she texted.

A reply came in less than a minute: *Keep an eye on the guy with the cheap blue suit and the Converse All Stars. Looks a little suspicious.*

Victoria had already checked him out. He was the somewhat eccentric head of BB&L's commercial litigation department, one of the top-ranked trial lawyers in America, known for showing up in court wearing wrinkled suits and sneakers. It was part of his jury appeal.

Know him. Not a POI, she texted back.

The immediate family took their places in the front row. Most of the guests had found seats, and latecomers were filling in the few random openings. It was standing room only, and Victoria made one last pass through the parlor, pretending to be looking for a seat near someone she knew, hunting for a killer she was dying to know. Her search led her to the back of the room. No suspects. She stepped into the lobby and checked for any messages from the officers. Nothing. The parlor doors were closed, and she was the lone guest in the lobby as the speaker in the ceiling crackled with the voice of a minister.

"The Lord be with you," he said in a solemn voice.

Victoria prayed with them, albeit from the next room, but she stepped outside before the first eulogy. The temperature had dropped since sunset, and the cool night air was refreshing. The area around the funeral home felt more residential than commercial, and many of the nearby businesses were on large lots, formerly single-family homes. It was a moonless night, and the dense canopy of broad-limbed oaks and sprawling poinciana trees turned the neighborhood into a dark suburban forest. Hundreds of parked cars lined the street, but the police were redirecting traffic at the intersections on either end, so it was completely quiet. Eerily quiet.

Victoria stepped to the porch railing and looked out into the darkness, taking it all in. A young couple came running up the sidewalk, obviously late. Victoria opened the door and let them pass. Other than the squad car monitoring the main lot, there was little else to take note of. The occasional rustle of leaves in the breeze. A distant chorus of crickets. And a tiny, glowing orange dot in the overflow parking lot across the street.

What is that?

She narrowed her eyes, straining for a better look. The orange dot was still there, but ever so slightly it seemed to have moved. Someone was standing there smoking.

Jeffrey Dahmer had been a chain smoker. So had many of the other serial killers she'd studied and even profiled.

Victoria texted one of the officers outside, alerting him to check out the orange dot, but before she could hit send, the orange dot disappeared.

"Shit!"

Victoria hurried down the steps and ran straight to the officer in the parking lot. No one wanted a scene at Tyla's memorial service, but Victoria had to trust her own instincts. Several squad cars were in the area for traffic control, but she'd heard no engine start and seen no car lights after the cigarette was extinguished. She grabbed the officer's radio and sent the best be-on-the-lookout alert that she could articulate.

"Intercept subject on foot leaving Seaver's overflow lot. No ID as yet. Definitely a smoker, so may smell of cigarettes or have them on his person."

"A smoker?" the cop beside her asked. "That's all you got?"

"That's all we'll ever have if you don't help. Fan out!"

Victoria kept his radio, drew her weapon, and ran across the street into the overflow lot. The officer swept to the left, approaching the lot from another street entrance. One of the squad cars from traffic control pulled up, beacons flashing. A pair of officers jumped out. One switched on the spotlight and scanned the overflow lot, while the other checked between rows of parked vehicles, his gun drawn. In a sea of cars, law enforcement was the only sign of movement.

One of the officers circled back to Victoria and asked, "What did you see, exactly?"

"Someone smoking a cigarette, standing right around here. Watching."

This officer had some seniority, and he seemed to grasp the significance of a man standing in the dark and watching a young woman's funeral from across the street. He keyed his radio and reiterated Victoria's earlier message.

Victoria breathed deep, appreciating the officer's follow-through, but knowing that the window of opportunity was closing. The orange dot had vanished. So had the smoker. There wasn't much to go on. At this point, unless the guy was stupid enough to be caught running down the street with a lit cigarette in his hand, no amount of perimeter control in the neighborhood was likely to be of help.

"Check this out," another officer said. He was down on one knee, his flashlight illuminating a black patch of asphalt behind a parked car. Victoria knelt for a closer look.

Sprinkled across the ground were traces of ash, the droppings from someone's cigarette. Ashes wouldn't yield DNA from saliva or anything else she could work with. But there was hope.

"Check for cigarette butts, everywhere, the whole parking lot." She rose slowly, gazing across the street toward the packed funeral home. "One mistake. That's all it takes. And we find this guy."

Chapter Twenty-Two

Brian Belter peered out the helicopter window, the black Atlantic below him, the south Florida Gold Coast on the western horizon, a continuous blur of lights from Miami to Palm Beach.

Belter was in his usual leather cabin seat of a Eurocopter EC225 Super Puma helicopter. It was the fastest of three helicopters used by the lawyers for Cortinas Sugar, big enough to transport an entire trial team at speeds up to 170 mph above the south Florida gridlock. Tonight, it was just Belter and a trusted associate, the only BB&L lawyers not attending Tyla's memorial service, in the spacious cabin, even though it had been Belter's full intention to deliver the eulogy. He'd massaged the draft for hours, choosing just the right words, striking exactly the right tone, touching precisely the right emotions. Of course he had run it by Alberto Cortinas well in advance.

"Nice," Cortinas had told him. "Get someone else to deliver it."

"Why?"

"I need you in the Dominican Republic tonight. Take the helicopter to Palm Beach. The jet leaves for La Romana at seven."

That had been the end of the matter. Brian Belter would miss Tyla Tomkins' memorial service, which was no big deal in the larger scheme of things. Belter had missed countless funerals and weddings over the years, missed his wife's fortieth birthday celebration, missed the forty-fifth birthday celebration that she had planned for him, missed the births of both their children, missed saying good-bye to his mother on her deathbed, and, yes, even missed her memorial service. All for one good reason.

Because Alberto Cortinas needed him.

The chopper touched down gently on the helipad at Palm Beach County International Airport. Belter's associate reached across the narrow aisle and handed him the phone. The pilot was powering down the Eurocopter, and the roar of twin engines was quickly cut in half, making it unnecessary to use headsets or even raise their voices when talking.

"I have Mr. Cortinas on the line," his associate said.

Belter took the call. Immediately he could hear that Cortinas was not happy.

"I just saw an e-mail from Maggie Green," said Cortinas. "What the hell is this nonsense about a subpoena?"

Belter signaled to the younger lawyer that he needed to be alone. An ejection seat couldn't have popped her from the cabin any faster.

"The subpoena was inevitable," he said into the phone.

"So is death. That doesn't make it pleasant. What right does the government have to review Tyla's e-mails and computer records at your law firm?"

"Tyla is the victim of a homicide. The FBI is coordinating the investigation. They're being thorough."

"Bullshit. The FBI is charging ahead with a subpoena before the state attorney is even on board, and I know exactly what this is about. This is shades of the Clinton administration, when that US attorney down in Miami sued the state of Florida for failing to enforce environmental regulations against us. Don't ever forget history, Brian. The feds have been aching to bring criminal charges against the sugar companies since their slavery indictment got tossed out of court in 1941. They're using Tyla's murder as an excuse to go on a fishing expedition, dredge up anything they can find. Frankly, there's probably plenty to sink their teeth into in Tyla's files. And you know exactly what I'm talking about."

Belter did. "We'll make sure that doesn't happen."

"How?"

"Maggie is on it," said Belter. "Our position will be that everything is protected by the attorney-client privilege. The government can't have it."

"That's lame," Cortinas said, scoffing. "It's not enough to say they can't have it. Before we even get into that fight, we need to know exactly what's in there. I don't want any more surprises like your phone number turning up on Tyla's prepaid phone."

Mere mention of it made Belter cringe. "I hear you."

"I'm going to send in a couple of my IT guys to search Tyla's computers."

"When?"

"Tonight."

Belter glanced out the window, toward the corporate jet on the runway. "The helicopter just landed. I'm about to leave for La Romana."

"I know. Unfortunately, you've been called away on business out of the country and are unable to supervise this process. Of course, it would be a shame if some of Tyla's files or e-mails were inadvertently deleted, but I trust these men will do their very best."

The helicopter engine shut down completely, and the whirring blades overhead faded into silence. Belter shifted uncomfortably but said nothing.

"Brian, do you hear what I'm saying?"

Belter cleared his throat, then spoke in a firm voice. "We need to be very careful here. Depending on how this investigation plays out, a court could order an independent expert to examine our computer system and determine if any of Tyla's files were deleted after her death. That would be a very simple analysis for any tech expert. And it would be very difficult for us to explain. My law firm has been served with a court-issued subpoena. There are criminal penalties for spoliation of evidence."

"I'm not worried about that."

"You need to be. I'm not just talking about corporate fines and a slap on the wrist. There could be jail time for anyone involved."

"Understood. But here's the thing, Brian: I'm not involved."

Belter was silent.

"Isn't that right, Brian?"

Belter still did not reply.

"Brian, I didn't hear you."

"Yeah," he said in a clipped voice.

"Yeah what?"

"That's exactly right. You're not involved."

"I'll send the driver to pick you up when the plane lands in La Romana. See you in a couple hours."

"Sure thing," said Belter. "See you then."

Chapter Twenty-Three

I joined Carmen for dinner after the memorial service. She picked the restaurant, a trendy place north of downtown in the design district called—of all things—Sugarcane. I hadn't eaten since lunch and I was starving, but I had too much on my mind to enjoy the food, which was served tapas-style. I basically drank while Carmen gushed about the crispy Florida frog legs potato purée with salsa verde, surpassed only by the duck and waffle crispy leg confit. I nibbled on a honey-glazed sparerib between beers, and Carmen cut me off after two bottles of some import that provided much more kick than the typical American brew. The last thing the state attorney needed was for one of her senior trial counsel to be pulled over for drunk driving.

I was home before eleven. Angelina was still out. I was tired and wanted to go to bed, but I had to wonder if my claim to half the mattress had been at least temporarily suspended. I got another beer from the refrigerator, plopped on the couch in front of the television, and channel-surfed for a while. The bottle was empty and I was nodding off when the front door opened. Angelina was by herself, which came as a relief. I was deep enough in the doghouse without her mother's involvement.

"How's your mom?"

"Fine."

That four-letter word again. Angelina left her keys in the dish by the door and crossed the room behind me. "We're doing a spa day tomorrow, so you should make plans."

I already had plans to go back to Belle Glade. "That's cool."

She stopped. "What does that mean?"

"What does what mean?"

" 'That's cool?' Who talks to his wife like that? I'm not one of your buddies. Who've you been hanging out with all day? J.T.?"

Sometimes I could have sworn that Angelina had ESP. "Are we circling back to J.T. now? Really?"

A look of surprise came over her, followed by a knowing expression that marked the realization that she was onto something. "You *did* go see him, didn't you?"

"I took him to visit Luther at the nursing home."

She dropped her purse on the cocktail table, stood between me and the television, and looked straight at me. "We might as well discuss this now. Mom and I had a talk."

Oh boy.

"Don't roll your eyes, Abe."

"I didn't." At least I didn't think so.

"This J.T. nonsense has to stop. I'm tired of you taking care of him. I'm tired of you going back to where you used to live, tired of you looking after Luther, tired of the whole stupid extended family thing."

"I can't just cut them off."

"Why not?"

"Because J.T. will end up living under a bridge again."

"That's not our problem, Abe."

"He's my brother-in-law."

"He *scares* me, okay?"

"There is nothing to be scared of."

"Abe, he kissed me on the mouth in our own house last Thanksgiving."

"We've been over this, Angelina. J.T. did not kiss you on the mouth. I saw the whole thing. He went to kiss you on the cheek, and you turned your head."

"That's not how it happened."

"That's *exactly* how it happened."

"Abe, this is the kind of thing that families don't talk about, and they put up with it, and they pretend nothing's wrong. Until one day it ends up on the six o'clock news because some crazed family member shows up at Christmas dinner with a semiautomatic pistol and blows everyone away."

"I've talked to J.T.'s psychiatrist. He's not violent."

"I don't want to take that risk, okay? Two days ago we talked about starting our own family—though frankly, the thought of having sex with you right now is not at the top of my list. But whatever. No sane mother would want J.T. around her child. You need to tell him he's not welcome here anymore."

I looked away, but I couldn't say that she was entirely wrong. "All right. J.T. doesn't visit our house anymore."

"I don't want you going over there, either. I don't want you to have anything to do with him."

"It's not that simple."

"Make it simple, Abe. This has gone on too long. I've tried to be understanding, and as complicated and confusing as this may sound, I truly feel sorry that your wife died. I know it seems like I've turned into a nag, but I just can't take it any—"

My focus drifted past her, toward the image on the flat-screen. The volume was low, but the lead story on the eleven o'clock news was the memorial service for "prominent Miami attorney Tyla Tomkins." Angelina turned and followed my gaze to the screen. Her annoyance that I had looked away from the conversation quickly turned to anger. There, on television, was me, alongside the state attorney, walking into the funeral home.

Angelina looked at me in disbelief. "You went to that woman's memorial service?"

"Carmen asked me to go with her."

"And you couldn't say no?"

"She's my boss."

"I'm your *wife*. Do you have no respect for me at all?"

"You're making way too much of this."

She glared at me like she'd never glared before. I wasn't sure if she was about to burst into tears or erupt in a rage.

"Get out, Abe."

"What?"

She wasn't screaming, but she was on the verge. She came to me, grabbed me by the arm, pulling me from the couch. "Just get out. Go stay with J.T."

"Angelina, please."

"Go!"

Tears were beginning to flow.

"Please don't—" I started to say, but she was pulling me toward the door and screaming.

"Go, Abe. Just get the hell out!"

She was so loud that I was afraid the neighbors might hear, not to mention one of the extra MDPD officers who had been patrolling our neighborhood since Thursday night and the arrival of those photographs of Tyla and me.

"Get out!"

Angelina pulled me across the room and yanked open the front door. I grabbed my keys as she literally pushed me out, and the door slammed behind me.

I stood outside on the porch for a minute, debating whether I should actually leave. I heard my empty beer bottle smash against the door, a direct hit from across the room, which was confirmation enough.

I walked slowly across the lawn to my car in the driveway, got inside, and started the engine. I didn't want to leave, but I didn't blame Angelina. The steering wheel was the closest target available, and I pounded it so hard that I thought I'd broken my fist.

"Idiot!" I shouted, and it had nothing to do with my throbbing hand.

The porch light went out, and the front window went dark. Angelina's final punctuation mark. I backed out of our driveway and drove away, not sure where I was headed.

Chapter Twenty-Four

I ended up at J.T.'s apartment.

J.T. had his definite downside, but one thing that could be counted on was that if ever you showed up at his door at midnight after an argument with your wife, not a word of it would end up on Facebook, Twitter, or any other social media. He didn't do any of it. I assured him that nothing was wrong, but even someone as self-centered as J.T. could see the worry lines etched on my face.

"Did you and Angelina have a fight?"

"No."

"Was it about me?"

Everybody but me had ESP, and I was getting tired of it. "I just need a place to sleep."

His interrogation continued, and finally my only exit was to close my eyes and pretend to fall asleep on the couch. He was a late sleeper on his medication, and I made a point of leaving the next morning long before he woke.

Belle Glade was a ninety-minute drive north, and I didn't even have to stop by my house to freshen up. Not to prove Angelina's point, but "emergency" overnighters at J.T.'s apartment had become so commonplace that I kept clean clothes and a toothbrush there. I reached the Farm Aid office by nine thirty. Ed drove from there. After such a horrendous week, I must have been desperate for comic relief, because it struck me as the funniest thing on earth that Ed actually owned an old Volkswagen bus, and I just couldn't stop laughing.

"What's so funny?"

I got control of myself. "Nothing, Shaggy."

I burst out laughing again.

We drove west out of the town of Belle Glade for about ten minutes, until we had to stop at a railroad crossing deep in the middle of cane-covered farmland. An endless string of railcars passed before my eyes, brimming with mounds of freshly cut cane stalks headed for the grinding mill.

"Six hundred thousand tons of cane every cutting season," said Ed. "And that's just Cortinas."

"How much sugar comes out of that?"

"A shitload. And with the artificial price supports from Uncle Sam, they sell it wholesale at a guaranteed minimum of twenty-two cents a pound, compared to about eight cents for sugar grown in other countries. Big Sugar will spit in your eye and call your mother dirty names if you ever utter the words 'corporate welfare,' but if you add it all up across the industry, the sugar subsidy puts an extra two-point-five billion on the backs of American consumers each year."

Ed had an assortment of rants against the sugar industry, each packaged separately and as neatly as the pink, blue, and yellow sugar substitutes on the coffee bar. "Sounds like your next lawsuit," I said.

"Don't get me started."

The end of the train finally passed, and the warning lights stopped flashing. The old van rocked over the rough crossing, but the next ten miles on the other side of the tracks looked exactly like the previous ten. The Cortinas family owned 12 percent of all the land in Palm Beach County, about 155,000 acres, not counting Alberto's $20 million Mediterranean-style estate on the island of Palm Beach. Neat rows of cane sprouted from the rich bed of black soil that the slow flow of the Everglades had deposited over the last hundred thousand years, most of it decayed saw grass. Here, on Cortinas land, the waters flowed no more, except in the rainy season, when the runoff of phosphates and other pollutants from the drained wetlands found their way into the waterways and canals and became someone else's problem.

Ed slowed the van, and we stopped on the gravel shoulder of the road. It seemed to be no place special, sugarcane fields to the south, the mirror image to the north.

"We're here," he said.

"Where is 'here'?"

Ed reached across to the glove compartment, removed a yellowed newspaper, and handed it to me. It was the front page of the *Palm Beach Post*, dated January 17, 1986.

"Car Crash Kills State Rep," read the headline below the fold. The first paragraph told me why Ed had brought me to this spot:

State representative Marshall Conrad (D. Sebring) died in a single-car crash twelve miles west of Belle Glade. The charred remains of his vehicle were found early Wednesday in a cane field. The field was undergoing a controlled burn late Tuesday night in preparation for harvesting, and workers for the Cortinas sugar company discovered the vehicle the next morning. Florida Highway Patrol reports that there were no known witnesses and that the accident is under investigation.

I skimmed the rest of the story, but it was mostly a discussion of the victim's record for fiscal conservatism as a state legislator and his plans to run for Congress in the upcoming fall election. Nothing further about the crash.

"So what happened?"

"You just read it."

I flicked the newspaper with my finger. "This hardly tells me anything."

Ed smiled and shook his head. "Welcome to the Cortinas world of privacy, power, and influence. Not another detail was ever released to the public."

"There must have been a police report," I said.

"Sealed."

"Medical examiner's report?"

"Sealed."

"Investigative file?"

"Sealed."

"Why?"

"Good question. This guy Conrad was a rising star in Florida politics. Not much help on the Everglades, but he hated Big Sugar on pure economics. He was gearing up to run a congressional campaign that would lay out the incumbent as the sugar industry's boy—a puppet on Capitol Hill who lines the pockets of the Cortinas family with artificial price supports from the federal government."

Now I understood his corporate welfare rant as we'd watched the train pass. "So you're serious? There's no public account of *how* this happened?"

"None."

I checked the masthead one more time, noting the year. "Nineteen eighty-six."

"The same year that Vernon Gallagher ended his cane cutting career."

"So, you're thinking—what?"

"Oh, I don't know," said Ed playfully. "A rising star in Florida politics dies in a fiery crash in a Cortinas cane field before he can challenge the sugar industry's biggest supporter in Congress. And within months the Michael Phelps of cane cutting hangs up his machete. Coincidence? Or not?"

I took his meaning. "The implication being that Vernon Gallagher was out in the field and knows something about the accident."

"Yeah," said Ed. "Like maybe the accident was no accident."

"A homicide," I said, "which has no statute of limitations."

"Which Tyla Tomkins would have reason to bring to your attention all these years later."

I glanced out the passenger side window, toward the thick cane field, then back at Ed. "We're getting way ahead of ourselves here."

"Yeah, I know." Ed restarted the engine.

"The good news is that our next trip should be much more interesting."

"Next trip?" he asked.

"Jamaica."

"Excellent. You're going to Jamaica?"

"No, *we* are," I said. "Time for a little talk with Vernon Gallagher."

I called Angelina on the drive back from Palm Beach County. She didn't answer, and I decided not to leave a message. Little more than twelve hours had passed since she'd thrown me out of the house. If she wasn't ready to talk, pushing her wasn't going to help.

I was cruising down the turnpike, south of cane country, but my thoughts drifted back to the Cortinas family. I was trying not to run too fast with Ed's theory about 1986. He was, after all, the ponytailed crusader who had taken on the sugar industry in a twelve-year legal battle, with nothing to show for it but an office full of archive boxes and ten thousand Jamaicans out of

work. But a day trip to Kingston wasn't a huge invest-
ment on my part, and if we could actually find Vernon
Gallagher, the payoff could be huge, and not just from
the standpoint of law enforcement. If Tyla's phone calls
to me did in fact prove to be a genuine crime tip, it
might soften some of Angelina's anger over my decision to attend the memorial service with Carmen. Of
course, there were still the dinner photographs from
Orlando. For that, I would simply have to beg for
Angelina's forgiveness.

Flowers? But not a bouquet. I could send her one
long-stemmed rose at a time. The first time we'd moved
in together, I'd told Angelina to choose her side of the
walk-in closet, select the dresser drawers she wanted,
and mark off the "Angelina only" section of the shared
master bathroom. After she fell asleep, I got up and
placed a single red rose in each drawer, each cabinet,
and every space she'd chosen, so that she'd find them
when she woke. We'd both missed work that morning.
That would evoke a nice memory. Or would it?

It occurred to me that I was again reaching back to
the pre-Samantha days of Abe and Angelina.

My cell rang through the Bluetooth. I checked the
digital display on the dashboard, which alerted me to
two facts: that I was doing eighty-five, and that the
call was from a New York area code. My hope was

that Angelina was calling me on her mother's phone. I cut my speed and answered on speaker. It was my mother-in-law.

"Abe, do you know where Angelina is?"

It was a strange question—not because I didn't know the answer, but because they were supposed to be at the spa together. "No, I've been in Palm Beach all day."

"When's the last time you saw her?"

The strangeness was giving way to a certain urgency in her voice. "Is everything okay?"

"Yes. No. I mean—I don't know. When did you see her last?"

"Just before midnight. I spent the night at J.T.'s apartment. Margaret, what is going on?"

"We were supposed to meet at my hotel two hours ago. Angelina never showed up. I've been calling her on her cell, and no one answers."

"I tried, too," I said. "Has anyone gone by the house?"

"Yes, I'm standing on the front porch right now. That's what has me so worried. Her car is here in the driveway, but no one answers the door."

It was premature for this to be a missing person case under normal protocol, but those photographs she'd received—possibly from a serial killer—changed everything.

"Margaret, I want you to stay calm, okay? There have been extra patrol cars in our neighborhood since Thursday night."

"Oh, my God, Abe. What is going on?"

"Help will be there soon," I told her. "I'm going to hang up and dial nine-one-one right now."

Chapter Twenty-Five

I felt like a switchboard operator on the ride home, dialing numbers, taking callbacks, making follow-ups.

My first call was to Carmen, who got right on it, and then to Rid. Two minutes later, Carmen called back to let me know that a pair of first responders had forced their way into our house. The good news was that the police hadn't found Angelina hurt, or worse.

"The concern is that no one knows where she is," said Carmen.

"What about the extra patrol officers in our neighborhood? Did any of them see her come or go from the house?"

"No."

I recalled my drive home Thursday night, when I'd spotted the extra officer sitting in his squad car, texting. "Is Angelina's car still in the driveway?"

"Yeah. That's one of the confusing things."

"She's a jogger. Did anyone see her out running this morning?"

"No, Abe. But they're interviewing neighbors as we speak."

We agreed that the FBI should be involved. Santos had made her mark at the bureau as a pioneer of what was then known as the Child Abduction and Serial Killer Unit. Despite the recent tension between Santos and me, it seemed like a godsend that she was at our disposal. Even so, my next call was to Rid, who conferenced in the other MDPD lieutenant overseeing the investigation, which was centered at my house. I shared everything I thought it was important for them to know about Angelina's habits, hangouts, and friends. Explaining why I hadn't been home with my wife last night was awkward, but I had to get everyone to move past it.

"You guys need to keep checking the neighborhood, checking her phone, her iPad. There must be something."

"We're on it," said Rid.

I wanted to be right on the scene, but I fully trusted that Rid was indeed "on it." I knew that every neighbor in the area would be interviewed, every emergency room in the county contacted, and that everything from Angelina's cell phone to her Facebook page would be tracked and monitored. Any activity on her credit cards would be an immediate red flag. But I needed to do something. I had only a mental list of names for Angelina's girlfriends and coworkers. Dialing 411 was something I could do from my car, and I called everyone I could think of. Some were good friends who could be trusted to act responsibly. But some of the names that came to mind were fringe friends, ex-friends, or coworkers I'd never met. There were bound to be a few gossips who might start rumors that Angelina was shacking up with an old boyfriend and would show up eventually. This was no time to be concerned about what others might think. To a point. I tempered the message with people I didn't really know, striking the right balance of urgency without feeding the salacious grapevine.

"Have you spoken to Angelina today?"

"No. Is something wrong, Abe?"

"I don't know. We're afraid she may have gotten into an accident or something."

I knew that was a lie, even before I came speeding down the street and spotted Angelina's car still in our driveway. I'd run three stop signs and two red lights

since leaving the turnpike. On the grassy swale outside the house were several squad cars parked beside a green-and-white van from the MDPD crime scene investigation unit. My car skidded to a stop behind the flashing beacons. Our front door was wide open, and I took it as a positive sign that no ambulance or medical examiner's van was on the scene, confirmation of Santos' earlier report of no body inside. Still, you don't have to be in law enforcement to recognize a cadaver-sniffing dog, and the canine unit was on the scene.

"Please, please, God," I said softly as I jumped out of the car.

My heart was pounding, and I sprinted up the sidewalk, stopping at the yellow police tape in the doorway. Santos was standing in the living room, on the other side of the tape, watching over one of the investigators.

"Has anyone heard from Angelina?" I asked, breathless. I had tried Angelina's cell several times from my car with no answer. Santos came one step closer and then stopped, leaving a good ten feet between herself and the open doorway.

"No," she said.

"Where's her mom?"

"One of the officers drove her back to the hotel. We wanted her by the telephone in case Angelina calls her room."

That made sense. I glanced around the doorjamb and noticed another investigator on his hands and knees with a penlight, combing through the carpeting between the couch and the front door.

The broken beer bottle. I had forgotten all about it in my conference call from the car with Rid, and I'd made no mention of it.

"I can explain that," I said.

"Good, but don't come in. I'll be right there. Oh, while I'm thinking of it, can you toss me your car keys?"

"What for?"

"I need to have one of the investigators go through your car. Just standard procedure. You don't mind, do you?"

If it hadn't come up immediately after the beer bottle, I probably would have minded less. "That's fine." I tossed her the keys.

Santos headed for the kitchen, our back entrance, and I waited on the front porch for her to walk around the house. My anxiety level was already high, but the thought of having to explain a broken beer bottle sent my stress level skyrocketing. I may have come across as a bit too defensive, but I wanted to address the bottle up front. I stepped down from the porch and met Santos halfway across our front yard.

"That broken bottle is not from an intruder," I said.

"How do you know that?"

"It's mine."

Her expression cut right through me. "Is this a tradition in your house? Angelina smashes her wine-glasses, you smash your beer bottles?"

My mouth fell open. I had forgotten about the broken wineglass Santos had found by the photographs. "This must look really bad," I said.

Santos was deadpan, no response.

"We're not a violent couple," I said. "Throwing bottles across the room is not what we do. It's important for you to know that."

"You want to tell me what happened?"

"Angelina came home around eleven last night. I was on the couch, half asleep. Somehow we got into an argument about J.T."

"What about J.T.?"

"Looking after him. It's more of an ongoing discussion and disagreement than an argument. What really set her off was when she found out that I went to Tyla's memorial service."

"You didn't tell her before you went?"

Her tone was much calmer than Angelina's had been, but it sounded worse coming from an FBI agent. "No. Carmen asked me to go with her, and I decided at the last minute."

"So you told Angelina when she got home?"

"Well, actually, she saw Carmen and me on television."

"So you never even *intended* to tell Angelina?"

"No, that's not right."

"But she obviously thinks you slept with Tyla."

"That's not right either," I said. "In fact, the opposite is true. Angelina told me—"

"She told you what?"

"The night the photographs came, she told me that she believed me when I said nothing happened between Tyla and me. But now that you say it, and seeing how she reacted, maybe that's what Angelina took away from my decision to go to Tyla's memorial service. She lost her temper, told me to get out, and slammed the door. I was outside on the porch when I heard the bottle smash."

"Did she hit you at any point?"

"No."

"Did you hit her?"

"Of course not."

"Did she threaten you?"

"Not really."

"Did you threaten her?"

"No way."

"Did she push you?"

That question was more difficult. "I wouldn't say she pushed me. She took me by the arm, sort of hurrying me to the door."

"Did you push back?"

"Not at all. Look, can we stop making this a domestic violence investigation, please? We know that a serial killer was standing on my front porch two days ago, delivering an ash-covered photograph of his latest victim, and now my wife is missing."

"I'm not convinced those photos came from Cutter."

"But you are convinced that Angelina and I were throwing beer bottles and wineglasses at each other, is that it?"

"I've seen the broken glass. In Cutter's case, I have yet to see a white victim who wasn't dating a black man."

"I was married to a black woman. Who knows how this killer's mind works? And the white woman/black man paradigm isn't ironclad anyway. Tyla was a black woman."

"It hasn't been confirmed that Tyla was one of Cutter's victims."

My head was starting to spin. "Okay, no disrespect to Tyla or any of the other victims, but what the hell is going on here? The clock is ticking, and all we've done so far is talk about a broken beer bottle and the psychological nuances of the Cutter profile. You were the first person Carmen and I agreed we should turn to when Angelina went missing because we thought the FBI would ramp up the search immediately. Are you on board, or not?"

She was about to say something, but one of the investigators walked over and interrupted. "Agent Santos, could you come inside a moment?"

I recognized the investigator. Early in my career I had prosecuted a case with her. "Mirna, are you working homicide and missing persons now?"

"No," she said. "I'm still with the domestic crimes section."

"I recommended the involvement of several units," said Santos. "We're covering all bases."

I could see which one was first base.

"Excuse me," said Santos.

It wasn't clear that I was invited to join them, but my wife was missing, this was our house, and I didn't like the way this was turning. I followed Santos and the investigator up the driveway. We walked right past my car. The trunk was open, the doors open, the hood up. The "standard" investigation apparently involved everything but turning the car upside down and shaking it. We entered the house through the garage and continued down the hall into the living room. Another crime scene investigator held a small piece of broken green glass on an evidence tray, her penlight illuminating the find.

"Looks like blood to me," said the investigator.

Santos examined the specimen more closely. Then her head turned, and her gaze fixed right on me. "Looks like blood to me, too."

It chilled me, but in addition to being a concerned husband, I was a prosecutor who understood how the criminal justice system worked. I felt compelled to say something in my own defense. "Maybe Angelina cut herself trying to clean up the broken glass. You know, after I was gone."

Santos nodded, but not because she was buying my explanation. It seemed more like the mere expression of her expectation that I would have one.

"Let's get it out to the lab."

Her directive had been to the investigator, but Santos had locked eyes with me. "And we'll need a cheek swab from you, Mr. Beckham. We need to be able to determine whether this blood or any other DNA we find here belongs to a stranger."

It was a standard request in a missing person case, but her timing made it seem otherwise. "That's fine," I said. One of the technicians had her kit ready and came right at my mouth. It took just a few seconds. I looked at Santos and asked, "What's next?"

"I want to continue our discussion outside, with Detective Reyes' involvement," she said, meaning the domestic crimes investigator.

"We're wasting way too much time talking," I said.

"Excuse me?"

"No offense to the team you're assembling, Santos. Domestic crime investigations have their place. But if you're so damned determined to make this into something it's not, I have a ton of things on my to-do list."

"Beckham—" She stopped me as I reached the hallway. "There's something I find very curious," she said, stepping toward me.

"Curious?"

She nodded, looking me in the eye. We were standing close, and she spoke low enough that no one else could hear.

"Now that Angelina has gone missing, you're gripped with fear that Cutter is out there stalking your neighborhood like the bogeyman. But fourteen hours ago you left your wife in this house, all alone. How do you explain that?"

I didn't like the implication, and I could feel her studying me, gauging my reaction, taking my criminological pulse. But worse than that, it was a level of guilt I wasn't sure I could ever come to terms with.

"That's quite a bedside manner you've got there, Dr. Santos. Is this how you talk to every husband with a missing wife?"

"No," she said, her gaze tightening. "Just certain ones."

I tried not to flinch, but I was locking eyes with a pro who had studied far more crime scenes than I ever would.

"I need to find my wife," I said, then turned and left through the garage, avoiding the broken glass at our front door. I was halfway down the driveway when another investigator stopped me.

"Before you leave, we need to check your hands for gunshot residue. It's standard procedure."

I glanced back toward the house. Agent Santos was watching through the window.

"Of course it is," I said.

Chapter Twenty-Six

I borrowed our neighbor's car—mine was still being searched—and hit the road.

I knew most of Angelina's local hangouts—restaurants, coffee shop, fitness center, and favorite places to shop. I mapped out the circuit in my head, checking each location off, one by one. I talked to waitresses, manicurists, personal trainers, and even random patrons who happened to be inside when I got there. It took two hours. No sign of Angelina, but I did link up with her best friend, Sloane, who promised to pull together teams to work the grassroots angle, both in the virtual world of social media and the real world of old-fashioned legwork. By late afternoon we had twenty volunteers outside my house. I also worked a few connections to bring out the local news stations.

"How do you pronounce your wife's name again?" the reporter asked. "Is it Ange-*lie*-nuh, like North Carolina?"

We were standing on the sidewalk in front of our house, thirty seconds from going on camera. The squad cars were still parked in the driveway. Crime scene investigators crisscrossed the yard behind us, coming and going from the house. A line of media vans was parked across the street.

"No, it's Ange*leena*, like Lena Horne."

The cameraman was ready. The reporter fixed her hair for the fifteenth time and smiled.

"Not so toothy," the cameraman said. "The poor guy's wife is missing."

I was starting to feel like I wasn't even there.

"Sorry," she said, losing the grin.

The cameraman raised his fingers—"Three, two, one"—and we were on the air.

"Good evening," said the reporter, taking the cue from the anchorwoman in the local studio. "Tonight, law enforcement is looking to help one of its own. I'm standing outside the home of Abe and Angelina—"

"*Leena*," I said. "Ange*leena*."

"Abe and Angelina Beckham," she continued, "where a search is under way . . ."

The entire spot lasted thirty seconds. Apart from the mispronunciation, I had no memory of it. I just prayed that they'd managed to put up the right picture on television screens across south Florida. I did three more interviews—*bang, bang, bang*—for the other network affiliates. They promised to air it again on the eleven o'clock broadcasts.

"Good job," Sloane told me.

I was in such a daze that I hadn't even noticed her standing on the sidewalk, watching the television interviews. Several other friends of Angelina were with her, all wearing comfortable shoes and toting flashlights. Some daylight was remaining, but they looked ready to search all night, if that was what it took.

"Thanks for coming out," I told her. I expressed the same gratitude to each of Angelina's friends, which went smoothly enough, until one of them sniffled back tears and hugged me, saying, "I'm so sorry, Abe." I thanked her, even if it was premature for sympathies and condolences, and I could hear the others taking her to task after I turned away.

The investigators had already confirmed that Angelina's running shoes were in her closet, but it still seemed worth a shot to trace her route. Maybe she'd caught on to the barefoot running craze. Who knew? Checking *somewhere* was better than standing around.

I didn't know Angelina's jogging route, but Sloane was able to lead me, a handful of volunteers, and one of the MDPD officers on a walk from start to finish. I held my breath a couple of times, but it turned out to be a milk carton in the ditch and the remains of a flattened raccoon on the road. Darkness was falling by the time we finished. I needed a break, but another shot of adrenaline kicked in. I called my mother-in-law at the hotel and offered to bring dinner.

"I'll just order room service," said Margaret.

"Are you sure?"

"Yes," she said, but even her one-word response cracked. "Abe, I'm scared."

"It's going to be okay."

"This serial killer wasn't news in New York, so I haven't been following the story. But this sounds like it could be—"

"Margaret, don't go there. We don't know anything yet."

"*Exactly.* We don't know *anything.* That's what has me so worried. They sent a detective over here to the hotel to get some information on Angelina. He told me that there's been no activity on her cell since late last night. It was her text to me. It's funny, even after a child is all grown up and married, a mother worries. When Angelina dropped me off at the hotel, I told her to text me to let me know she got home safely. So she did. She texted me and said . . . she said 'I'm home. Love U.' "

She was starting to unravel. "Margaret, I can come by the hotel."

"No, no. That's not necessary. But I can't understand this. It's as if Angelina has fallen off the map. The last person to see her was you, and that was eighteen hours ago."

Last person to see her. Santos had made the same point while following me out of the house, right up until I'd jumped in the car to go hunt for Angelina.

"Let's stay close on this," I said. "We'll call each other as soon as we hear anything. Deal?"

"Okay, deal. Jake is flying down later tonight. He'll stay with me here at the hotel."

Jake was Angelina's father. "That's good."

"Are Joe and Sandy on their way down?"

My parents. I'd called earlier to tell them there was nothing they could do, which was true. They truly liked Angelina, but things had been awkward between us since Samantha, and I don't mean her death. My parents were too well mannered to be obnoxious about their disapproval, and they had actually smiled and behaved themselves through the wedding. The tipping point didn't come until about six months later, when

Samantha and I visited them in Charlottesville and spent the night in their guest room. All was well until we left. Five miles down the road I realized that I'd forgotten my sunglasses. I drove back and found that my mother had not only stripped the bed that Samantha and I had slept in but also thrown the sheets into the garbage. And it wasn't because we'd had sex on them.

"Not yet," I said. "They may come later." *Like when, the funeral? Dumb-ass thing to say.* "Let me know if Jake needs a ride from the airport."

"He'll be fine. You should just keep doing what you're doing. I saw the piece you did on the news. That was a . . ."

Her voice faded. I could hear her swallow back her emotions. "Margaret?"

"Sorry. That interview for the news channel that you did was a good idea."

"Are you sure you don't want me to come by until Jake gets in?"

"No, that's not the best use of your time. Besides, one of your friends is coming to see me. I won't be alone."

"One of *my* friends? Or one of Angelina's?"

"Yours. Agent Santos."

It was like an ice bath, and I hated that it made me feel that way. The FBI *should* have been "a friend."

"Is that what Agent Santos told you, that she was my friend?"

"I'm not sure. Maybe I just assumed. The police officer already took my statement, so I figured she was just being nice and checking on me. Why, is she not your friend?"

That was complicated. "She's fine."

"Would you rather I not talk to her?"

The last thing I needed was for my mother-in-law to tell the FBI that I'd instructed her not to talk to the agent who was investigating Angelina's disappearance. "Not at all," I said. "Just let me know how it goes."

"Okay, I will. Thank you again, Abe. And stay positive."

I promised I would, said good-bye, and hung up.

"Stay positive" was good advice. We had the media involved. The community was activated. All afternoon I'd been fielding calls of support from cops I'd worked with over the years, some of whom had long since retired. Carmen had the entire state attorney's office at my disposal. The *Eyewitness News* reporter had gotten one thing right: local law enforcement was mobilized to help "one of its own." With one apparent exception. Agent Santos. And it was starting to make me crazy.

I needed to get to the bottom of it.

It was Saturday night, but Carmen had told me to call anytime. I reached out to her. She picked up the phone, but she was attending a banquet at the Four Seasons and was minutes away from accepting another community service award, this one from the Cuban American Bar Association. She promised to stop by my house afterward, which prompted my next move. I started up the sidewalk to check with the crime scene investigators. They seemed to be wrapping things up, but this was taking way too long. If the domestic crime investigator wasn't running the show, she was at least one of its executive producers.

I was stepping onto the front porch when I saw Rid's car pull into the driveway. He jumped out quickly, and the expression on his face as he crossed the lawn gave me concern. I went to him, meeting him halfway, my heart pounding.

"It's okay," he said. "This is not the final piece of bad news that no one wants to hear."

My anxiety level dropped a notch, but it was still high.

"We found Angelina's cell phone."

I caught my breath. "Where?"

"On the side of the road. Scuffed up, scratch marks, the glass is shattered. It looks like it was tossed out of a moving car."

I went cold. I knew the statistics; I'd attended the police lectures. Never get in the car. Never, never, *never*. Kick, scream, punch, squirm, spit, claw—do whatever it takes, but don't get in that vehicle. A woman's chances of survival plummeted.

"What road?" I asked.

"Calle Ocho," he said, then paused. "West end. Just before it becomes the Tamiami Trail."

The road into the Everglades. I felt my knees buckle. "Dear God," was all I could say.

Chapter Twenty-Seven

Victoria was at the Ritz-Carlton having a talk with Angelina's mother when the phone call came from Detective Riddel. She broke things off and drove straight to the recovery scene. Her advice to Margaret was to wait at the hotel.

Their conversation had been moving along exactly as Victoria had expected. The last thing the mother of a missing daughter wants to believe is that her model son-in-law is in any way responsible. Difficult questions, at this early stage, were bound to draw a defensive posture, perhaps even indignation. Extremely difficult questions, like those about the broken beer bottle, could wait for round two. The goal in round one had been simply to open Margaret's mind to possibilities, however unthinkable.

It was a twenty-minute drive to the Everglades, giving her time aplenty to replay the predictable responses of a distraught mother—and to analyze a few surprises.

"When did Angelina ask you to come down from New York?"

There were three women in the hotel room. Margaret sat in the armchair by the window. Victoria took the edge of the bed, facing her. Detective Reyes from the Miami-Dade domestic crimes section was seated in the desk chair. Margaret was the seventy-year-old version of Grace Kelly, and the strong resemblance between mother and daughter made it plain to see how Angelina had become such a classic beauty. The unimaginable stress, however, was already taking a toll. Margaret was holding it together, but barely. A week of this, Victoria knew, and the worry lines would be carved in stone.

"Sometime Friday morning was when she called," said Margaret.

"When did you get on the airplane?"

"Friday afternoon."

"What was the rush?"

"No rush."

"Sounds to me like you got on the first flight available."

"One of the first, I guess."

"Was Angelina upset about something?"

"Of course she was upset. Angelina is a newlywed. She and Abe had just had their first argument as a married couple. These things happen. I needed to be there for her."

"Did she tell you what the argument was about?"

Margaret sighed deeply. Her hand shook as she sipped from a glass of water. "Abe's brother-in-law, J.T."

"What about him?"

Her voice tightened. "He scares Angelina. Frankly, he scares me a little, too."

"Why does he scare you?"

"*Why?*" asked Margaret. "Have you ever met him?"

"Briefly. At his apartment."

"Well, that's not *his* apartment. That's where Abe used to live. I don't know all the details, but I understand J.T. was homeless for a while. You know, he practically ruined Angelina's whole wedding."

"How?"

"He stood up at the reception and made this bizarre toast about Abe being a true brother now because he went from an African-American wife to a blonde. He's a very strange person. Abe needed to be more sensitive about that."

"Do you think Abe is insensitive?"

"No, not in general. Just about this."

"Do you think J.T. could have anything to do with Angelina's disappearance?"

She considered the question for quite some time, as if not ruling it out. "I don't know. But I don't really see how. Isn't he under house arrest?"

"Do you think Abe could?"

"Do I think Abe could what?"

Victoria paused long enough to let Margaret know that she couldn't make the tough questions go away by pretending not to understand them. Then she asked again.

"Do you think Abe could have had something to do with Angelina's disappearance?"

"Oh, for God's sake, no. You can't be serious."

Victoria drove west on Southwest Eighth Street, past Florida International University, until the lights of strip malls were behind them and the darkness of the Everglades lay ahead. A night trip on the Tamiami Trail was like a midnight drive across the plains of Kansas, only the drop-off from civilization was more sudden. The Everglades marked the abrupt end of westward development and city lights, and the chain of headlight beams along the Trail stretched like a stray filament into utter blackness.

It was the GPS chip in Angelina's smartphone that had led to its recovery. The night search for Angelina was focused on the north side of the Trail, the side on which the cell had been found. The staging area for law enforcement's search and recovery mission was the same gravel parking lot used by crews working on the new bridge. Victoria parked beside a colossal earthmover and walked along the shoulder of the road. Detective Reyes was with her. Traffic wasn't any heavier than usual, but it was beginning to back up in both directions. A team of traffic cops kept rubberneckers from bringing the Trail to a standstill.

Victoria spotted Riddel at the center of activity near a portable tree of vapor lights. A pair of noisy generators powered six trees in all, setting the flat waters of the Everglades aglow, but only for a distance of twenty-five yards or so. A police helicopter whirred overhead, the sweep of its searchlight reaching deeper into the saw grass. Rescue workers on pontoons trolled slowly across the canal, the beams from high-powered navigation lights crisscrossing in the night. In the darkness beyond, countless pairs of alligator eyes caught just a hint of the artificial light and glowed like fireflies in the darkness.

The north side of the Trail was for law enforcement only. Police tape stretched for a hundred yards along the shoulder. On the other side of the highway, behind a secondary perimeter, stood Abe Beckham. Swirling police beacons turned his face alternating shades of red and orange. Beckham didn't seem to notice Victoria or Detective Reyes as they passed beneath the tape, and they didn't try to get his attention. They went straight to Riddel.

"How goes it?" asked Victoria.

Riddel stepped toward her, away from the noisy generator. "Nothing but her cell phone so far."

"How far are we from the recovery site for Tyla Tomkins?"

"I clocked it. Tomkins was a mile and two-tenths due west. It makes a big difference. More shoulder area and dry ground here."

"Any tire tracks or footprints?"

"Yeah, a million of them. The work crews walk from the construction staging area to the bridge and back every day. But there's nothing closer to the water. Not a footprint, not a tire track, not a broken weed. Honestly, I don't see this being a recovery site."

"How do you think the phone got here?"

"My take is that the guy got this far down the Trail and suddenly remembered that smartphones have GPS tracking chips. He panicked, tossed it out the window, and kept right on going. You can check out the phone for yourself, but it looks like it was thrown from a moving vehicle. I'm hoping that's the case. Never a good scenario for a woman to be in the car of her abductor on the way to who knows where. But she could still be alive."

"She could be," said Victoria.

Riddel glanced farther down the road. "Worse case, he drove halfway to Naples before stopping to dispose of the body in the middle of the Everglades. Or he drove to Naples and just kept driving north, maybe with her still alive."

Victoria glanced in Abe's direction, then back at Riddel. "Anything is possible at this point."

"I just issued a BOLO for the west coast, from Collier County on up," said Riddel.

"I issued one six hours ago," said Santos.

"I know. It's consistent with yours."

"I don't care if it is. You need to coordinate with me. Exactly what did you tell them to be on the lookout for?"

"Here, look for yourself." He pulled up the BOLO on his phone, and Victoria read from the screen.

"No better than mine," she said. "No worse."

"The situation is what it is," said Riddel. "Other than a photograph of Angelina and your criminal profile of Cutter—white male in his thirties—what else can we say? Angelina's car is still parked in the driveway, so we don't even know what kind of vehicle to look for, unless again we go with the stereotypical serial killer profile and hunt down commercial vans with no windows."

"Any thoughts on how to find out what vehicles crossed the Trail in the last twenty-four hours?"

Riddel shook his head. "There aren't any toll booths on the Tamiami Trail, so no cameras checking plates. I asked Collier County sheriffs to visit service stations around Naples. They're talking to sales clerks, checking security cameras. People often stop for gas after a ride across the Trail. Maybe something will turn up."

A commotion in the westbound lane caught Victoria's attention. A media van was trying to force its way closer to the crime scene, and traffic cops were doing their job. Many more vans were sure to follow.

"We need to work out a press release," said Victoria.

"I got it covered," said Riddel.

"I'd like to see it."

He hesitated.

"*Before* you issue it," she said. "Unlike the BOLO."

Riddel glanced over his shoulder, toward his friend Abe, then gave Victoria a stern expression. "Let me say this up front. We all know the statistics on married women murdered by their husbands, and I felt a certain vibe coursing through Abe's house tonight. But at this point, I won't say a damn thing to even hint that Abe Beckham is in any way, shape, or form under a cloud of suspicion. Period."

Victoria neither agreed nor disagreed. "Communication with the media is a task force function. I need to see it."

He locked eyes with her a moment, as if to reemphasize that certain things were not negotiable. "It's in my car. I'll get it."

Victoria waited on the side of the road with Detective Reyes, both women watching the search and rescue team at work. Reyes broke the silence.

"I agree with Riddel," she said. There was almost an apologetic quality to the detective's voice.

Victoria's gaze remained fixed, cast out toward the Everglades. She said nothing.

"Abe is a stand-up guy," Reyes continued. "I've worked with him. He's highly respected."

"He's also a liar," said Victoria. "He had an affair with Tyla Tomkins. He lied to his wife about it. He lied to his boss about it with me in the room."

"We don't even know for sure that he was having an affair."

" 'For sure,' as in one hundred percent certain? No. And Tyla is dead, so we may never know."

"Even if he was having an affair, that doesn't make him a murderer."

"No, but it explains a lot. Angelina gets the photos of Abe with Tyla. She calls her mom down from New York. She comes home from dinner only to hear that while she and her mother were trying to figure out how to save her marriage, Abe went to his lover's memorial service. She tells him to get out, the marriage is over. They argue. A beer bottle sails across the room. One thing leads to another, and when it's over, Abe has a dead body on his hands. He tosses Angelina's cell phone on the Tamiami Trail to make us think Cutter did it. God only knows where he dumped Angelina's body."

"Lots of suppositions in there."

"Be honest," said Victoria. "Many a model husband has jumped to the top of your list of suspects based on far less than this."

"I would be more in your camp if we had a history of domestic violence."

"Two nights ago I found a broken wineglass on their cocktail table."

"That's not what I mean. Nothing I heard from Angelina's mother even raised the possibility of an abusive relationship."

"Mom lives in New York. She knows what her daughter wanted her to know. We need to focus on local witnesses."

"Angelina's girlfriends?"

"They're on the list. But I'm going to break the mold here. Start where Abe wouldn't expect me to start."

"Where's that?"

Victoria checked her watch. Only nine. Still early, time enough to follow another lead. "A twofer," she said. "The only person with a front-row seat in both of Abe's marriages."

Reyes thought for a moment. "You don't mean his brother-in-law, do you?"

Victoria's expression turned very serious. "That's exactly who I mean."

Chapter Twenty-Eight

From behind the yellow police tape, I watched Agent Santos and her new sidekick from the domestic violence section. They were pretending not to notice me. I was pretending that it didn't bother me.

A cold shoulder from Detective Reyes was especially hard for me to swallow.

Many career prosecutors in our office, myself included, did a stint in domestic violence somewhere along the line. Some of my best work had been with Reyes, the whole gamut of cases—battery, sexual assault, violation of injunctions, stalking. The head of domestic crime had been one of my biggest supporters for promotion to homicide, where I went on to prosecute four cases of uxoricide. All involved infidelity. Two were cheaters whose wives had promised to take everything in the divorce. One couldn't handle it when his wife said she was leaving him for another man. A fourth was just bizarre, a guy who liked to masturbate while watching his wife engage in rough sex, and who did nothing to stop a 'roided-up weight lifter from strangling her to death. Aside from cases involving a confession, they were among the easiest convictions I'd ever won. They all got the death penalty.

I tried not to seem angry as Rid walked in my direction. He stopped at the tape. He looked exhausted, as if he'd just gone ten rounds with the heavyweight champion of the world.

"Santos wants to see my press release."

The champion had just landed another blow, and this time it was on me. I was the author of that release.

"What did you tell her?"

"That it was in the car."

"Are you going to show it to her?"

He glanced across the road, in the direction of Santos, then back. "I can't really say no. Santos is the task force coordinator for the Cutter investigation."

I'd been dealing with the fears and realities all day long, but it still chilled me to hear him speak of a serial killer in such matter-of-fact terms. "Is that where you're coming out?" I asked. "Angelina belongs in the Cutter investigation?"

"No, no, Abe. We're not there yet. We may never get there. Don't give up hope. God forbid it's a homicide, but if things move in that direction, for certain people the only two possibilities seem to be Cutter or—"

"Or me."

"Yeah. You."

"Why?" I asked, but it was almost rhetorical. "How could Santos think I would kill my wife?"

He didn't answer right away, but I could see from his expression that Rid had been wondering the same thing. "You want my honest opinion?"

"Yeah, I do."

"I've dealt with these FBI types before—the rising stars who make it all way to the Behavioral Analysis Unit and do one serial killer investigation after another. The burnout rate in my job is ridiculous, but compared to those guys, it's nothing. They have the worst rate in law enforcement. There comes a point in time when you've finally crawled inside the head of one too many psychopaths, looked into the eyes of too many lifeless victims of the worst of the worst. Santos hasn't told me this, but I'm guessing that's why she got reassigned to Miami. The bureau is hoping that a little time in the field will breathe some life back into her."

"So what are you saying? She got demoted, and she's taking it out on me?"

"No, you're completely missing my point. I think Santos has written so many profiles of sexually sadistic serial killers that her brain is preprogrammed. Something about Angelina doesn't fit in that program."

I gave it some consideration before responding. The hum of the generators was the only sound around us. "I guess if you flip it around, look at the positive side, I should take some comfort in this."

"Comfort?"

"Yeah. It's actually a good thing, right? One of the best-trained minds in the country seems convinced that my wife was not the victim of a serial killer."

"That is a positive," said Rid.

"But it raises a question, right? If it wasn't Cutter, and it wasn't me . . . then where is she?"

"I promise you this, Abe. I won't stop looking until I have an answer."

One of the generators roared, sending a surge of industrial light across the highway and down the embankment, toward the search and rescue team trolling for another body in the Everglades.

An answer.

"Let's hope it's one I can live with," I said.

Chapter Twenty-Nine

Brian Belter was with his best client, at his favorite restaurant, in his most beloved place in all of the Dominican Republic. And he was miserable.

Belter was one of eight at a dinner hosted by Alberto Cortinas and his wife at La Piazzetta, a gourmet Italian restaurant in Altos de Chavón, an ambitious re-creation of a sixteenth-century Mediterranean village that sits high on a bluff in La Romana. The pumpkin risotto and fillet of hake were memorable, but truly unforgettable were the views of the river valley far below. A torchlit table beneath the stars out on the stone terrace was highly coveted, especially on a Saturday night, but the privileged guests in the Cortinas party had the entire terrace to themselves.

"Más vino, Señor Belter?"

His wineglass was empty, but he was at his limit. "No, gracias."

The drinking had started on the golf course at noon. One Cuba Libre led to another. Belter was a scratch golfer and had birdied the first two holes, but it was downhill from there. Teeth of the Dog was the premier course in the Caribbean, a challenge even for sober professionals. It was built on a bed of coral, which made for unforgiving hazards, all created by Dominican work crews whose only tools were sledgehammers, pickaxes, and chisels. By the eighth hole, Belter needed a pickax to find his tee shot. He'd been drinking rum and Cokes like Kool-Aid, and no one had warned him that it was Bacardi 151. The pressure behind his eyes was almost unbearable. He was starting to feel nauseous. Maybe it was the alcohol. Maybe it was the altitude.

Maybe it was Tyla Tomkins.

"Agua, por favor," he told the waiter.

Alberto Cortinas was seated at the head of a rectangular table, holding court for the six most influential Dominican lawmakers, all men. With growing opposition to sugar growers in the Everglades, Cortinas was planning to expand production in the DR. The goal was to convince the Dominican senate to approve a proposed tax on fructose corn syrup. Big Sugar hated competition. All lawmakers could be persuaded. It would take much more than a round of golf, a pricey restaurant, and a penthouse suite at a world-class resort, even if the room did come with a pair of Latina hookers who could command five thousand a night in New York City. *El hombre con los regalos verde*—the man with the green gifts—would visit each of the lawmakers in the morning. Money talked. But not when Alberto Cortinas was anywhere nearby.

I'm not involved, Brian.

A headache of this magnitude made it nearly impossible for Belter to keep up with the lively conversation in Spanish at the other end of the table. His mind needed a break. He excused himself, walked across the stone terrace, and went inside to the restroom. He checked for messages while taking care of business, then went to the home page for the *Miami Tribune*. The headline grabbed him—to the point that he nearly dropped his phone in the urinal.

Ho-lee shit.

He was so engrossed in the article that he forgot to tip the bathroom attendant after washing his hands. He quickly returned to the terrace, went straight to the head of the table, and politely interrupted his client.

Cortinas did not look pleased. He was in the middle of one of his favorite stories, the one about the insider at the US Department of Agriculture who would tip off Alberto whenever the secretary was at his desk getting a blow job. It was the only time Alberto ever called him, because he knew the secretary had no choice but to take his call.

"What is it?" Alberto asked in English.

"I need your attention for just a minute," said Belter. "In private."

Alberto rose reluctantly and excused himself. Belter led him away from the dining table, across the terrace, out of sight of the guests. They found a quiet place around the stone pillars that marked the entrance to the restaurant. It was a setting out of Shakespeare, two men of power whispering in the dark, standing across from little shops and artist dens on a narrow cobblestone street lined with lanterns, wrought-iron balconies, and other markings of a Renaissance village.

"Abe Beckham's wife has gone missing," said Belter. "There's an all-out search about a mile or so from where they found Tyla's body."

Cortinas pulled a cigar from the pocket of his guayabera and snipped off the tip. "That's very sad."

Belter watched him light up, waiting for him to say more. But Cortinas' only concern seemed to be an even burn on his cigar.

"Is that all you have to say?" asked Belter. "Very sad?"

Cortinas took a long drag, the ashes glowing in the night. "This is not something that demands my immediate attention."

"Don't you see the obvious problem here?"

"The only problem I see is a table full of guests wondering what the hell is so damned important that you pull me away in the middle of a story."

Belter moved closer, lowering his voice. "Tyla Tomkins was murdered. Now Abe Beckham's wife is missing. The media will go nuts on this."

"So what? Let them."

"You're being way too cavalier."

"You make it sound like this is our fault."

"It's *always* our fault!" Belter said, keeping his voice low but speaking with greater urgency. "Big Sugar is Florida's all-time favorite whipping boy. Like it or not, we are connected to this circus through Tyla Tomkins."

"We've got this covered, Brian. Everything is being taken care of. Some very high-priced techies are at work on Tyla's computer files and e-mails as we speak."

"Dodging one subpoena from the US attorney is not the entire ball game. This is shaping up to be the info-tainment story of the century. It will put my law firm and your companies under the microscope. That's no place to be. You didn't often agree with your old man, but he was dead right about one thing: Big Sugar does better with a low profile."

"What do you want me to do, Brian? Turn back the hands of time and make it all go away?"

"No, but—damn it, Alberto! This isn't just business we're talking about. This is my family, *my life*. Agent Santos and that smartass detective who came to my office last week know about me and Tyla. Jenny will leave me if that comes out. What am I supposed to tell her? What am I going to tell my kids?"

"That's really up to you, Brian. But there are a couple of choices." Cortinas took another long drag on his cigar, a cloud of smoke pouring across his lips and into Belter's face as he spoke. "One, you could tell them that when Tyla called you on her prepaid cell phone, you should have had a prepaid phone of your own, which would have made the numbers untraceable on both ends. But you were too stupid to figure that one out. Unlike me."

Belter froze, silent.

"Or," said Cortinas, "you can simply tell them it's been a really lousy week for women who like to fuck Abe Beckham."

Belter looked at him, confused. When it came to insanely arrogant remarks, even *he* had difficulty telling when Cortinas was serious, half serious, or just kidding around.

Finally Cortinas smiled, clenching the big cigar in his teeth. "Come, my friend. It's time to return to our guests."

Belter walked with him, but he wanted to pull his client aside, look him in the eye, and find out if he was serious about the prepaid cell phone. If something had been going on between him and Tyla, it was news to Belter. Disturbing news. It wasn't just ego and idle curiosity pulling at him.

Once upon a time, Belter had thought he was the only one.

He was about to ask, and a simple follow-up question would have been the most natural thing in the world between two men who'd known each other nearly their entire adult lives. But he followed his instincts, just as he had in so many other dealings with Alberto Cortinas.

Better not to know.

The two men returned to the dinner party on the terrace, where Belter laughed with the others about "Cortinas interruptus" and the US secretary of agriculture.

Chapter Thirty

It was almost nine in the evening when Victoria knocked on J.T.'s door. Detective Reyes was with her on the front porch. The chain lock was engaged, and J.T. spoke to them with his face wedged between the door and the frame.

"What do you want?"

"I'm Agent—"

"I know who you are," he said. "You came to my house with Detective Riddel to take my answering machine. Who's she?"

Reyes introduced herself and showed her badge.

"We'd like to talk to you about Angelina," said Victoria.

"I can't talk to you now. I'm watching a movie."

The television was blasting in the background. It sounded like a total guy movie, something high on special effects, perhaps *Transformers* or *Iron Man*. "You do know that Angelina has gone missing, right?"

"Yeah. Abe told me."

"And you can't make five minutes to talk to us?"

He made a face like a teenager caught playing video games after midnight. "Oh, all right. I'll pause it."

His face disappeared, the chain rattled, and the door opened. J.T. was wearing only a pair of baggy basketball shorts that reached all the way to his knees, no shirt, and no shoes. The ankle bracelet was in place, Victoria noted. He led them into the TV room and paused the movie. Victoria's guess had been right on: *Iron Man 2.*

"Have a seat," said J.T.

The women took the couch. J.T. fell into a bright orange beanbag chair. The rest of the room was tastefully decorated with a woman's touch, and Victoria would have bet that the orange beanbag was the one piece of furniture that had not been of his late sister's choosing. Victoria used it as a starting point.

"Nice apartment, J.T. Did your sister pick out all these beautiful things?"

"Yup. Except the beanbag."

Two for two. "Is that your contribution, or was that Abe's touch?"

"Beanbag's mine. Two bucks at a garage sale. Abe never woulda brung a piece of shit like this into Samantha's house. He went with whatever she wanted."

The conversation was moving in exactly the right direction. "They got along well?"

"Oh, hell yeah. Made for each other, if you ask me."

"What makes you say that?"

He cast a suspicious look. "Nothing *makes* me say it. What's that supposed to mean, anyway? You think I'm on drugs or something?"

"No, I wasn't suggesting—"

"You asked what *makes* me say that. I say it because I think it. Not because something made me say it. That's all there is to it. I don't do drugs. You cool with that?"

"Yes, we're cool. I was just trying to understand what you were saying. Abe and Samantha were made for each other. So I guess they never argued?"

He took a deep breath, and his sudden anger seemed to pass. "Argued? Not really. Not that I saw."

"What about Abe and Angelina?"

"What about them?"

"You ever see them argue?"

He hesitated, then answered. "Yeah. They argued."

"Argued? Or argue?"

"Is that a trick question?"

"No," she said. " 'Argued' just puts Angelina in the past. 'Argue,' on the other hand—"

"So it *is* a trick question," he said sharply. "You're trying to trip me up."

"Forget I asked that."

"Forget nothin'. Abe's wife is missing, and you show up at my apartment and start asking trick questions. You think I did something to her, don't you?"

"We're just having a conversation."

"Well, how about having a conversation that makes some damn sense? I can't even leave my own apartment. In case you haven't noticed, I'm wearing an ankle bracelet."

He stuck his foot in the air, and Victoria got more than an eyeful. He wasn't wearing any underwear. "You can put your leg down now, J.T."

He lowered it.

"What kind of things do Abe and Angelina argue about?" she asked.

"I don't know. They argue about everything."

"Everything?"

"Not *everything*. Lots of things."

"You've heard them raise their voices?"

"Sure."

"Have you ever seen any physicality between them?"

"You mean do I watch them have sex?"

She knew he was playing dumb, a clear signal that he would rather avoid the question—which only heightened Victoria's interest in hearing the answer. "No. I mean 'physicality,' as in Abe raising a hand to her."

"Abe never hit Angelina."

"Are you sure about that?"

"Yeah, I'm sure."

She leaned forward, making eye contact with him. "This is important, J.T. If Abe has ever hit Angelina, I need to know about it."

He looked right back at her, never breaking eye contact. "Abe never hit her."

Victoria let his answer linger. She had stared down many a witness, many a suspect, many a liar. Polygraph examinations had their place, but sometimes there was nothing like two decades of law enforcement experience. J.T. wasn't lying, at least not in her estimation. Finally he looked away.

"But . . ."

She waited a moment, then prompted him. "But what?"

He didn't answer, his gaze cast downward.

"But what, J.T.?"

He raised his eyes, meeting her stare. "She hits him."

Victoria tried not to react, keeping an even keel. "Angelina hits Abe?"

"Yeah," he said, matter of fact. "That's what I'm saying."

She nodded slowly. "Now, when you say she hits him, do you mean this has happened on more than one occasion?"

"Mm-hmm. More than once."

Victoria exchanged glances with Detective Reyes beside her on the couch, and then turned her attention back to J.T.

"Okay," she said. "I want you to tell us all about this, J.T."

Chapter Thirty-One

That's simply not true," I said.

It had taken all my strength to look Agent Santos in the eye and deliver a controlled and level response. I was angry at J.T. for saying that Angelina hit me. I was furious with Agent Santos for bringing it up on this night, under these circumstances, right across the road from the ongoing search for Angelina's body.

"Why would J.T. lie about this?" asked Santos.

J.T. had been psycho calling me for the past thirty minutes, but I just didn't want to take his call. I wish I had. I would have asked him the same question. And I wouldn't have been ambushed by Santos and Detective Reyes.

"Why does J.T. do any of the things he does?" I said. "If the court puts an ankle bracelet on him, he'll tell you the government is spying on him. If there's a serial killer named Cutter in south Florida, he'll tell you he used to cut sugarcane. He says a lot of things to see how people react."

"So that's your answer? He lies for the sake of lying?"

How to explain J.T. to an outsider? "He's in his own world. We visited his father in the nursing home Friday, and J.T. denied that he was his father's son. It's not *lying*. He knows he's not fooling anyone. These are the things he does. Sometimes he'll say the exact opposite of what he and everyone else knows is true."

"So if J.T.'s brother-in-law hits his wife, J.T. might say the wife hits his brother-in-law?"

I should have seen that coming, but I hadn't, which only confirmed my level of stress. "I've never hit a woman in my life."

"There's an easy way to settle this."

"Yeah, you could stop playing the abusive-husband card and find out what really happened to my wife."

"I could. Or you could take a polygraph."

"No," I said firmly, no hesitation.

"Glad you took some time to think about it," she said, sarcastic.

"I'm not going to play this game," I said. "If I allow you to treat me like a suspect, you will continue to treat me like one. If I pass the polygraph, then you'll want a strip search to see if I have any bruises or scratches. If the strip search shows nothing, you'll want to take another polygraph. If I pass again, you'll find another angle. Every minute you spend trying to build a bullshit case against me is a minute wasted. Go find the real killer."

I froze, realizing what I'd just said. Santos caught it. *Killer.* She didn't have to ask, but I could see the question written all over her face. *How do you know she's dead?*

"Think about that polygraph," she said.

"The answer is no."

"Sorry to hear that."

She started away, but I stopped her. "Hey, what is going on here?"

"Excuse me?"

"This started as a hunt for a serial killer. Now it's a witch hunt, and I'm the guy tied to the stake. I've been standing out here for two hours, watching and praying as search and rescue does its work. But I've also been wondering—about you. I even made a phone call."

"You're checking up on me?"

"I Googled you on my iPhone and read about that serial killer investigation you did with help from the *Miami Tribune*. It occurred to me that you must have known the old crime reporter at the *Tribune*. He left about five years ago. Twenty-two years on the beat. Pulitzer Prize winner. Really good guy. Covered my first capital trial and lots of others. His name's Mike Posten."

She said nothing, but I could see in her eyes that Mike's name meant something to her.

"Anyway, I gave Mike a call," I said. "You know what he says?"

"No idea. Haven't seen him in years."

"Well, Mike's bet is that your gut, heart, and mind aren't telling you that Abe Beckham is your man. He thinks someone is pushing your buttons. He says that the Victoria Santos he knows is much smarter than this."

She took a step closer, looking me in the eye. "The Victoria that Mike knows was a thirty-two-year-old newbie. No one is pushing my buttons."

"I'm just telling you what Mike thinks."

She seemed to be searching for a response, but then changed her mind. She turned and started away.

"Hey, Santos," I said.

She took two more steps, as if wishing she could drop the whole "Mike" conversation, but something made her stop and listen to what I had to say.

"What would that thirty-two-year-old newbie think?"

It was dark in the shadows, away from the portable light trees, and I couldn't really read Santos' expression. My sense, however, was that my last punch had landed.

But Santos did not go down easily. She came right back at me, stopping on the other side of the tape. "That newbie would think exactly what I think," said Santos, a definite edge to her tone. "It might take her a little longer to get there, because of her inexperience, but her conclusion would be the same.

"Our serial killer has yet to strike out of Palm Beach County. Cutter didn't kill Tyla Tomkins. And he didn't take your wife, either."

Before I could even begin to respond, she turned sharply and left. I wanted to duck under the tape and ask the flood of follow-up questions that were suddenly coming to mind, but contamination of a crime scene with my footprints was not something I needed to add to my list of troubles. More to the point, I knew she was done talking to me.

I let it go for now, watching in silence as Santos walked back into the glow of the search and rescue vapor lights.

Chapter Thirty-Two

Victoria felt a chill as she walked across the Tamiami Trail, through stopped traffic, and toward the search and recovery team leader on the bank. It wasn't nearly as cold as it had been on the morning of Tyla Tomkins' recovery, but it was only ten p.m., and temperatures drop fast in the Everglades after midnight.

Victoria had tried not to show it, but Beckham had gotten to her. Mike Posten had been the first low blow, and then he'd hit even lower.

What would that thirty-two-year-old newbie think?

It was an interesting question. She would probably think a lot of things. That task force coordinator for the Miami field office was the last thing she would be at this stage of her career. That burnout would never get her. That it had been true back then, and that it would be true forever, at least from the standpoint of homicide statistics: the most dangerous place for a woman to be was in a relationship with a man.

But those were not excuses for losing her cool. Sparring with Abe Beckham, speaking out of anger, was no way to share her professional opinion that Tyla had been murdered by someone other than Cutter.

And there was the whole Mike Posten thing. A married man who'd faced temptation and remained true to his wife. *Beckham could have learned a thing or two from him.*

Her cell rang. It was from the Palm Beach County Sheriff's Department. Her task force contact was calling at ten thirty on a Saturday night, which was not a good sign. She braced herself and took the call.

"What is it, Juan?" she asked.

"Looks like we have another victim," he said.

She swallowed the news bitterly, internalizing it as the price every law enforcement officer paid for moving too slowly to catch a monster. "Where?"

"Cane field off Route Twenty-Seven. That's a good ways west of the other recovery sites, but still on Cortinas property."

"Do you have an ID yet?"

"No. The body was found nude, no identification on her. White female, possibly in her thirties, is all I can tell you at this point."

"Cutter's signature?"

"Yeah," he said. "Signature confirmed."

Ash on the face.

She glanced in Abe's direction, still on the phone. "Juan, do me a favor. Check the Angelina Beckham BOLO that went out today from Miami-Dade. There's a photograph with it. Just for comparison."

"Okay."

"And Juan," she added.

"Yeah?"

"Call me right back on that. I mean *right* back, as soon as you can."

"Will do," he said.

Victoria hung up, but she didn't put her phone away. She held on to it, waiting for the vibration in her hand to signal a callback. A light breeze sent ripples across the illuminated waters of the black Everglades, and it made her heart pound to think that, in a matter of moments, she might officially call off the search. Or not.

Either way, she would be on her way to Palm Beach soon. It was going to be a long and painful night.

Chapter Thirty-Three

Agent Santos had me worried.

I watched her take a phone call, then hurry across the highway, jump in her car, and speed away, not toward the Everglades but toward Florida's Turnpike. Within minutes, I noticed a dramatic change in the search activities. Scuba divers popped to the surface and came to shore. Searchlights no longer swept the saw grass. Cadaver dogs obeyed the "sit" command. A squad car pulled away, then another. Law enforcement had reduced itself to clusters of idle conversation alongside the canal, the sense of urgency dissipating in the darkness. Way too many people standing around, nothing to do. I continued to respect the police perimeter, but I wasn't sure how much longer I could stay put on the onlooker side of the Tamiami Trail. I couldn't spot Rid anywhere in the crowd. I left a voice-mail message.

"I don't like what I'm seeing. Call me right back. What is going on?"

I watched the traffic crawl past me, my heart in my throat. I studied the long line of approaching vehicles, looking for the medical examiner's van, looking for something I did not want to see. My phone vibrated with Rid's callback, and he told me about Palm Beach. It was suddenly hard to breathe.

"Tell me it's not her," I said.

"We don't know yet."

"Don't bullshit me!"

"Abe, I'm telling you what I know."

I watched him cross the highway, his cell pressed to his ear, and as he approached we put away our phones. Even though he was standing just on the other side of the yellow tape, it was difficult to see his face. All but one of the light trees along the road had been cut off, and we were standing in the darkness that was the Everglades.

"They have Angelina's photograph," I said. "Can't somebody make a comparison?"

Rid looked at the ground. "It was a particularly vicious attack, I'm told. Officers on the scene confirmed traces of ash, but even that wasn't easy. The face is not really recognizable."

"Oh, God." I tried to hold it together. "What about fingerprints? The investigation team must have pulled a set of prints from Angelina's hairbrush or blow dryer—some damn thing."

"They did," said Rid. "But, again, given the severity of the wounds, not sure fingerprints will give us an answer."

My mind raced to another place I didn't want to go, and I tried to shake the horrific image of stumps at the wrists, no hands, no fingerprints. "How fast can we get DNA results?"

"It will be on a rush basis, not just for victim identification but for the killer's DNA, too. But the lab can't get started until DNA is collected, which has to be done carefully. It won't happen till the body is in the medical examiner's office."

The body. I knew it like no one else. Rid was on the same page.

"Abe, the most helpful thing to do right now is come up with a list of distinctive markings. I'll pass them along to the Palm Beach ME."

The mole on her inner thigh, the freckles on her shoulders, the details that not even Angelina knew about Angelina. Sure, we could make a list. In the car.

"I need to go," I said.

I **drove** straight up the turnpike. Fast. And alone. Rid had to stay behind. The search along Tamiami Trail was on hold, not shut down. I took that as a good sign; you take what you can get.

I was dictating into my phone, up to number fourteen on my list of distinctive Angelina body marks, when Ed Brumbel called from Belle Glade.

"You may know this," he said, "but the police found a body in the cane fields about a mile from my house."

By "house," I knew he meant the legal aid clinic. "I heard. I'm headed up to the medical examiner's office now."

"Is it—"

"We don't know yet."

"I'll meet you there," he said, no hesitation.

"That's not necessary."

"Who's with you?"

"No one."

"Abe, don't do this alone. I'll meet you there."

I thanked him and kept driving. I finished my Angelina list while crossing the Miami-Dade county line. I was passing one of those too-far-west developments that had sprouted up on the edge of civilization during the building boom, where new residents soon learned the mosquitoes' indifference to the end of suburbia and the start of the Everglades.

I e-mailed my list to Rid, then made the call I was dreading: Angelina's mother. Margaret and I had promised to keep each other informed. Angelina's father answered her phone.

"Margaret's asleep," he told me. "She was going crazy when I got here. I gave her an Ambien."

I told him where I was headed. The silence on the line made me wonder if my phone had dropped the call, but finally he spoke.

"Should Margaret and I meet you there?"

"I don't think that's a good idea, Jake."

"Are you sure?"

I struggled to find a positive spin. "We have multiple fronts to cover. If this is not Angelina, the search to find her alive will kick right back up again. We need family in Miami-Dade County."

"Right, that makes sense."

"I'll call you as soon as I know," I said.

We hung up. I drove faster.

Chapter Thirty-Four

I reached the medical examiner's office just before midnight. Ed was waiting outside the entrance. We walked inside together, through the pneumatic doors and down the hallway.

I heard crying from the lobby ahead of us. Not little sniffles. Great, racking grief, the kind of wailing that attends only one misery on earth: a mother's loss of her child.

I stopped at the end of the hall, unable to enter the brightly lit lobby. A handful of chairs lined the far wall. Seated in one was a man about Jake's age, consoling the woman next to him. She had the Palm Beach look, a well-dressed and attractive woman who could have easily passed for one of my mother-in-law's girlfriends. Agent Santos was seated beside her, holding her hand.

Santos spotted me, excused herself from the couple, and whispered as she came toward me.

"It's not your wife."

There was no serious sense of relief. I suddenly felt . . . selfish, self-centered. It hit me between the eyes, the fact that we were dealing with a serial killer, which by definition meant multiple victims and exponential grief. Other families were suffering. The sobbing mother of Cutter's latest victim leaned on her husband's shoulder. I wanted to walk over and hold them both up.

"I wasn't jerking you around," said Santos. "We just confirmed the identification. I needed to tell them before I told you."

"I understand."

"I've instructed Riddel to resume the search in Miami-Dade. You should go now."

"Okay. I'll let Angelina's parents know."

"Can you make that call outside, please? I don't want these folks to overhear."

"Sure," I said. Santos went back to the grieving parents. Ed followed me down the hall toward the exit.

"That's some good news," said Ed.

"Yeah. For us."

We kept walking. "By the way, Vernon Gallagher didn't pan out."

"Vernon who?"

"Remember? The Michael Phelps of cane cutting? The old cutter Tyla Tomkins might have been talking about in her message to you?"

"Right, right."

"I really thought there was something fishy about that car accident that killed the state rep. Especially the way all the investigative records were sealed. But I talked to Conrad's widow. It turns out that the Conrad family got the records sealed, not Big Sugar. Conrad was drunk as shit and driving too fast when he came up on the burning field. The fire jumped the road, and that was that. He crashed."

Ed was wandering so far off track that I could barely follow. "That's a shame."

"My point is that I don't think the car crash has anything to do with the crime that Tyla was trying to tell you about."

"Agreed. Let's drop the whole thing."

"No, no, no," he said, stopping me. "I didn't mean we should give up. If Tyla was trying to tip you off about a crime committed by Cortinas Sugar, we definitely need to find out what it was."

"Ed, right now all I want to do is update my in-laws." I started down the hall, walking faster. He kept up.

"Hear me out on this, okay? I think the crime Tyla was trying to tell you about has something to do with the land deal that her law firm worked on."

My footfall struck the rubber mat, the doors opened automatically, and we continued outside. "The land deal?"

"Four years ago Big Sugar cut a billion-dollar deal to sell farmland back to the state of Florida. It was way over market price, but the environmentalists went along with it because the plan was to retire all those acres from sugar production and return the Everglades to a natural state. But then Big Sugar got the politicians to lease the same land back to them for another twenty years of sugar production at some ridiculously low sweetheart rental rate. It's outright thievery."

We were outside the building. I tried my phone. Zero bars. "Damn it." I followed the sidewalk along the front of the building, searching for reception. The parking lot was around the corner. Ed kept stride.

"So this land deal—"

"Ed, enough," I said, annoyed. "What does a land deal have to do with anything?"

"Stay with me," said Ed. "I'm sure no one has figured this out yet, but I can show you a map. This serial killer has dumped each of his Palm Beach victims in a cane field. So far, every single one of those fields is a leased-back parcel."

I stopped, incredulous. "Are you out of your mind? What do you think this is, *The Da Vinci Code*?"

"Huh?"

"Ed, I don't want to hear about a sweetheart land deal."

"You're missing the point. It all ties in with the serial killer. I think there's a message here."

I walked faster still, but an absurd image came to mind of an old cartoon that my mentor had once taped to his door, until Carmen made him take it down: two detectives staring at a city map, push pins marking each crime scene, the dots spelling out "Fuck You," and one detective asking the other, "You think there's a pattern here?"

I checked my phone. Still no reception. I needed to get around to the other side of the building. I kept walking.

"Abe, are you listening to what I'm saying?"

"Not anymore. I thought you came here out of friendship. Instead, you're bending my ear about a *lawsuit*?"

"We can nail these guys once and for all, Abe."

"I'm not interested."

"Abe, you and me, a team. We can beat Big Sugar."

"That's your thing, not mine, Ed."

"*Make* it your thing, damn it. Cutter isn't the only murderer in town, you know. These sugar-baron bastards are killing the Everglades, and they're getting away with it."

"Ed, I have bigger things on my mind, my wife is missing, *and I honestly don't give a shit!*"

I stopped cold. We had just rounded the corner of the building and nearly collided with a television news crew. An appalled reporter was staring right at me. I had been yelling, the part the reporter had heard was completely out of context, and the cameraman had heard it, too. I was about to explain, but she wouldn't give me a chance, at least not off camera. At the snap of her fingers, the video was rolling.

"Excuse me, sir," she said. "Aren't you Abe Beckham?"

The microphone was in my face. The red eye of the camera was staring at me.

Another man might have learned his lesson from the one-word lie in Carmen's office, the one about how long it had been since my last encounter with Tyla Tomkins. But I was desperate for a quick out.

"No," I said, and I hurried to my car.

Chapter Thirty-Five

I couldn't go home. Not tonight. My house was still a crime scene, and the investigators would return in the morning. If I planned on being there, I needed sleep. I headed for J.T.'s apartment.

I called Angelina's parents. Her father was relieved, but he asked the obvious question:

"So, where do they think she is?"

"We have to keep looking."

"I know we have the tip line through the police, but I want to offer a reward to go with it. You know, anyone with information please call us. No questions asked. Maybe . . . how much do you think? Twenty-five thousand? Fifty thousand? I don't know. How do people come up with these numbers?"

How indeed. Is it what someone's worth? What the family can afford? Another question with no answer. "A reward is a good idea, Jake. We'll figure out the amount in the morning."

I told him not to give up hope, he told me the same, and we hung up. I slapped myself across the face six or seven times on the drive down the turnpike just to stay awake. They didn't hurt as much as the next call. I answered only because I thought the Palm Beach area code could have been from someone on the task force. Somehow that TV reporter had hunted down my cell number.

"Mr. Beckham, I know that was you."

My first instinct was to hang up, but damage control had its place. "I apologize. That was very rude of me, but this is a difficult time. Please respect my privacy."

"I heard what you said. I'd like to give you an opportunity to explain."

I needed to be smart here. "I tell you what, Ms. . . . what's your name?"

"Heather. Heather Hunt."

Of course it is. "I love my wife, and I'm doing everything humanly possible to find her. What you heard was completely out of context. Now, if you promise to leave me alone, I promise that the next time I have an update for the media, you'll be the first person I call."

"Mr. Beckham, I don't mean to sound insensitive, but your wife is a Miami story. I want to talk to you about Cortinas Sugar."

"What?"

"After you ran off, literally, Mr. Brumbel explained what you meant when you said you didn't give a you-know-what. He said that right before Tyla Tomkins was killed she contacted you about criminal activity and a cover-up at Cortinas Sugar."

Damn it, Ed. From the get-go, I'd made it clear to him that Tyla's message was confidential.

"I'm sorry, I can't talk to you about that."

"Mr. Brumbel gave me your cell and said you'd be happy to explain."

Shit, Ed! "No, I can't."

"So you really don't give a S-H-I-T about a possible connection between Tyla Tomkins and criminal activity at Cortinas Sugar?"

"I really have to go now. I'm sorry, Hunter."

"Heather. Heather Hunt."

"I'm driving down the turnpike at seventy miles per hour, I'm tired, and I'm talking on the phone. This is dangerous. Good night."

She called right back, but I ignored it. I fumbled with the phone to dial Ed. Yes, he'd come out after midnight to support me, and perhaps I could have found a more delicate way to say that finding Angelina was a higher priority than suing Big Sugar. But blabbering to a reporter about Tyla and me was pretty harsh payback.

The call went to voice mail. My mind suddenly filled with thoughts of Ed on the other line, feeding Heather Hunt more quotes about Tyla, me, and whatever lawsuit he was trying to build against Cortinas Sugar. I left a message: "Ed, I trusted you to keep it confidential that Tyla may have been a whistleblower. Please, not another word to the media. You're compromising a homicide investigation. That's all I have to say." I put the phone away, but my anger simmered all the way back to Miami. Maybe some of it was misdirected.

There was still my brother-in-law's mess to deal with.

It was one thirty in the morning when I reached J.T.'s complex. I flew over three sets of speed bumps, pulled my car into the same spot I'd parked in when Samantha and I had lived here, and dropped my keys in the same dish by the front door. Two trips to and from Palm Beach in the last sixteen hours, and that had been the easy part of my day. I was exhausted, but sleep was not my first order of business. The Cortinas connection had me wound up, but I couldn't waste energy on it. I had to stay focused. I still wanted to hear J.T.'s version of his conversation with Agent Santos, and I didn't care if I was waking him up in the middle of the night to get it. I went into his room, switched on the lamp, and nudged him till he woke.

"Did you tell Agent Santos that Angelina hits me?"

He blinked, trying to get his bearings. "What?"

I peeled back the blankets, pulled him up from his pillow, and sat him on the edge of the mattress, facing me. He was wearing his usual basketball shorts and T-shirt. I repeated my question, trying not to sound too accusatory, but at this stage of the game I was losing my bedside manner. His eyes were adjusting to the light, but that wasn't the only reason for the slow response. Finally he answered.

"I might have," he said.

"J.T, why would you do that?"

"I—uh." His leg got restless, his right heel bouncing up and down on the floor like a jackhammer. The SCRAM bracelet rattled on his ankle.

"I'm not going to get mad. I promise."

Both his legs were going now. The bed was actually squeaking. I needed to back off a bit.

"J.T., breathe for me, okay? I want you to relax and tell me why you told Agent Santos that Angelina hits me."

He inhaled through his mouth, exhaled through his nose. It seemed backward to me, but so did most of J.T.'s world.

"I was just . . . just trying to help."

"Help? Help who?"

"You."

"Me? How was that going to help me?"

"She was trying to get me to say that you hit her. She didn't believe me when I said no. So—I don't know, Abe. I just went too far. You know, people push me, and I push back. So it was like, Oh yeah, you think Abe hits Angelina? That's not only bullshit. It's *double* bullshit. Angelina hits *him*. In your face, lady."

In a weird J.T. way, it made sense. He was breathing so hard that there was a whistling through his nose on each exhale. "J.T., don't hyperventilate."

His breathing slowed, but the restless legs continued.

"It's nice that you want to help me," I said. "But it doesn't help to say that Angelina hit me. Agent Santos will turn that around and say that this was a violent relationship, Angelina hit me one too many times, and I finally hit back, and Angelina ended up missing. Or worse."

"Is that what happened?"

"No, J.T.! Shit, no!"

"Don't yell at me, Abe!"

He sprang to his feet. I recoiled defensively, but J.T. went right past me. His body was simply responding to that uncontrollable urge to pace the floor. Innocent enough, but it brought back Angelina's words to me. *He scares me, Abe.*

"J.T., have you been taking your pills every day?"

"Uh-huh, yeah." He was in constant motion, back and forth at the foot of the bed, from one end of the room to the other.

"Are you sure?"

"Don't call me no liar, Abe."

"I'm just asking. Because I know you want to help me, right?"

"Yeah, yeah," he said, but his words were just grunts.

"J.T., the best way you can help me right now is to take care of yourself. Can you do that for me?"

"Wanna help, wanna help, wanna help. That's all."

"J.T., can you promise me that?"

"I just wanted to help, that's all I was trying to do, but now I fucked up everything, and no one will ever want my help again. I should have just said no, go away, I can't talk now, see you later, bitchy FBI woman who I caught looking up my shorts at my black dick."

I went to him, but he was pacing too furiously. If I didn't do something fast, he'd be skipping across the room, and as funny as people thought that sounded, there was nothing funny about it.

"I shouldn't have said nothin', Abe!"

"Don't worry about it. I need you to calm down, okay?"

"I'm just stupid."

"J.T., come on."

"Stupid, stupid, stupid," he said, slapping his forehead with each *stupid*.

"J.T., stop it!"

I was so loud that I'd startled myself, but it didn't faze J.T. He dropped to the floor and started working at the ankle bracelet. "We gotta get this thing off me, Abe."

"Don't!"

"I can't wear this shit no more!"

This was trouble we didn't need. *I* didn't need. Instinctively, I lunged toward him before we had a swarm of squad cars in the parking lot and the police beating on the door. My foot caught the corner of the bed and I fell forward. My reflex was to throw a stiff arm to break my fall, and I banged my tricep so hard on the bedpost that I practically saw stars.

"Damn it, J.T.!"

He didn't hear, didn't even notice me. My arm was killing me, but the problem was the ankle bracelet.

"Got to get this fucking thing off me, Abe!"

I was desperate. I had one card to play, one I'd been holding for nineteen months. I wasn't sure I could actually pull it off, but if ever there would be a time to try, this was it.

I started singing.

I was off key, and my voice cracked, partly because I was a terrible singer, mostly because I wasn't doing justice to a special memory. It was a song that I'd heard Samantha sing to her brother in bad situations, some worse than this. Samantha had a beautiful voice. It was no surprise that it had worked for her. I was doing the best I could.

"Can you sing it with me, J.T.?"

I sang the first verse alone, lacking the power the composer had intended, sounding not at all like the choir at J.T. and Samantha's old church. But it was enough to make J.T. stop pacing and sit on the edge of the mattress. I didn't know the second verse, so I started over, and J.T. joined me.

God gives me a rainbow
after a storm.
All winter God tells me
It'll get warm.
Through hard times
His Grace
In good times
His Grace

Makes me grateful, so grateful.
I'm grateful He's great.
Be grateful.

We sang it twice. J.T. went quiet. No more pacing, no restless legs. The room was oddly still, a rarity in my life with J.T., and I savored it. "Try to go back to sleep," I told him.

J.T. climbed into the bed and slid under the sheets. I switched off the lamp and started toward the door.

"Abe?" he called in the darkness.

I stopped in the doorway.

"What are you grateful for?" he asked.

The question cut right through me, sliced me in two. Half of me inside a room that was thick with memories of Samantha. Half out there, somewhere, searching for Angelina.

"Good night, J.T.," I said as I closed the door.

I made up the couch and lay in the darkness. Even with J.T.'s bedroom door closed, I could hear him snoring. But that wasn't what kept me awake. I couldn't close my eyes without going back to the hospital. I closed them anyway.

It had been a hot summer morning, but Samantha was unaware. We were in a hospital in name only. It was hospice care, and even though everyone meant well, my head was going to explode if I heard the words "make her comfortable" one more time. Samantha had been in and out of sleep brought on by painkillers. I was half asleep myself, in the chair beside her bed, when her eyes opened.

"Abe?"

"What, honey?"

She waved me closer. I leaned over the rail.

"Promise me something," she whispered.

I thought it might be our Ryan O'Neal and Ali MacGraw moment, our own personal *Love Story*, where my dying wife tells me that she wants me to remarry.

"Anything," I said.

"Promise me that you will look after J.T."

I took her hand, her bony hand. "Okay."

She would have propped herself up on an elbow, but she lacked the strength. She looked straight into my eyes. "No, don't just say okay. Tell it to me. Say, 'Samantha, I promise you, I will look after J.T.'"

I swallowed hard. I was trying not to squeeze her fingers too tightly, she seemed so fragile, but she was crushing mine with whatever strength she had left.

"Samantha, I promise you I will look after J.T."

A peacefulness seemed to wash over her. She let go of my hand, settled into her pillow, and closed her eyes.

It wasn't the last thing I said to my wife. But I'm pretty sure—in fact, I'm certain—that those were the last words Samantha Vine ever heard.

Chapter Thirty-Six

I slept till seven. The music woke me.

Be-e-e-e-e grateful. J.T. had the gospel revival choir version of our song blasting on the old CD player. It was Sunday morning indeed.

My arm felt sore as I pushed myself up from the couch, but it was no big deal. I was lucky I hadn't broken my neck, the way I had fallen. I checked my phone. I had eleven messages from Heather, Hunter, whatever her name was. I deleted all of them.

"Abe, can you go shopping for me today? I got hardly nothin' left to eat."

Yeah, that was right at the top of my list. Sounded like a great job for one of the many people who had asked if there was anything they could do to help.

"J.T., I just went shopping for you on Friday."

"I think it was contaminated. I had to put most of it down the disposal."

Really? REALLY? I took a deep breath. *Be grateful.* "I'll take care of it."

"Can you go now?"

"No, I can't go now, J.T."

"I'm really hungry."

We ordered pizza. Yes, at seven in the morning. There was a place on South Beach that only delivered after 4:00 a.m. Living in a city where people partied in shifts had its advantages.

I checked in with Rid. The search along the Tamiami Trail had been scaled back but was ongoing. It would wrap up by noon. They didn't have the manpower to search beyond the one-mile bridge area. I called Angelina's friend Sloane. By eight thirty she had forty volunteers to walk the Trail. We met at the parking lot east of the bridge. It was mostly women, lots of broad hats, water bottles, and sunscreen. Sloane played camp counselor.

"I want two lines, single file," she said to the group. "One line will walk the north shoulder, and the other walks the south. Don't touch or pick up anything. If you see anything, I mean *anything*, dial my cell. Don't play cop. Let the police check it out."

"How far are we walking?" someone asked.

"As far as we can go."

Someone in the crowd pointed out that the Trail was 275 miles long, and I overheard one or two others muttering something to the effect that "she," presumably Sloane, must be out of her fucking mind.

"If you get tired, just let me know," said Sloane. "We have a couple of volunteers with SUVs who will run a shuttle back to the staging area."

That drew a collective sigh of relief from the volunteers. Off they went. I didn't. I flagged down Rid. We talked near the bridge, just outside the police tape.

"Is Santos coming today?" I asked.

"She's in Palm Beach."

"Pardon the stupid question, but are they sure this latest homicide was Cutter?"

"Yeah. Ash on the face. White woman with black boyfriend. Other indicators that—sorry, pal—I can't share with you."

"I understand."

"The thing is," said Rid, "this makes it even more unlikely that Angelina is one of Cutter's victims. That's not his pattern, two in one weekend. It's not any serial killer's pattern. Some of them sleep for days after a kill."

"That's the typical profile," I said, and I knew something about this. "Not that I'm hoping this Cutter has something to do with Angelina, but serial killers can become spree killers, especially at the end of their run."

"True. But spree killer ain't where Santos' head is at."

"Is she still looking at me?" My bet was fifty-fifty that he would answer.

"She hasn't ruled you out. That's all I can say."

"I need more," I said.

Rid didn't answer. But he didn't shut me down, either. "I spoke to J.T.," I said. "He told Santos that Angelina hits me."

"I know," said Rid. "That's not helpful. For you, I mean."

"There's a good explanation. Basically, J.T. was talking shit. You know that, and I know that. I need your help to make Santos understand it, too."

Rid looked away, toward the line of volunteers streaming across the bridge like army ants. "Did he give her any specifics?"

"No. He just said Angelina hits me. When Santos pressed for details, he told her that she needed to ask me about it."

"Did she ask you?"

"Yeah."

"Did you tell her?"

"I told her it wasn't true."

He looked right at me. "So you didn't tell her that Angelina broke your nose?"

I caught my breath. That was three years earlier. "I broke my nose playing basketball."

"No, you didn't, Abe. That was your story. Nuke and you went up for a rebound and his elbow caught you square in the nose. That shit happens all the time in the Carver gym. Except I talked to Nuke. I know it didn't happen."

I'd given Nuke a new pair of LeBron high-tops to tell that story. Apparently his memory did not extend beyond the life of the shoes. "That was a long time ago," I said.

"Not that long," said Rid.

"Angelina and I dated for almost three years, lived together for over half that time. It was hard on her when things broke off. When she found out I was leaving her for Samantha—"

"A black chick."

He said it, not me. "She didn't take it well."

"*Didn't take it well?* Abe, she smashed your face in."

"It really wasn't—"

"Wasn't her fault? Is that what you were going to say? What the shit, Abe? Now you sound like the battered women who go back home to a husband who's so sorry for what he did, then end up getting carried out the front door in a body bag."

I knew those women. I'd prosecuted their husbands. That wasn't Angelina and me. "There's been nothing like that since we got married."

"What about the smashed beer bottle?"

"There's been *nothing*," I said, more forceful.

"Okay. Whatever." He looked away again.

"Hey," I said, forcing him to make eye contact. "Santos doesn't need to know about the nose."

It took a while, and for the longest time, I thought I might not have him. But finally I saw that look on his face, the one that told me we were friends, not just colleagues, and that we had an understanding.

"Nosebleeds," he said. "Part of fucking round ball."

"Thank you, man. I thank you very much."

Chapter Thirty-Seven

Victoria wasn't in Palm Beach. She was in Miami, meeting with the chief assistant to the US attorney, Matthew Lewis. In any organization, no one works longer hours than the chief assistant to the top banana, and the US attorney's office was no exception. Lewis arrived early and stayed late, routinely working weekends and holidays, occasionally stepping out for a cigarette. They talked at a patio table in the courtyard outside the Federal Building, a handful of dead cigarettes in the ashtray between them. Smoking was not allowed in the building, and this was the chief assistant's regular spot.

"Got a sugar war brewing," Victoria said.

Lewis smiled and lit another cigarette. Early in his career, Lewis had been one of the hard-nosed government lawyers in a save-the-Everglades law-suit against the state of Florida for failure to enforce clean-water regulations against Big Sugar. No one in Tallahassee would admit it, but Cortinas controlled the state officials who negotiated the settlement.

"What'd the bastards do this time? Drown day-old kittens?"

She smiled a little, then turned serious. "I'm not sure where this is headed, but the Ed Brumbel segment on the news this morning got me thinking."

Lewis took a drag on his cigarette. "Who?"

"Farm Aid lawyer in Belle Glade. Spent the last twenty years of his career trying to nail Big Sugar for something. He's a doofus, but we all know the story about the blind pig and the acorn. There actually may be a Big Sugar connection to my Cutter investigation."

"Tell me."

"Basically, we have five victims recovered from the sugarcane fields in Palm Beach County. No problem linking them all to one killer. Then we have two outliers in Miami-Dade. One is Tyla Tomkins, the lawyer from Belter, Benning and Lang. I'm almost one hundred percent sure that Cutter is not her killer."

"Copycat?"

"Maybe. The other is Abe Beckham's wife, still missing. Search is ongoing, and we have no body to examine, so I can't be as sure about her. But my guess: not Cutter."

"Where does the sugar war fit in?"

"Brian Belter was sleeping with Tyla Tomkins. I have no doubt about that. And we have a voice-mail message from Tyla Tomkins to Abe Beckham. It sounds like she was offering up incriminating information about the business activities of Cortinas Sugar. Tomkins, it turns out, did some of the most sensitive legal work, both for the companies and for the Cortinas family."

"So Tomkins was in a position to destroy Brian Belter's marriage and do serious damage to his best client."

"You got it."

Lewis flicked the ash. "So your theory is what? Belter turned into Dexter?"

"No, my theory is that Belter had a big problem that could be solved only by getting rid of Tyla Tomkins. Not only was Cutter in the news, but the bodies were turning up in his client's sugarcane fields. Maybe it put an idea in his head. Kill Tyla and make it look like Cutter did it."

Lewis thought for a moment. "I've met Belter. He doesn't strike me as a machete-swinging kind of guy."

"Cortinas still uses cane cutters outside the States. It wouldn't take much to fly one over, have him do the deed, and pay him enough pesos to keep his mouth shut."

"Maybe."

"Some of these cutters are of questionable background. One they hired in Brazil was an ex-con on parole. Put his girlfriend in a coma for five days when he hit her over the head with the flat side of his cane knife. A little turn of his wrist, and she would have been dead."

"Could he be your serial killer?"

"He's back in jail. But there are tens of thousands of cane cutters in Central America, South America, the Caribbean. All Belter needed to find was one who was willing to whack Tyla Tomkins."

"What have you done on this so far?"

"One of your AUSAs helped with a subpoena. We want access to Tyla's computers and e-mails at BB&L."

"That will be a dogfight."

"Yeah. Maggie Green is running major interference."

"I'll look into that. But how do you connect Belter to the disappearance of Beckham's wife? Why would Belter have anything to do with her?"

"He wouldn't."

"So who are you looking at there?"

"Abe Beckham."

"Ah, the husband. The twenty-first-century Colonel Mustard."

"What?"

"Sorry. I played too much Clue as a kid. My question is, other than the fact that he's the husband, why would you think he did it?"

"I'm pretty sure he was having an affair. With Tyla Tomkins."

Lewis shook his head. "So a woman puts her career at risk to call him with a crime tip, and he can't keep his wick dry. He always was an arrogant son of a bitch."

"Do you know Beckham?"

"Can't stand him. Typical state prosecutor with the my-dick's-bigger-than-your-dick mentality. Thinks all feds are white-collar pansies and the only real prosecutors are the ones doing murder, rape, robbery."

"He didn't really strike me that way."

"Probably because you've got him by the balls. Are you looking at Beckham for both Tyla Tomkins and his wife?"

"Looking at him. Yes."

"So that gives you two possibles in the murder of Tyla Tomkins: Belter and Beckham."

"Three, really. Can't rule out a copycat."

"Okay, three. But only one has an obvious connection to both Tyla and Angelina."

"That's true."

"So if I were you, I'd keep the Brian Belter angle alive. But in the short term, blaze down the path of least resistance. See where it leads."

"Meaning Beckham. I totally agree. But I don't have the time, the budget, or the stomach for a witch hunt. Whatever Beckham's role in this may be, I have a serial killer to catch. That's why I've been doing my best to keep any suspicion about Beckham off the record. A media circus about another husband killing his pretty wife will only hurt the search for Cutter. I need your help."

"Name it."

"I want Beckham to sit for a polygraph. If he passes, I turn the page."

"Did you ask him to sit for one?"

"Yeah. He refused."

Lewis took another long drag, smoke billowing into the air. "I can't get a court order that requires anyone to sit for a polygraph."

"I know. But here's how I want to play it: 'Mr. Beckham, you can refuse to take a polygraph, but that won't make me happy. In fact, it could make me so unhappy that I might say screw it. Let's arrest you on a lesser charge, something far less serious than murder.

If we arrest you, we'd have to lock you up for the night, and if we have to lock you up, even for a misdemeanor, and even for just one night, we can strip-search you. So says the Supreme Court.'"

"You're right on the law. But what lesser charge are you talking about?"

"Old Reliable. One-zero-zero-one," she said, meaning section 1001 of the US criminal code.

"Ah, the Martha Stewart strategy. If you can't make the real crime stick, put them in prison for making a false statement to an FBI agent."

"It sounds lame, I know, but this is just posturing. Beckham's wife is missing. The last thing he needs is for us to haul him downtown for lying to an FBI agent, strip-search him, and stick him in the slammer overnight. People hear 'lying' and 'strip search,' and they think 'This guy's guilty and dangerous.' He'd be on the fast track for conviction by millions of TV jurors who can't get enough of this shit. It's all horse trading: 'Look, Mr. Beckham. Let's spare you the stigma and embarrassment of an arrest and a strip search. Just sit for a polygraph, and no charges will be brought.'"

"Good angle," said Lewis. "But only if he made a false statement."

"He lied to the state attorney, to a Miami-Dade homicide detective, and to an FBI agent—namely, me."

"Seriously? When?"

"Monday morning. We were sitting in Carmen Jimenez's office. Beckham told us that he hadn't seen Tyla Tomkins in ten years. We have photos of him having dinner with her last September."

"No shit?"

"No shit," said Victoria, her eyes narrowing. "So I'm asking for your help. I want to look Abe Beckham in the eye and tell him that if he doesn't sit for a polygraph, the chief assistant to the US attorney is prepared to go before a grand jury and indict him for lying to an FBI agent."

Lewis crushed out his cigarette and smiled wryly. "Nice work, Agent Santos. You may have enough for a strip search *and* a polygraph."

Chapter Thirty-Eight

I was naked. Completely naked. And not enjoying it in the least.

"Turn around, please," the cop said.

I turned. The wind from the AC vent rushed between my thighs. The penlight roamed my privates. This was not the typical strip search that police do for concealed contraband or weapons that could present a danger to prison guards or other inmates. This was a full-body examination for bruises, scratches, or any other physical evidence of an altercation between Angelina and me. According to the Miami-Dade Police Department form that I'd signed, the examination was being done with my "full and knowing consent." Sort of. Agent Santos had been quite persuasive: "I want a polygraph and a complete physical examination. Or we literally make a federal case out of the lie you told me about Tyla Tomkins."

Had I not been a prosecutor, it would have sounded like bullshit. But I knew that lying to a cop or an FBI agent in the course of a criminal investigation was a felony punishable by up to five years in prison, even if the statement wasn't made under oath. I wasn't convinced that Santos would act on the threat, but I was in no position to call her bluff. So I took the polygraph. And then I got naked.

"Raise your arms," said the examiner.

I complied. We were in a small, windowless room. The walls were yellow-painted cinder blocks. Bright fluorescent lighting assaulted my eyes. The examiner had clearly done this before, and I was coming around to the view that the pooper scooper who trailed behind the elephants in the Ringling Brothers parade did not have the un-greatest job on earth after all. Not many people had familiarized themselves with the obscure ligament that separated my testicles from my rectum, but he found it. The examiner narrated his findings into a recorder, and his assistant took notes. *Left groin, clear; right groin, clear.* Rid stood in the corner, averting his eyes the way men did when standing at the urinals in a public restroom, where the singular goal was never to get caught looking. Rid wasn't there just for moral support. He was one of the lead detectives in the search for Angelina.

"Let's get a photograph of that," said the examiner.

My arms were up over my head. The examiner was aiming his penlight at the inside of my left tricep. "A photograph of what?" I asked.

"The consent form includes photographs," he said.

"I know. I just want to know what you're photographing."

Rid spoke up from the corner. "It's a bruise, Abe."

I craned my neck, trying to see a part of my tricep muscle that wasn't in my normal line of sight. "I wasn't even aware it was there."

"No yellowing," said the examiner. "Probably less than two days old."

The assistant wrote that down.

"I can't think of anything in the last couple of days," I said.

"Maybe you got it playing basketball," said Rid.

I caught Rid's eye. He looked away, but I could read his mind: *Just like the broken nose.*

The assistant snapped the photograph, several of them actually, the flash blinking machine-gun style. I suddenly remembered my fall in J.T.'s bedroom.

"Oh, now I know how that happened. Last night with J.T. there was a minor crisis, I guess you'd call it. I tripped on the edge of the bed and—"

"Abe," said Rid, giving me a subtle "cut" sign. My explanation sounded like bullshit, and in his mind he was doing me a favor by telling me to put a sock in it. Maybe he was. I zipped it.

If the examiner found other bruises, he didn't tell me about them. The entire examination took less than twenty minutes.

"You can get dressed now."

The examiner left with his assistant. It had been bad enough standing in the room naked with three other men, but alone with Rid was beyond awkward.

"Let me check on the polygraph," he said, and then he left, too.

I gathered my clothes and got dressed. The bruise was a potential problem, given what J.T. had told Santos, but I wasn't worried. I was convinced that the results of the polygraph examination would quickly put an end to this nonsense. I'd never taken one before, but I'd seen it administered to suspects many times. Santos had insisted that it be administered by an FBI examiner, so I didn't know him, which was fine by me. All had gone as I'd expected. The examiner asked the usual control questions on irrelevant matters. *Do you like ice cream? Is your hair purple?* These were designed to give the examiner a baseline for my truth telling as measured by his instruments. Then he moved to the heart of the matter. Three questions—it was typically three—that would either rule me out or propel me to the top of the list of suspects.

Have you ever seen your wife dead?

Did you kill your wife?

Did you have anything to do with your wife's disappearance?

My answers, of course, had been no, no, and no.

There was a knock at the door. Rid entered and closed the door. I didn't like the expression on his face, and the first question out of my mouth was a reflection of my mounting paranoia.

"Don't tell me I failed," I said.

"No, no. The FBI won't share the results."

"Huh?"

"Santos' position is that you agreed to take a polygraph. She never agreed to share the results."

"What the fuck is that about?"

"Sorry. I didn't see that coming either. I guess that's why she insisted that we use an FBI examiner."

"This is bullshit," I said. "I passed, and now she doesn't want me to be able to state publicly that I passed."

"I'll straighten this out. But for now, forget that."

"Forget nothing—"

"Abe, listen to me. I need you to go into Little Havana with me."

"What for?"

"We've been checking all the pawnshops along Eighth Street leading to the Tamiami Trail. We found one in Little Havana that looks like it could have something for us. A guy who never came into the shop before showed up early Saturday morning selling a diamond engagement ring. No negotiation. He took whatever he could get for it, way less than what it was worth."

My heart sank.

"Come on," he said. "I need you to tell me if it's Angelina's."

Chapter Thirty-Nine

We didn't talk in the car. Rid drove. I stared out the passenger-side window.

Calle Ocho was once the heart of a community of Cuban exiles, a place where old men could be found in José Martí Park playing dominoes, smoking cigars, and talking *béisbol*. Many of the neighborhood *tiendas* were gone, either squeezed out by El Costco or simply a casualty of changing demographics. Pawnshops continued to flourish, resilient as ever, catering to Miami's unending stream of new arrivals who lacked credit and needed fast cash, no questions asked.

Pawn 24 was one of those shops that never closed, but the door was always locked. Iron security bars reinforced a storefront window where, a decade or two earlier, anything from lawn statues of the Virgin Mary to Cuban wedding cakes might have been on display. Rid and I went to the entrance and rang the bell. A twenty-something man came to the door. Tattoos covered his arms. A toothpick wagged from his mouth as he spoke from the other side of the glass.

"What you want?"

Rid showed his badge. The man checked it, unlocked the door, and let us in. He immediately relocked it.

"Sunday afternoon is prime time for holdups," he said. "My uncle says keep the door locked."

"Your uncle's a smart man," said Rid.

His name was Manny. His uncle owned the shop, and Manny worked the late shift and on weekends. We shook hands—just one shake, a formality. Rid introduced me as a state prosecutor first, then as Angelina's husband.

"I saw you on the news," he said. "Sorry about your wife."

"Thank you for that," I said.

"Not sure I can help, but when the cops were here this morning, they asked if anyone suspicious came in after midnight Friday. I told 'em everybody's suspicious after midnight on Friday."

"Were you here alone when the guy came in to sell the diamond?" asked Rid.

" 'Course I was alone. What do you think this is, Walmart? Basically it's either me or my uncle running the place."

"What did the guy look like?" asked Rid.

"Homeless, if you ask me. Maybe six feet tall, dark hair. But that's not the suspicious part. The cops asked if anyone came by looking to get quick cash for a woman's personal effects. Diamond ring, earrings, necklace, a designer handbag, expensive shoes, that sort of thing. That's when I mentioned the ring."

"Why didn't you show it to them?"

"Because my uncle would kick my ass if he knew I had a bunch of cops snooping around the shop inspecting his merchandise, okay? If the ring belongs to this man's wife, he can tell me, and then you guys can follow up with my uncle. If it doesn't belong to her, then we're done. My uncle doesn't even need to know you were here."

"I'm pretty anxious to see it," I said.

"It's back in the vault," said Manny. "I'll get it."

"We'll go with you," said Rid.

"No need."

"I want to minimize the amount of handling," said Rid.

"If you're hoping to lift fingerprints, forget it. It's like I told the cops this morning. I cleaned that baby good, soaked it in solution all day yesterday, polished it up."

"Got it," said Rid. "But it's still better if we keep the handling to a minimum."

Manny's voice tightened. "I need you to back off, all right? I didn't have to be a good citizen here. I could have just kept my mouth shut and let my uncle sell the ring. Unless you have a warrant, you're not going into the storeroom. Period."

"No need to get your back up," said Rid.

"No need for me to lose my job, either. You're making me sorry I even got involved. I put the ring in a little jewel box, so I don't even have to touch it to bring it out here. Do you want to see it or don't you?"

Not all pawnshops were fencers, but my bet was on a load of stolen merchandise in the back of this one. I didn't give a hoot about his uncle's stash.

"Get the ring, Manny. We'll wait."

"But *don't* touch it," said Rid.

He turned and went. Rid and I waited at the counter. Pawn 24 was not the kind of place to keep fine jewelry on display. Most of the items on the shelves sold in the range of seventy-five to two hundred bucks. Power tools were apparently hot items. Musical instruments were not far behind. Handguns were the biggest seller of all. The sign at the cash register read, "No credit cards excepted," which, semantically speaking, was the opposite of what was meant.

"Here we go," said Manny. He laid the case on the counter. Most of the blue velvet on the outside had worn away.

"Open it, please," said Rid.

He lifted the cover on the old case. The diamond caught the light and sparkled in my eye. I froze.

"A real beauty," said Manny. "About a karat and a half."

Yes, it was. Exactly. Marquis cut. Platinum band. I couldn't look away, but I felt the weight of Rid's stare—on *me*. It was as if he knew something was up before I even opened my mouth.

"It's not Angelina's," I said.

"Say what?"

I knew it was going to sound crazy, and I wasn't sure Rid would believe me. I could hardly believe it myself.

"The ring is not Angelina's," I said again. "It was Samantha's."

Chapter Forty

For seven hundred dollars I bought back Samantha's ring from the pawnshop, which was less than 10 percent of retail, but a couple hundred bucks more than Manny had paid for it.

At first, Manny's uncle had flat-out refused to give up the ring. We could have gone to court to force the issue, but there was little doubt in my mind that the ring would be "lost" by then. After telling me how much he hoped my wife was okay, Uncle Asshole tried to tack on an additional fifty-dollar fee for paying by check. Luckily, Rid was there to prevent another homicide. Crime scene investigators collected the ring as evidence and took it to the lab. The ring still smelled of the strong ammonia-based solution Manny had used to clean it, so there was little hope of lifting fingerprints, but it was worth a shot.

A Miami-Dade detective took Manny to the station to review mug shots of recent arrests in the area. Two other officers canvassed the neighborhood, talking to homeless people, since that was Manny's description of the man who sold the ring.

Rid and I went back to my house, which was still a secure crime scene. Agent Santos met us there. I still had a bone to pick with her over the polygraph results, but at the moment, the ring was more important. We talked in the driveway, standing beside Rid's car.

"Where did you keep the ring?" asked Santos.

I'd already gone over this with Rid. "There's a strongbox in the closet."

"Ever heard of a safe deposit box?" asked Santos.

"I had one," I said.

I'd put Samantha's wedding set in there after the funeral. I continued to wear my ring for many months afterward, until Angelina and I started dating. When I decided to remarry, it had been my plan to put my old wedding ring in the box with Samantha's. I got all the way to the bank and opened the box. Samantha's rings were there. I held them exactly as I had held them when I'd slipped them on her finger. When I felt ready, I put them back. I removed my ring, took a breath, and tried to lay it beside those bejeweled expressions of love for Samantha. Then I read the inscription that Samantha had engraved inside my ring. It wasn't the usual initials, date, and romantic sentiment. "Put me back on," it read. Samantha's love and sense of humor came flooding over me. My heart ached. At that moment, it was simply no longer possible for me to drop my ring in a cold metal box in a bank vault and walk away. I couldn't leave hers behind either. I brought her rings and mine back to the house and placed them in a locked strongbox, fully intending to take them back to the bank when I was ready.

"I guess I never got around to using it," I told Santos.

"Let's have a look inside," she said. "There's no strongbox on the inventory list, but let's see if it's here and the investigators just missed it."

Rid unlocked the door and opened it.

"Freezing in here," said Rid.

So cold, in fact, that the windows were sweating with condensation. It was hard to keep an active crime scene cool with investigators coming and going, the doors opening and closing constantly. Someone on the team had turned down the AC to sixty degrees and had forgotten to dial up the temperature before leaving.

Rid and Santos followed me down the hall to the master bedroom. I went to the walk-in closet. The chair I sat on every morning when tying my shoes was where it always was. I moved it to the back of the closet, directly in front of the built-in set of shelves, cabinets, and open storage cubicles that covered the entire wall. I climbed up on the chair so that I could reach the small cabinet all the way at the top. I opened it. An empty feeling washed over me, as empty as the space I was staring into.

"It's gone," I said.

I stared into the cabinet for a moment longer, then climbed down from the chair. We stepped out of the closet and into the bedroom.

"Other than her wedding set, what else was in the box?" asked Santos.

"A pair of diamond earrings I bought her for our first anniversary. And a watch that Luther bought for her. I have other mementos, but they're not really valuable to anyone but me."

"Abe and I already covered this," said Rid. "Metro-Dade police are checking other pawnshops to see if those other items were hocked, too."

"Good," said Santos. "This changes the analysis."

I knew it did, but I wanted to know her thinking. "How so?"

"It's not unusual for serial killers to take keepsakes from their victims. Rings, pendants, that sort of thing. But Samantha's rings are not a trophy. This is more like a robbery."

"A robbery and an abduction?" I asked.

"Possibly," said Rid. "Except there's no sign that anyone went rummaging through drawers and closets looking for valuables."

"Could have been a home invasion," I said. "I know of two of them in our area in the last year or so. The homeowner answers the door, and as soon as it opens, the guy forces himself inside, pulls a gun, and demands to be led to whatever money or jewelry there is in the house. There's no sign of struggle because there is no struggle. It's the element of surprise."

"Did Angelina know about the rings?" asked Riddel.

"I never mentioned them to her," I said. "But obviously she couldn't have led a home invader to the box if she didn't know about it. Maybe she found it on her own. It's not like I had it hidden in the attic."

"But there's another problem," said Santos.

"What?"

She walked to the dresser where Angelina's jewelry box lay in plain view. Santos opened it. "Angelina's engagement ring is still here."

I walked over. The diamond ring was right where Angelina placed it every night before going to sleep. Rid looked at me, and I at him, both searching for an explanation.

"That's a puzzler, ain't it?" said Rid.

"Yeah," said Santos, looking at me. "Got an answer for that?"

I stared at Angelina's ring, thinking. "No. I really don't."

Santos told Rid to follow up with the investigators. "Make sure they covered the cabinet area thoroughly," she added.

Rid and I followed her out of the bedroom and back to the living room. I adjusted the thermostat to a normal level, one that wouldn't bankrupt me. Rid got a phone call and stepped into the kitchen. I had a moment alone with Santos.

"I want the polygraph results," I said.

"You can't have them. I never promised—"

"I know, I know. Riddel told me. You never promised to share the results. That's bullshit. The right to the results is part of any agreement to take a polygraph."

"It wasn't part of *our* agreement."

"That's just sleazy," I said.

"Excuse me?"

"You have this awesome reputation as a stellar FBI agent. But I don't see it. I've dealt with criminal defense lawyers so slimy that I want to wear a wetsuit whenever I'm in the same room with them. Even they wouldn't pull a stunt like this one."

"You need to be careful here, Mr. Beckham."

"Why? Because you might turn against me? You convicted me a long time ago, before you even saw the evidence."

"That is not true."

"It *is* true." I was building up steam, and probably should have stopped, but I couldn't. "You had it all figured out. A pretty wife, an old fling with Tyla Tomkins, and a broken beer bottle all add up to a guilty husband. And then what happens? Guilty husband sits for a polygraph. And guess what? Husband passes."

"You don't know what you're talking about."

"You won't share the results because I *passed*. That doesn't fit very well with your theory of the case, does it? I passed, but you don't want me to be able to tell anyone that I passed. That is the shittiest thing I've ever seen a law enforcement officer do, and you suck for doing it. You suck, and I'm telling you to your face."

I shouldn't have said it, but it felt good. For the first time in a long time, *something* felt good. I didn't care that Santos was so steaming mad that I almost needed to turn the AC back down to sixty.

She took a step closer, her eyes like embers. "I was doing you a favor."

I stared back at her, confused.

"Until now, you could honestly say that you were willing to take a polygraph, that you took a polygraph, and that the FBI refused to share the results. Now you have to tell the truth, Mr. Beckham."

I felt it coming, but I didn't want to believe it. Then the hammer dropped.

"You failed," she said.

I suddenly lost all ability to speak. Santos walked away, leaving me alone in the room where I had last seen my wife.

Chapter Forty-One

Rid drove me to the Find Angelina Beckham command center. It was news to me that one existed. I had Angelina's friend Sloane to thank.

Sloane had convinced the manager of a motor lodge on busy US 1, right across from the University of Miami, to donate a ballroom for the next two weeks. About a hundred civilian volunteers were inside when Rid and I arrived. People were lining up to distribute flyers, leaflets, and posters with Angelina's picture on them. A group of women at another table were busily tying yellow ribbons into bows. A dozen others were tapping away on their laptops, tablets, and other devices, spreading the word in the virtual world of social media. It was an impressive operation, but they had enough coffee, fruit, and snacks spread across three tables to serve at least double the turnout. It was like Samantha's funeral: anyone who didn't know what to do brought food.

The door was open, but I stopped at the entrance. Across the ballroom, on the wall behind the tables of food, a much-larger-than-life-size head shot of Angelina was staring at me. Of course I'd been dealing with the crisis and was painfully aware of what I was up against, but the word MISSING in bold black letters beneath her face still hit me like a mule kick.

Angelina's sister came to me. She and her husband had just arrived from Jacksonville. I introduced Rid, but he quickly excused himself to check out the food and give us time alone.

"Good news," she said. "The reward is up to twenty-five thousand dollars."

"Nice work," I said. "Thanks for all you're doing."

"Oh, it's not me," she said, her eyes welling. "It's all Sloane."

She hugged me so hard and for so long that it was awkward. I wasn't sure what had brought it on. Maybe it was the big sister embarrassed by having been so outdone by the best friend. Maybe it was driving her crazy that Angelina, the prettier of the two Miller sisters, was getting all the attention yet again. Maybe I was going to burn in hell for thinking such things. I couldn't say. Weird shit, whatever it was.

Probably just me, on edge, knowing that I'd failed a polygraph examination.

I spotted Sloane across the room. She was in supervisory mode, iPad in hand and a hands-free wireless headset to facilitate the multitasking. She and Angelina had once cochaired an art festival on the University of Miami campus, and I suddenly had a vision of Sloane busting some hapless artist's ass for driving his truck on the lawn.

"Facebook ads will start running in a few hours," she told me. "Local news coverage wouldn't give me an exact time, but all the networks will be here at some point before the six o'clock broadcast."

"That's excellent," I said.

"I'm working on Angelina's supervisor to see if the bank will match the existing donations to bring the reward up to a hundred thousand."

"Terrific. I've been getting e-mails all afternoon from people at the state attorney's office, offering to pitch in, too."

"Forward those to me, if you want. Let's shoot for five o'clock to have a firm number. Then we should do a news conference."

"That sounds like a good plan."

"You should talk to your in-laws," she said. "They don't want to do a news conference, but it's important that we get their faces out there to appeal to the community."

"Well, if they don't want to, I—"

"Abe, no. *They* need to do it."

The emphasis was on "they," not "need." I got the message. *I* wasn't enough.

Did she know I'd failed a lie detector test? "Okay, I'll talk to them," I said.

Sloane brought up an image on her iPad and showed it to me. "Right now, we're going with the reward for information leading to Angelina's safe return. You and your in-laws will have to decide when we run this one."

I looked at the screen. The reward for Angelina's safe return was in big red letters. Below it, in black letters and a slightly smaller font, was a smaller reward "for information leading to the location and recovery of Angelina's body."

"I'll let you know on that," I said.

She thanked me—for what, I wasn't sure. Then she closed out her iPad screen, excused herself, and walked over to the ribbon-tying table to step up production. Rid was on his third cupcake at the food table. He grabbed two more and came back to me.

"You hungry?" he asked.

"Not really."

"You need to eat something."

"Later."

A few more volunteers arrived. Sloane was right on them.

"That girl is good," said Rid. "She's been going around the room telling the volunteers to leave you alone. It was getting so bad that your in-laws had to step out for a while."

I had been wondering where they were.

Rid swallowed the rest of his cupcake. "It's better to give you space. A command center doesn't work for the family if it turns into a constant greeting line of mourners paying their respects. Especially when it's people you don't even know."

My attention shifted toward the entrance. Angelina's father was back. Margaret wasn't with him. A few people hadn't gotten the message about space, and they swarmed around him. He shook hands graciously, then spotted me and came across the room. The expression on his face spelled trouble.

"I just spoke with Agent Santos on the phone," he said. Then he checked over his shoulder, leaned closer, and said in a low voice, "Why didn't you tell me you were taking a polygraph?"

This was not a conversation I wanted to have in the middle of the Find Angelina command center. "Can we talk about this outside?"

"Abe, did you take a polygraph?"

"Yes, I did."

He seemed afraid to ask the follow-up. He was waiting for me to volunteer the information he wanted to hear.

"Let's step out where we can talk," I said.

He looked at me, confused. I told Rid we'd be right back, and Jake followed me out of the ballroom. We found a place to talk down the hall, just me, my father-in-law, and the proverbial elephant in the room. He was still asking that follow-up question, but only with his eyes: *You passed, right?*

I gave him the best answer I could.

"Do you know anything about polygraphs, Jake?"

"Just what I've seen on TV."

"Basically the examiner asks a lot of questions, but only three questions really matter. A lot turns on how the examiner phrases those key questions. In every polygraph examination I've ever been involved in at the state attorney's office, prosecutors and defense lawyers will negotiate for hours, back and forth, about the exact wording of the questions. Then when everyone is in agreement, you sit for the examination. We didn't have that kind of back-and-forth here. There wasn't time. I just sat for the exam."

"What were the three questions they asked you?"

I told him. "It's the last one that's . . . problematic," I said, looking for the right word.

"Problematic?"

"The examiner asked me: 'Did you have anything to do with Angelina's disappearance?' My answer was the same as it was to the other questions: 'no.' "

"What did the examination say about your answer?"

"I haven't seen the polygraph examiner's report," I said, which was true. "But I could definitely understand how someone might see signs of deception in a straight 'no' answer, without any ability to explain."

Jake was speechless, his eyes burning through me as they never had before. "What are you telling me?"

"It's a bad question, is what I'm telling you. Did I have anything to do with Angelina's disappearance? Jake, a serial killer sent photographs to our house. Angelina and I had an argument. I spent the night at J.T.'s apartment. I left Angelina alone in our house. Of course I feel like I had something to do with her disappearance."

He was silent. I was trying to read his expression, but I couldn't possibly know what was inside his head. If he didn't speak soon, he might as well have said it: *You killed my daughter.*

"I want to see the examiner's report," he said.

"I'm not sure I can get it for you."

"Get it," he said, his voice a few degrees colder.

"Okay, I'll make it happen."

He stepped closer, his nose less than a foot from mine, our eyes even. "I want to believe you, Abe. It was always important to Angelina that her mother and I love you like a son. But if the 'something' you had to do with her disappearance turns out to be something more than you just described, I will fucking kill you."

His glare held me a moment longer. Then he turned and walked back to the ballroom without me.

Chapter Forty-Two

Victoria was working at the Cutter task force command center at the Miami field office, away from volunteers. Angelina was still on her mind, but so were Cutter and the victims he'd left in Palm Beach cane fields. Their photographs were posted on the bulletin board, along with personal data and a brief physical description. Elizabeth, twenty-three years old; Caitlin, twenty-five years old; Holly, twenty-one years old; Amanda, twenty-eight years old. And now his latest: Megan, thirty-one years old. Lives cut short by a monster with a machete. Across south Florida, white women with black husbands or boyfriends were on edge, but relatively little had been said about the Palm Beach victims since the murder of Tyla Tomkins and the disappearance of Angelina Beckham. For every homicide that became a TV obsession, dozens went unnoticed. Too many went unsolved.

Not you girls. I promise.

Victoria sat alone at the conference table, her laptop in front of her, boxes of files and materials scattered across the table. She was dialing on a secure line for a follow-up with a tech agent when her cell rang. It was Abe Beckham. She hung up the landline and took Abe's call.

"I need to see a copy of the polygraph examiner's report," he said.

"The answer is still no," she said.

"My father-in-law wants to see it."

"He can't have it either."

"Why did you tell him I took one?"

"Because he asked."

She could almost feel Beckham's surprise. "Jake asked you if I had taken a polygraph?"

"Yes."

"Just to be clear," he said, his voice tinged with disbelief. "Jake asked if I had taken a polygraph before you said anything about one. Is that what you're saying?"

"Yes." She wasn't messing with him. It was true.

"Did you tell him the results?"

"No. I told him to ask you how it went. Mr. Beckham, I need to make another call. I have to go."

"Wait. I want that report."

"You don't want it, and you can't have it."

"Oh, I don't want it? What, are you doing me a favor again?"

"No. I'm doing *me* a favor. Good-bye."

She hung up and went to the microwave on the counter to make "dinner." Some agents couldn't live without a coffeemaker, but for Victoria, a command center wasn't officially up and running without micro-waved popcorn.

She knew she had probably sounded like a smart-ass, but she *was* doing herself a favor. And Elizabeth, Caitlin, Holly, Amanda, and Megan. If she shared the exam-iner's report with Abe Beckham, his father-in-law, or anyone else, it was sure to leak to the press. Overnight, the Angelina Beckham disappearance would be the media equivalent of Laci and Scott Peterson. Victoria had worked enough cases to know that sensationalism on that level wouldn't help her catch Cutter.

And it wouldn't help her find out what had hap-pened to Angelina, either.

The popcorn stopped popping. She opened the bag to let it cool, went back to the phone, and dialed on the secure line. She talked through the "appetizer," clementine wedges, her other dietary staple.

"Is this a good time, Albert?"

Albert was little more than half Victoria's age, a talented agent who had worked his way up from general technology matters to a coveted spot in the FBI Cyber Unit in Washington. He was eager to please, the way Victoria had been on her way up, and she exploited his ambition, the way her supervisors had exploited hers. He was more than happy to help on a weekend, even if he was merely double-checking the findings of the Miami tech agents. Victoria wanted to be right about this, and she was sure that the Miami agents were fine. But Albert was someone she knew, and Albert was always right.

"Okay, I got something for you," said Albert. "First, on those four voice-mail messages that Tyla Tomkins left on Abe Beckham's cell phone. Your Miami agents got it right: each of them was listened to and deleted on the same day it was received."

"You're sure of that?"

"Yes. But here's something interesting that, no offense, the boys in Miami didn't catch. When it comes to voice-mail messages, there's deleted, and then there's *permanently* deleted. The difference is what the word *permanent* implies: you can't ever get it back. It's gone. Even though each of these messages was received on a different day, all four were permanently deleted on *the same day.*"

Victoria salted her popcorn. "When?"

"Sunday, January nineteenth."

"The medical examiner puts Tyla Tomkins' death on Saturday night or very early that Sunday morning."

"If that's the case," said Albert, "this is an even more interesting finding than I thought."

"Yeah. It means that whoever deleted those messages knew that Tyla Tomkins was dead at least a day before her body was found in the Everglades, at least two days before it was identified."

"Well, then, you're welcome," said Albert.

"What about Tyla's prepaid phone?" she asked, shifting gears. "Anything on the number that we couldn't identify?"

"I'm afraid I can't help you there. Five of the six numbers she dialed were to registered cell phones. That includes Beckham. But this sixth number is to a phone just like Tyla's. It's prepaid, disposable, no registered user. There's no way to know who owned that phone or who Tyla was talking to. Unless you find the physical phone and pull fingerprints from it."

The Miami tech agent had told her the same thing. But now she was doubly sure. "Okay, we'll have to work with that. Thanks so much."

They hung up. Victoria dug into her bag of popcorn, sat back, and thought things through. Sometimes all the pieces to the puzzle were scattered on the table right in front of you. It was just a matter of configuring them the right way. But sometimes a piece was missing. If you were lucky, you knew which piece was missing. Or you at least had a hunch about what piece was missing. Victoria had a hunch.

No way to know who Tyla was talking to. Unless you find the physical phone and pull fingerprints from it.

Victoria picked up the phone again and dialed Detective Reyes, her domestic violence contact at MDPD.

"I need you to do an affidavit in support of an application for a search warrant in state court."

"What are we searching for?"

"A cell phone."

"When?"

"Right away."

"You mean tonight?"

"Yes," said Victoria. "Definitely tonight."

Chapter Forty-Three

The phone call surprised me. It was Brian Belter. He wanted to meet me for coffee, without delay.

"It's beyond important, well worth your time, and not anything I can discuss on the telephone," he said.

"Can you come to the command center?" I asked. I told him where it was. He suggested a coffee shop two blocks away. We agreed to meet there in twenty minutes.

The urgency in his voice had piqued my interest, but I wasn't sure what to make of it. I knew what Ed Brumbel would tell me to do, but I was in no frame of mind to cross-examine Belter until he broke down, cried, and admitted that Big Sugar had enslaved its workers, destroyed the Everglades, and sunk the *Titanic*. I went alone, and I told no one where I was going.

Belter was waiting in a booth at the back. He was wearing a golf shirt from the Cortinas resort in the Dominican Republic, which reminded me that less than forty-eight hours had passed since the unexpected business travel that had rendered him a no-show at Tyla's memorial service. It felt more like a month.

He rose to greet me. "Thanks for coming," he said.

I slid into the booth, and he returned to his seat, facing me. A steaming demitasse of espresso was on the table in front of him.

"Can I order you a coffee?" he asked.

"No. My stomach is churning enough."

Belter lowered his eyes, stirring his espresso. "I'm sorry you have to go through this. Truly, I am."

"Thank you. I can't stay long."

"I understand. I wanted to tell you that I would like to contribute to the reward fund for your wife."

That hardly seemed like something that couldn't be done on the phone. "That's very kind of you," I said.

"Twenty-five thousand dollars."

I was taken aback. "That's *very* kind. Thank you."

"All I ask in return is one small favor. More a show of support, really."

"Ah," I said. This had to be the face-to-face component. "Support on what?"

"The truth. I never slept with Tyla Tomkins."

My instinct was to leave, but this was the first I'd sat down in hours, and my body refused to get up. "I wouldn't know anything about that."

"I'm sure Tyla must have mentioned that to you."

"Actually, I never—"

"Abe," he said, stopping me before I could close the door on whatever proposal he had in mind. "I'm *sure* Tyla *must* have mentioned it to you."

Belter pulled his checkbook from his coat pocket, opened his Montblanc fountain pen, but then paused before filling in the number. "How much did I say my contribution would be?"

"Twenty-five thousand."

"I'm sorry. My mistake. I left off a zero."

I watched in disbelief as he wrote out a check for a quarter million dollars.

"Is there a fund you've established that I should make this payable to?" Then he lifted his eyes, looking at me. "Or should I just make it out to you?"

"To *me*?"

"Or we could dispense with these silly paper checks altogether, and I could wire the funds. To an account of your choosing, in a country of your liking."

"Are you actually trying to bribe an assistant state attorney?"

He didn't even blink. His expression was all business, nothing more, nothing less, as if to remind me who I was dealing with. As if to say, *Big Sugar has bribed much bigger fish than you, Abe Beckham.*

"Keep your money," I said, rising.

He grabbed my wrist before I could leave the table, but it was the intensity in his eyes that would not release me. "I know who the unknown caller is," he said.

"What unknown caller?"

"Tyla dialed six different numbers on her prepaid phone," he said in a low, even voice, his words flowing in machine-gun cadence. "Five of those numbers have been linked to five married men who cheated on their wives: you, me, and three other schmucks who will have a lot of explaining to do when the Tyla Tomkins murder investigation comes knocking on their door. Please don't take offense—I'm only being realistic, not cruel—but your wife is probably dead, which takes you off the hook, no explanation owed to her or to anyone else. On the other hand, my wife is very much alive, she is most unforgiving, and our prenuptial agreement expired eighteen months ago on the joyous occasion of our twentieth wedding anniversary."

"How romantic."

"Listen to me. The sixth telephone number that showed up on Tyla's prepaid phone record has never been identified. That's because the call was from another prepaid phone, one just as untraceable as Tyla's. But I know who was on that other phone."

"Who?"

"*Someone else*," he said, leaning closer. "My point is this: I never slept with Tyla. The only time I spoke to her on her prepaid cell phone was to make arrangements for her 'afternoons' with *someone else.*"

I knew exactly who he meant.

Belter slid the check across the table. It was payable to me. "I was just a go-between. Tyla *must* have made mention of that to you," he said.

I stared right back at him. There were a lot of things I could have said, many names I could have called him. But my body was running on empty, and even the launch of a verbal attack seemed like wasted effort.

"Don't ever call me again," I said.

I walked away, leaving the check on the table, and went back to the command center.

Chapter Forty-Four

The two-block walk from the coffee shop back to the command center did me good. My temper cooled, and I refocused. But I would never forget.

Brian Belter had not heard the last from me.

We were thirty minutes out from our press conference. I wanted to check in with Margaret and Jake to see how they were holding up. Rid intercepted me in the hallway before I reached the ballroom. He took me to a conference room near the business suite that had been converted into a makeshift green room. Someone had pushed the large rectangular table against the wall and brought in a couch and two additional armchairs for extra seating. Carmen Jimenez rose to greet me. It was just the three of us.

"How are you, Abe?" she said in a sincere voice.

I could have lied; I could have told the truth. What would it have mattered? "Thanks for coming, but you didn't have to," I said.

"I wanted to," she said. "First, some good news. People in the office are totally behind you. There's another five thousand dollars to kick in to the reward fund."

"Thank you. That means a lot," I said. But I knew that good news was usually paired with bad.

"Sit down, Abe," she said.

Especially when someone tells you to sit. I took the armchair. She took the other one. Rid was behind her, leaning on the edge of the desk.

"I know about the polygraph," she said.

"Carmen, I did not kill Angelina."

"I know you failed."

"I'll say it again: I did not kill my wife. The questions were bad. Just look at that third question, where he asked—"

"Abe, you failed on all three questions."

I went cold. *Have you ever seen your wife dead? Did you kill your wife? Did you have anything to do with your wife's disappearance?*

"That's not possible," I said.

"I know the examiner," said Carmen. "I talked to him."

"Did he show you the report?"

"Santos won't let him share it with anyone. But he wouldn't lie to me about that. You failed."

"They're bad questions, Carmen. The first question, *Have you ever seen your wife dead?* There was no opportunity for me to clarify the question, but I knew he was asking about Angelina, so my answer was simply no. But *yes*, of course I've seen my wife dead. For God's sake, I buried Samantha!"

"I agree with you," said Carmen. "Number three is bad, too. But it's question two that troubles me."

Did you kill your wife?

"Polygraphs are not infallible," I said. "You know that. We all know that. That's why no court in America has ever allowed them into evidence at trial."

"I understand," said Carmen. "It could have been the series of questions, it could have been the examiner, it could have been fatigue on your part, it could have been the stress of everything that has happened."

"It could have been all those things," I said.

"Could have been," said Carmen. "Here's the deal, Abe. First, I want you out of the news conference. I'll do it with Angelina's parents."

"Why?"

"Two reasons," said Carmen. "I don't want anyone blindsiding you with a polygraph question. Rumors are circulating, and this could go badly for you."

"I can handle myself," I said.

"Possibly. But that doesn't solve the bigger problem: Jake doesn't want you there."

I wasn't shocked. But it still hurt. "I want to be there."

"Don't force it, Abe. You did your job with the local media yesterday. Let Angelina's parents take the lead and announce the reward tonight. They're putting in twenty-five grand of their own money as it is."

"It will look odd if I'm not there."

"It will look worse if Jake refuses to stand within twenty-five feet of you."

"Far worse," said Rid.

It was two against one, and the one was wavering. "Media coverage is only going to intensify," I said. "I can't go around dodging cameras and microphones and saying 'no comment.'"

"I couldn't agree more," said Carmen. "So here's the plan. Your in-laws and I will do the press conference. You and Riddel will leave before it even starts, and I will explain that you are busy assisting investigators in the search for your wife. Tonight, you do whatever it takes to get a good night's sleep. Take an Ambien if you have to. In the morning, you will be rested, and we are going to redo the polygraph examination. When it's over, you can face all the media questions you want."

When it's over. What she really meant was, *If you pass.* I left that alone. "Will it be the same examiner?"

"No. The FBI will not be part of this. We'll use someone I know and trust and who will frame the questions properly."

"But not someone *I* know," I said. "If I'm going to do this, I don't want anyone claiming that the redo was rigged."

"No one you know," said Carmen.

I was trying to find the flaw in it, but I couldn't. This all made sense. And it felt good to know that there were at least two people—two people who really mattered—who didn't have me at the top of their list of suspects.

"Okay," I said. "We have a plan."

Carmen seemed pleased. The three of us shook on it and went to the door. Carmen went one way, toward the ballroom. Rid and I went the other way, avoiding the crowd. We took a side exit to the parking lot and got in his car. No one saw us as we drove away and merged into traffic on US 1.

It was a stupid thing to say, but I couldn't help myself. "Now all I have to do is pass the stupid test," I said, chuckling nervously.

"Don't redo it if you don't want to, Abe."

I was looking at him from the passenger seat, but his eyes remained fixed on the road. "No, I like Carmen's plan," I said. "This is something I need to do."

We stopped at a red light. Rid glanced across the console, looking right at me. "Abe, I'm speaking to you as a friend now, not a detective."

"Okay, let's hear it, friend."

"What you probably need is a lawyer."

Rid and I watched the Find Angelina news conference on the TV at the police station. Easy viewing it wasn't. Jake spoke first, reading from a prepared script, which was the only way to get through it.

"Angelina's family and friends are pleading with *anyone* who may know anything about her disappearance, her whereabouts, or"—he paused, his voice quaking—"or her fate. Please call the Miami-Dade Police Department at the number on your television screen, or leave information at the Find Angelina Beckham website. A reward of one hundred thousand dollars is being offered for information leading to her safe return."

The microphone passed from Jake to Carmen, but the camera angle was wide enough for me to see Margaret at Jake's side. Carmen said exactly the right thing, my esteemed and credible proxy, but I hardly processed a word of it. My entire focus was on Angelina's mother. I could almost feel the sadness, the exhaustion, the worry, the dwindling sense of hope pressing down on her shoulders. Her heart was not merely broken. It was shredded, the pieces falling away live and on camera for all the world to see, the sadness gathering in pools of despair around her, bottomless pools that could drown the most robust spirit.

I truly wondered if Margaret was going to live through this.

Chapter Forty-Five

We left the Miami-Dade police station at eight o'clock. Rid drove me to my car and went home to his wife. I wasn't sure where to spend the night. I wasn't sure I could handle J.T. I drove west on the Tamiami Trail until I reached the one-mile bridge. I parked on the shoulder and walked to the guardrail and looked out into the night. Nothing but the unending blackness of the Everglades lay before me. The shoreline along the canal was no longer a crime scene. The search for Angelina along this stretch of the highway was over, at least for the night. Maybe they'd return in the morning. Maybe a new lead would break overnight and shift the search to another location. Maybe grim news would end all hopes.

The thought made my head spin.

We were closing in on that all-important forty-eight-hour mark since Angelina had gone missing. Time was ticking. Some people said it was the first sixty hours that were crucial, but if you hear that, you are probably speaking to a man who is in hour forty-nine of the search for his wife. I had questions that needed to be answered before it was too late. I called Rid.

"How long did Cutter hold his victims before he killed them?"

"Abe, don't do this to yourself."

"I need to know. How much time do we have?"

"It varied."

"What was the longest he held any of them?"

"This is not an exact science. You have to know exactly when the victim disappeared, and the medical estimate of time of death is always just that, an estimate."

"Fine, we're estimating. What's the longest he held any of his victims before he killed them? Three days? Two days? One?"

Rid didn't answer right away. "Less," he said finally.

"A matter of hours, then?"

"Yes. Except the first victim."

"She was held longer?" I asked, hopeful.

"Her body was found burned in the cane field. No way to estimate her time of death, so no way to know how much time elapsed between her disappearance and her death."

I took a breath. "Okay. Thanks. That's helpful."

"No, it's not. Take Carmen's advice and get some sleep, Abe. *That* would be helpful."

We hung up. I took another long look at the Everglades, a panoramic view, my gaze sweeping across utter blackness. I wondered how many bodies this amazing body of water had never given up. I wondered if Angelina's would be among them.

She had warned me, actually. I daresay she had *predicted* this moment. I had forgotten the conversation, but it came flooding back to me in J.T.'s bedroom after we sang that song together, when J.T. called out to me in the darkness and asked, "What are you grateful for, Abe?" Angelina had asked me the same thing in a little different way, and a very different tone of voice. In fact, she had been screaming, tears streaming down her face.

"Damn it, Abe! I'm nice, I'm pretty, I deserve to be treated better than this. Someday you're going to stop licking your wounds, stop living in the past, and wake up. But it's going to be too late! Because I'll be gone, and then you'll realize how much you miss me."

Be grateful.

I started the car. My phone rang. It was J.T. I almost didn't answer. I was sure he wanted me to come over.

Just one more ring, and it would have gone to voice mail. Something made me pick up. He sounded anything but calm.

"Abe, you gotta get over here right now!"

I knew it. "What is it now, J.T.?"

"The cops are here."

"What? Why?"

"They have a search warrant."

It was hard to think straight, but it was Rid's offhanded advice that rang most clearly in my mind. *What you probably need is a lawyer.* A huge heads-up from a friend who couldn't come right out and tell me what was in the works, and I had ignored it.

"J.T., listen to me carefully. Do not interfere with the police. But I want you to repeat these words: Officer, I do not consent to the search for any item not listed in the warrant, and I do not consent to the search of any place not described in the warrant."

"Okay."

"No, don't say 'Okay.' Repeat what I just said."

He tried. He flubbed it.

"J.T., where are the cops now?"

"My bedroom."

"Stay on the phone, walk into the bedroom, and stand in a place where the cops can hear you. I'll tell you exactly what to say to them."

"Okay," he said, and I could sense that he was moving. "I'm in the room."

I fed him the mantra in bite-size segments, and I told him to say it loud enough for the cops, the neighbors, and even the dead to hear him. *Officer, I do not consent . . .*

"Good job," I told him. "Now sit tight. I'll be right there."

Chapter Forty-Six

The search was ongoing when I reached J.T.'s apartment. Two MDPD squad cars were parked out front. A uniformed officer was posted at the door. Rather than trying to explain that I was the brother-in-law who used to live there and still paid the rent, I simply flashed my badge, identified myself as an assistant state attorney, and walked in. I found J.T. right inside the front door, sitting on the floor with his back against the wall, clutching an empty box of Raisin Bran. His hands were shaking, his body a bundle of nerves.

"Are you okay?" I asked.

I'd seen the apartment a mess before, but nothing like this. Rugs peeled back. Furniture pulled away from the walls. Seat cushions scattered across the floor.

And that was just in the living room. J.T. was staring straight ahead, a blank expression on his face.

"They dumped out the last of my food."

I glanced toward the kitchen, which was quiet, and there wasn't a cop in sight. But I could hear them down the hall in J.T.'s bedroom.

"Did they give you a copy of the warrant?"

J.T. opened his fist, offering up the warrant, which he'd squeezed into a tight ball of legal mumbo-jumbo. I unwound the wad and read the description of the item to be confiscated: "one prepaid cellular phone, manufacturer unknown." I suddenly realized what this was about, and not just because Brian Belter had mentioned the prepaid cellular phone at the coffee shop three hours earlier.

"I knew they'd come for me," J.T. said, breathless, the way he got on the verge of a panic attack. "Bad shit happens when you put on these fucking bracelets. I gotta get this thing off me, Abe."

"No one is coming for you, J.T. I'm here now. This is a problem we can fix. Just wait here."

"Right, okay."

His voice shook, not a good sign, but I had to sort this out. I walked to the bedroom, where I found Agent Santos and Detective Reyes. A Miami-Dade officer was rummaging through dresser drawers. Another was picking apart the closet.

Santos stopped me in the doorway. "Wait in the hall, please."

I took a step back, technically outside the bedroom. "You know it's not here," I said.

"Excuse me?"

"You know damn well that my brother-in-law wasn't speaking to Tyla Tomkins on a prepaid cell phone."

"We'll find out."

One of the officers lifted the mattress and pushed it against the wall. He found nothing.

"This is a fishing expedition," I said. "That pesky Fourth Amendment keeps you from barging in here without probable cause, so you pretend to search for a cell phone, which you know isn't here, and you hope something else turns up. Are you really this desperate?"

"Are you really this concerned that *something else* might turn up?"

"J.T. has already put you on notice that he does not consent to a search for anything not listed in the warrant."

"Good luck with that," she said.

Prosecutors and defense lawyers argued every day over confiscated items not listed in the warrant: a gun found in a search for contraband, a knife found in a search for a pair of shoes. If the police search for a murder weapon and don't find it, the defense exploits that point at trial. Better to search for a phone and hope for a bloody machete.

"What are you looking for, Santos?"

"A cell phone."

"What are you *really* looking for? Just tell me. If I know where it is, I'll give it to you, and we don't have to tear apart J.T.'s apartment."

She didn't answer. An officer emerged from the walk-in closet. He was finished. Nothing.

"Try outside on the deck," Santos told him.

"Hold on," I said as I checked the warrant. J.T.'s apartment had a backyard no bigger than the living room. Home Depot and I had built that deck to Samantha's specifications.

The officer walked past me and started down the hall. I followed.

"You don't have a warrant to search outside," I said.

He continued through the living room, toward the sliding glass doors off the kitchen. I pulled out my iPhone and videoed him. "Stop right there," I said. "Your warrant does not cover the deck or any area outside the apartment. This is an illegal search."

It got the attention of Agent Santos.

"Don't go out," she told the officer. Santos didn't look happy, but my reading of the warrant was correct.

The other officer called her back to the bedroom. I followed her back down the hallway, starting to feel a bit like a yo-yo. She made me stop in the doorway, but I had a clear view into the room.

"Take a look at this," he told her. The bottom drawer of J.T.'s nightstand was open. A small stack of magazines was piled up on the floor, as if the officer had pulled them from the drawer, one by one, then stopped when something caught his interest. Santos peered into the drawer, but I couldn't see that far.

"If it's not a phone, put it back," I said.

Santos pulled on latex gloves, reached inside, and retrieved a newspaper.

I was getting nervous. All kinds of things were wrapped in newspaper. "Didn't see periodicals listed in the search warrant," I said.

She opened the newspaper. It didn't seem to be concealing anything, at least not from where I was standing. But Santos was riveted, apparently by the story. She came toward me, newspaper in hand, and stopped a few feet in front of me in the doorway. The newspaper was yellowed with age. She showed me the headline.

Sugar Company Indicted for Slavery.

It was a copy of the *Miami Tribune*—from 1941.

"I know what you're thinking," I said. "A serial killer attacks his victims with a machete and dumps their bodies in a cane field. Here's J.T., a guy with a criminal record, a history of emotional illness, and who's probably never read a newspaper in his life. But for some reason he keeps an old newspaper about sugarcane cutters at his bedside."

"If you have an explanation, I'm all ears."

"J.T.'s father was a cane cutter for National Sugar Corporation in 1941. It was guys like him who got the company indicted."

"Are you saying that this newspaper belongs to J.T.'s father?"

I started to answer, then stopped. "Actually, I'm not saying anything. And neither is J.T. Except to point out, once again, that the only item listed in the search warrant is a cell phone."

She walked across the room and laid the newspaper on the nightstand. "Keep looking," she told the officer.

"This is a waste of time," I said. "You know J.T. doesn't have the phone. And you know he's not the killer. J.T. was right here, under house arrest with a bracelet on this ankle, when the last victim was murdered."

She looked at me from across the room, but I still felt it. "J.T. was under house arrest when the last victim was *found*. The medical examiner puts her time of death at least two days before J.T. went under house arrest."

I suddenly realized why it had been so difficult to compare Angelina's photograph to the face of the victim. After that much time in the Everglades, bloating and decomposition could make facial recognition problematic.

Santos walked toward me again. "Do you know where your brother-in-law was on that night?"

I didn't answer.

"I didn't think so," she said.

"Bag the newspaper," she told the officer. "As far as I'm concerned, it's evidence. We'll let the judge decide if it's admissible."

Chapter Forty-Seven

I got the newspaper from Samantha," J.T. said.

It was just J.T. and me in his TV room. The police were gone. No cell phone. They'd left only with the old copy of the *Miami Tribune*. I gathered up the couch cushions from the floor, arranged them exactly as they'd been before the search, and told J.T. to have a seat. He ignored me and took his beanbag chair.

"It's your fucking couch, Abe. You sit on it."

I did. "When you say you got it from Samantha, do you mean it was left behind here, like the couch and all the other furniture, and you happened to find it when you moved in? Or do you mean she literally *gave* it to you?"

"It was a gift," he said.

"When did she give it to you?"

"Right before she went into the hospital," he said, then swallowed. "The last time she went in."

Not our favorite subject. "Tell me what happened."

He groaned, pressing the heels of his palms to his eyes, clearly not wanting to make this journey.

"J.T., this is very important."

"All right!" he said in an angry voice.

I gave him a minute. He collected himself.

"She told me she probably wasn't coming home again." He paused to catch his breath. "She says, 'J.T., Momma's gone. Devon's gone. Daddy won't be here much longer. When I go, that leaves you.'"

Devon was the oldest brother, whom I'd never met. "Go on," I said.

"That's when she told me the story," he said.

"What story?"

"The fucking story in the newspaper, Abe. My old man was one of the men that these sugar companies brought down from Memphis like slaves. It's part of our family. It's a piece of history. We need to keep it, pass it on. Let people know that fucking slavery didn't end in 1865."

"Where did she get the newspaper?"

"Where do you think? She said there was other stuff, too."

"Other stuff?"

"Yeah, Luther had all kinds of crap from when he cut cane. The sugar company made him buy it with his own money—a blanket, all that gear and equipment. He's such a cheap son of a bitch. He paid for it, so he kept it."

I remembered that part of the story. Before the first row of cane was cut, the men were so far in debt that they could never leave the plantation. As I recalled, they'd also made each worker buy a machete. I didn't go there. Not specifically.

"Where's the other stuff?"

"I don't know, Abe. She gave me the newspaper article and said more shit was in a box somewhere. I never looked for it. Samantha says I needed to pass it on to the next generation, but who the hell am I gonna pass anything on to, Abe?"

"Did Samantha tell you where that box is?"

"It's with all my old man's shit. I don't know where. Whatever happened to it when you guys moved him into the nursing home?"

Finally, a question I could answer. "It's in mini storage," I said. Along with some other personal items of Samantha's, things that I couldn't bring myself to just donate to Goodwill and that I knew Angelina wouldn't want around our house.

"Then that's where it is," said J.T. "In storage. But why does it matter? Why does any of this matter?"

"It doesn't," I said.

J.T. popped up from the beanbag, pacing. "It matters to Santos. That bitch is crazy. She comes to my house last night, asking questions like you was the one who killed Angelina. Now she comes to my house with a search warrant, acting like I killed her. Or maybe she thinks I killed all these women. Is that what she thinks, Abe?"

"J.T., relax. She doesn't think you killed anyone. She's putting pressure on you in order to put pressure on me."

"So she doesn't think I did anything?"

"No."

"She thinks you did it?"

I looked away from J.T., toward the middle distance. "Honestly, I don't know what she thinks anymore."

I rose from the couch and dug my car keys from my pocket.

"Where you going?" asked J.T.

"Nowhere," I said as I headed for the door.

He followed me. "What do you mean, *nowhere?* You're going *somewhere.*"

I pulled the door open. "Get some sleep, J.T."

He grabbed me by the arm. "Where you going, Abe?"

I said nothing, but my expression was stern enough to make him release my arm. "I'm going to get some answers. Lock the door and go to sleep."

I didn't wait for daylight. AAA Mini Storage was open twenty-four hours, seven days a week. I drove home, got the key to the unit, and went to the warehouse. The five-story building was deserted, more like a mausoleum. Sensors triggered the lights in the lobby as I entered.

Pod 403 was on the fourth floor. The elevator was out of service, so I walked up. Technically the building was air-conditioned, but I was breaking a sweat in the stairwell. More sweat as I walked down the hallway. Maybe it was the stale air. Maybe it was nerves.

I unlocked the garage-style metal door and rolled it open. It was cooler inside the unit than in the hallway, but that was my only sense of relief. Memories stared back at me, making it difficult to enter.

My last visit to Pod 403 had been about six months after Samantha's funeral. Some of her things I had given away. Some things I felt like I should keep, though not necessarily keep around the house, especially after I started dating Angelina. Carmen had gone through the same exercise with the passing of her husband. She'd told me to tackle one drawer, one closet, at a time, and to create three piles: the save pile, the donation/trash pile, and the not-sure-what-I-want-to-do-with-it pile. It was a fine line between "Save" and "Not sure." On the one hand, it was pointless to save a framed college diploma, but it represented four years of Samantha's life. And what about the enormous dollhouse that Luther had made for her with his own two hands, and that Samantha had been saving for her own daughter?

I stepped into the unit and saw the boxes I'd packed so carefully, still not sure what to do with these things. They had all ended up in Pod 403—along with the personal effects that Samantha had gathered from Luther's apartment when he went to the nursing home. Samantha had sealed up the boxes, etched Luther's name on them with a black marker, and stored them in our garage. I had never looked inside any of those boxes. They had remained sealed from the day Samantha had packed them. When Samantha died, "Luther Vine" was the bulk of my "Not sure" pile, but it was mostly procrastination on my part. I had planned to go through them some day.

This was the day.

The boxes were stacked floor-to-ceiling on the left. I started at the top, taking two boxes at a time into the hallway, cutting through the tape with the key. Some of Luther's stuff, I had no idea why Samantha had kept. Who needs a *TV Guide* from 1972? My guess was that she'd packed up his entire apartment without deciding what to save and what to discard. If Luther kept something, it was important. I understood. It was a safe bet that, ten minutes after throwing out that *TV Guide*, Samantha would have gotten an urgent phone call from the nursing home: *Hey, whatever happened to that 1972 . . .*

The ninth box got my attention, but only after I'd pulled it down from the very top of the fourth stack of boxes. On the side that had been shoved against the wall and hidden from sight, in black letters, Samantha had written: "Luther Vine 1941. *SAVE*."

I carried the box into the hallway and placed it on the floor. The sharp edge of the key ripped through the tape. I peeled open the flaps. It had all the anticipation of opening a time capsule, except that I knew exactly what I was looking for.

An old blanket was on top, neatly folded. I removed it and laid it on the floor. Beneath it I found a loose collection of things. Some were easily recognizable, and I removed those first. A water canteen. A lunch pail. A pair of work gloves. Heavy boots with steel toes. Other things I had to examine more closely to figure out what they were. A pair of metal knee guards. Wrist shields. There was even a badge with Luther's name on it, which identified him as an employee of the National Sugar Corporation. The wage record and task log was interesting. It said that Luther cut forty-three tons of cane his first week on the job. He owed the company nineteen dollars and twenty-seven cents.

I emptied the box completely, Luther's dark piece of history laid out across the floor. I went back inside the unit and searched for more boxes, but there was just the one from 1941. I looked a second time. I was there till midnight.

I found no cane-cutting knife.

Chapter Forty-Eight

I should have gone to bed, but sleep was out of the question.

Part of me wanted to go see Luther and ask what had happened to his machete. There were two problems with that. One, he was surely asleep at this hour. Two, he probably had no memory of it. For all I knew, he'd lost it doing yard work when Truman was president.

Get a good night's sleep. That had been Carmen's advice. I was supposed to sit for another polygraph examination in the morning, one with "better" questions. I needed to be rested and ready for it. But I was tired of other people dictating my needs.

I needed to find my wife.

Monday was half an hour old when I reached Little Havana. I parked down the street from Pawn 24, which of course was open for business. From the sidewalk, through the iron security bars over the plateglass window, I could see Manny with a client at the counter. They were haggling over the "loan" value on a stolen wristwatch or some such thing. I didn't go inside. Manny and his uncle had already given us all the help they were willing to give. Manny had reviewed dozens of photographs at the police station, and not one of them was the guy who had sold him Samantha's ring. The police had walked the streets for hours and asked every homeless person in the neighborhood about the ring. Nothing. The problem was that the police had done their search in the afternoon, not after midnight, when the sale had been made. They had told me to leave the investigation to them, but we were beyond that forty-eight-hour mark since Angelina had gone missing, no leads. My choice was to lie in bed awake or give it a shot myself. It was an easy decision.

"Hey, got a second?" I asked the first guy I saw. He was standing in the recessed doorway of a *farmacia* that had closed at midnight, straightening out his bed of cardboard.

"Get lost," he grumbled. "This is my spot."

I handed him a couple bucks, then flashed a photograph of Samantha's ring on my iPhone. "Know anyone selling a ring like this?"

"Nope."

I flashed a photo of Angelina. "I'm looking for this woman."

He looked closely, as if he might actually want to help, then turned away. "Don't waste your time. Lousiest blow job I ever got."

This wasn't going to be easy. The next six conversations were even less productive, and not just because my Spanish was marginal. The seventh guy grabbed my phone. I managed to hang on to it, but he wouldn't let go until I pushed him to the ground.

"Asshole! Why'd you hand me the phone if you don't want me to have it?"

He stayed down, which made me feel even worse. He reminded me a little of J.T. I was heading back to my car when I spotted a woman outside a cigar shop. Her world was wrapped in a green garbage bag inside the shopping cart that she pushed along the sidewalk.

"Ask you a question?"

She stopped, seemingly surprised that I'd spoken to her. I showed her the photograph of the ring and asked the same question I'd asked the others.

"Jerko sold that," she said.

My turn to be surprised. "What did you say?"

"My friend Jerko sold a diamond ring like that."

"When?"

"This weekend. Five hundred bucks. Or so he says. Shithead wouldn't give me ten cents, so I calls him a liar."

My heart was pounding. "Is your friend dangerous?"

"If you were dangerous, would you let people call you Jerko?"

That made sense, but he didn't exactly sound like a prime suspect in my wife's disappearance. "How do I find this Jerko?"

She raised an eyebrow, negotiating. "How bad do you want to find him?"

"I'll give you ten bucks." I didn't want to appear too eager.

"I wouldn't tell you what city he's in for ten bucks."

To hell with looking eager. "How much, then?"

"Fifty. I'll take you right where he sleeps."

"Twenty to take me to his spot," I said, fishing the bill from my wallet. "Fifty if he's actually there."

She snatched the twenty from my hand. "Done."

I offered to push her cart, but she would have sooner cut off her arm. Or mine. She led, and I followed behind the rattle of the wheels on the cracked sidewalk. This stretch of Calle Ocho was a one-way street, still a couple miles from downtown Miami, but we were headed in that direction. We walked five blocks, and just as the journey was starting to seem pointless, she stopped outside El Presidente Supermarket. Across the street was a vacant lot. A huge For Sale sign said it was suitable for commercial or residential, "approved for 323 units." My gaze drifted beyond the chain-link fence toward the far corner of the lot, where the homeless had decided not to wait for the approved units to be built.

"He's over there," she said.

"You need to point him out to me if you want your money," I said.

"Cheapskate," she muttered.

I followed her across the street, and she knew exactly where to find the unauthorized opening in the chain-link fence, which was more than big enough to accommodate her cart. The ground was packed hard, patches of grass and weeds here and there. Bulldozers had left a few trees standing across the back of the lot, and the farther away from the street we walked, the more homeless we saw. Cardboard houses stood beneath the trees. Sheets of plastic served as blankets. The pungent odor of urine wafted from behind the bushes. If I squinted, turning the night into grainy black-and-white footage, it was like a scene from *The Grapes of Wrath.*

At the very back of the lot were several picnic tables, presumably stolen from a nearby park and brought here for shelter. We were beyond the glow of streetlights, but in the moonlight I saw the silhouette of a man lying on the ground beneath one of the tables.

"That's him," she said.

I started toward the table, but she stopped me. "You owe me thirty bucks," she said.

I kept my end of the deal. "Ten more if you'll make a nice introduction."

She smiled, took the extra ten, and shouted into the darkness. "Hey, asshole! There's a fucking idiot here to see you!"

She stuffed the money into one of her many pockets and pushed her cart across the lot, back toward Calle Ocho. The man stirred and then sat up, but he didn't come out from under the picnic table.

I made a quick judgment. I knew I wasn't dealing with Cutter, a serial killer with the wherewithal to dump multiple victims in the Palm Beach County cane fields ninety miles from here and to avoid detection for over two months. In theory, it was still possible that this was the man who had taken my wife, perhaps even killed her. But something told me that if Jerko had indeed pawned Samantha's ring, he'd come into possession of it secondhand, maybe even third. I went with my gut and operated from that premise.

"Can I talk to you?" I said, walking toward him.

"Stay where you are!"

I stopped a few feet away. Slowly I lowered myself into a crouch. We were at eye level, but in the shadows beneath the table, his face was barely visible.

"Your friend says you sold a diamond ring this weekend."

"She's not my friend."

No disavowal of the sale. "Can you tell me where you got the ring?"

"Can you go fuck yourself?"

Jerko was indeed a jerk. "Look, pal. I'm not a cop. I'm not here to make trouble for you. I just need some information."

He didn't answer, and I still couldn't read his face. He was shrouded in total darkness beneath the table, the trees overhead.

"Just tell me how you got the ring," I said. "I'll pay you for your help."

"How much?"

I was running out of cash. "Twenty bucks."

"A hundred."

"I don't have that much on me." I wasn't lying.

"I'll take your phone."

"I can't give you my phone."

"Then I can't help you."

Patience, I told myself, but the anger was working its way up from somewhere deep inside, unstoppable.

"Tell me where you got the ring," I said. It was a voice so threatening that I barely recognized it as my own. It was fair warning to him, even if he couldn't see the anger in my eyes.

"Hand over your phone," he said.

"I don't have one."

"Everybody has one."

I opened my wallet, dug out all my cash. "I'll give you sixty dollars."

"And your phone."

On another night, I might have played his game, or at least called for a squad car and done this by the book. But my wife was missing, and after Tyla's murder, J.T.'s house arrest, and a mountain of aggravation from Agent Santos, something snapped. I lunged at him, grabbed him by the shirt, and pulled him from under the table. He was much smaller than me, and in no time I had him facedown, under control. I was sitting on his kidneys, my hand at the base of his skull, pushing his forehead into the ground.

"Don't hurt me!" he said, pleading.

I grabbed his greasy hair and jerked his head back. "You want my phone?" I said in a harsh voice. "Here's my phone. Look, you son of a bitch. Look at this picture!"

I held his head still, the phone in my free hand. Angelina's head shot was right before his eyes. "Look at her! What do you know about this woman?"

It was a demand, not a question. He didn't answer. I shoved his face into the ground, then yanked his head back far enough to see Angelina's photo again. "*What do you know?*" I shouted.

"That's her," he said.

"That's who?"

"That's the woman who asked me to pawn the ring."

"Don't lie to me!"

"I'm not lying! She said if I went inside the pawnshop and sold the ring for her, I could keep fifty bucks."

"That's a damn lie."

"It's the truth."

His body was shaking beneath my weight. I tightened my grip on his hair. "Don't you dare lie to me!"

His body was no longer shaking. These were seismic undulations, the difference between 5.0 and 7.0 on the Richter scale. He was crying uncontrollably.

"I'm not lying! It was her. That's the lady!"

I felt my grip loosen and his hair slip through my fingers. His chin dropped, and he was crying into the dirt. I climbed to my feet and stood over him, not knowing what to think.

"If I find out you hurt that woman in the picture, I will—"

"I never touched her! I just sold a stupid ring."

I wanted to call him a liar, a bald-faced liar, but my head was spinning, and the accusation wouldn't come. I grabbed him by the collar and pulled him to his feet.

"What are you doing, man?"

I kept a tight hold on his shirt, forcing him to walk with me. He was half jogging to keep up as we crossed the vacant lot to the hole in the fence. He was too scared, too tired, and too much of a wimp to resist.

"Where you taking me?"

I didn't answer, but we were less than two blocks from Pawn 24. I'd seen Manny through the window earlier, so I knew he was working the early a.m. shift. It took less than a minute to get there, even while dragging Jerko along with me. I rang the bell outside the entrance. Manny came to the door, but I didn't wait for him to unlock it. I shoved Jerko's face against the glass, and with the other hand I showed my badge. Manny seemed startled for a moment, but he recognized me from that morning.

"Is this the guy?" I shouted. "Is this who sold you the ring?"

Manny studied the man's face through the glass. Only a few seconds were needed. Then he nodded.

"I'll give the money back to you," said Jerko. "Just don't hurt me, okay?"

I pulled him away from the door and forced him to sit on the sidewalk.

"Don't you move an inch," I said, dialing Rid's number. "We're gonna find out what the hell is going on."

Chapter Forty-Nine

Jerko sobbed and cried, begging me to let him go, right up until the Miami-Dade police arrived and put him in the back of the squad car. I followed in my car to the station. Rid met us there, but he immediately took me out of the loop. I found a bench in the hallway and waited outside the interrogation room while Rid and another detective did their teamwork. Just before 1:00 a.m., the door opened, and Rid came to me.

"Jerko has no idea what happened to Angelina," he said.

It was hard to know if that was good or bad news. "Are you sure?"

"There are older detectives here, Abe. But I've been doing this a while. Long enough to know. But don't get me wrong. This guy is a piece of shit."

"Tell me."

"He's a registered sex offender in the state of New York. That was his last known address."

"What was his offense?"

"Multiple acts of sexual misconduct. Apparently he's a huge fan of high-school girls' soccer. So long as he can stand on the other side of the fence and jerk off."

Finally a definitive explanation for the name Jerko. It hardly put me at ease. "But if he's a sex offender, doesn't that make him even more of a suspect?"

"Abe, here's the situation. Your wife, and Samantha's ring, went missing, but there's no sign of any break-in at your house. One possibility is that the perp was someone she knew, and Angelina let him in."

"Or he lived there," I said. "Agent Santos' theory."

"Right," said Rid. "Or he was a stranger and had a key. That's why we've been checking every conceivable place Angelina may have valeted her car for the last month, to see if anyone copied her house key. Jerko doesn't exactly fit the profile of someone who could get his hands on a key to your house, much less someone who'd manage to find Samantha's ring and make your wife vanish, all without leaving a shred of evidence."

"Then how did Jerko get the ring?"

"I don't know."

"He said he got it from Angelina."

"That's his story, and he's sticking to it," said Rid. "He's obviously lying, covering for a friend, or afraid to name names."

"Is it really obvious that it's a lie?"

"It is to me."

I walked to the bench, tried to sit, but my mind was racing. I went right back at Rid. "Isn't it possible that he got the ring from Angelina?"

He sighed, exasperated. "Abe, I just walked you through the likely scenarios: someone she knew or a stranger who had a key."

"What about the *unlikely* scenarios?" I paused, careful to deliver this properly. "What if she just left?"

"Just took off? Middle of the night. Poof. That's what you're saying?"

"Yeah."

"Why in the hell would she do that?"

"To teach me a lesson."

Rid scoffed. "Abe, you need some sleep."

"I'm serious, Rid. Hear me out. It's always bugged Angelina the way I hung on to Samantha's memory. Suddenly she disappears, and the only thing missing from the house is Samantha's jewelry, including her engagement ring, which is hocked at a Little Havana pawnshop for a fraction of its value. Isn't that sending a message: 'Get this worthless thing out of our house'?"

"Abe, it's been a long week. You're really tired."

"And to top it off, Angelina's ring was left sitting right on the dresser. What thief would climb all the way up to the top shelf in the closet for Samantha's rings but leave the low-hanging fruit right on the dresser?"

"It's odd, okay, I give you that. But there has to be a better explanation than Angelina trying to teach you a lesson."

"Not one I can think of, and I've been thinking about this a lot. She even said it herself one time—that I'd miss her when she was gone. That's when I'd appreciate her."

A couple officers walked by us in the hall. Rid waited for them to pass, then shook his head at me. "Abe, drop this. You're hoping your wife is alive and safe. That's natural. And the thought that Angelina up and left you is a lot better scenario than some of the other possibilities that must be going through your mind. But don't go sharing this theory with anyone but me."

"Why are you so closed-minded?"

"Because if you weren't shell-shocked and sleep-deprived, I'd say it's the most egotistical thing any man has ever said."

"What are you talking about?"

"First off, it's fucking crazy to say your wife went missing just to make you appreciate her more. I know

Angelina has a temper, and she even popped you in the nose when you left her for Samantha, but unless there's some really abusive shit going on between you two—"

"There's not," I said.

"Fine, there's not. But for argument's sake, let's say Angelina is the nuttiest fruitcake on the block and has a mile-long mean streak. You saw Angelina's parents on TV tonight. I *know* you saw her mother practically falling apart in front of the camera. The idea that Angelina would do this to her own *mother and father* just to teach you a lesson is—Abe, it's . . ."

I could have waited for him to finish his thought, but it wasn't necessary. "Unthinkable?" I offered.

"That would be my word for it," said Rid.

Mine, too. Maybe I did need sleep. "Okay. That's valid. But the fact remains that Jerko ended up with the ring. I showed him the picture of Angelina on my phone. He admitted that he got it from her. He told you the same thing."

"Yeah, he did. But—"

"But what?"

He took me by the arm, pulling me toward the interrogation room. "Come inside with me."

"What for?"

"You want to know why it's bullshit that Jerko got the ring straight from your wife? I'll show you."

He opened the door, and I followed him inside. Jerko was seated across the table from another Miami-Dade detective. He recoiled at the sight of me, the memory of our earlier "discussion" still fresh. I stood in the corner by the door. Rid crossed the room and leaned on the table, staring Jerko down. There was a manila file on the tabletop. Rid opened it. I couldn't see what was inside, and until he put his question to Jerko, I didn't know it was a photograph.

"Is this the woman who asked you to pawn the ring?" asked Rid.

Jerko nodded quickly, nervously. "Yeah, that's her. That's the woman."

Rid tucked the photograph into the file and brought it with him as he led me back into the hallway, the door closing behind us. Then he showed me the photograph.

I blinked, confused. "That looks like Charlize Theron."

"It *is* Charlize Theron. Jerko said the same thing when we showed him Reese Witherspoon fifteen minutes ago. And Kirsten Dunst ten minutes before that. They're all beautiful blond women, just like your wife in the picture you showed him, and they all asked him to pawn the ring."

Whatever remained inside of me quickly drained away—all the excitement of a solid lead, all the hope of a break in the investigation. "But clearly he got the ring from somebody."

"From somebody. But not from Angelina. Not if you ask me."

I checked the clock on the wall. Almost 2:00 a.m. "It's late," I said.

"Get some sleep," said Rid. "You have a polygraph exam in seven hours."

I took a deep breath, then let it out. "Yeah. Maybe this time I should study."

Chapter Fifty

I slept for three hours, but no more. I could have stayed in bed and stared at J.T.'s ceiling for the next two hours. Instead, I got up, showered, and drove to Sunny Garden Nursing Home.

Luther was an early riser, and each passing year pushed back the hands on his internal alarm clock. Six a.m., no problem. Hell, it was practically his lunchtime. When I walked into his room, he was sitting in a chair by the window, wide awake and dressed, his flannel shirt buttoned all the way up to his Adam's apple. Even better, he was himself.

"Well, shut my mouth, it's Mr. Lincoln."

"Don't get up," I said.

"Don't worry."

I smiled as if there were nothing wrong, and in Luther's mind, there wasn't. I hadn't said a word to him about Angelina, and he was the antithesis of a news junkie. If it wasn't on ESPN, it didn't exist.

I pulled up another chair. "How are you, old man?"

"Old. That 'bout covers it."

It just about did. Half of the time he couldn't remember that I had remarried, so even under the best of circumstances, any mention of Angelina was confusing to him. A conversation about her disappearance would surely have gone off the rails. After Samantha died, I'd wondered how long it might be till the next funeral, thinking it would be Luther's. I sure as hell didn't think it would be for my second wife.

There was a noise in the hallway, right outside the open door to Luther's room. I craned my neck for a glimpse and saw the paramedics wheeling a gurney out of the room across the hall. A white sheet covered the body. I went to close the door, but Luther stopped me.

"We lose someone?" he asked.

"Looks that way. Across the hall."

"Oh, that's Barbara. Sad, sad, sad. Not her time."

"How old was she?"

"Ninety-four."

I looked away, then back. "No offense, Luther, but she was ninety-four years old. Not her time?"

"I know what you think. She's old. She's ready. But she wasn't. Ready, I mean."

"Did she want to make it to a hundred?"

"No, no. Barbara wished herself to death fifty years ago."

"She did what?"

He leaned forward and looked me in the eye, even if he did have that one eye that kind of pointed off in another direction. "Pay attention, boy. There's a difference between wantin' to die and bein' ready to die."

I thought about it, and decided he was making sense. "Why wasn't she ready?"

"Same reason she wished she was dead. Broken heart."

"How did her heart get broken?"

He sat back, arms folded. "I ain't got a clue."

"Then how do you know she had one?"

"I'm as old as Noah. I know a broken heart when I see it. Yes, sir. That heart stopped beatin' last night. But Barbara died a long, long time ago."

"That's sad."

"Nothin' sadder." Again he leaned closer, this time raising a finger to make his point. "You know what I always say, don't you, Abe?"

I nodded. "Ain't no shame in dyin'."

And then Luther finished it: "But it's a cryin' shame to die of a broken heart."

I could have slipped away right then, let my mind drift back to the first time I'd heard Luther tell me about broken hearts. But I refused to go there.

Luther pointed at the pitcher on the tray. "Pour me some water there, would you?"

"Sure."

I got up and filled his cup. The sound and sight of it made me think of the tab he'd run up at the National Sugar Corporation, as recorded on seventy-year-old task sheets and pay stubs I'd seen earlier at the warehouse. The company had charged him for water that wasn't too dirty to drink, part of the nineteen dollars he owed at the end of the first week of cutting cane.

I handed him his cup and returned to my chair. "Luther, have we ever talked about your days of cutting sugarcane?"

He steadied his cup and sipped from it. "Probably not."

"You mind if I ask about it?"

"What you wanna know?"

"I found a box that Samantha kept. It had some old things in it from when you cut cane."

His eyes brightened a bit, not from the memory of the cane fields, but from my mention of his daughter's name.

"Samantha said that stuff belonged in a museum. I guess she never got anyone interested in havin' it."

"I guess not. It's all still there," I said, pausing just a second before getting to the real point. "All except the machete."

"My cuttin' knife not there?"

"No. Everything else. But not the knife."

"Damn, I paid a buck-fifty for that knife. Another fifty cent for the file."

It made me think of J.T.'s remark: *He paid for it, he was gonna keep it.*

"Luther, I want you to think very hard. When is the last time you saw that knife?"

"Hell, I don't know."

"Was it after you cut cane for National Sugar? I just want to know if you're sure you brought it home from the camp."

"Oh, I'm sure. If there was anything worth keepin', it was the knife."

"Okay, that's helpful. Now think about this before you answer: Did you keep the knife with all the other things from your cane-cutting days?"

"I ain't seen that stuff in years, Abe."

"I know. It's been a long time. But this is important. Is it possible you kept the knife somewhere else. A toolbox, a shed?"

"Possible, I guess."

"Could it have gotten lost somewhere? Or thrown away? Maybe even someone stole it?"

"When?"

"Anytime."

"Shit, Abe. We're talkin' more than seventy years."

"*I know*," I said, my tone more urgent than I intended. "But I need to know: Is it possible?"

"Abe, of course it's possible. This goes back before the Second World War. Who knows where that knife ended up? Could be anywhere."

I sat back and took a breath. It was the best answer he could give me, and it was the reality of the situation, whether I liked it or not.

"You're right," I said. "Anywhere."

Chapter Fifty-One

A predawn fog crept across the darkness of Shadow Wood Park. In silence, Victoria and a SWAT unit of eight rode in the rear compartment of a special-response vehicle.

The tip had come from an alert customer at a self-serve gas station. The tipster, a Vietnam veteran, had been driving all night from Tallahassee. He pulled up behind a sedan, climbed out of his truck, and squeezed between his front bumper and the back of the other vehicle on his way to the pump. "I smelled plenty of dead bodies in 'Nam," he'd told police. "You don't forget it. That was what I smelled coming from the trunk of that car."

The hope was that the body was not Angelina's, that Angelina was still alive and in the house. Any potential hostage situation called for action far more drastic than a car search. The FBI opted for a tactical response.

Shadow Wood Park was adjacent to the suspect's house in a quiet subdivision. It was a typical 1970s development in northwest Broward County, where homeowners chose from one of four models, bulldozers came in, good schools were built, and in two years a thousand ranch-style single-family homes stood where the Everglades had once flowed. It was a strategic decision for SWAT to launch before sunrise, and the park offered the added cover of forty-year-old trees and overgrown bushes. It was the designated staging area for the SWAT assault.

The vehicle stopped. Team leader Kyle Crawford ran through the prelaunch checklist.

The SWAT C-33 was a dual-purpose vehicle that delivered tactical support and served as a mobile command platform for response team planning and communications. A night-vision field camera mounted on Crawford's helmet would provide live video feed to a monitor inside the vehicle. Two other team members—"breachers," the first to enter—also had cameras. A bone microphone and headset provided audio communication. Victoria would be in constant contact with the team while watching the operation unfold in real time, through their eyes.

Crawford's checklist was finished. The rear doors opened, and the team filed out. The intensity was palpable, even if they were still in prelaunch mode. A second SWAT unit had followed in a separate vehicle and joined them. Dressed all in black, faces covered with greasepaint, the units were virtually invisible in the darkness. Victoria was armed only with her standard Sig Sauer 9 mm sidearm, but plenty more firepower would go in before her. Team members carried fully automatic M16s. Kevlar vests, helmets, and countless hours of training and experience would protect them from whatever might come in return.

A third vehicle arrived. Victoria's communications specialist and two forensic agents caught up with the team and went inside the mobile command center.

Crawford gave a hand signal. SWAT 1 deployed in silent unison.

Peering through night-vision goggles, Victoria watched the first wave of SWAT members fan out around the perimeter of the quarter-acre lot as they surrounded the suspect in his house. Mature olive trees partially blocked her view, but she could see the front yard, the walkway, and the front of the house. The windows were black, no sign of any lights burning inside, but a bug light on the porch cast an eerie amber pall.

Crawford adjusted his earpiece. He was getting audio from team one.

"Stand by," Crawford told his team. "Ten seconds to video."

Victoria went back inside the vehicle. The communications specialist was seated in front of five separate monitors, each linked to a different field camera. Victoria watched over his shoulder. Crawford and two other SWAT members joined her. The first monitor flickered, then fixed on an image. It was from the surveillance agents, the first to approach the house. Theirs was the all-important job of scoping out the scene in stealth, from outside the walls. They had already pulled the building plans and confirmed the floor plan for this particular model, which the team had reviewed and memorized. Infrared cameras couldn't see through brick walls or glass, but winter in Florida was the season for open windows. If the agents could find one, heat sensors would tell them if anyone was inside.

"Video confirmed," Victoria said into her microphone. "Go ahead. Over."

"Building plans are accurate," the surveillance agent reported, "no structural alterations detected. Two small bedrooms on south side of the house. Both vacant. Kitchen, dining, and TV room on the east side. Also vacant. Infrared sensor confirms one subject in master bedroom, north side. Large, probably male. Appears to be sleeping. Direct access through sliding glass doors facing rear screened-in patio. Over."

"Any sign of second subject? Over."

By "subject," Victoria meant "victim." They were looking for a serial killer, and Angelina was still missing.

"Can't get a visual. Infrared scan shows amorphous glow from master bathroom. Some source of heat."

Victoria leaned closer to the monitor. The image was weak, but the description had been accurate. Victoria had worked with infrared in many cases before, and she'd seen similar low-level glows from victims found in Dumpsters or hidden in the weeds. A human body would continue to give off detectable levels of warmth at least two or three hours after death.

Crawford went team-wide on his microphone. "Stand by," he said, not a hint of emotion in his voice. "On three we're yellow."

Yellow was the SWAT code for the final position of cover and concealment. Green was the assault, the moment of life and death, literally.

Crawford exited the communications van and joined the rest of Team 2. Victoria could no longer see him, but the image from the camera mounted on Crawford's helmet flashed on screen two. Images from other field cameras flashed on monitors three, four, and five.

Victoria had the total picture. And she had Crawford's command in her ear.

"Three, two, one."

The monitors showed SWAT on the move, a silent and well-choreographed wave through the woods, out of the park, and into the yard. Victoria could almost feel their steps—toes first, then heels, knees bent to absorb the recoil in case they were forced to fire. Monitor two captured the approach from the east to cover the back door. Monitor three showed street-side containment, SWAT within striking distance of the front door, but not too close, the approach coming to a stop just beyond the reach of the glowing yellow porch light. Crawford and two others went around to the patio, but his camera feed wasn't clear. The fog and the patio screens made for a blur on the monitor, which only added to Victoria's anxiety.

She wondered about that ghostly aura of warmth emanating from the bathroom.

The images froze. Movement had stopped. A round of microphone checks confirmed it: SWAT was in position.

"On three we're green," Crawford whispered, his voice breaking the radio squelch in Victoria's ear. He counted slowly, deliberately, a man with ice water in his veins. At the count of three, the monitors were a blur of motion. Victoria's headset resounded with the simultaneous crash of the front and rear doors, and the shattering of the sliding glass in the master bedroom. She braced for the crack of gunfire, but she heard only the shouts of Crawford and his team as they swept through the house and into the bedroom.

"Down, down! Get down on the floor!"

Victoria stared at the night-vision feed on the monitors, all images converging on the man on the mattress, the man going down, the man surrounded.

There was a crackling on the radio, more commands. Monitor one showed a subject under control. The others flashed with the sweep of the house. Camera five was in the bathroom, where the infrared scan had detected warmth.

"Nothing here," the agent reported.

Victoria looked more closely at the monitor. An empty bathroom.

"All clear," said Crawford.

Victoria and her forensic specialists sprang into action and ran toward the house. Two tech agents were right behind her. Only the communications specialists remained behind.

Victoria cut across the lawn at full speed. The patch of warmth was still a mystery, but if they had indeed found Cutter, Victoria didn't want some clever defense lawyer arguing that he had confessed to a crime with an M16 rifle pointed at his head. The front door was barely hanging on its hinges, damaged from the breach. She hurried inside. The tech agents followed SWAT to the subject's computer. Victoria and the forensic specialists went to the master suite. Crawford and two other agents were standing over a large man who was facedown on the floor beside the bed. He was wearing only pajama bottoms and a white T-shirt. His hands were clasped behind his waist with plastic cuffs.

"Where is Angelina Beckham?" Victoria shouted.

"I don't know!" he said into the carpet.

"What did you do with her?"

"Nothing. I don't know who you're talking about!"

She wasn't sure he was lying.

"Santos, got something," the forensic specialist said from the bathroom. Victoria hurried toward the bathroom. The forensic specialist was on the floor.

"Here's your heat source on the infrared," he said.

Victoria didn't see anything but white tile. "What?"

"Chemical cleaner," he said. "Some concentration of sulfuric acid or hydrochloric acid, which increases hydronium ions in a solution and attracts electrons from whatever mess you're trying to clean up. The hydronium ions react chemically with the material they're cleaning, which releases heat."

"Enough heat to be picked up by an infrared scan?"

"If there's enough acid. And a big enough mess."

"What kind of mess?"

He took his bottle of Luminol and sprayed one of the ceramic floor tiles. Victoria switched off the light. The blue glow told the story.

"Blood," he said. "From the amount of heat that showed up on the infrared scan, I'd say he was using one hell of a lot of chemical cleaners, wiping up *a lot* of blood."

A SWAT agent entered the suite. "No body in the trunk of the car," he told Victoria. "But the cadaver dog's going nuts. Our tipster from the gas station was right on. Definitely was a body in there at some point."

"Let's get forensics on it," said Victoria.

"Something else you need to see."

Victoria followed him out of the master bedroom, down the hall. Another agent opened the door, and she entered what should have been the garage. Somehow, she knew what she was about to see, but it still took her breath away.

"Oh, my God," she said, stopping in the doorway.

The rear half of a two-car garage had been built out and converted into a windowless room. The walls and ceiling were painted black. The floor was unfinished concrete. Three spotlights were mounted in the ceiling, their blinding beams targeting the very center of the room, where four sets of metal cuffs—two for the wrists, two for the ankles—were bolted into the concrete. The lighting was so tightly focused that the perimeter remained in the shadows, but there was just enough light to see the workbench against the wall. Slowly, Victoria walked toward it. The tools of a sadist came into view. Leather straps. Bullwhips. Pliers. Scissors. Alligator clips, leashes, handcuffs, pins, and dildos of varying length and thickness, the largest about eighteen inches. They were laid out meticulously across the bench. But it was the tool hanging on the wall, right above the bench, that distinguished this killer from so many other sociopaths who might have fit the criminal profile.

It was a cane cutter's machete.

Victoria felt a wave of . . . something. *Accomplishment* perhaps summed it up; the tragedy of so many young victims made it impossible to call it success.

"Got him," she said quietly.

Chapter Fifty-Two

I was a good half hour ahead of peak rush hour, cruising past the University of Miami campus in the first wave of morning commuters, heading to the Find Angelina command center, no plan in mind, just feeling like I needed to be doing something. The Dadeland Publix opened at seven, and I'd already been there and delivered three bags of groceries to J.T.'s apartment, putting an end to the I-got-no-food mantra. That was when Rid called from his house.

"Cutter is in custody."

Countless questions clogged my mind, but I whittled the jumble of confusion down to the most important one. "What about Angelina?"

"We don't know."

My hands shook on the wheel. I had to pull off US 1 and park at a gas station, but I left the motor running. "You don't know if he took her," I asked, "or he took her, and you don't know what he did with her?"

"The first one. Be glad for that, Abe. If this monster is in any way involved, there's not much doubt what he did."

I cranked the AC to max, anything to help me breathe again. "Who is he?"

"His name is Tommy Salvo. He works for Cortinas Sugar."

My mouth fell open. "He *works* for the fucking sugar company? How could Santos not zero in on this guy sooner?"

"Keep in mind that the sugar industry has hundreds of thousands of employees and former employees. A computer search ruled him out in the first run through the database. Salvo has a house in Broward County, but he lives and works in Nicaragua during the harvest season, October to May. Apparently they still cut by hand there."

"He actually is a cane cutter?"

"No. The cutting is done by very low-wage Nicaraguans. Salvo is an American citizen and has a supervisory role in field operations. Anyway, he slipped through the computer search because he has no criminal record, and immigration records showed that he was in Nicaragua at the time of the murders."

"So he came back illegally."

"Right. The FBI's thinking is that he flew Managua–Havana–Nassau on Cuba Jet, then paid someone under the table for a boat ride to the states from the Bahamas. A circuitous route, but if you're a serial killer who wants law enforcement to think you're out of the country, it's worth the effort. No one knew he was here."

"Except—" I started to say, then stopped.

"Except who?" asked Rid.

"Except maybe Tyla Tomkins. Could that be why she was calling me and leaving me messages on my voice mail?"

Rid didn't answer me.

"Did Salvo kill Tyla?" I asked.

"That's not clear."

"That's a shitty answer."

"Abe, my hands are tied as to what I can tell you. Santos is interrogating the suspect now. This is all very confidential."

"Don't give me that 'confidential' bullshit!" I shouted, my words a bolt of anger. "Knowing what happened to Tyla could mean the difference between finding and not finding my wife. Tell me what you know—good, bad, everything. Fucking tell me, Rid!"

A soccer mom in an SUV pulled into the gas station and maneuvered toward the pump in front of me, a pack of kids in the rear seats. She drove right past the pump and steered back onto the highway. My windows were up, but I must have looked like a lunatic, yelling into my phone and pounding the steering wheel.

"Okay, here's what I know," he said. "Salvo had his kill room set up like an amateur movie studio. Black walls, spotlights, soundproofing, the whole bit. The FBI confiscated his computer, but Santos is being tight-lipped about what they found. It's a pretty safe bet that this sick son of a bitch liked to film what he did to his victims, but I have no idea if that means five women from Palm Beach County, or if it means more than that. I don't want to lead you wrong with half-baked information. This could turn out to be good news for you. Or it could be godawful news."

I practically fell forward, my forehead landing on the steering wheel. It was a struggle to talk. "Where's the interrogation?"

"FBI field office."

"I'm going up there."

"It's pointless. Santos won't let you near the interrogation."

"Rid, I'm going up. Are you in the game or on the sidelines?"

He hesitated, but only for a second. "I'll let Carmen know your polygraph is off and meet you there."

I hung up, put the car in drive, and said a prayer as I pulled out of the gas station and onto US 1.

Chapter Fifty-Three

Victoria knew she was going to break him.

Despite having led law enforcement to believe that he was in Nicaragua, Cutter was not a clever one. Victoria had spent the first two hours of the interrogation making him understand that there was no talking his way out of this: she had the goods to fry his ass. Then she and her partner had left the room, let him sit alone at the table and stare at the bare walls for ten minutes, twenty minutes, half an hour. The two FBI agents watched from the viewing room, behind the one-way mirror. With them were Bert Franklin and his partner, both homicide detectives from the Palm Beach County Sheriff's Department.

"How much longer are you going to let him stew?" asked Franklin.

"A few more minutes," she said.

"This is a foolish strategy," he said. "You let him sit much longer, he's going to demand a lawyer."

Franklin was still fuming over the fact that he was strictly an observer. The FBI had asserted jurisdiction based on reams of hard-core child pornography found on Cutter's computer—a federal offense. It was the hook that allowed Victoria to seize the lead in what otherwise would have been strictly a violation of state law: homicide. Victoria had invited Franklin and his partner as a professional courtesy to the multiagency task force.

"I got this covered," she said.

Victoria stepped closer to the one-way glass, studying her subject. Salvo was a big man, six-foot-three, well over two hundred pounds. Muscular, but not like a gym rat. He had the physique and weathered look of a farmer who'd spent his life working the field. His salt-and-pepper beard was not at all groomed, just the scruff of a man who didn't like to shave. A buzz cut made it less obvious that his hair was thinning. At forty-eight he was older than Victoria had profiled, which explained the Viagra they'd confiscated from his residence. Erectile dysfunction only partially explained the abundance of dildos, all black, all of which fit Victoria's profile of an angry white male who targeted white women with black boyfriends. *Still like it black, bitch?*

"Phase two," said Victoria. It was time to go back inside.

Victoria had done this many times before in so many cases. This was when the smart ones started to bargain. *I'll tell you where I dumped the five bodies you don't know about if you don't go for the death penalty.* Victoria didn't expect that from Cutter. He needed to show her how smart he was. *Look how many clues you missed, how I was right under your nose and laughing at your incompetence.* Cutter was a bragger. She could feel it.

She laid a pack of Marlboros in front of him. "Cigarette?"

He took it. She slid a lighter across the table, and he lit up.

"I knew you smoked," she said.

"Good one, Sherlock. Was it the ashtrays all over my house or the cigarette cartons that tipped you off?"

Bragger. "It was the burn marks on your victims," she said.

He breathed out a cloud of smoke, saying nothing.

Victoria methodically laid four autopsy photographs in front of him, four of the five Palm Beach County victims, excluding the one who had been burned beyond recognition in the field. Only their faces were in the photos.

"But that's not cigarette ash smeared all over their faces," she said. "Is it?"

He took another drag. "You know what it is."

"Why don't you tell me?"

He sat back, flicking his ash on the floor. Getting comfortable, thought Victoria.

"Do you know why women used to be called the fair sex?" he asked.

She knew it had to do with an archaic sense of beauty and purity—*Mirror, mirror, on the wall*—but she wanted his view. "I've never really given it much thought."

"It's because when you compare them to men, they really are fairer."

"In what way?" asked Victoria.

"Are you even trying to pay attention? What do you think we're talking about here? I mean their skin. There's a difference in pigmentation between men and women."

"I would have thought it depends on the person."

"That's because you're stupid," he said. "And I'm much smarter than I look."

Talk to me, smart boy.

"It's a chemical and molecular fact," he said. "Obviously it's not as dramatic as the difference between a black man and a white man. But if you compare a white man to a white woman, or a black man to a black woman, the male has more melanin and hemoglobin. Men are darker. Women are paler. The female is the fair sex."

Victoria couldn't wait to see what this guy had been reading on the Internet. "Is that so?"

"Don't talk down to me."

"I'm not."

"I see that look on your face. You think I'm a Confederate-flag-waving racist and card-carrying member of the Ku Klux Klan."

"I didn't say that."

"People think because I went into farming and didn't go to college, I couldn't hack it in school. I was actually a good student. Chemistry was my best subject."

Translation: you cooked meth.

"And I've lived all over the world. Nicaragua, Dominican Republic, Brazil."

"That's impressive."

"I'm not trying to impress you. I'm making a point. My brain, and what I see with my own two eyes, tells me that skin color is less and less about race."

"I'm not sure I understand what you just said."

"Pay attention, will you? It's simple. You go to a place like Managua or Santo Domingo or São Paulo, who the fuck knows what race those people are? Black? White? Hispanic? Indian? Multiracial, whatever that means? Truth is, the labels are all bullshit. It's a thousand-year process, but the world is evolving into a single human race where skin color is important for one thing only: sex. The darker male is attracted to the lighter female."

"That's your theory?"

"Not a theory. It's factual. That's why black men have always wanted our women."

"Does that make you angry?"

"Not at all. I've been surrounded by dark-skinned men in the cane fields all my adult life. Got no problem with them. Physical attraction to the fair sex is completely natural." He leaned closer, the smoke from his cigarette trailing toward Victoria. "What pisses me off is white women who want to pop out little brown babies."

Victoria had heard enough. With the homemade videos of his victims on his computer, the physical evidence collected by the forensic team, and his demonstrated desire to fill the world with anthropological bullshit, Cutter was on his way to a very long sleep at the end of Death Row. It was time to see what he knew about the crimes outside of Palm Beach County.

Victoria collected the victims' photographs and tucked them into the file. "There's another reason I knew you smoked," she said. "Aside from the burn marks on the victims, I mean."

He crushed out his cigarette and lit another. "Is this part of your brilliant criminal profile? White male chain smoker?"

She opened another file and laid a single photograph of Tyla Tomkins on the table. Not Tyla the victim. It was Tyla the lawyer, a professional black-and-white image from the BB&L website.

"I saw you standing across the street from Tyla Tomkins' memorial service," said Victoria.

He smiled.

"That *was* you, wasn't it? That glowing orange dot in the overflow parking lot?"

Silence.

She leaned closer, staring him down from across the table. "Did you kill Tyla Tomkins?"

"Nope," he said, no hesitation. "We would have liked to, though."

"What do you mean, 'we'?"

"All of us in Nicaragua. She was part of the team of Miami lawyers who came over to bust our balls."

This wasn't a turn Victoria had expected. "Who else was on that team?"

"Bunch of suits. I don't remember."

"They came to bust your balls about what?"

"Everything. The whole cane-cutting operation in Nicaragua."

"What, specifically?"

"Same old bullshit. Labor issues. Ask the lawyers if you want to know more."

Victoria glanced at her partner, who made a note of it. They *would* ask the lawyers.

She laid another photograph on the table. It was a frame from the security camera at the restaurant in Orlando, Tyla having dinner with Abe Beckham.

"Why did you send this to Angelina Beckham?"

"Who's Angelina Beckham?"

Victoria ignored his question. She laid a duplicate of the restaurant photograph on the table, right beside the other, but this one showed the smudge of ash on Tyla's face.

"Angelina Beckham found these photos in her mailbox. I know it was you who sent them. That's your signature."

"My signature?"

"Sugarcane ash on Tyla's face."

He took a closer look, almost chuckling. "Why would anyone smear black ash on a face that's already black?"

"I don't know. Why would they?"

He took a long drag from his cigarette. "Doesn't make any sense to me."

It didn't to Victoria, either. She laid a photograph of Angelina on the table. "Where is Angelina Beckham?"

"Is that her?"

"You know it is."

"Never heard of her," he said.

"Why did you go to Tyla Tomkins' memorial service?" she asked, a quick gear shift, just to trip him up.

"I didn't go to her service."

"Why were you having a smoke in the parking lot across the street?"

"I got a better question: Why did you dumb shits think Cutter killed her?"

Cutter, a name the media had created. Obviously he'd been following the story in the news. "Did Cutter kill her?"

"Ask Cutter."

"I am asking."

He took another drag on his cigarette, his eyes narrowing. It was one of those breakthrough moments that could never be duplicated, and Victoria could only hope that the video would show that he was talking about himself in the third person. "Cutter doesn't do that black shit," he said. "You should know that, genius."

Victoria pushed the other photograph toward him. She hated to talk on a psychopath's level, but sometimes it was necessary. "Did Cutter 'do' Angelina Beckham?"

He glanced at the photo, a sick smile creasing his lips. "He would. If she needed to be reminded to suck the pink finger."

"Did Angelina need that reminder?"

He shook his head, then shrugged. "Fuck if I know. Never seen the woman before."

Victoria locked eyes with him, refusing to blink. He didn't look away. She could have worked him harder, pushed his buttons, asked him the same question over and over, fifty different ways. But she didn't see the point.

She believed him.

Chapter Fifty-Four

Rid met me at the entrance to the FBI's Miami field office. He'd been right. I got through the security clearance checkpoint in the main lobby but no farther. Santos was keeping a tight fist on the interrogation. She probably wouldn't have even allowed me in the building if Rid hadn't been with me.

"She should at least let you observe," I said. "You're one of the lead Miami-Dade detectives on the task force."

We were alone in a windowless waiting area. I was pacing. Rid was on the couch, seated beneath a bronze plaque that honored fallen agents from the Miami office.

"She thinks I'm a pipeline to you," he said.

"Maybe we shouldn't have canceled that redo of the polygraph this morning."

"Abe, you're in no shape to take another polygraph."

"You can see that. You're sitting right here with me. But what if Carmen thinks I'm just afraid to retake the test?"

Rid gave me a sobering look. "You know how I feel about it."

He'd said it when Carmen had suggested a second examination. He wasn't going to come right out and say it again, but his advice "as a friend" was reheard nonetheless: *What you probably need is a lawyer.*

"Let's see how this plays out," I said.

I stopped and dialed Angelina's mother again. No answer. It was the same with her father. I didn't bother leaving a fourth message for them to call me. I wanted to be the one to tell them about Cutter in custody. After the way Jake had spoken to me before their press conference, it troubled me that neither one would answer.

"You go ahead and call them, Rid. See if they pick up."

He dialed. First Margaret. Then Jake. Neither one answered. I dialed the main number at the hotel, then Angelina's sister. I tried Sloane at the command center. No sign of Angelina's parents.

"This is getting weird," I said.

Getting weird? The expression on Rid's face had almost asked that question, but he'd caught himself. It could have been funny if this weren't so unfunny.

My phone rang, and I answered without even checking the number, hoping that it was Jake or Margaret. It was Ed Brumbel.

"I heard they got Cutter."

We hadn't talked since the message I'd left him about talking to the reporter, but that already seemed like ancient history. "How did you hear?"

"I read every press release the sugar industry issues. Cortinas just put one out on Tommy Salvo, basically disowning him."

"Can you send that to me?"

"Sure. I can also tell you a thing or two about Tommy Salvo. I took his deposition twenty years ago in the class action lawsuits."

"The wage-shorting cases?"

"Right. He was one of the supervisors who reviewed the task wages. And a lying son of a bitch."

"My understanding is that he's in the Nicaragua operations now."

"I saw that in the press release. And that's what really interests me. Compared to Central America, the old H-2 program on the Florida plantations was like Club Med."

"Ed, I'm looking for my wife. I don't have time to talk—"

"I understand. And, hey, I'm really sorry about slipping up and mentioning Tyla to that reporter

Saturday night. Or Sunday morning, whenever it was."

"Forget it."

"But listen to me. Cortinas issued this press release proactively for damage control. They know the company is going to take serious heat."

"Because one of their ten thousand employees turns out to be a killer? I don't buy it."

"No. Because Salvo left Nicaragua three months ago, just before the harvest season started in Central America, right before these killings started in Florida. Cortinas obviously knew he wasn't showing up for work, and they must have known he had a house that isn't very far from where the bodies were being dumped in the cane fields. But the company never told the FBI that Salvo should be on the radar. As far as the FBI knew, Salvo was in Nicaragua the whole time."

"That seems like an important point," I said. "But I'm having trouble connecting it to the only thing that matters right now, which is finding my wife."

"It's one piece of the bigger puzzle," he said. "It explains Tyla Tomkins."

We were getting warm. "How?"

"Tyla was trying to tell you about some kind of criminal conduct involving the Cortinas companies. The Central American operation is out of control. Do you know what the second most common killer of men in Nicaragua and El Salvador is? Chronic kidney disease. You know where ninety-nine percent of those men work? In the sugarcane fields. It's a mystery illness. They don't know if it's exposure to pesticides or if the sugar companies are literally working these men to death. They call it 'the malady of the sugarcane.' Healthy men in their twenties are ending up on dialysis and dropping dead. This is criminal, Abe."

"Yeah, but I'm a prosecutor in Miami. Why would Tyla come to me about crimes in Central America?"

"She was blowing the whistle on her own client, and she trusted you. Something or someone told her that Tommy Salvo was deep into what was happening in Central America. It bugged her that Cortinas didn't want local law enforcement interviewing him—even if he was involved in these serial killings."

"Wait a minute. Are you saying that Cortinas knew he was the killer?"

"No. I'm saying they didn't give a shit if he was or he wasn't. Which is the way that this company has always operated. The only thing they cared about was the fact that Tommy Salvo has information about 'the malady of the sugarcane,' and the last thing the company wanted was Salvo talking to the FBI. I think *that's* what Tyla Tomkins was trying to tell you. Maybe she uncovered something about his background, or maybe she just had a hunch about this guy because he was back in Florida illegally. But she was trying to tell you that local law enforcement needed to talk to Tommy Salvo."

I had to discount anything Ed said about Big Sugar. But he was actually making sense.

"It might have gotten her killed," he added.

"Except that Agent Santos seems pretty certain that Cutter didn't kill Tyla."

"Maybe Agent Santos is wrong."

She also didn't think Cutter had anything to do with Angelina's disappearance. "She could be wrong," I said. "Or we could be missing something."

My phone vibrated with an incoming text. It was from Angelina's mother.

"Ed, thanks, I'll call you later," I said, and quickly hung up. Rid asked me something about the call, but I was too focused on Margaret's message to hear him.

IMPORTANT. You are going to get a phone call from the law office of Jeffrey Winters. Pick up the call. Do not ignore it!!!

I knew Winters. He'd left the state attorney's office when Carmen promoted me, and not him, to senior trial counsel. Hard to say who "won." He was one of the top criminal defense lawyers in Miami.

"Rid, what do you know about this call from Jeffrey Winters?"

Rid looked at me, confused. "Winters? Nothing."

I wasn't buying it. "You're the one who's been telling me I need a lawyer. Did you and Margaret cook this up?"

"I haven't talked to Margaret."

I was getting angry. "Rid, I can sniff this one out a mile away. Jake is not on my side. Margaret is. You told her I need a lawyer. She's paying for Winters behind Jake's back. That's what this call is about, isn't it?"

"Abe, I got nothing to do with this."

The door opened. One of the FBI agents on the Cutter task force stepped into the waiting area. "Detective Riddel, you can come in, if you like. Agent Santos and I are available now."

"What about Abe?" he asked.

"Sorry. Task force only."

My phone rang. The caller ID said it was the law office of Jeffrey Winters.

"You go ahead," I said. "I'll wait."

Rid and the agent disappeared behind the door. My phone continued to ring. I had no desire to talk to Jeffrey Winters, but I suddenly did want to know if Rid had "nothing to do with this"—or if, for the first time since I'd known him, he'd lied to my face.

One more ring and it would have gone to voice mail. I picked up and said hello.

"Abe?"

I froze.

"Abe, it's me."

I nearly dropped the phone.

It was my wife.

Chapter Fifty-Five

I reached the law office of Jeffrey Winters in ten minutes.

My phone conversation with Angelina had been short. Winters didn't want us talking on an unsecure line. It was important that we speak in private. She told me only that she was unhurt and that she had never been in any danger.

"*Never been in danger?*"

"I'll explain when you get here," she'd told me. "And don't say a word to anyone until you meet with Jeffrey and me."

"I have to tell your parents."

"They know."

And they didn't tell me? Weird was turning to weirder.

The law firm occupied the entire penthouse floor in a new high-rise in an old neighborhood along the Miami River, less than a mile from the criminal courts. Winters' spacious corner office had an impressive view of downtown Miami. To the south, I could see where he used to work. My office. The Boomerang. It had an ironic connotation as my once-missing wife rushed toward me and threw her arms around me.

"I'm so sorry, Abe."

She was squeezing me tight and shaking with emotion. I squeezed back, looking over the top of her head and toward the window. There was not a sliver of space between us, and she was speaking into my shoulder.

"I'm sorry I ran."

I broke the embrace. Her expression was tight with stress, but I'd seen women who'd actually been on the run, and Angelina bore none of the markings. She hadn't cut or colored her hair. No spray tan to darken her skin, no phony eyeglasses, no tinted contact lenses to make her blue eyes brown. If she'd been trying to look frumpy or heavier, the designer jeans and thin cashmere sweater weren't exactly doing the trick.

"Ran from what?" I asked.

Winters came toward us. "Let's talk this out, shall we?"

Angelina took my hand and led me to the couch. We were sitting next to each other, but with so much unexplained the hand-holding felt awkward, and we both let go. We were only inches apart, but it felt like much more. Her lawyer sat across from us in a leather armchair.

Winters had always been a sharp dresser, even while on a government salary, but if the office furnishings were any indication of his success in private practice, his wardrobe no longer depended on the once-a-year Hugo Boss sale. The French cuffs and perfectly pressed suit made me even more aware of my disheveled appearance. I was powered by caffeine, looking as though I'd been sleeping in my clothes, if I'd slept at all.

"First off, Abe," he said. "I want to be clear that even though I am Angelina's attorney and not yours, everything said in this room is privileged and protected under the marital privilege. Agreed?"

"Fine," I said, looking at Angelina. "But why do you have a lawyer?"

"My mother hired him for me," she said.

"When?"

"This morning. After I called her."

That explained why my in-laws had not returned my calls. "So you spoke to your parents *and* hired a lawyer before you even called me?"

"Yes, but don't say it as if I did something wrong. I saw my mom on TV last night. She looked more upset than anyone. I had to call her first."

"I understand that part. It's talking to *him* first that bothers me."

Winters sat forward, addressing me. "The timeline is that Angelina called her mother, and Margaret called me. Her concern was that the family could bear financial responsibility for the costs that law enforcement incurred in the emergency response."

I looked at Angelina. "Because there was no actual emergency?"

She looked at Winters before answering.

"Go ahead and walk Abe through this from the beginning," he said. "It will make more sense that way."

I was getting the distinct impression that they had rehearsed this, but I listened. Angelina drew a breath and then began.

"Friday night was a bad night."

She quickly summarized what I already knew. It seemed hard to believe that barely a weekend had passed since the shattered beer bottle against our front door.

"After you left, I was scared to be alone in the house. I was too angry to ask you to come back, and I didn't want my mother to see me this upset. So I sucked it up and stayed."

She asked for some water, and Winters brought it to her. Then she continued.

"I couldn't fall asleep. I got up and watched TV for a while. The house started to make noises. Creaking windows. The AC turning on and off. Even with the television on, I could hear those things. Or imagine them. I went back to bed and lay there, wide awake, afraid to turn out the lights. Thoughts were running through my mind. A serial killer was on the loose. Five women were dead. A photograph of his latest victim was sitting on my cocktail table, hand delivered to my mailbox by her killer. Why did he do that? Was he coming back for me? Who was going to stop him? A squad car was parked on our block, which made me feel a little safer. But why would the police agree to provide protection if I wasn't in serious danger? And what could they really do to stop a psychopath who was determined to make Abe Beckham's wife the next victim? I was starting to freak out. I decided— . . ."

She drank more water.

"Take your time," said Winters.

"I couldn't just sit in my house and wait for a homicidal maniac to show up with a machete. But then it occurred to me: Cutter can't kill me if he doesn't know where I am. And he can't threaten my family at knife-point and force them to divulge where I am if *no one* knows where I went. I decided to . . . vanish."

"How? Where?" I asked.

"I didn't know. I was flying by the seat of my pants."

Winters interjected. "This is an important point, Abe. There is no evidence that Angelina's disappearance was anything but spontaneous and driven by fear. She didn't hoard cash in advance. She didn't change her appearance. She didn't have any fraudulent identification with her. She left her passport behind and had no prepaid tickets for domestic or international travel."

"How did you expect to pull this off?" I asked her.

"I panicked. You watch enough movies, and you start to think that if you pin your hair up under a hat and put on a pair of sunglasses, you're good to go. But you have to buy things to live, and it has to be cash, because credit cards leave a trail. All I could scrape together in the house was about $175. I wasn't sure what to do, but one of the shows that came on while I was watching TV with all the other insomniacs was *Pawn Stars*. It's about normal-looking people getting cash for just about anything at a pawnshop. That's when I decided to pawn the jewelry."

"Samantha's jewelry, you mean."

She averted her eyes, but only for a second, and then looked back at me. "Would it make you happier if I had sold my own ring?"

There was only one answer to that question. "No."

"I knew about the strongbox, Abe. I'm the only one in the house who cleans closets."

Angelina rose, went to her purse on the credenza, and removed a plastic bag. "I'm sorry," she said as she handed it to me. "I got rid of the strongbox, but everything is here, except for the rings, which you already have."

I opened it. Samantha's diamond earrings and the wristwatch from Luther were inside, as well as some other things that weren't nearly as valuable. I was glad Angelina hadn't pawned them, but I wasn't in an appreciative frame of mind. My prosecutorial instincts were taking over, and I wanted to be the one asking questions. "How did you get to the pawnshop?"

"I walked."

"Past the police officer who was parked on our street?"

"I went out the back and left the car in the driveway so he wouldn't see me."

"Why did you pick Pawn 24 in Little Havana?"

"I could walk there. It was the closest pawnshop to our house that was open twenty-four hours."

"How did Jerko get the ring?"

"Who?"

"The homeless guy who sold the ring to the pawn-shop. How did he get his hands on it?"

"I knew the police would be looking for me, and I was afraid the shop owner might remember me. This guy happened to be sitting on the sidewalk a few doors down from the shop. I told him I'd pay him fifty dollars if he went inside and sold the ring for me."

"You trusted him?"

"I shouldn't have. When he came out, he refused to hand over the money unless I gave him my iPhone on top of his fifty-dollar cut."

I remembered my encounter with Jerko and the way he'd insisted that I give him my phone. "You gave your phone to him?"

"Yes. I needed the money. I couldn't power on the phone anyway. I could be tracked."

"How did your phone end up on the side of the Tamiami Trail?"

"You'll need to ask Jerko."

"You didn't put it there?"

"No."

I pressed harder, perhaps a bit too prosecutorial. "You didn't toss the phone onto the side of the road to make police think you had been murdered and dumped in the Everglades, like Tyla Tomkins?"

"I was running from the man who killed Tyla. Dumping my phone there wasn't going to make him think he killed me. That makes no sense."

"Unless you were running from something else."

"Do I have to say it again? *No*. I didn't toss my phone on the Tamiami Trail. You're asking the wrong person."

It was getting a little icy in the room, and Winters felt the need to intervene. "Let's all take a deep breath," he said.

I kept quiet. Angelina rose from the couch and took the armchair beside her lawyer, both of them facing me now.

"Where did you go after you sold the ring?" I asked in a tone less accusatory.

"The hotel and casino on the Miccosukee Indian Reservation. It's the one place where you can wear sunglasses indoors and at night and blend in with all the other poker players."

"It's also outside the jurisdiction of local law enforcement," I said.

"Yes, I'm aware of that. I panicked, but I'm not totally stupid."

"How did you get there?"

"I got a ride."

"From a stranger?"

"There's a coffee shop not far from Pawn 24. I didn't go in. I waited outside until someone who seemed safe came along. A couple of girls came by for a jolt of caffeine after a night of clubbing. I told them that my asshole boyfriend hooked up with another woman and left me stranded, that I needed a ride back to my hotel at the casino, and that I was afraid to call a taxi at three in the morning because just last week a woman had been raped by a Miami cabdriver."

The part about the "asshole boyfriend" made me squirm a little. "Weren't you afraid that they might see your picture on the news the next day and identify you?"

"It seemed worth the risk. The only thing newsworthy to these girls is their personal Facebook posts."

I sank a little deeper into the couch, my emotions all over the map. I didn't believe all of it, but if any of it was true, I was sorry that I'd left her alone in the house. I tried to keep reminding myself to be glad that she was alive and that she hadn't been butchered by a sociopath, but I was mad as hell that she'd put me and everyone else through this nightmare.

"So you just sat in a hotel room the entire weekend while all this was going on?"

"I was exhausted when I got to the room. By the time I woke Saturday afternoon, this had snowballed into something I hadn't really envisioned."

426 · JAMES GRIPPANDO

"You went *missing*. What did you think it would become?"

"I don't know, Abe!"

She was so loud it startled both of us.

"Sorry, I didn't mean to yell," she said. "I panicked, and I realized pretty quickly that it was a terrible idea. People were going to think I was nuts. The thought of having to explain myself to the police and the media was making me sick to my stomach. Then on Sunday I saw my mother on television at that press conference with my father, and I knew this had to end."

"Which leads us to where we are now," said Winters. "Here's the plan that Angelina and I have agreed to."

"Plan for what?"

"The announcement of her return. There is no upside to holding a press conference and throwing her to the wolves. We'll release a YouTube video. The videographer is setting up now in the main conference room. Angelina will read a statement that has been prepared by my media-relations consultant."

"You hired a publicist?"

"No, a media-relations consultant."

"It's the same thing."

"We're not promoting a reality television show here, Abe. Everything down to the titles of the people on our team must reinforce the notion that we are not spinning anything. Our focus is only on the clarity of our message."

"What's the message?"

"Simple," he said. "We are grateful to the law enforcement agencies that apprehended Mr. Salvo and brought an end to this series of brutal murders. We are thankful that Angelina is no longer living in constant fear for her life. We regret the inconvenience caused by a poor decision that was driven by that fear."

" 'We' meaning Angelina and me?"

"And her parents. The four of you will appear together in the video."

"Where are your parents?" I asked my wife.

Winters answered for her. "They're in the conference room with the videographer."

"Am I supposed to say anything?"

"No. You and Angelina's folks are there for support. But the written press release will contain a quote from you," he said as he handed me the one-page draft.

I read it. My line was a single sentence: "I'm just happy to have Angelina back, and we're really looking forward to getting our lives back to normal."

"You good with that?" asked Winters.

I still had questions, even some doubts about Angelina's explanation. Angelina seemed to pick up on my hesitation. She returned to a seat right beside me on the couch, and she squeezed my hand. "Abe, you are glad I'm back, aren't you?"

What kind of husband would hesitate to say that he was happy to have his wife back? That wasn't the issue.

"We need to get this out now," Winters said firmly. "Are you on board or not, Abe?"

I recognized that tone of voice. I'd used it myself when nudging reluctant witnesses. Winters was telling me to be glad that my wife was about to say to the world that she had run only out of her fear of Cutter, and not because she feared her husband as well. The Angelina Express was leaving the station. I could get on the train, or I could stand aside and give her attorney good reason to advise his client to throw me under it.

"The statement's fine," I said.

"Thank you," he said. "I'll tell my consultant to blast it right now."

Winters had his consultant on speed dial. He told her to "let it rip" and then hung up and advised me of the next step. "In ten minutes I'll follow up with a personal phone call to Agent Santos and each of the agencies on the Cutter task force."

"I'd like to call Detective Riddel myself," I said.

"No. We have to stay on message and speak with one voice," he said, meaning his.

"Riddel is my friend."

"He's a cop," said Winters.

"Please listen to him, Abe. He knows what he's doing."

And I don't?

Winters got another call. I assumed it was his publicist—er, media-relations consultant. It was a brief conversation, and he seemed even more energized as he hung up and spoke to us.

"The script for the YouTube video is ready. Angelina, let's go down to the conference room and do a dry run. I want the video to launch as soon after the press release as possible. Abe, the most important thing you can do right now is work on those bags under your eyes."

"I have bags?"

"No. That's my point. You should, and the world needs to see them. I'll have the videographer's assistant come and do your makeup."

Angelina gave me a half smile. "See? He's good, right?"

I nodded without heart. " 'Good' isn't the word for it," I said, as my wife and her lawyer walked out the door.

Chapter Fifty-Six

W e did the video in one take. The only glitch was me. I refused to wear makeup, bags or no bags beneath my eyes. It really didn't matter. I was the loving husband seated on my wife's right. Jake and Margaret were the relieved parents on their daughter's left. The focus was on Angelina, who was pitch-perfect as she read her prepared statement.

"I am deeply sorry for the pain I have caused my family and friends, and for the trouble and inconvenience I caused law enforcement and so many volunteers who came forward to help. Decisions made out of fear are never good, and I made a terrible decision that deceived all of you. I have no right to your forgiveness, but I hope you will understand that I truly was acting out of fear for my life. It was only because I felt as though I had no choice . . ."

She paused in the right places. Her voice quaked convincingly. The videographer needed thirty minutes to finalize it. The YouTube launch was scheduled for 9:00 a.m. sharp, but the media frenzy had begun even earlier with the written press release, which by 8:30 had gone viral. I'd turned off my phone for the video shoot, and when I powered it on, my in-box populated with a flood of messages and missed-call updates. Most were from people I didn't know, random journalists and bloggers looking for quotes to flesh out the press release. But others mattered. I owed Carmen and Rid an explanation. Agent Santos as well.

"I need to return some calls," I told Winters.

"We speak with one voice," he reminded me.

"Horseshit."

"Abe, please," said Angelina. "At least until the media frenzy dies down, let the press release and the YouTube video do the talking for us, and let Jeffrey handle any questions."

My cell rang again. Another number I didn't recognize. I ignored it and put the phone on vibrate. "That's fine for strangers," I said. "Not for my friends. Especially my friends in law enforcement. They stepped up to help without me even asking."

"The major players are all on my call list," said Winters.

"It needs to come from me. I'm a prosecutor, for God's sake. I work with these folks. I can't look them in the eye again if I don't give them a personal explanation of what happened."

Winters seemed to understand that there was no debating it. "Fine," he said. "But stay on message. And be careful using a cell phone. This goes for you, too, Angelina. The media is filled with eavesdroppers, and your only safe bet is a landline or a face-to-face conversation."

I agreed. But if I used his landline, "Law Office of Jeffrey Winters" would pop up on caller ID every time I phoned a friend in law enforcement. Not cool. It was time for me to leave, and not just to make phone calls. I had questions for my wife, and I wanted answers away from her lawyer.

"When can you and I talk alone?" I asked her.

"Let's discuss that," said Winters.

"I was talking to Angelina," I said.

"I understand. But the question of where everyone goes from here is next on my agenda."

"I just want to have a conversation with my wife."

"And you will, as soon as we've sorted this out. I've made arrangements for Angelina's parents to change hotels and stay here in Miami for a couple days. The media won't be able to reach them. By the end of the week or so, when they feel rested and ready to travel, they'll take a nice long vacation."

"They're looking into New Zealand," said Angelina.

"Perfect," said Winters.

"I have a job," I said. "I'm not going into hiding or running to the other side of the world."

"That's not what I have in mind for you and Angelina. Your lives should return to normal."

"Agreed," I said. "The sooner the better."

"My plan is to get Miami-Dade police to lift the crime scene designation from your house immediately. I'd like to see you sleep there tonight."

I wondered if that meant in the same bed. "That sounds good to me," I said, glancing at Angelina.

"Me too," she said without making eye contact.

"Then that's our goal," said Winters. "But first there's work to do. The media presence will be huge. My preference is that neither of you leave this building until my consultant and I have choreographed everything from the car ride home to the way you look at each other as you walk through the front door."

"That's not necessary," I said. "Angelina, I say we do this right now and get it over with."

"No, no, no," said Winters. "The only image I want out for public consumption today is the YouTube video.

Let it play out for a good eight to twelve hours. That gives us time to rehearse."

"I don't need to rehearse walking into my own house."

"You'll be peppered with questions the minute you step out of the car. Saying the wrong thing or even just looking into the camera the wrong way can undo all the good we've just done. My consultant will role-play with you and make sure you're prepared for that first live encounter with the media."

I looked at my wife. "Angelina, let's go home."

"Why are you being so difficult?" she asked.

"*I'm* being difficult? Why have we not spoken a word to each other so far without your lawyer in the room?"

"That's not fair, Abe. I've made some terrible decisions in the last few days. I need good advice."

"Mine's free."

"Jeffrey's is objective."

"Jeffrey is looking out for Jeffrey."

There. It needed to be said. I'd believed it from the day I'd first met him at the state attorney's office. His determination to turn Angelina into a media darling and YouTube sensation had convinced me that it was truer than ever.

"Abe, you should apologize to Jeffrey right now."

"No need," said Winters. "Abe is entitled to his opinion."

They were both right, but this charade was all wrong, and I was not about to apologize.

"Abe?" she said, nudging. I wasn't biting.

"I've seen this before," said Winters. "Cops, prosecutors, anyone in law enforcement. They have no use for criminal defense lawyers. Nothing personal, Abe, but I prepared Angelina for your reaction."

"All I want is thirty minutes of alone time with my wife."

"And you'll get it," he said, "maybe as soon as tonight, if all goes well. But these next twelve hours are crucial. Angelina needs a lawyer. As her attorney, I have advised her to avoid spending time alone with anyone who will try to convince her that she doesn't need one. Even her husband."

"Especially her husband?"

"I didn't say that," said Winters. "I suspected that you would fall into that category. Your behavior this morning confirms it."

"I'm going to make a few phone calls," I said, rising.

Winters seemed happy that I was leaving. "Remember what I said about the cell phone. The receptionist can set you up in a conference room with a landline."

"Thanks, but I'll make the calls from my office."

"You're leaving?" asked Angelina.

"Yeah. Are you coming?"

She looked at her lawyer, but she didn't move. Winters had her under a sit-and-stay command worthy of the Westminster Kennel Club.

"I didn't think so," I said, and I left the room.

The morning rush hour had the courthouse district in a chokehold, and it made no sense to put off my calls until I could get to a landline. I phoned Carmen from my car while stuck in traffic.

"This could turn into one hell of a mess," she said.

My first call had been to Rid, but it went to voice mail. Carmen was next. She'd read the press release from Jeffrey Winters, and I told her about the YouTube video that was ready to launch. Of course she was glad that Angelina was unharmed, but that didn't alleviate her concerns about the growing "mess."

"You mean the media?" I asked.

"That part I can handle," she said. "I'm talking about Agent Santos."

"Have you talked to her?"

"Yes. She has questions that I simply can't answer, and if she doesn't get answers, this is going to snowball into a very bad situation. It's a federal crime to fake your own disappearance and disrupt the investigative work of a multijurisdictional task force."

"We know. That's why Angelina has a lawyer."

"Listen to what I'm saying, Abe. Santos doesn't believe that your wife pulled this off alone. She thinks that the only way this could have happened was if someone on the inside ran misdirection and got the cops to ignore leads and look the other away. Someone like her husband."

"That's crazy. Even if she said that, it must have been in some kind of brainstorming session. She can't actually *believe* it. Why would I get involved in a stunt like that?"

"You're right. I don't know what's inside Santos' head. But I can think of one reason you might: maybe you and Angelina both came to the conclusion that the only way to keep her safe from Cutter was to make Cutter think she was killed by a copycat."

A copycat. I thought again of how Angelina's phone had ended up on the Tamiami Trail, not far from where Tyla's body had been recovered.

"Carmen, you know I would never do something like this. I could be disbarred."

"Yes, you could."

"Is that what Santos wants?"

"As I said, I don't know where Santos is headed with this. Maybe she's just pissed off that the media is paying more attention to Angelina's return than to the FBI's apprehension of a serial killer. But my advice to you is to get to the bottom of it."

"Good advice," I said. "I will."

I hung up and stopped at the traffic light. I was about to call Santos, but my thoughts returned to Carmen's mention of a copycat killer, Angelina's cell phone, and her emphatic denial of any knowledge of how it had ended up near Tyla's recovery site.

No. I didn't toss my phone on the Tamiami Trail. You're asking the wrong person.

It made me wonder. Who was the right person?

Traffic was finally moving, but I pulled into a gas station and called Rid. It went to voice mail again. I dialed three more times without success. It was possible that he'd been tied up all morning, and it ran against my better judgment to think that he was anything other than too busy to answer his phone. But I was pretty sure Rid was avoiding my calls.

I made a quick three-point turn, and the tires squealed as I started back to the law office.

Chapter Fifty-Seven

Victoria Santos had one priority: find Tyla Tomkins' killer.

She knew it wasn't Cutter, and not just because a black woman from Miami-Dade didn't meet the victim profile of a white female from Palm Beach County who dated black men. There was no sadistic video of Tyla in Tommy Salvo's computer and no sign of Tyla's DNA in his kill room or anywhere else in his house or car. It technically wasn't the FBI's jurisdiction to solve a homicide unrelated to a federal offense, but legal technicalities aside, this one was different: Victoria had been lied to.

The YouTube video had nearly sent Victoria over the edge. It was vintage Jeffrey Winters, a lightweight criminal defense showman who fancied himself a master in the courtroom of public opinion. Nothing would satisfy Victoria more than to hoist Winters by his own petard, to use his own strategy against him to crack the Tyla Tomkins case. She'd watched Angelina's mea culpa video three times, then drove herself to the Beckham residence. An army of television journalists rushed toward her vehicle. She had to force the driver's-side door open and push back the crowd just to get out of her car. They surrounded her as she cut across the lawn, and questions hit her from every direction.

Does the FBI have any comment on this morning's video?

Will any charges be brought?

Why is the Beckham house still a crime scene?

At this stage, it was in Victoria's interest not to answer any of those questions. She forged ahead, eyes forward, "No comment." The reporters followed her all the way to the police tape at the front steps. Victoria ducked under the yellow ribbon of authority, went inside, and closed the door behind her. Detective Reyes of the Miami-Dade domestic violence unit was waiting in the living room.

"A media circus out there," said Reyes.

Victoria looked out the front window. She recognized many of the same teams that had provided Find Angelina news coverage over the weekend, but even more had joined the frenzy for this latest development.

"They smell blood." Victoria took another step into the living room, then glanced back at the spot where they'd found the shattered beer bottle on Saturday morning. "And I smell spouse abuse."

"Smell won't get me a conviction," said Reyes.

"No. But I'm pretty certain that a physical examination of Angelina's body will. A woman doesn't run out of her house after midnight and fake her own disappearance if she isn't scared to death of her husband. There has to be a bruise or a cut somewhere on her body."

The detective shook her head. "You can't force a victim to submit to a physical examination. I've tried."

"That's where I can help you," said Victoria.

"How?"

"You can't force Angelina to submit to an examination. But if she's staring at federal charges and five years in prison for faking her disappearance and obstruction of justice, she might very well 'consent' to it."

"Good of you to help," said Reyes. "But I'm assuming that you didn't throw yourself back into this mess out of the goodness of your heart. What do you want from me?"

Victoria stepped closer, her expression very serious. "Spouse abuse is the tip of the iceberg here. I'm looking for Tyla Tomkins' killer."

"Don't you have that in Cutter?"

"No."

"You should be talking to Detective Riddel about this."

"Detective Riddel talks too much to Abe Beckham."

"Are you sure Cutter is not your man? Is there nothing to connect him to Tyla Tomkins?"

Victoria wasn't ready to share Tommy Salvo's mention of his encounter with Tyla at the Cortinas plantation in Nicaragua. Not yet. "Let me put it this way. I have one thing that may connect Cutter to Tyla Tomkins. On the night of Tyla's memorial service, I looked across the street from the funeral home and saw a glowing orange dot in the dark parking lot. Someone was standing there watching and smoking a cigarette. Tommy Salvo is a chain smoker."

"So it was him?"

"He denied it at first. Then we started talking about Cutter in the third person, and he insinuated that it might have been him, but I led him there in my questioning. It fits the stereotype of the serial killer who watches the funeral or visits the grave of his victims. Except that Tyla wasn't his victim."

"Maybe he went there out of curiosity just to see why people thought Tyla Tomkins was one of Cutter's victims."

"Maybe. But I don't think so."

"Okay. You know *someone* was smoking in the dark and watching from across the street. If not him, who?"

"That is the question," said Victoria. "The answer depends on what you find here as part of your domestic violence investigation."

"I hope this doesn't make me sound like I have sawdust between my ears, but you want to tell me exactly what you're hoping I find here?"

Victoria slowly crossed the living room, walking around the cocktail table and past each of the end tables. "There's not a single ashtray anywhere in this house, is there?"

"None that I've seen, and none listed in the initial CIS inventory," said Reyes.

She walked to the drapes and sniffed the fabric. "No obvious smoking odor?"

"I can't say that I've detected any, but that wasn't the focus of the forensic team's investigation when Mrs. Beckham went missing."

"Here's what I'm looking for," said Victoria. "Anything—and I mean *anything*—that tells you Angelina Beckham is a closet smoker."

"How does that relate to my domestic violence investigation?"

It doesn't. "Trust me on this," said Victoria. "You'll see."

Chapter Fifty-Eight

I parked right beside Jeffrey Winters' shiny new Tesla and hurried into his building. The elevator was packed, no room for me, so I ran up the stairwell. Sweat beaded at my brow, and I was breathing heavily as I entered his suite, raced past the receptionist, and entered his office. Angelina and her parents were with him.

"Angelina, I have to talk to you," I said.

They looked at me with confusion, probably wondering why I was panting like a Saint Bernard.

"Sorry, I ran up the steps," I explained. "But Angelina, this is urgent. Give me five minutes alone and hear what I have to say. I didn't rush all the way back here to tell you to fire your lawyer."

She glanced at Winters, who gave her the green light. "You can use the conference room," he said.

We walked across the hall together. It wasn't as large as Winters' office, but it was plenty big for the two of us. As I closed the door, I wondered if the room was bugged and if Winters could hear everything. I didn't care. I was just glad to have Angelina's undivided ear. We took seats at the conference table.

"What is going on, Abe?"

I was still winded and took a moment. "I've been thinking about your story."

"It's not a 'story,'" she said. "It's the truth."

She was starting to sound like her lawyer. "Okay, let me start again."

I paused. I knew Winters would hold me to my five-minute limit and would knock on the door soon. But what I needed to say wasn't something I could just blurt out. It was a delicate situation.

"Angelina, I've met a lot of victims as a prosecutor. A lot of them have had horrible things done to them. No one ever wants to talk about it. It's never easy. Some are able to recall everything, and they can describe it in amazing detail. Some remember what happened, but they just can't talk about it. A few seem to have no memory of it. They've blocked it out for the sake of their own survival."

"What are you talking about?"

"I'm talking about you," I said.

"It doesn't sound like it."

"I'm worried about your story."

"It's not a—"

"Sorry, your statement. It may be 'the truth,'" I said, making air quotes, "but not all of it sounds true. It has holes. I'm having trouble believing it. I don't think the public is going to believe it either."

"That's your opinion."

"Let me be more specific. I believe you got scared after I left. You did leave the house thinking that you'd be safer from Cutter if you went into hiding. Maybe you were even so pissed off at me that you decided to hurt me and sell Samantha's ring for money."

"I didn't do it to spite you."

"Stay with me on this," I said. "Maybe you got yourself into a sketchy neighborhood at two o'clock in the morning, and something bad happened."

"I didn't do anything wrong."

"I know you didn't. When I say something bad happened, I mean something bad happened *to* you."

She didn't answer.

"Something that you don't want to talk about. That you don't want to have to describe in painful detail to me, your mother, your father, the police, a jury, or anyone else."

She shook her head, but I read it more as confusion than disagreement. "Why would you think that?"

"It started with your phone. You don't really have a good explanation of how it ended up on the Tamiami Trail near the recovery site for Tyla's body. You said Jerko made you give it to him. When I pushed for a better answer, all you could say is that I wasn't asking the right person. It suddenly occurred to me that maybe the 'right person' did more than take your phone."

"You're overanalyzing this, Abe."

"Am I? Anyone who has watched the news in the last two weeks knows all about Tyla Tomkins, knows where the body was found, and knows that the police are looking for a serial killer. That's the kind of information a guy can use to his advantage if he spots a woman alone in the pawnshop district of Little Havana. Let's say it's late, the woman is desperate, and she needs a ride. He stops. She knows better than to get in, but he pulls her into his car and violates her. For some reason he lets her go, or maybe she fights and gets away. But he has her purse and her cell phone, and he wants to throw the police off his trail. He tosses the victim's phone out the car window on the Tamiami Trail. He gets the police looking for Cutter, not him."

We were pushing up against the five-minute deadline, but I gave Angelina thirty seconds to consider my words. Had she been a stranger, I would have known what to say next. I would have told her that none of this was her fault, that there was no shame in having once been a victim, and that now she was a survivor. I would have explained that too many sexual assaults went unreported, and that it was important to catch the guy who had done this to her and make sure he didn't do it again. But the script went out the window when speaking to Angelina, and for the life of me, I couldn't tell what was going through her head. Finally, she spoke.

"Abe, I understand what you're doing. I know you're trying to help. But you can't put words in my mouth. *That* would be a story."

"Angelina, please."

"No, Abe. What you just said may sound more like the truth. But I'm sticking with the *real* truth."

There was a crisp knock on the door, and Winters entered.

"Can we have another minute, please," I said, annoyed.

"Both of you need to see this," he said as he grabbed the television remote. The flat-screen TV on the wall switched on, and Winters put on the local morning edition of the Action News channel.

"They're at your house again," said Winters.

"The media?" I asked.

"The police," he said as he increased the volume.

On screen was the same Action News reporter who had interviewed me on Saturday after Angelina's disappearance. She appeared much less subdued in this broadcast, a genuine air of excitement about her.

"We expected to see Angelina Beckham return home this morning," she said into the camera, microphone in hand. "Instead, it is the Miami-Dade police who have returned. While we have no word yet as to what law enforcement is looking for, clearly the Beckham residence remains an active crime scene."

The camera switched to a broader angle from the sidewalk and panned across our front yard and driveway. I recognized Agent Santos' car parked behind the MDPD squad cars.

"Isn't that your friend?" asked Angelina.

"You mean Santos?"

"No. The guy behind the reporter. Isn't that Detective Riddel?"

I rose and walked around the conference table for a closer look at the TV. In the background, behind the Action News reporter, a man was running up the driveway and trying to break free from other reporters on his way toward my house.

"It sure is," I said.

Winters went to the phone. "This needs to end. I'll speak directly to the chief of police about this."

I stepped around the table and pressed the disconnect button, ending his call in mid-dial.

"What are you doing?" he asked.

I looked at Angelina. "Do you swear I'm wrong? That I was totally off base? That what I just said to you didn't happen?"

She met my stare. "It didn't happen."

"Then I'll take care of Riddel."

She looked at me with concern. "How?"

"I'm going home."

"That's crazy," said Winters. "It's a hornets' nest. You can't go there."

"Watch me," I said.

"What the hell do you think you're going to do when you get there?" he asked.

I glanced back at the television to see a mob of reporters pushing against the crime scene tape and calling my friend's name as he disappeared through my front door.

"I'm gonna get right in Rid's face," I said.

Chapter Fifty-Nine

The media assault began the instant I stepped out of my car. Reporters pushed, shoved, and jockeyed for position as I walked up the sidewalk. This wasn't the first time that microphones had been thrust in my face, but past experiences had been on the courthouse steps, never on my front lawn. I didn't run or bully my way through the crowd, and I tried not to look annoyed as I stopped and delivered the short and innocuous statement that I'd rehearsed during the car ride.

"I want to thank each of you for the professional manner in which the media did its job while respecting our privacy after Angelina went missing. The apology that she issued this morning was from the heart. I hope you will continue to respect our privacy, especially around our home, now that this is behind us. Again, thank you."

I continued toward the house. The mob moved with me, surrounding me. I was the glob of jelly trying to find some way to squish his way out of the center of the doughnut. Their questions ran together—*Where is Angelina, why are the police here, what are they looking for?*—but I ignored them. I ducked beneath the police tape, well aware of how it would look on the news if I ran up the front steps and slammed the door on the media. I walked calmly, turned and waved to the cameras, and went inside.

My camera smile disappeared immediately. Santos was waiting for me.

"Your house is still a crime scene," she said. "You can't come in here."

"This is bullshit," I said. "There can't be a crime scene where there's no crime."

Detective Reyes stepped out of the kitchen and joined us. "It's a domestic violence investigation, Abe."

"That's not true. I was watching the TV coverage and saw Riddel come into the house."

"I sent him away. Homicide is not involved."

"Right, I'm an abuser," I said with a shake of my head. "We're back to this again? Really?"

"I'm doing my job," said Reyes. "There was a broken beer bottle on the floor. The lab confirmed that the blood on one of the shards was Angelina's."

I knew about the blood but not the lab report. The confirmation of the connection to Angelina didn't come as a shock. "She probably stepped on it."

"Your physical examination revealed a bruise on your arm."

"I already explained this once. I banged my arm when I fell at my brother-in-law's apartment."

"Maybe you did. And maybe we'd believe you, if we were to conduct a physical examination of Angelina's body and found nothing."

I kept my anger in check, but I couldn't take the edge off my voice entirely. "The only *abuse* in this house is an abuse of police power. If you're looking for something, get a search warrant. And by the way," I said, my gaze shifting toward Santos, "since when is the FBI involved in a domestic violence investigation?"

We were locked in a stare-down, and I seriously wanted an answer.

"Let's talk in the kitchen," she said.

Reyes seemed befuddled to be out of the loop so suddenly, but she deferred and stayed behind. I followed Santos into the kitchen. We stood on opposite sides of the counter, where fewer than three days earlier Rid had wolfed down a plate of Angelina's osso buco.

"You could force us to get a warrant," Santos said. "But if you think the media is stirred up now, wait until they hear that a warrant has been issued and the police are searching your house. I'm actually doing you a favor by keeping it low-key and at least creating the impression that we're here simply to wrap up a crime scene."

"You're doing *me* a favor?" I said, scoffing. "The FBI is doing *itself* a favor. I see what's going on here. My house was a task force crime scene. Now that Cutter is in custody, your authority as task force coordinator ends, and the FBI goes back to catching bank robbers and to life as J. Edgar Hoover intended it. You're using Detective Reyes and this domestic violence bullshit to reach beyond federal jurisdiction and get inside my house. What are you looking for, Santos? What are you *really* looking for?"

"Cutter didn't kill Tyla Tomkins. I want to know who did."

"If she wasn't one of Cutter's victims, then it's none of your business. Step aside and let the locals investigate."

She came closer, her eyes narrowing. "You'd like that, wouldn't you? Let your buddy Riddel handle the investigation into Tyla Tomkins' murder."

I wanted to push back, but I could see that it would get me nowhere. I needed to go on the offensive.

"All right, if you're determined to stick your FBI nose where it doesn't belong, you might as well stick it in the right place. When's the last time you knocked on Brian Belter's door?"

"I'm on to Belter."

"Not as much as you should be. He's in big-time cover-up mode."

"It's not surprising that a law firm would fight a subpoena to examine the e-mails and computers of one of its partners. Especially a partner like Tyla, who was one of Big Sugar's most trusted advisers."

"I'm not talking about your subpoena. Belter offered me a bribe yesterday. A quarter million dollars."

"Yesterday? And you're just getting around to telling me today?"

"I told Carmen last night." I lied, and I wasn't entirely sure why. It was becoming a bad habit when questions from Santos made me uncomfortable.

"Is the state attorney's office going to convene a grand jury?"

"I don't know. I haven't even written up a full report yet. Believe it or not, I've had other things on my mind in the last sixteen hours." That much was true.

"What did Belter want you to do for a quarter million dollars?"

I hesitated, not sure how much to tell Santos before having a fuller discussion with Carmen. But Carmen wasn't the one I needed out of my house. A little cooperation among law enforcement officers could go a long way. At least, that had been my experience prior to meeting Agent Santos.

"He was dancing around a bit, and I shut him down hard. But I have a pretty good idea of where he was going."

"You want to share it?"

"You want to quit busting my ass?"

"Maybe. Let's hear your theory."

Again I hesitated. I had no reason to believe that "my theory" would completely knock me off her shit list. But I could at least slow down the train.

"All right, but bear in mind that this involves some supposition on my part. Belter believes that the prime suspect in Tyla Tomkins' murder will be someone who slept with her. I think he was angling for a truce between the two of us. He won't point the finger at me if I don't point the finger at him, so long as we both point the finger at Mr. Cortinas."

"Cortinas was sleeping with Tyla Tomkins? Do you know that for a fact?"

"I know that Tyla used a prepaid cell phone to talk to certain men. One of the numbers connected to her phone still has never been linked to an identifiable caller. Am I right?"

She didn't answer.

"I thought so," I said. "Belter says it was Alberto Cortinas. He had his own prepaid cell that he used when he and Tyla talked rendezvous."

Santos studied my expression carefully as she considered my words. My candor seemed to have repaired some of the damage. For the time being, at least.

"Thank you for this," she said.

"You're welcome."

"We'll be out of your house in one hour. The crime scene tape will be gone. You and your wife are free to return. Fair enough?"

"Fair enough," I said.

She turned and went back into the living room. I left through the back door and cut through the neighbor's yard to the next street over. The media could have my car. A cab would suit me just fine.

Chapter Sixty

I walked four blocks from my house and decided against a taxi. I took a shot and called Rid instead. This time he answered.

"Why have you been avoiding me all morning?" I asked.

"You think I got one case I work on?"

"Don't bullshit me, Rid. I went by my house after I saw you on the news, but you were already gone. Did Santos and Detective Reyes actually tell you to leave?"

"Yup. They said it's not a homicide investigation, but that's not the real reason they kicked me out."

"What's the real reason?"

"I talk too much. To you. Which needs to stop, Abe."

He sounded downtrodden, which usually meant he was fed up with police bureaucracy. "Did someone come down on you for being too chummy with me in this investigation?"

"Nahhhh," he said with a heavy dose of sarcasm. "What would give you that idea?"

"I tell you what," I said. "How about you just swing by and give me a ride?"

"Didn't you hear what I just said?"

"You don't have to tell me a thing. I talk, you listen. Give me that much."

"I know what I should give you," he said, grumbling. Then he hung up. I took that as a yes and texted him my location. Five minutes later, Rid picked me up at a gas station in an unmarked police car. "Where to?" he asked.

"Boomerang."

He knew the joke, but he wasn't smiling. He pulled into traffic and headed toward my office. I wasn't sure where to begin, so he started.

"You got a big problem on your hands, Abe. Bigger than you think."

He hung a left turn toward the river. It was the long way to the state attorney's office, the scenic route. I could see that he was conflicted about whether he should even be having a conversation with me, but there was something he needed to tell me.

"I've been thinking about the photographs of you and Tyla Tomkins at the restaurant," he said, keeping his eyes on the road.

"What about them?"

"How did Angelina get them?"

"They were left in her mailbox."

"Who left them there?"

"Cutter."

"How did Cutter get them?"

"Cutter was stalking his victims. We've been over this."

He made another turn. We were cruising along the riverfront, past a Panamanian freighter that was headed upriver at no-wake speed. "That's bullshit," said Rid.

"You sound like Santos," I said.

He glanced over in my direction. "I agree with Santos."

"Agree with her on what?"

"I watched the video of Cutter's interview. He denies he killed Tyla. He denies he sent the photos to Angelina, denies that he even knew who Angelina was. The black ash on Tyla's face doesn't fit into Cutter's profile. The crazy son of a bitch summed it up pretty good himself: why color a black face black? It makes no sense. Unless you're trying to make it *look like* Cutter sent the photos."

I waited for him to continue, but he stopped. We drove another block. I got the impression that he would have liked to tell me more, but he'd already gone further than allowed. I nudged him along. "Who would do that, Rid? If Cutter didn't send the photos, who did?"

"I was going to ask you that question."

"I'd give you the same answer I gave Carmen," I said. "We talked back when all this started, right after you and Santos went to Belter's office and accused him of sleeping with Tyla. Sending those photographs was his return shot across the bow, his way of saying 'You ruin my marriage, I'll ruin Abe Beckham.'"

"Whoever sent those photographs had to know the killer's signature. That's not Belter."

"So it's probably Cutter. The only other option is someone in law enforcement."

"Or someone married to law enforcement." A siren wailed behind us. Rid steered to the right to let an ambulance pass. "Santos says it was Angelina."

He was pulling back into traffic, not looking at me as he spoke, and I wondered if I'd heard him correctly.

"What did you say?"

"Santos thinks Angelina sent them to herself."

The ambulance siren faded, but things were no less clear to me. "How would she know the signature of the ash on the face?"

"Maybe you slipped. Maybe she overheard you talking on the telephone."

"I'm more careful than that, but let's put that aside. *Why* would she send those photographs to herself?"

"To create the impression that she didn't know you were cheating on her until after Tyla was dead."

"I didn't cheat on Angelina."

"You're missing the point. It's not a matter of whether you were or you weren't actually cheating on your wife. It matters only if she thought you were, and when she thought it. It's a question of motive."

"Motive . . . to kill Tyla Tomkins?"

"Bingo."

"Rid, come on. This was a gruesome, bloody murder with a machete."

"Was it? We never recovered Tyla's head. No way to examine it for blunt trauma. Maybe it was as clean as someone sneaking up from behind and hitting her in the back of the skull with a fucking rolling pin."

"The medical examiner says it was a blow to the back of the neck with a large knife."

"Yeah, and maybe Tyla was already dead when that blow was delivered. Maybe the only point of that machete wound was to make it *look* like Cutter."

I wasn't comfortable with this discussion at all, but I couldn't *disprove* any of it. "Angelina is not a killer."

I expected him to second the notion, but he didn't. "Like I told you, Abe. I've been thinking about those photographs. I've been studying them, in fact."

"And?"

We stopped at a red light, and Rid handed me his phone. One of the photographs of Tyla and me was on the screen. "Look closely," he said.

"I am looking," I said.

"Look at your dinner plate."

I enlarged the image and zoomed in on my plate.

Rid asked, "What were you eating at the restaurant that night with Tyla?"

I was staring at the screen, my entrée clearly visible in the photograph. It was a dish I'd never heard of before meeting Angelina, but after tasting hers, I ordered it whenever a restaurant had it on the menu. "Osso buco."

"What did Angelina cook for you on the night she disappeared?"

I didn't answer right away.

"I know you remember," he said, "because I ate it, loved it, and told you it was better than oxtail."

"Osso buco," I said.

"Yeah," said Rid. "If you think that's a coincidence, you're a fucking moron. Angelina was messing with you, Abe. She's *been* messing with you."

I handed the phone back to him. The traffic light turned green. Rid drove another block closer to the Boomerang and pulled up to the curb. "This close enough?" he asked.

"Yeah, thanks."

I opened the passenger-side door, but he stopped me before I climbed out. "Abe, you know we can't talk any more about this, right?"

I nodded.

"We cool then?"

"Yeah," I said. "We're cool."

I stepped out onto the sidewalk, shut the door, and watched him drive away.

Chapter Sixty-One

Victoria left the Beckham residence at 10:00 a.m. Detective Reyes stayed behind to wrap up the crime scene.

The law office of Jeffrey Winters was Victoria's destination, but she took a circuitous route. She hopped onto the expressway, exited north of downtown at Overtown, and cut across the design district in a zigzag pattern of one-way streets. She'd refused any comment to the media outside the Beckham house, and several reporters had followed her, curious to know where she and the story were headed. At least two remained on her tail all through the design district.

"Let's go 'round again, boys," she said as she checked her mirror.

She got back on the expressway and started the pointless journey all over again, determined to repeat as necessary until the tail was gone. Her concern wasn't so much the media, per se. Rather, she didn't want Abe to find out through media coverage or otherwise that the FBI was about to speak to his wife without him.

By the third loop around the city, the last of the media vans had given up and disappeared from her rearview mirror. She parked on the street outside Winters' building, went inside, and rode the elevator to the penthouse. The young and pretty receptionist struck Victoria as polite but not too bright—a ditz, in fact, someone who might show up for an *American Idol* audition wearing a string bikini and leave in tears because no one had told her that a voice was required. The young woman offered a warm greeting, which cooled a bit when Victoria introduced herself.

"You're an FBI agent? Seriously?"

"Yes, seriously."

"Is Mr. Winters expecting you?"

"Only if he's really smart."

The receptionist had no idea how to handle that one. Flustered, she buzzed Winters' assistant, told her that "Agent Smart" was in the lobby, and asked Victoria to have a seat. Victoria went to the waiting area and perused the law firm's impressive art collection, which leaned toward the ultramodern. Probably from Art Basel. Or from a drug dealer who couldn't pay his lawyer in cash.

"I'm sorry," said the receptionist. "What was your name again?"

Victoria had wondered how long it would take her to correct the "Agent Smart" mix up. She set the girl straight and turned back to the art.

Beckham's story about the attempted bribe had been intriguing, and Victoria knew exactly where Abe was going with it. A follow-up with Brian Belter was definitely in order. But first she wanted to know what Angelina's lawyer thought about it.

"Mr. Winters will see you now," said the receptionist.

Victoria followed her down the hallway to an empty conference room. She took a seat at the glass-topped table and waited. It wasn't long before Winters and one of his associates entered. They seemed a little surprised that Victoria was alone, not the usual FBI duo. Victoria didn't bother to explain that she had her own way of doing things when she pushed the outer limits of her FBI authority, which was one reason she was back in a field office and no longer working out of Quantico at what should have been the height of her career. They exchanged introductions and sat on opposite sides of the table, two against one.

"Your client is welcome to join us," said Victoria.

"Pass," said Winters, smiling.

"That's fine. Her husband has done plenty of talking for her."

His smile faded. "Talking where?"

"I didn't mean any place specifically. Everywhere."

The lawyers exchanged uneasy glances, and then Winters focused his gaze on Victoria. "Has Mr. Beckham been talking directly to you?"

"Of course."

"About what?"

"That's what I wanted to discuss with you. See, I've been working very hard on the Cutter task force, and it's my very firm conclusion that Tommy Salvo had nothing to do with the murder of Tyla Tomkins. I've spoken to Abe Beckham about this, and he is pushing hard in the direction of Brian Belter. You know Mr. Belter, I'm sure."

"Yes, I know him. Managing partner of BB&L, lawyer for Big Sugar."

"And Tyla Tomkins' supervising partner. So I totally get Abe's theory. The senior partner is bedding Tyla Tomkins, rising star. Tyla gains the kind of access to Cortinas Sugar that only someone who's sleeping with

Brian Belter could get. She visits the company's plantation in Nicaragua and witnesses appalling business practices, then comes back to Miami and calls 'an old friend' at the state attorney's office to see if anything can be done about it. Belter finds out she's talking to law enforcement—maybe he even discovers that Abe Beckham is her new favorite married man to sleep with, which makes Belter even crazier. Belter suddenly stands to lose his wife, his mistress, his best client, and everything else that matters to him. Tyla Tomkins ends up dead."

"I honestly have no idea what you're talking about," said Winters.

"Your client does, so take good notes, Junior," she said, glancing at the associate.

"My client knows nothing about the death of Tyla Tomkins," said Winters.

"Let's hope you're right. But Angelina still needs to be very concerned. Her husband's theory about Brian Belter has holes, and I intend to blow those holes wide open. When I do, Abe Beckham will realize that it's pointless to keep pointing the finger at Brian Belter. When that happens, he is going to point in another direction."

Winters didn't answer, but it was clear that he fully grasped Victoria's implication: Angelina would be Abe's next scapegoat.

"There's been an awful lot of talk about homicide," said Winters. "Right now, Angelina's only concern is a potential criminal charge for making herself disappear."

"It all ties together," said Victoria. "See, I watched the YouTube video, and I don't think Angelina ran out of fear of Cutter. I think she ran out of fear of her husband. But unlike some of my friends in the domestic violence unit at MDPD, I don't believe that Abe was a habitual abuser. I see it as an isolated incident. Angelina uncovered something about Tyla. Specifically, about her murder. I think she confronted Abe with it. Abe had his own version of events, and Angelina was afraid or refused to go along with it. So she ran."

Winters showed no reaction, but the associate beside him was scribbling furiously. Victoria had planted the seeds.

"This is all very interesting," said Winters.

"There's more," said Victoria. She laid her iPad on the table and brought up the photographs of Tyla and Abe at the restaurant.

"I've seen these," said Winters. "Those are the pictures that the killer left in her mailbox."

"Another misstatement in Angelina's video," said Victoria. "She didn't get these from Cutter."

"Then who sent them?"

Victoria leaned closer, making sure she had his full attention. "Abe Beckham."

The associate stopped writing. Even Winters was unable to hide his surprise. "Why would he do that?"

"To create the impression that Cutter killed Tyla and that Abe Beckham did not. Outing yourself as a cheater is better than being convicted as a murderer."

"You know this for a fact?" asked Winters. "Abe sent these photographs?"

"Not yet," said Victoria. "But I am going to prove it. And if your client knows what's good for her, she will stop playing her husband's game and help me."

Chapter Sixty-Two

We waited until 11:35 p.m. and the end of the late local news broadcasts. The camera crews packed up their equipment, our front lawn darkened, and the media vans drove away. Across the networks, the gist of the "breaking news at eleven" had been that "the Beckham house is no longer a crime scene, but there is no sign of Abe and Angelina Beckham and no word when they will return."

Then Angelina and I went home. Together.

Angelina entered first. I closed the door and secured it with both the dead bolt and the chain. I noticed the mark on the panel where Angelina had nailed it with a beer bottle on Friday night. So did she. We ignored it.

"Home sweet home," she said flatly.

I went to the landline on the table and checked our voice mail. "Thirty-eight messages," I told Angelina. "Probably all from reporters."

I didn't have the energy to listen to them. I hung up and silenced the ringer so that we could get through the night.

"What do we do if the news people come back?"

"Turn on the sprinklers." I was only half kidding. She didn't laugh.

"I'm getting ready for bed." She turned and disappeared down the hallway to the master. I went to the couch and sat in front of the TV. My hand was pre-programmed to reach for the remote and surf, but I resisted. I opted for no television, not even satellite radio. Silence.

The previous twelve hours had been a marital stand-off, me refusing to return to the law office of Jeffrey Winters and Angelina refusing to leave until her lawyer said it was time. The state attorney's office became my fortress. No media ambushes. No phone calls I didn't want to take. I told Carmen and the head of our public corruption unit about Belter's attempted bribery of an assistant state attorney, namely, me. I intended to follow up later in the week, but my plan for the rest of the day had simply been to retreat from reality and throw myself into one of my pending cases, which proved to be impossible. One colleague after another popped by my office to show support. All had seen Angelina's YouTube video. No one said he believed her. No one said he didn't. I did notice that not a single prosecutor from our domestic violence unit came by to talk. I kept most of the conversations short. Only once had I been tempted to discuss matters in greater depth. Our head of the sexual assault unit would have been a great sounding board for my fears that something awful had happened to Angelina in the wee hours of the morning in Little Havana, something so traumatizing that she'd decided to tell no one. The most experienced sexual-assault prosecutor in the state of Florida had been standing right in my office, but on the heels of my talk with Rid and his view that Angelina was "messing with me," I chose not to bring it up. I wondered if I should have.

"Abe?"

I glanced over my shoulder. Angelina was standing in the shadows at the end of the hallway, not quite inside the living room. She was wearing her nightgown.

"Are you coming to bed?" she asked.

"In a little bit."

"You should come now." She turned and went into the bedroom.

I blinked, confused. What did that mean, "You should come now?" I want to lie down beside my husband? I want you to hold me? I want to make love to you? Don't sit out here till two and then come crawling into bed and wake me up, asshole?

"Okay," I said, even though she was gone.

I walked to the bathroom, brushed my teeth, and pulled on a clean pair of running shorts and a T-shirt. Angelina was on her side of the bed, lying in the dark, when I entered the master. I crossed the room, peeled back the comforter, and climbed in beside her. She rolled onto her back. So did I. We lay in silence, eyes open, staring at the ceiling.

Darkness. Stillness. Utter quiet. There was no place like a bed, and nothing was more palpable than the line that ran down the middle of one.

"I talked to Rid finally," I said.

"What did he say?"

I hesitated, not sure how to answer. *That you've been messing with me? That Santos thinks you killed Tyla Tomkins?*

"He says he can't talk to me anymore about any of this."

"I'm not surprised," she said.

More silence. The air conditioner kicked on, and chilly air breathed on us from above. My pupils were adjusting to the darkness, and I could see cracks in the ceiling. Long, meandering cracks that reached from wall to wall. Cracks that had existed since Angelina and I had moved in and that I had never noticed. Until now.

"Abe, there's something I have to tell you."

My mind raced. Was Rid right, and was a confession coming? Was I right, and was she about to tell me what really happened to her in Little Havana?

"What is it?" I asked.

"Agent Santos met with my lawyer today."

Not what I was expecting. "When?"

"Sometime before lunch. It wasn't a planned thing. Santos just showed up and wanted to talk."

"Why?"

"I wasn't there. But Jeffrey said she's investigating the murder of Tyla Tomkins. And she's targeting you."

I propped myself up on one elbow and looked at her. She remained on her back. "Why didn't you tell me this earlier?"

"Jeffrey didn't say anything about it till an hour ago. He was against my decision to come home with you. Telling me this was his last attempt to convince me that I shouldn't."

I was glad that she'd ignored his advice, but I still didn't like it that she'd waited until we were in bed to tell me. "This goes without saying, but you know I didn't kill Tyla Tomkins."

"I know. Technically speaking, Agent Santos doesn't think you did, either."

"You just said she was targeting me."

"She thinks you're responsible, but she doesn't think you're the one who physically hit Tyla with a machete."

It felt as if someone had just hit *me* with the machete. I rolled onto my back again and stared at those cracks in the ceiling. "Somehow I knew they would try to drag J.T. into this."

"Do you think it's possible?"

"No."

"He's always scared me."

"He's not a violent person."

"He attacked that bus driver."

"That was more of a misunderstanding than an attack."

"His father was a cane cutter."

"Angelina, it makes no sense. What reason would J.T. have to kill Tyla Tomkins?"

She didn't answer.

"See," I said. "No motive. There was no reason for him to commit this crime. None."

"None," she said with a hint of nervousness. "Unless you asked him to."

I was up on my elbow again and looking straight at her. "Is that what you think?"

"No, Abe. That's what Agent Santos thinks."

I moved a little closer to her, but I didn't cross that line in the bed. "Angelina, this is a game Santos is playing. She's trying to drive a wedge between us. She talks to my friend Rid and says you killed Tyla. She talks to your lawyer and says I got J.T. to kill her."

"She told Riddel that *I* killed Tyla?"

"Yes."

She was suddenly up on her elbow, the same reaction I'd had to her lawyer's meeting with Santos. We were eye to eye, staring at each other from opposite sides of that imaginary line down our mattress like two soldiers in the trenches.

"Santos thinks I killed Tyla, and you didn't *tell me?* Why didn't you tell me?"

"I thought it was so preposterous that I didn't need to," I said.

"Really?"

"Yes, really. Tyla was hacked to death with a machete. It was a bloody, gruesome death."

"Oh, so if it had been a nice clean bullet to the back of the head, that would be different. That's something you could see me doing?"

This wasn't the time to get into "rolling pins" and Rid's alternative theories on cause of death. "No. I didn't say that."

She lowered herself onto her back and folded her arms atop the comforter.

"Angelina, please, let's not get like this. We're playing right into Agent Santos' hands. Her strategy is to break down the trust between us. She wants us to turn against each other."

"Do you trust me?" she asked.

It was a simple question, but the answer felt complicated. I hesitated too long.

"Abe, *do you trust me?*" she asked again.

"Yes, of course."

"Don't say 'of course.' Nothing is *of course* anymore. We have to rebuild. I *want* to rebuild. But not if you're going to say dumbass things like 'Of course I trust you, honey.' It's dismissive of me and everything that's happened."

She had a point. "I'm sorry."

She took a breath and sank a little deeper into the mattress. I lay back and did the same.

"I didn't kill Tyla," I said. "J.T. didn't kill Tyla. I didn't get J.T. to kill Tyla."

I heard her take another deep breath in the darkness. "Thank you," she said.

"You're welcome. Anything else you want to know?"

"Not right now."

"Good."

"Well, maybe one thing," she said.

"What?"

"Just to be clear: when I close my eyes to go to sleep, J.T. isn't going to jump out of the closet with a machete, is he?"

I knew it was a joke, and maybe I should have appreciated the attempt at humor, but it didn't work for me, and I sensed that she regretted it.

"No," I said. "That's definitely not going to happen."

A minute passed. I wondered if she had more to say. She didn't.

"Good night, Abe."

"Good night."

There was no kiss. I rolled onto my side and really tried to find sleep. I was exhausted, but I couldn't clear my head and disengage. The air conditioner went through another cycle. Ten minutes or more passed. I shifted onto my left side, glancing at Angelina as I rolled over.

She was still on her back. Her eyes were open.

I wondered if her mind was so busy that, try as she might, she just couldn't close them. Or was she dead tired and fighting to keep them open, waiting for me to fall asleep first?

I breathed in and out and wished the night would end.

Chapter Sixty-Three

At 5:30 a.m. something woke me. I sat up in bed and listened. I was certain that I'd heard a noise in the living room. Angelina was still asleep. I slid out of bed, walked quietly down the hall, and entered the living room. With sunrise more than an hour away, it was dark inside the house, and the windows were black with night. I listened for that noise again but heard nothing.

A crisp knock on the door startled me.

I checked through the peephole and saw a woman on my front porch. She was holding a microphone. Behind her was a man with a camera resting on his shoulder. It was the same *Eyewitness News* team that had interviewed me on Saturday.

You gotta be kidding me.

She knocked again. I didn't dare open the door. I was tempted to sneak out the back and turn the hose on her. Instead, I got my phone from the charger and tapped out a text message. I chose my words carefully, making sure that no matter how she tried to slice it up for her report, she would be the one to look like an ass:

Thank you for coming by our house at 5:30 a.m. Like most people, we are asleep at 5:30 a.m. Please be off our property no later than 5:31 a.m. so that I may return to sleep by 5:32 a.m. Otherwise, I will call the police at 5:33 a.m. Once again, thank you for your predawn concern and consideration.

That would do it. I hit send, gave it a minute to transmit, and then watched through the peephole as she read it. She was required to leave once told to do so. It was the law, and I was a prosecutor. She texted back something along the lines of *Please, pretty please, I'm a nice person,* which I read as, *My razor-sharp claws come out only if you're stupid enough to open the door.* I didn't bite. She wedged her business card into the doorframe—*Oh, yeah, I will definitely call you, lady*—and left with her crew.

I returned to the bedroom. Angelina had slept right through the knocking, which surprised me, until

I noticed the molded wax earplugs. They were for swimming laps, and with that watertight seal she probably would have kept right on sleeping even if the news team had used shock grenades and a battering ram.

I, however, was officially wide awake. I decided to let her sleep. I took a quick shower and dressed for the office, but I didn't feel like going in so early. I needed a diversion, a person I could talk to about something other than Tyla Tomkins, Cutter, and, frankly, Angelina. Only one such person fit the bill, and it just so happened that he was also the only guy on earth who would be happy to see me before 6:30 a.m. I backed my car out of the garage, waved as I passed the *Eyewitness News* team on the street, and drove to the nursing home. Luther had already eaten breakfast and was sitting outside in the courtyard, tearing off pieces of leftover wheat toast and feeding the pigeons.

"Now don't fight," he said. "Can't we all just get along?"

Good advice for the birds. Good advice for humans. "Rodney King couldn't have said it better," I said as I approached.

Luther probably didn't catch my allusion to the 1992 LA riots, but he was glad to see me. I told him not to get up, and he told me not to worry. It was the worn-out joke between me and an old man who was almost too frail to stand, but it still made me smile. I took a seat on the bench beside him.

"Why you up so early?" he asked.

"The McRib is back. I wanted to be first in line."

He laughed and shook his head. "You are definitely the funniest white man I know."

We talked about him for a few minutes, and I heard all about the new physical therapist with the nice smile and soft hands. Then he told me about a friend of mine who had come to visit him.

"One of *my* friends?" I asked.

"Victoria," was her name. "Victoria Santos."

I was about to explode. This was the second time Santos had pulled this stunt, first with Angelina's mother and now with Samantha's father.

"What did you two talk about?"

"Me, mostly. Nice girl, but she sure asks a lot of questions."

"What about?"

He tossed another piece of bread to the birds. They climbed all over each other in the scramble for it. "She wanted to know about my days cuttin' sugarcane."

I closed my eyes and opened them slowly, trying to keep my anger at bay. "Did J.T.'s name come up?"

He nodded. "Yes. Yes, it did."

"How so?"

"I can't remember exactly how, Abe. Honestly, I tuned her out at that point. She was asking me things like, 'Are you sure J.T. never cut sugarcane?' And, 'Did you pass on the tradition to your son?' Kind of like asking Obama if anyone in his family kept up the tradition of pickin' cotton."

I would have laughed under different circumstances. But the notion that J.T. fancied himself a sugarcane cutter wasn't just idle curiosity. It fit perfectly with Santos' theory behind the murder of Tyla Tomkins.

Luther signaled for one of the nurses, and she started toward us from across the courtyard. "Sorry, Abe," he said. "I gotta pee."

"That's okay. Time for me to go anyway."

We said good-bye, and I went quickly to my car. Part of me wanted to drive straight to Santos' apartment and bang on her door, *Eyewitness News* style. Nothing good would come of that. Instead I called Rid. He was running on a treadmill, which struck me as an interesting metaphor, and breathing heavily on the other end of the line.

"Did you know what Santos did now?"

"Abe," he said, his speech halting from the run. "We said we weren't . . . going to talk about this anymore."

"She went to see Luther."

The treadmill stopped whining in the background. I had his attention.

"Why?" he asked.

"Because he's an old cane cutter, and now Santos wants to prove that J.T. and I cooked up a plan to kill Tyla Tomkins and make it look like Cutter did it."

"She shouldn't drag the old man into this."

"She shouldn't drag me and J.T. into it either. Rid, you gotta help me out here."

"What do you want?"

"Tell me what she was looking for in my house yesterday."

"Abe," he said, groaning.

"Come on, Rid. This shit has gone far enough. I've been strip-searched, I sat for a polygraph, she searched J.T.'s house, she searched my house without a warrant, she ambushed my father-in-law in a nursing home, and that's just the stuff I know about. What's Santos gonna do next, exhume Samantha's body?"

He paused, but I could almost feel him coming around. Then he gave it to me.

"She's looking for evidence that Angelina is a smoker."

"She doesn't smoke."

"A closet smoker."

"What the hell is this about?"

He told me about the glowing orange dot in the parking lot across the street from the funeral home on the night of Tyla's memorial service.

"That sounds like something a serial killer would do," I said. "Case the funeral home of one of his victims."

"She doesn't think it was Cutter."

"She thinks it was Angelina?"

"Let's just say she doesn't think you and Angelina have a healthy relationship."

"No, I need more than that. I need to know what Santos is thinking, Rid. Does she see Angelina as some kind of crazy stalker wife who followed me to Tyla's memorial service?"

"Something made her smash a beer bottle against the door after throwing you out of the house, Abe. And let's not forget the broken nose."

I didn't want to get into that again with Rid. "Okay. This is helpful. Anything else you can tell me?"

"Just one thing," said Rid. "This is *really* the last time we talk about this, Abe."

He hung up. I put my phone away. I'd heard the finality in his voice, and he'd meant it: this would be the last favor.

I hoped I wouldn't need another.

Chapter Sixty-Four

Angelina was awake and in the kitchen when I got home. The media vans were no longer outside our house. I wondered if Angelina had stolen my idea.

"What'd you do, turn the hose on *Eyewitness News?*"

She was wearing her bathrobe with her wet hair wrapped in a towel, having just showered. "Jeffrey took care of them," she said as she poured a cup of coffee.

"How?"

She stirred in a pink pack of sweetener. "I told him what networks were out there. He called the producers and promised an exclusive first interview with me if their van disappeared."

"You can't promise exclusive first interviews to everyone."

She tasted her coffee and shrugged. "Jeffrey can. It worked."

"When are these exclusive interviews supposed to take place?"

"Four o'clock, in plenty of time to air on the evening news. Unfortunately, I'm coming down with the flu at three thirty."

I was getting tired of this game. "Get dressed. I want us to have a meeting with your lawyer."

"What about?"

"I want to refinance our mortgage. Come on, Angelina, can we just go?"

"Sor-ree." She took her coffee into the bedroom and closed the door. I called her lawyer's office and set up a meeting with Winters for 8:30. I could not imagine why it took Angelina so long to figure out what to wear, but we didn't leave the house until 8:15. I managed to get there on time. Somehow, so did Angelina's mother.

"Margaret? What are you doing here?" I asked.

"Jeffrey tells me whenever there's a meeting, since I'm paying the bills."

"Hi, Mommy."

"Hello, sweetheart," Margaret said as mother and daughter embraced.

I was getting *really* tired of this game. "Margaret, I understand that it was your idea to hire a lawyer, but Angelina and I will pay the bill."

"I want to pay," she said.

"No. *We'll* pay. But even if you were paying, that doesn't make you the client, and this morning, the lawyer is meeting only with his client and her husband."

Margaret took a few seconds to compute what I was saying. "So . . . you want me to wait out here?"

"Please."

"Well. Okay. I guess that's okay."

"It's okay, Mommy."

"Have a good meeting then. I'll be right out here. If you need me."

The receptionist escorted Angelina and me to Winters' office. He was on the telephone but waved us in. We took seats in the armchairs facing his desk. He wrapped up the call but didn't come around his desk to greet us. He seemed under the gun and dispensed with the usual pleasantries.

"Sorry to be rush-rush, but I'm picking a jury at nine thirty," he said. "How can I help you?"

"Abe thinks our mortgage rate is too high. Don't you, honey?"

Right back at me.

"He what?" asked Winters.

"I have some concerns about Agent Santos. There are really two—"

"Sorry, Abe," said Winters. "I hate to interrupt, but can you excuse us?"

"Excuse you?"

"Yes. Would you step out for a few minutes? Before the three of us talk, I'd like to have a word with my client."

Man, was I tired of this game. "Fine. Have a word. Have a paragraph. Have a whole fucking dictionary."

"Abe, stop it," said Angelina.

"I'll be outside," I said as I crossed the room. I closed the door behind me and continued down the hall. I was in no mood to wait, and with each step toward the lobby I felt more like continuing straight to the elevator. Margaret spotted me. She was seated on the black leather couch in front of the flat-screen television.

"That was a short meeting," she said.

"Yeah. Shorter than planned."

"Well, just because you pay the bill doesn't mean you're the client."

I pushed the elevator call button six times. If it didn't come soon, I figured I'd just jump out the window. Margaret sank deeper into the couch and sighed.

"The TV news people sure aren't warming up to Angelina's video," she said.

The bell chimed as the elevator doors opened. I let it go and walked toward Margaret. "Why do you say that?" I asked.

"They've been picking it apart all morning." She switched the channel back to *Eyewitness News* morning edition and turned up the volume. "Look, they're still talking about it."

I walked around the table for a better look at the TV, careful not to knock over the priceless work of art made out of coat hangers and Ping-Pong balls. The former US attorney for the Southern District of Florida was the legal-know-it-all du jour on the local morning news show.

"In theory," he said, "law enforcement could seek reimbursement of all costs of this investigation. But that would be very unlikely, in my view, if law enforcement believes what Angelina Beckham is telling us, that she ran out of a legitimate fear that she was about to be a serial killer's next victim."

"Do you believe her?" asked the interviewer.

"I think the verdict is still out. A YouTube video isn't going to do it. She and everyone around her will have to answer some very tough questions."

Margaret rose from the couch. "I can't watch this anymore," she said as she stepped out of the lobby and headed down the hallway. I didn't ask where she was going. The television had me riveted. It was a good thing that Margaret had left. The network was replaying Sunday evening's news conference, Jake and Margaret's plea for their daughter's return. Jake had done all the talking, but my eyes were on Margaret. The first time I'd watched it, I'd wondered if Margaret was going to live through this. It wasn't any easier to watch a second time.

The receptionist came to me. "Mr. Winters is ready to see you now."

I followed her through the reception area and then stopped. The lobby area in Winters' penthouse had more glass walls than a fun house, and I wanted to make sure I'd seen what I thought I'd seen. I was looking through three panes: a wall of beveled glass behind the receptionist, the glass door to the main conference room, and another glass door to a balcony off the conference room. Margaret was outside, on the balcony, surely unaware that I or anyone else was watching.

I'd never known her to smoke, never smelled it on her. But she was lighting up a cigarette.

Angelina's mother was a closet smoker.

I stood in the hallway and watched, imagining the glowing orange dot in the dark parking lot across the street from Tyla's memorial service. She'd been watching me. Angelina's mother had been watching me.

"Mr. Beckham, are you all right?" asked the receptionist.

"Yeah," I said as we continued toward Winters' office. "I will be."

Chapter Sixty-Five

The receptionist tapped lightly on the door to Winters' office and opened it. My phone rang as I was about to enter. The display read "Triple-A Storage." I took the call, which was from the property manager.

"Is this Mr. Beckham?"

"Yes, it is."

"I'm calling to advise you that I am about to open your storage unit."

"Why? Did I forget to pay the bill?"

"No. The police are here with a search warrant."

My first thought was Santos. "What police?"

"Miami-Dade."

"Put one of the officers on the line."

"They aren't going to talk to you, dude. I already asked them to give you a call, but they don't need you to be here. They don't *want* you to be here. That's the way these things work."

I knew that. "What are they looking for?"

"I don't know."

"It's on the warrant."

"Look, I don't get involved in the details. I just give my customers a heads-up in case they want to come over. Or get out of town."

"Thanks. I'll be right there." I hung up and stuck my head in the office. "Sorry, I gotta go."

"What?" said Winters.

"Something came up."

"What's this about?" asked Angelina.

"I don't have time to explain. Just stay here."

"What am I supposed to do?"

"I don't know. Have another word with your attorney. Start on the thesaurus. I *really* have to go."

I turned and ran down the hall, through the lobby to the elevator. A courier held the door open for me, and in three minutes I was down in the main lobby, through the revolving entrance doors, and in my car.

The manager had said it was MDPD, and I believed him, but I was certain that Santos was somehow behind the search. I wasn't sure how she would have found out about the storage unit. Perhaps it had come up in her visit with Luther. I dialed Santos from my car, but she didn't answer. Rid didn't take my call either. I drove faster, weaving between slower-moving cars in the morning traffic. I parked next to the squad cars outside the storage warehouse and ran upstairs to the fourth floor. The roll-up door to my unit was open. The search was in progress. Agent Santos was standing in the hallway, a tacit acknowledgment that she was operating outside her jurisdiction, the supervisor masquerading as an observer.

"Let me see the warrant," I said.

"This is a Miami-Dade police search," she said. "Get it from Detective Reyes."

MDPD, my ass. I went toward my unit. A team of officers was stacking boxes in the hallway. Some were open. Loose items were scattered across the floor. It felt wrong to see the police rummaging through Samantha's belongings, her mementos, my memories. Detective Reyes stepped out of the unit and handed me the warrant. I immediately focused on the box that listed the items covered by the search.

"A cane-cutting machete?" I asked. "Are you kidding me?"

Santos walked over and joined us. "Your father-in-law told me he still had his old equipment."

"Let me count the problems I have with that," I said, glowering. "One, you should have called me if you wanted to talk to Luther. Two, you said this was a Miami-Dade search, not yours. Three, even if it is technically an MDPD search, what the hell does a machete have to do with Detective Reyes and the domestic violence unit, other than the fact that you two have become Detective Frick and Agent Frack? Four, there's no machete here."

"What did you do with it?"

"Nothing."

"How do you know it's not here?"

I gave it some thought before answering. *Because I wanted to know if my brother-in-law was a serial killer?* "Why don't you just look and see for yourself?"

"We will."

The team continued its work in silence, taking inventory, checking off each box searched. I watched for a few minutes, smoldering with anger.

"Do you have any other warrants?" I asked.

Reyes ignored the question. Santos didn't even look in my direction.

I walked to the stairwell at the end of the hallway, closed the door behind me, and dialed J.T. on my cell.

"Where you been, Abe? I'm almost out of food again."

"J.T., listen to me. This is important."

"Food's important."

"Yes, food is definitely important. But this is even more important. Do you remember when the police came to your apartment with a search warrant?"

"Duh. You're not talking to Forrest Gump. I hate when people treat me like I'm stupid. I'm a smart man, Abe. Samantha even said I was a genius once."

"I know, I'm sorry. What I meant to ask is if you remember how the police wanted to go outside your apartment and search the deck?"

"Uhm . . ."

"Forget it. It doesn't matter if you remember or not. My point is that the first warrant didn't allow them to search outside. But the police always have the option to come back with another warrant."

"Oh, shit! They're coming back?"

"Calm down, okay? I don't know for sure that they're coming back."

"Don't bullshit me. Why would you call me if they wasn't?"

"I just want you to be ready."

"*Ready?*" he shouted. "How do I get *ready?* I can't do this again. I can't, Abe."

"J.T., it's going to be okay. Just—"

"It's this bracelet, Abe!"

"It's not the bracelet."

"All this bad shit happened after I put on this fucking bracelet!"

"That has nothing to do with any of this."

"I gotta get out of here."

"J.T., you can't go anywhere with that bracelet on. That judge will throw you in jail if you do."

"I don't care. They're coming. You said it. I heard you say it. They're coming back here!"

"J.T., I'm on the way. Stay right there."

"I gotta get out, Abe!"

"J.T., just—"

I stopped myself. He was gone. "Damn, it, J.T.!"

I tucked my phone away and ran down the stairwell to my car. Gravel flew and a cloud of dust rose over the squad cars as I raced out of the parking lot. With everything else that was going on, the last thing I needed was for J.T. to be arrested and hauled into court for violation of his house arrest. I dialed his number twice from the road but got no answer. Again I was weaving between cars, even passing the ones that were exceeding the speed limit. I was less than a block away when I got behind a pack of cyclists who were dressed for the Tour de France but moving at the speed of a French waltz. The pack leader flipped me the bird as I passed on the right to get around them, half on the shoulder and half on the grassy swale. My car screeched to a halt in the parking space in front of J.T.'s apartment. I ran to the door but it was locked. I knocked hard.

"J.T., open the door!"

I gave him a minute. I knocked again and put my ear to the door. I heard nothing from inside the apartment, but if he was gone, having fled out of fear that "they" were coming back, he wouldn't have taken the time to lock the door on his way out. I ran around the building to the rear entrance to his apartment. A fragrant burst of gardenia hit me as I rounded the corner. The tree I'd planted when Samantha and I moved in was in full bloom. The backyard was just big enough for the deck and one tree, and it was surrounded by a five-foot wood fence. I tried the gate, but it was locked—another sign to me that J.T. had to be inside. I hopped over the fence and caught my shirt on a thorny bougainvillea bush. My sleeve ripped as I fell to the ground and rolled, and when I climbed to my feet I was facing the deck. I froze at the sight. The pressure-treated planks that Samantha and I had laid were covered with blood. Wide, dark pools of blood.

"J.T.!"

My heart pounded as I lunged toward the deck. I stumbled, and fell to my knees. Blood soaked through my pant legs, and I saw the crimson trail leading back into the kitchen. I knew that J.T. was in there, but I couldn't go in yet. It was probably only a split-second hesitation, but the image was searing so deeply into my brain that my delay seemed much longer. My gaze was locked on a deck painted in blood. An old cane cutter's machete lay in the middle of it. Beside the blade was the ankle bracelet. It was still attached to J.T.'s foot, a white spear of bone protruding from the ankle.

"Oh, shit, J.T.! *Shit, shit!*"

I dialed 911 on my cell as I ran into the apartment through the open doorway. I followed the trail of blood across the kitchen, across the TV room, and all the way to the foyer. That was as far as J.T.'s one-footed escape had carried him. His body was a motionless heap on the floor at the front door. I called his name and went to him. I shouted details to the 911 dispatcher as I slapped J.T.'s face and pried his eyes open, anything to bring him back.

"His foot is cut off!" I told the dispatcher. "He's bleeding to death! Just send an ambulance!"

My shirt was already ripped from the thorns. I tore it into strips for a tourniquet and tied it as tightly as I could around J.T.'s calf. I rolled him on his back and started CPR.

"Come on, brother! Come on!"

I went back and forth, three quick chest compressions and then pressure on the leg wound, until the paramedics arrived.

Chapter Sixty-Six

We held a graveside service for J.T. at Mount Olive Cemetery, where members of the Vine family had been laid to rest beneath the sprawling limbs of giant oak trees for more than half a century.

My efforts to revive J.T. had been fruitless. The paramedics were too late. The massive blood loss had sent him into cardiac arrest. He was dead before they reached the hospital.

A simple metal casket rested on pilings above the open grave. A green canopy shaded us from the afternoon sun. It was low-key and private: Luther, me, and the same minister who had presided at Samantha's service. I couldn't blame Angelina for not wanting to attend.

Not after Tyla Tomkins' blood was found on the machete.

It was Luther's cane knife. J.T. had gotten it from Samantha. It was one of the heirlooms that she entrusted him with after she got sick, along with the yellowed 1941 newspapers that the police had found in J.T.'s nightstand, their mother's watch, and other personal items. J.T. had kept it in a safe place in the apartment after Samantha's death. He buried it in the backyard under the deck after using it to kill Tyla. Samantha had made him promise that he'd never lose it and that he would give it away only to a museum, so it was easy to look into J.T.'s mind and understand why he'd kept it even after he'd turned it into a murder weapon.

The harder thing to understand was why he had wanted Tyla dead.

"We do not gather here today to dwell on the why or what of sin," the Reverend Otis Brown said, standing beside the casket. "The Bible teaches that 'Whoever keeps the whole law but fails in one point has become accountable for all of it. For He who said, "Do not commit adultery," also said, "Do not murder." ' "

I blinked, for he who mentioned murder had been looking right at me when he said "adultery."

"It is not the size of the sin but the lack of faith that separates us from God. J.T. was a troubled man, but he was not the face of evil. Let us pray that he has met the face of forgiveness and found eternal life. Can I get an *A-men?*"

"Amen," Luther and I said softly.

A pair of blue jays cawed in the pine tree behind us. The preacher returned to the folding chair beside Luther and consoled him. I rose and went to the CD player. I'd selected one piece. It was the song that J.T. and I had sung together in his apartment, the one Samantha used to sing to her brother. *Be grateful.*

The service ended by three o'clock. Luther and I said good-bye to the minister. We were less than fifty yards from Samantha's grave, and I suggested that we visit it.

"You go on," said Luther. "I want to sit a spell."

I let him be and walked down the gravel path to visit Samantha's grave. It was a quiet and peaceful walk. And lonely. Literally hundreds of mourners had followed me down this same path for Samantha's burial. I'd heard many of them sobbing and crying behind me. I could still hear them.

"How you holding up, Abe?"

I stopped. I wasn't imagining things. Rid was standing in the shade of the biggest oak tree in the cemetery. We were a dozen or more gravestones away from Samantha's marker.

"Okay, I guess. A little worried about Luther. Can't believe it was his knife, you know, that—"

"I know."

The sun was beating down and forcing me to squint. I moved into the shade, closer to Rid. "You were welcome to join us," I said. "You didn't have to watch from a distance."

"This is close enough," he said. "Don't want to disrespect Tyla's family."

"I understand."

He went to the bench beneath the tree and sat. "You know this isn't over."

"Yes, it is. J.T. killed her. End of story."

The knife wasn't the only proof. Until Rid showed me the rental agreement signed on the day of Tyla's death, I'd been under the outdated impression that all rental car companies required a credit card. The irony was that I had pushed J.T. to get his license and even cosigned for his debit card as part of getting his life together. The debit charge led MDPD to the rental office, and from there they tracked down the car. Traces of Tyla's blood were still in the trunk.

"Santos isn't going to go away," Rid said. "The motive is a sticking point."

Exactly *where* he had killed Tyla was also unknown. Such a tiny amount of blood in the trunk suggested that the fatal blow had been delivered after the car ride, probably not far from where he'd dumped the body, most of the bloody evidence swallowed by the Everglades. The lack of ligature marks meant that he'd probably knocked her unconscious before taking her there, perhaps hitting her with the flat side of the blade—but as Rid had pointed out earlier that week, a headless corpse offered no way to confirm a skull fracture or contusion. Had J.T. followed her in his rental car and abducted her while she was out jogging? Had he used the fact that he was Abe Beckham's brother-in-law to trick her into meeting him somewhere?

Only one question really mattered anymore: Why?

"Motives can be complicated," I said. "Especially for someone like J.T."

He leaned forward, his expression serious. "Santos doesn't believe that J.T. wanted Tyla dead. She believes he killed her because someone else wanted her dead."

"J.T. the hit man?"

"You need to take this seriously, Abe. There are lots of possibilities. Santos will consider all of them. And most involve you."

I went to the bench and sat beside him. We were facing in the direction of Samantha's grave, a long row of stone monuments before us.

"What is she thinking?"

"That you're a married man who needed to eliminate one of the world's oldest problems. One theory has you asking J.T. to kill Tyla. Another has J.T. doing it on his own, thinking he was doing you a favor."

"That didn't happen."

"It makes more sense than J.T. killing Tyla for no reason at all."

"He had a reason."

"You gonna just keep it all to yourself?"

I stared off into the middle distance. "Yup."

He shook his head and rose. "Okay. Hope that works out for you."

"Me too. At least as long as Luther is alive."

He laid a hand on my shoulder. "Take care of yourself."

I nodded and watched him walk away. I remained seated on the bench for a minute longer. Then I got up slowly and started toward Samantha's grave. It hurt to put one foot in front of the other, but only on the inside. Probably not unlike the hurt that had tormented J.T. after Samantha's death.

Tyla had called the apartment where Samantha and I once lived. Maybe she really did want to blow the whistle on Cortinas Sugar for crimes committed in Nicaragua. More likely it was all an excuse to hook up with me again, since a Miami prosecutor was powerless to do anything about crimes in Nicaragua. The first time she'd called, J.T. didn't answer. She'd left a message for me on our old answering machine, which had never been erased, and which Santos, Rid, and I had listened to. But was that the only call? How was anyone to know that Tyla hadn't called again?

And what if J.T. had spoken to her? There would have been no record of it, because J.T. had picked up the landline. He could have spoken to Tyla, and no one but Tyla and J.T. would have known about it. Santos, Rid, and I had focused only on the voice-mail message. But maybe it was their conversation—a conversation we knew nothing about—that had convinced J.T. that Tyla was gunning for me.

I stopped before Samantha's grave. The grass was freshly mowed. A recent visitor had left a bouquet of fresh flowers. There was no card. Anonymous. Samantha had so many friends, so many people who loved her.

"I'm sorry, Samantha."

Killing Tyla was J.T.'s redemption. Tyla's punishment was the price of sin, a sin that J.T. had known about only because he'd been fooling around with my phone one day and seen the explicit evidence of its commission. Tyla was a little younger and a lot more careless in those days, and I could only assume that

J.T.'s uncovering of her sexting to me was the reason she would later take the extreme precaution of a pre-paid cell phone, no texting. In any event, that dirty old secret was now entirely with me. The other sinner.

There's no shame in dyin'. It's a cryin' shame to die of a broken heart.

Samantha didn't die of a broken heart. She died *with* a broken heart. I never cheated on Angelina. But I had cheated on my wife.

I fell to my knees and touched the grass on Samantha's grave. "So sorry," I whispered.

Tyla's death was an imperfect justice, but it was justice in J.T.'s mind. Right or wrong, J.T. never blamed me for my "mistake" with Tyla, at least not after Samantha told him that she'd forgiven me and that he, too, must forgive me. J.T. blamed Tyla alone for Samantha's broken heart. He blamed himself for the fact that he couldn't save his own sister with a bone marrow transplant because he wasn't a match. He did what he thought he had to do to make things right.

In a manner of speaking, Tyla Tomkins died of a broken heart.

Samantha's.

Epilogue

Ten months later

Christmas cane. Some say it is the sweetest sugarcane of all. That's a lie, of course, just an excuse cooked up to justify Big Sugar's refusal to stop the harvest and give its workers a day off on Christmas.

Over time, lies and excuses can become truth.

Angelina was one of those people who couldn't wait for Christmas. The Thanksgiving turkey was barely cold before she ran to the firefighters' lot to buy the perfect Fraser fir.

Most people had predicted that our marriage would be over by Easter, Memorial Day, or at the latest, the Fourth of July. We'd taken a two-month "break," our marriage counselor's euphemism for separation, but we were back together, which was more than could be said for Brian Belter and his soon-to-be ex-wife. They had all but resorted to chemical, nuclear, and other weapons of mass destruction in their very public divorce war. Step two in his personal and professional demise was just around the corner, a criminal indictment on charges of attempted bribery. Happy New Year.

But speculation about the Beckhams was not unwarranted.

"Abe, honey, can you run to the store and buy some shallots?"

Angelina was in the kitchen. I was sitting in front of the television watching two college football teams in a Christmas Eve bowl game that I didn't care about. "Sure," I shouted back. *What the hell's a shallot?*

"And some brown sugar?"

"Yup."

"They close at four today, so hurry."

I grabbed my car keys and headed out the door.

Angelina and I had stopped trying to have a baby. Not that we'd ever gotten started. Making love was off the agenda during our separation. At the two-month mark, our counselor suggested a "reunion" to see where we were. The theory was that I'd never given Angelina a shot, that no woman would have stood a chance on the heels of Samantha's death. Sex wasn't supposed to be part of the reunion weekend. In fact, the counselor had advised against it. When it happened, I pulled out at climax. "Good call," she'd whispered in my ear. "I'll go back on the pill." End of discussion. It still seemed curious that the first time Angelina had ever mentioned a baby—lunch at the Big Fish restaurant on the Miami River—was the same day the news stations reported that Tyla Tomkins was dead. Strange coincidence. Or not. Whenever I thought of it, Rid's words came back to me.

Angelina's messing with you, Abe. She's been messin' with you.

I backed the car out of the garage and stopped at the end of the driveway. *Brown sugar and what?* It came to me, and I drove to the grocery store, past palm trees covered with twinkling lights and other signs of the holidays in south Florida.

Agent Santos had moved on. Literally. I never found out what she had done to piss off the powers that be at FBI headquarters, but she'd done her penance in the Miami field office, and her reassignment was short-lived. She was back in Quantico with the Behavioral Analysis Unit, where she belonged. I'd thought about sending her a congratulatory note but never got around to it. Or maybe I feared that her reply would be some-thing along the lines of *I'm not finished with you, Beckham. Or your wife.*

"Excuse me, where are your Skittles?" I asked the stock boy.

"Aisle seven."

I wasted five minutes in the candy section before realizing that I'd misspoken. I found the shallots and brown sugar, spent another fifteen minutes in the so-called express checkout lane, and headed home.

Angelina and I didn't talk about Tyla's death anymore. Or J.T.'s. It had taken months for her to open up to me. I was still undecided about what to do with her confession.

There had been no second phone call from Tyla to J.T. The lone voice-mail message had been their only communication, which by itself wasn't nearly enough to set J.T. off and convince him that Tyla was coming back for me. The photographs of Tyla and me in the restaurant had pushed J.T. over the edge. He'd gotten them from Angelina.

I dialed Angelina from my car. "Got what you needed," I said.

"Thanks, honey. Hurry home."

Angelina's mother was a smart woman. Smart enough to have seen how unhappy her daughter was in her marriage. The proverbial "other woman" had been Margaret's immediate suspicion. The private investigator that Margaret had hired to follow me on my trip to

Orlando had earned his money with those photographs of Tyla and me. Why Angelina had shown them to J.T. was a mystery to me. We'd talked about it for the last time over the Labor Day weekend. She'd told me that she was merely gathering all the information she could about Tyla, and that she wanted to see if J.T. knew the truth about Tyla and me. Her explanation was plausible. But there was another possibility, one that played on J.T.'s paranoia, fears, and vulnerability: Had Angelina gone to J.T. and presented Tyla Tomkins as a common enemy that needed to be eliminated?

No, she'd told me. Absolutely not, Abe.

But I had my suspicions. Back then, I was still using Samantha's birthday as my iPhone password, and it would only have made Angelina angrier when she guessed it. Who else would have answered my ringing cell phone when I was in the shower and had a two-minute conversation with Tyla? Who else would have continued to check my voice mail and deleted four separate messages from Tyla? Who else could have overheard me talking to Rid or Santos about Cutter's signature, and why else would she have smeared ash on the photographs and sent them to herself, making it look as though Cutter had killed Tyla and was coming after her?

Why else would she run?

Angelina didn't run because she thought she was going to be Cutter's next victim. She didn't run to teach me a lesson or because she was afraid of me. Angelina ran because she knew J.T. had killed Tyla Tomkins. She feared that he was going to name her as his accomplice—the person who had put the idea in his head and perhaps encouraged him to do it. Maybe she'd gone even further, convinced Tyla to meet someplace private to talk woman to "other woman," sent J.T. in her place, and then helped J.T. rent the car that he—or they—had used to dump the body in the Everglades. She'd panicked in the middle of the night, hocked Samantha's ring at a pawnshop, bummed a ride from two young women to the Miccosukee Resort in the Everglades, and tossed her cell phone on the Tamiami Trail as they passed the spot where Tyla's body had been recovered—*Hey girls, I'm feeling carsick back here, I'm going to roll down the window.* She'd tried to disappear, only to return two days later after realizing how much work it really is to make yourself vanish.

I couldn't prove that. I didn't even want to think it. But sometimes I wondered. Sometimes I still thought she was messing with me.

I laid the shallots and brown sugar on the kitchen counter. "Here you go."

"Thanks, honey."

She was smiling. Angelina was happy these days, and getting really big. The pill, our ob/gyn explained, was 99.5 percent effective, not 100 percent. I sometimes wondered if Angelina had really been taking it, and if our "reunion" had been planned around her most fertile time of the month. But I put bad thoughts aside. We had a baby girl on the way. Life was good, right?

"Dinner will be ready at six."

"Great," I said. "What are we having?"

"Your favorite. Osso buco."

Yes, Angelina was still messing with me.

It made me wonder which dinner would be our last.

Acknowledgments

Twenty-five years ago I started writing a novel about Florida's sugarcane cutters, a mystery set in the Everglades. At the time I was a young lawyer in a large Miami law firm, and after four years of coming home from my day job and writing late into the night, the result was not so sweet. My agent, Artie Pine, told me I'd gotten "the most encouraging rejection letters" he'd ever seen. Seriously. Those were his exact words. "Put the sugar story aside," he told me, "and write another novel." So I did. Twenty-two more, to be exact.

Cane and Abe bears no resemblance to that first stumble, but my return to sugar and the Everglades after more than two decades had me thinking often of "Artie the optimist," whom we all miss. His son, Richard, continues to be my agent, and I'm forever grateful for his guidance. My editor, Carolyn Marino, has been part of the dynamic trio almost from the very beginning. Her experience and expertise continue to make me a better writer.

My beta readers, Janis Koch and Gloria Villa, have become indispensable members of this team effort. Thank you for the keen eye and attention to detail that is becoming a lost art in this "auto-correct" world. Assistant editor Emily Krump is the newest member of the team. Welcome aboard!

I also want to express my special thanks to Rex Hamilton and the Everglades Foundation. Our daytrips into the Everglades and Florida Bay were unforgettable experiences, highly educational, and invaluable sources of inspiration for *Cane and Abe*. My son Ryan especially dug the airboats.

Incidentally, I was single and dating a beautiful woman who held a degree in English literature when my first sugar novel crashed and burned. She married me anyway. Thanks, Tiffany, for sharing the highs and lows and making it all so much sweeter.

JMG, fall 2014

About the Author

J ames Grippando is a *New York Times* bestsell-
ing author whose novels are enjoyed worldwide in
twenty-six languages. *Cane and Abe* is his twenty-first
novel published by HarperCollins, and it comes on the
twentieth anniversary of his debut thriller, *The Pardon*
(fall 1994). He is also the author of *Leapholes* for young
adults. James was a trial lawyer for twelve years before
he became a writer, and he is now counsel at the law
firm of Boies, Schiller & Flexner LLP. He lives and
writes in south Florida.

HARPER (LUXE)

THE NEW LUXURY IN READING

We hope you enjoyed reading
our new, comfortable print size and found it
an experience you would like to repeat.

Well – you're in luck!

HarperLuxe offers the finest in fiction and
nonfiction books in this same larger print size and
paperback format. Light and easy to read, HarperLuxe
paperbacks are for book lovers who want to see
what they are reading without the strain.

For a full listing of titles and
new releases to come, please visit our website:

www.HarperLuxe.com